THE RIVALS OF COPPER COUNTY

COPPER COUNTY
BOOK 2

MAY ARCHER

Cover Art: Natasha Snow Designs
Editing: One Love Editing
Proofreading: Jodi Duggan

All the good bits are theirs, and any mistakes are my own!

My childhood friend. My biggest rival. The only man I've ever wanted.

If there were a prize for the most contented man in Copper County, I'd win it every time. I've got my business. My son. My family. My friends... and no romantic prospects, sure, but only because I don't need any. My life's great as it is. Seriously. Could not be better. I'm practically bleeding serenity over here.

At least until Jasper Wrigley shows up in Copper County after twenty years–as my son's temporary hockey coach, no less, though the man could barely lace up his skates back in the day–and throws my carefully ordered life into chaos.

Once upon a time, magnetic, confident Jasper was my best friend and greatest rival, and his summer visits to town were the best part of my year. Our competitions were fierce. Our dares were thrilling. We talked about everything under the sun, and he made me believe in the possibility of a bright, hazy future somewhere just out of reach.

But then he left, and I grew up. Now the last thing I need is Jasper back in my space, provoking me, challenging me, and making me question... freaking *everything*.

Like whether my life's as perfect as I claim.
Like whether I'm as straight as I think.
Like whether there might be something better than "contentment" out there for me if I'm brave enough to look for it.
And whether the man who was always my greatest rival...
might just be the love of my life.

CHAPTER ONE

"Watt! Yoo-hoo! Watt Bartlett!" a feminine voice called as I walked down Weaver Street one pretty autumn morning.

I cringed, snapped my eyes to the ground, and tried like hell not to indicate I'd heard it.

Autumn in Western New York was supposed to be glorious and delightful.

In my hometown of Copper County, every front porch was adorned with pumpkins and cornstalks, window boxes overflowed with gold and purple mums, the tree branches at the orchard were heavy with apples and pears, and the leaves around scenic Copper Lake were ablaze with color.

Here in O'Leary, the slightly larger neighbor of Copper County, sunlight bathed the street, and O'Learians bustled to and fro on their errands while the scent of smoke from some industrious person's woodstove mingled with the crisp breeze.

On days like this, it was impossible not to be perfectly content with my life.

At least until one *yoo-hoo* had caused my blood pressure to spike and my happy autumn vibe to be ruined.

The fact that my friend Ollie—and a dozen of our closest friends and neighbors—were there to hear it only made it worse.

"Watt? Watt *Bartlett*?" Ollie singsonged under his breath. "Don't you hear lover girl calling for you?"

Thankfully, he was able to give me shit without indicating that either one of us had noticed the woman dressed in high-visibility pink and hopping up and down in front of a table festooned with pumpkins and fundraising fliers.

I focused on avoiding the cracks in the sidewalk. Meticulously. "What were we talking about?" My voice came out tinged with desperation. "Your strange, recurring John Ruffian dream? Or football? Because I think Derry will be home from his mom's in time to watch the game, if you wanna come over. Or—?"

Kayla's voice cut through the air again. "Oh my heck, it *is* you! Watt! Watt, honey!"

I closed my eyes and inhaled a breath, trying to recenter myself in the autumnal reverie and contentment I'd been this-close to achieving—

"Watt! Come on over here and tell Missy and Tom about how we're going to prance together on the day after Thanksgiving!"

—but I couldn't achieve that ever-elusive contentment unless I could make it to the grocery store without having to tell anyone anything about *prancing*.

Suddenly, I was shoved through the front door of Nickerson's Books & More, nearly knocking over one of their customers. "Sorry, Bennett," I muttered to the man before glaring at Ollie. "What the hell?"

"I saved you," Ollie pointed out. "Just like John Ruffian

in that episode where he shoved Monica into the alley to protect her from the people who wanted to steal her grandma's pudding recipe. And all I want in exchange for my death-defying feat... is information."

"Oliver," I warned.

"Tell me everything there is to know about you and Kayla... *prancing*." He bounced his eyebrows.

I rolled my eyes and prayed for patience. "There's nothing to tell. It's a hockey fundraiser." I tried moving toward the door to continue toward Lyon's.

Ollie stopped me.

"Did something happen between the two of you?"

I shuddered. "No? I mean, other than those few dates last year. She's helping raise money for Derry's hockey summer camp, Camp Fair Shot. I agreed to help. That's all. Can we continue, please? I need to get back before the U-Pick opens."

Instead of walking out the front door, I snuck behind the register before making my way to the employees-only entrance that came out further down Weaver. It wasn't the first time I'd used the Nickersons' store as a handy cut-through... though admittedly not for anything like this.

Once we were back on the sidewalk—albeit a different one—Ollie started in on me again.

"Maybe the best way to get Kayla off your back is to date someone else. What about Lori Tiffner? I ran into her at the bakery the other day and—"

I gritted my teeth. "Subject change, please."

"I don't get why you're so aggressively allergic to dating, Watt."

"I don't recall it being any of your fucking business, Ollie," I said mildly. I paused to glance in the window of Hardison's Drugs, where a sign reminded passersby of the upcoming O'Leary Trunk or Treat event and to *BOO Your Candy Here, 20% Off!* "You're as bad as the town matchmakers."

Ollie sighed like I was being deliberately obtuse. "Not even remotely the same. *I'm* not trying to marry you off. I'm talking about dating. Dating's fun. And there are lots of nice folks in Copper County and O'Leary who dig your whole tall, buff Farmer Watt aesthetic. If you gave them a single wink, they'd be lining up to... you know, plant a garden or pick some apples with you."

I turned my head to give him a raised eyebrow. "Are those sex euphemisms? I can never tell with you."

"What? *No.*" Ollie looked briefly confused, then shook his head. "Watt, honey lamb, this is what I mean. You need to get out more."

I lifted a hand, indicating the street, the shops, the people, and Ollie himself. "Witness me, getting out."

He rolled his eyes. "Breakfast and groceries don't count. Derry's going off to college next year, and you'll be an empty nester. I'm concerned you might be... you know, lonely. So Chris and I were talking—"

I groaned. It was horrifying enough knowing that Copper County had clucked its collective tongues worriedly over the end of my marriage and each of the handful of women I'd dated since—*"Gosh, poor Watt. Wonder what happened this time? Should we bring him another casserole?"*—but the idea that my friends had been talking about my nonexistent love life was worse.

"—Chris and I were talking," Ollie continued stubbornly, "because we love you—we're *united by the sacred bonds of friendship,* as John Ruffian once said—and we were thinking you need to find a nice woman. A monogamous, steady woman. The same kind of thing Chris found with Reed, you know?"

I huffed out a breath. My friend Chris had been engaged to Reed Sunday for less than a week. Surely, he had better things to do than start matchmaking?

Then again, in Copper County—and O'Leary—there was practically a Must Enjoy Matchmaking bylaw, and as one of Copper County's newest residents, it made sense that Chris had jumped right in.

"But you're definitely not trying to marry me off, right? This is way different?" I said dryly. "Okay, first off." I turned toward Ollie so he'd know I was serious. "Derry hasn't left yet. He's barely started his senior year. He's got a whole hockey season to get through. And second… I don't want to date anyone. Dating leads to complications and expectations." I nodded firmly, a clear signal that the subject was closed, and kept walking.

Ollie apparently didn't seem to speak this universal language because he hurried to catch up to my side and kept right on talking.

"Relationships are the spice of life," he informed me. "They challenge you, yes, but the challenges make you a better person. Also, studies show that people in relationships live longer."

I stopped again. "Oliver, in the ten years I've known you, you've refused to swipe right on the same guy twice and have repeatedly referred to Copper County as '*a Grindr graveyard once the Copper-plates leave town on Labor Day*,' so I assume this is a theoretical knowledge. Or… wait, no! You read it in *AARP Magazine* while hanging out with your ladies, didn't you?"

Ollie's posse of blue-haired physical therapy patients, the hub of Copper County gossip, were a fearsome lot…

assuming the wheels on their walkers had been recently greased.

"That... might be accurate. I don't precisely recall," he sniffed. "Doesn't make it less true. And yes, *I* am a hookup guy. I am, not to put too fine a point on it, a player. But you... you're a relationship guy, Watt. You're kind and easygoing and steady. The word *settled* is practically tattooed on your forehead. You grow trees, for God's sake."

I wanted to ask what trees had to do with anything, but then he'd probably answer, so instead, I ignored him.

"Morning, Watt! Oliver!" Henry Lattimer called from the stoop of O'Leary Hardware, where he brandished a push broom, vigilantly guarding the tidy sidewalk against stray foliage.

Ollie and I waved back.

"Bartlett! Bringing the kids out to the U-Pick this afternoon. See you there?" Gideon called from a parking spot down the block, where he was buckling one of his twins into a car seat.

"Yep. Rena's bringing her goats and setting up a petting zoo," I called back. "Looking forward to it."

"Watt," Martha Cushman said as she passed, "I've been meaning to ask if I could get a bulk order of your Jonagolds. Call you this week?"

"Sure thing," I promised. "I'll get you a deal."

"See what I mean?" Ollie said in a low voice as we continued walking. "You've got roots, and you need to plant them in—"

"If you say Kayla, so help me..."

He sighed. "Not Kayla. She's a little too intense even for me. Besides, I heard she thinks you're not over Rachel."

I winced. "I may have... let her believe that when she threw it out as a possible reason. Honestly, I didn't have a better reason to give her. I can't exactly tell her that when she smiles at me and calls me honey, my whole body gets sweaty, and my stomach flips."

Ollie snorted. "Watt. Buddy. I'm not sure how to break it to you, but it sounds like she got your engine revving. She charged your battery. You're feeling *lust*."

I shook my head. "I promise you, she was nowhere near my battery."

I knew what lust felt like. I knew how it felt to want someone. The feeling I got with Kayla was not that. It was more like an intense discomfort. Like my body recognized that she wanted something from me I couldn't give her.

Admittedly, I didn't have a very good track record with... batteries. My first experience at being attracted to someone had ended in an utter fucking disaster of a kiss when I'd misread the signs and thought my friend returned my feelings.

Later, I'd loved my ex-wife, but as she'd pointed out when asking for a divorce, we'd mostly been friends who'd tried to make marriage work for the sake of our son.

I'd tried dating post-divorce, too, sort of wondering if my allergy to romance was like an aversion to beets and I might have grown out of it as I matured. I'd gone out with a couple of beautiful, kind women, and even though I'd never dated a guy, I'd looked hard at some gay men I knew, too. I'd thought maybe, you know, that a different *variety* of beets would do the trick.

Alas, no. Beets of all types still tasted like dirt, and as much as I might be meant for a relationship *in theory*, in reality, even thinking about dating or hooking up with someone left me feeling vaguely sweaty and anxious. I hated the idea of letting someone down, and it was practically a foregone conclusion when my libido was so… contrary.

As I grabbed a cart and we entered the relative safety of the grocery store produce aisle, I tried to explain. "Just yesterday, I ran into Kayla at the Gas n' Sip. She was all smiley, and I felt… terrible. Guilty. She's a nice person, and we should work, on paper, but there's nothing there for me."

And I couldn't help feeling like this was somewhat my fault. Like I was broken or… hadn't tried hard enough.

Ollie frowned. "Who *do* you work with? What gets your battery going?"

Staring at the display of bananas, I opened my mouth to respond, then shut it again.

Warm tan skin, cool blue eyes. Chiseled jaw, lean muscles. A teasing smile that made my teenaged heart skip more beats than could possibly be healthy. *You're gonna miss me so much when summer's over, Watt Bartlett.*

I swallowed hard. "Nothing. I mean… nobody. I mean… I don't want to talk about it." I grabbed a bunch of bananas at random and put it in my cart. "The point is, I felt so guilty for trying things on with Kayla and failing that I couldn't say no when she asked me to volunteer for her 5K fundraiser to support the kids' summer hockey camp." I rolled my eyes. "This is the kind of complication I'm trying to avoid."

Ollie snorted. "Jesus. Good thing she wasn't asking for a kidney." He frowned. "Wait, what's going on with the camp? I heard Brindley's Sports dropped them as a sponsor…"

"Yeah, and without a sponsor, they're toast. The best part about Fair Shot is that it's free. It's become kind of a rite of passage for the graduating seniors to volunteer the summer after graduation, and Derry was really looking forward to it. So was Kayla's son, Zach... all of which Kayla pointed out when pressing me to sign up." I sighed as I pushed the carriage down toward the meat aisle. "She also reminded me that the kids had to shorten their season because Coach Monroe is out on maternity leave, and wasn't that disappointing?"

"But I heard they got a history teacher who's covering for Tam and taking over the coaching, too. I heard the guy played for Boston—"

I nodded. I'd heard the same rumors. "Doesn't matter. She gave me sad eyes—*blink, blink*—" I batted my own lashes in demonstration. "—and said she knew I was the sort of person who wouldn't let her down, and I thought about how I *had* let her down, with the whole dating thing—"

"And you folded like a cheap card table." He shook his head sadly.

"No!" I considered and sighed in disgust. "Or, effectively, yes. Next thing you know, I'm signed up to do the fucking Pilgrim Prance."

I could feel Ollie's stare. "The pilgrim..."

"Prance," I snapped. "You heard me."

"*Did* pilgrims prance, as a general rule?" he mused. "I thought they were fairly anti-prancing."

"I didn't ask her for details, Oliver," I bit out, tossing a couple of packages of ground beef into the cart. "I said okay because I love my kid and because... it felt like the right thing to do."

Ollie whistled. "Okay, I changed my mind. I think it's possible that you're *too* settled and easygoing."

"Clearly, since we're still fucking talking about this," I shot back. "Can we please talk about literally anything else?"

"Fine." He looked thoughtful for a minute, then brightened. "Oh! Chris said there was someone at the Wrigley Campground the other day. You have a new neighbor."

My chest seized. "Anything," I gritted out, "but that."

"Why?" Ollie demanded. "What's the story with the campground?"

"No story." My hands clenched too tightly on a package of chicken, and I forced myself to set it down gently. "I promised Mabel I'd take care of the place, but since she died, her lawyers haven't kept me in the loop. All I know is when Derry and I were eating dinner with Chris and Reed the other night, we saw a light on in the Wrigleys' window—"

When I leave this light on, Watt, that'll be our signal. Meet me at the dock.

"—but that doesn't mean anyone's moving in. More likely, Mabel's great-nephew finally sent someone out to settle the estate." I *hmphed*. "About damn time."

There was movement at the corner of my eye—a blond head standing in front of a display of candy corn—and I whirled around, the breath freezing in my lungs.

That hair. Summer blond, Mabel had called it. Gold streaked with white. Was it actually—?

The man turned, and his wrinkled face creased into a smile. "Hey, Watt! Candy corn on sale this week. Dollar a bag. Want some?"

I blinked, my heart banging madly against my rib cage, as I recognized David Siegel, the store owner... whose hair was definitely *gray*-white and not at all summer blond.

"No!" I said roughly. "No. Thanks."

"Oh." Dave frowned down at the candy, then sniffed and turned away, cradling it protectively. "Some people don't appreciate the classics."

Christ.

"I heard about the nephew from my ladies," Ollie went on, supremely unaware that I was losing my mind. "Heard he was a big model or something."

"Yeah." I gripped the carriage handle with both hands. "He's definitely a big something."

"You know him?" Ollie demanded. "Tell me everything."

I shook my head. "I don't. Not really. Back when I was in high school, Jasper's parents used to bring him from Boston to spend summers with Mabel and Abe at the campground. We hung out on the dock and swam in the lake sometimes... like *all* kids in Copper County do," I stressed.

"Jasper," Ollie repeated. "So you were friends."

That was the *opposite* of what I'd been trying to convey, but suddenly, Jasper's decades-old voice was in my head saying, *You're my best friend, Watt,* and I found I couldn't deny it.

"We... were," I admitted. "Rivals, too. We bickered. Insulted each other all the time. One-upped and challenged each other, that kind of thing. God, we used to dare each other to do the stupidest shit." I shook my head. "Think testosterone and bad decisions."

"Two of my favorite things ever." Ollie jabbed me lightly with his elbow. "FYI, that *was* a sex euphemism."

I rolled my eyes. "Anyway, he left the summer before senior year. I graduated and went to college, and when Rachel got pregnant, we came back... but as far as I know, Jasper never did. Not when Abe died. Not when Mabel had her stroke. Not after she passed last summer, even though he was her sole heir."

"Wonder why not," he mused.

I made a rude noise. "Who cares? He should've come. You don't just abandon people you care about." I frowned, surprised by my own outburst. "I mean... not that it matters to me, one way or another."

"Hmm," Ollie said. Then he sighed. "Can't lie, I was hoping for a fun and meaty love story here, buddy. Star-crossed teenage lovers. Maybe some good old-fashioned pining..."

"If you're looking for a love story, count me out. Go find one of your own."

At that exact moment, Ollie's phone let out a distinctive Grindr *blurp*, and he burst out laughing as he pulled it from his pocket. "Fuck love. I'm getting a nooner. Way more fun... and meaty, too." He waggled his eyebrows.

I groaned. "Your euphemisms need serious work."

Ollie typed out a text and slid the phone away with a grin. "Gotta go."

I clutched my chest. "But... what about the sacred bonds of friendship, buddy? Don't tell me your Grindr graveyard is coming back to life?"

"Eh. Every once in a while, a tourist comes through for the foliage, and I like to send 'em off with a little souvenir. My contribution to the town." He gave my cheek a conde-scending pat. "Don't sign up for any more fundraisers, you hear? And don't think you've heard the last of this relation-ship conversation, either. Chris and I care about you too much to let you be lonely. Our third *John Ruffian: Pretender* binge-watch begins a week from Friday, and I can guarantee this will be on the agenda."

"Great. Collectively, you're a giant pain in my ass," I called after him. "More you than him."

I tried to focus on my shopping after that, loading milk for Derry's smoothies into my cart, but since Ollie had brought it up—and made me seriously reconsider our friendship in doing so—I couldn't stop thinking about that damn light in the window of the Wrigleys' place.

That light was a total coincidence. The signal had ceased to have any meaning, twenty years on, and I'd meant it when I told Ollie that Jasper wouldn't be coming.

In fairness, Mabel had never asked him to. In fact, she'd insisted she wanted Jasper to focus on his own life and that you didn't have to be in the same place in order to love someone. "This place is his home, and his heart is here," she'd say.

Personally, I called bullshit on *all* of that. Jasper wasn't a Coppertian. Copper County wasn't his home. At best, he'd only ever been a Copper-plate. Temporary, like the other folks who vacationed on the lake in the summer.

Furthermore, when you loved someone, you were there for them when they needed you. You didn't wait for them to ask for help; you checked in on them yourself.

If I were a betting man, I'd say Jasper had finally arranged for someone to clear out the house. I'd see a For Sale sign soon, and then someone new would buy the place. Property on Copper Lake never stayed on the market for long.

And that was good. The past was the past.

Jasper Wrigley was none of my damn business.

I glanced up, realized I'd accidentally loaded six gallons of milk into my carriage, and cursed under my breath as I set five back.

Down the center aisle, someone burst into raucous laughter, and I instinctively turned to look. A lean man with shaggy, gold-tipped hair threw his arm over the shoulder of the woman beside him with easy grace and pulled her against his side.

My stomach somersaulted.

I felt the weight of that arm on my own shoulders like a phantom touch. Recalled the precise weight of it the way I remembered the weight of Derry against my chest when he was a newborn. Knew the warmth of it the way I knew the warmth of the quilt my mom had pieced for my bed.

"Holy shit," I said under my breath.

The man turned, caught me staring, and gave me a puzzled smile.

I squeezed my eyes shut briefly, then opened them and returned my friend Parker's greeting.

Losing. My. Mind.

This wasn't like me. I was easygoing, as Ollie had said. Steady and settled. Like a tree or whatever the fuck. I didn't jump at shadows. I didn't get overwhelmed with emotion.

I sure as heck didn't get emotional about *Jasper*.

I mean, yes, okay, I had missed him... briefly. We *had* been friends. Better friends than I'd let on with Ollie. Even, maybe, best friends. And once upon a time, for a single golden summer, I'd hoped we could be... more.

I could also admit that I'd felt... not great... about the way we'd left things. I'd fucked up by wanting more—and immediately regretted it—but then Jasper's parents had needed him home right away, and he'd left Copper County without giving me a chance to explain or apologize or say goodbye. It had felt even worse the following summer when I'd waited for a light in the window that had never come on.

But I'd been a kid—seventeen, eighteen, like Derry was now?—and the biggest worry in my life had been playing hockey. Stuff that was important then became trivial once I had a mortgage to pay and a kid to raise. So I genuinely wasn't sure where my strange mood was coming from, but it had to stop.

I mean, worst-case scenario, if Jasper Wrigley ever did

come back to town, I'd simply nod and shake his hand. I'd say in the calm, measured voice of an almost thirty-seven-year-old, "Jasper. How have you been?" Because that was what adults *did*.

I grabbed a container of Derry's pricey protein powder and threw a package of frozen berries in my cart.

At the last second, I grabbed a pack of candy corn and threw that in, too, as penance to Dave for my earlier outburst.

I chatted for a moment with Bennett Graham about the deer herd that had begun ransacking gardens around the lake.

I had a pleasant exchange about the carburetor on the Chevy I was restoring with Joe Cross, our local mechanic.

When I saw Dave up on a ladder, placing the final turkey on a giant pyramid of paper Thanksgiving center-pieces right in front of the checkout, I took a second to praise his artistic taste and engineering skill. Maybe what I needed was to stop thinking about things so hard.

"It's not as easy as it looks," Dave said, peering at the display with pride.

"At least you only have to do it once a year," I called back, basking in my contentment and all-around settled-ness as I turned to load my purchases onto the conveyor belt.

This time, when someone turned around to give me a friendly smile and even flashed a pair of startling blue eyes at me, I didn't flinch. I gave the man a polite, distracted smile. I could be a friendly neighbor without thinking everyone was a ghost from my past.

But then the guy opened his damn mouth.

"Watt?" the ghost whispered in a voice I knew—and would, as much as I loathed to admit it, never mistake for another for as long as I lived. "Hey, Watt. How have you been?"

Much later, I might remember that Jasper looked nervous and hopeful. I would definitely recall that I'd meant to be calm and adult.

Right then, all I could think was that Jasper Wrigley—beautiful, confident, too-smart-for-his-own-good-or-mine Jasper, my very first crush—was standing in front of me.

How was it possible?

Twenty years of time folded in on itself in an instant, and it felt like teenage Watt and I were standing on top of one another in the goddamn checkout aisle. All the frustrated longing and unrestrained joy that young and untried boy felt at this surprise appearance of his soul mate were living inside me.

But adult me was in there, too, noting that Jasper had somehow gotten even more beautiful while he was away. The strong cut of his jaw, the high cheekbones, and the full lips I'd last seen in a black-and-white magazine ad were suddenly in front of me, in living color. My chest heaved, my dick stirred, and a voice in my brain sighed, *Fucking finally.*

The world went blurry at the edges, and I could hear my heartbeat pounding like it was coming from the other end of a long tunnel as my brain overloaded. The recycled store air seared my lungs, and my palms itched to grab hold of something—possibly Jasper—to keep my balance.

I wasn't settled.

I couldn't remember what settled felt like.

My overloaded brain screamed at me to *say something, do something, MOVE*, and my legs obeyed. I took a step back... and then another, and another...

And I landed on my ass, smack in the display of holiday

decorations, sending the entire flock of turkeys flying through the air like spectacular poultry confetti.

Eyes still on Jasper, I scrambled to my feet. "I..." I held out a hand to ward him off. "You..."

But I still couldn't make my mouth work right, and I was very afraid I was going to say something I'd deeply regret.

So, ignoring the shocked gazes of a dozen Coppertians, O'Learians, and one unfairly beautiful Copper-plate... I bolted out the door.

CHAPTER TWO

JASPER

"Nicely done, Jasper," I whispered as my former best friend and once-upon-a-time first crush disappeared out the door. An ache settled under my breastbone, and I rubbed it absently. "Another failure. At least you're consistent."

I'd daydreamed about a reunion with Watt Bartlett many times since I'd left Copper County nearly twenty years ago.

In the earliest versions of the dream, it would happen after I'd accepted my Academy Award for Best Actor after I got randomly discovered (as you do) in Los Angeles. Watt would somehow appear backstage, hazel eyes glowing with pride and smiling the special smile he'd only ever smiled at me. He'd engulf me in a backbreaking hug before kissing me soundly, then promptly confess his undying love.

Later, when I'd been around long enough to know undying love was a fantasy, I'd imagined coming back to Copper County as the wealthy, successful partner in a modeling agency. I'd planned to shower Uncle Abe and Aunt Mabel with riches to thank them for their years of unfailing support. I'd known Watt had gotten married and had a family, but I'd dreamed of him greeting me with that same warm smile that let me know he still gave a shit about me after all these years.

By the time I'd crossed the Copper County border a few days ago, my heart sore with the knowledge that Abe and Mabel wouldn't be at the campground to greet me, my body tired from three days of cross-country driving, and my post-divorce wallet nearly empty, the only part of the dream I'd clung to was Watt's smile.

I sucked in a shuddering breath and let it out again, hearing my mindset coach's voice in my head. *Your breath is your anchor. Recenter.* But I wasn't entirely sure how to recenter myself if my last and most fiercely guarded dream was gone, too.

In none of my imaginings had Watt—still rawly beautiful and somehow more unconsciously sexy than ever— looked at me like I was patient zero in a zombie apocalypse, gasped in horror, and fled the scene.

Given what had happened the last time I saw him, though, I probably should have expected it.

Maybe I should have focused a little harder on the specifics of how I'd make amends for throwing our friendship in a wood chipper one sunny afternoon a billion years ago and a little less on the happy ever after.

At the very least, I should have spent the last two thousand miles thinking up something better to say than a wet-cardboard-nothing like, "How have you been?" As my college theater teacher had told me repeatedly, improv was not my strong suit.

"Sir? Um... sir? Excuse me." The teenage cashier dipped her head into my line of sight, and I realized I was still staring at the damn door, though Watt was long gone.

I quickly slapped on a smile to hide the fact that I'd been hollowed out. "Sorry... what?"

"I said that'll be forty-three sixty-seven," she said. She eyed Watt's abandoned grocery cart. "Unless... Did you want me to add those?"

I frowned in confusion. If I'd wanted more groceries, wouldn't I have gotten them? But then I realized that she meant buying them *for Watt*—the kind of friendly gesture that was such a part of Copper County and so foreign to the life I'd been living recently.

I wasn't sure what part of my interaction with Watt (let alone the heap of paper turkey carcasses littering the floor behind me) suggested Watt would appreciate the friendly gesture and wouldn't, say, greet me with a *Walking Dead*-style stake to the brain, but... but maybe it could be a peace offering.

An opening.

A *second* second chance.

The beginning of me making amends.

"You know what? Yeah. Add them in." I stacked the rest of Watt's groceries on the conveyor belt. "Great idea."

"Nice of you," the cashier commented, giving me a dimpled grin that showed off her cheek piercings. "I'm Liza. You new in town or just visiting?"

Exchanging personal info in the checkout line? *I don't think we're in Los Angeles anymore, Toto.*

"Uh... A little of both?" I tilted my head from side to side. "I'm—"

"Jasper?" a female voice shrieked. "Oh my heck!"

I turned to find a woman in bright pink had frozen, stock-still, at the end of the checkout lane, her hands pressed to her cheeks in a comical show of surprise.

"You probably don't remember me," she began,

brushing a nonexistent strand of hair from her face coquettishly. "It's been ages—"

Even if I hadn't remembered her face, I'd have remembered that falsetto shriek from my summers on Copper Lake. I pulled out my brightest smile. "Kayla. Kayla Tartaglione."

She beamed. "You *do* remember. But it's Kayla Milley now." She held up her bare left hand and—there was no other word for it—giggled. "Ditched the husband, kept the name."

I managed a short laugh. "I get it." Better than she knew.

"So how long are you in town?" she demanded. "Will we have time to catch up? Are you visiting... *oh*." Her pretty face crumpled. "Oh, gosh, listen to me. You must be here to settle Mabel's estate. I was so sorry to hear about her passing. She was a sweet lady."

My throat went hot and tight in an instant. I kept on smiling, though, past the dull, hollow longing in my chest at Watt's rejection, past the guilt and self-recrimination over Mabel that made my stomach churn. If there was one thing I'd learned over the years, it was how to fucking smile.

"She was the best," I agreed softly. "I'll, uh... I'll be in town for a while, actually. Until the new year, at least. The house is going to need some work before it's ready to sell, and Mabel had a lot of collectibles to sort through. I figure I owe it to her to do the job right."

This was partly true. Unbeknownst to me, Mabel's house hadn't been lived in for years or maintained in a decade, and at some point before that, her collections of teacups, kaleidoscopes, and figurines had gotten way out of control.

Like, *Hoarders*-level out of control.

And no, I hadn't known that, either.

The full truth—that I wasn't just a terrible great-nephew but also a nearly penniless idiot who needed to regroup before I could head back to LA and reclaim his life—was nobody else's business.

"Oh, this is so exciting." Kayla's eyes gleamed. "You're as gorgeous as ever, you know. And you must have so many modeling stories. I bet you've been everywhere and done everything."

My smile slipped for an instant before I righted it. If only Copper County had been hiring washed-up models. Or ex-modeling agency managers. Or, hell, anyone with business management skills at all. "Ha. Well. I don't know about every—"

"I can't wait to hear all the details," she insisted, grabbing my arm. "*All* the details. We can have lunch. No! *Dinner.*"

Back in LA, this would have been a meaningless offer, which I would have accepted without hesitation, knowing it would never actually happen. We would air-kiss goodbye and never think of each other again.

I vaguely recalled, though, that in Copper County, agreeing would be tantamount to signing my name in blood... or possibly posting the banns for our upcoming nuptials, depending on how the gossips spun it.

I scraped my bottom teeth over my lip and responded hesitantly, trying to remember how to communicate in a language I'd once spoken fluently. "Uh. Thank you. So much. For thinking of me? But I'll be working most days—"

"No way! You're working *here*? Are you shooting a campaign for something big? Can you share details?" She fairly vibrated with excitement. "Jasper Wrigley, local celebrity—"

"No," I said firmly. "Not that kind of job. I haven't modeled for a while." Not since I'd agreed to start "our" agency with my asshole ex. "And it's Jasper Lancaster, technically." I held up my bare left hand just as she'd done. "Ditched the husband, haven't quite ditched the name yet."

"Oh." Kayla blinked. "*Oh.*" Her smile dimmed for half a second, like she was recalibrating, then brightened again. "Right. Got it. You know, if you're looking for a date, I have *lots* of gay friends."

Liza and I exchanged a look, and she rolled her eyes slightly before ducking her head to hide her smile.

"Thank you," I told Kayla solemnly. "I'll keep that in mind."

"M'kay, well... I'll let you finish up. But welcome home, Jasper," she said as she headed for the back of the store. "Everyone's gonna be so excited you're back."

Not everyone was. Not the most important person. But I couldn't deny Kayla's words were nice to hear. This reunion had gone leagues better than the last.

That was what we called *progress*.

"Um, that'll be one hundred sixty-seven dollars and twelve cents," Liza informed me.

My eyes bugged. "How much?" I shook my head. "Never mind. It's fine." I swiped my card and tried to ignore the pulse of anxiety as I calculated the balance of my checking account.

Peace offerings weren't cheap, right?

The important thing here was to not panic. Not about Watt and definitely not about money.

Panicking caused a person to do all kinds of stupid stuff like, say, not call their best friend because they didn't know what to say... or get drunk and let their modeling agent blow them when they found out their ex-best friend had gotten married... or not do their due diligence when divorcing their modeling-agent-turned-husband, only to learn the asshole had been steadily siphoning clients from their co-owned agency to the business he'd started with his *new* client-turned-lover... that kind of thing.

I did have a job, so I'd be getting a paycheck soon enough, as long as I made sure the nice folks at Camden-O'Leary Regional High School didn't realize quite how much "on-the-job training" I was gonna need.

And since I was planning on being in Copper County for a few months, I'd have another chance to reconnect with Watt. Hopefully, lots of chances.

As I hefted the groceries through the sliding doors at the front of the store, I took a deep breath and tried to settle myself. I'd never been in Copper County—or O'Leary, technically, I supposed—in autumn before, and it definitely didn't suck. The whole town smelled like a Yankee Candle and looked like a Hollywood soundstage where the scene notes read "small-town autumn." I half expected to hear a harried director yelling, "More leaves! I need more falling leaves over here, people!"

There were worse places to hibernate while I got my life in order before going back to LA. In fact, I had an opportunity to reinvent myself in Copper County. To be a more logical, rational Jasper.

I might not have the first clue how to do that, but "fake it 'til you make it" had always been my motto. Determination was the key.

When I got to the parking lot and found Watt Bartlett standing one spot over from my car in front of a Bartlett Estates truck, though, my determination guttered out like a candle, and my stomach clenched with nerves.

Peace offering, I reminded myself. *Make amends.*

I took another deep, steady breath and prepared to offer a friendly greeting as I handed him his very expensive protein powder and frozen berry mea culpa...

But then I accidentally noticed how Watt's hip was cocked so his jeans pulled tight against his ass, how one enormous, dirty hand was braced on the truck's open hood, and how his biceps flexed against the confines of his shirt while he glared aggressively at the engine. All my rational, logical thoughts got lost in my churning blood, and what emerged from my mouth was a flirty, provoking...

"Want me to jump you?"

Watt wheeled around, eyes wide and panicked, like I wasn't just out to infect him with the zombie virus but shake him down for his lunch money, too. "What? No!"

"I meant jump your battery," I explained patiently, though my eyes might have rolled a little. "Does it need a charge?"

"Hell no. My battery is perfectly charged, thank you very much." Watt's cheeks went red. "I... I mean, this truck's brand-new, and anyway, the interior lights are on. It's not a... a battery issue, and my battery is none of your business."

My eyebrows winged up. "Oookay."

Part of me wanted to teasingly ask if he could say *battery* a couple more times, but no. *Bad Jasper.* I wasn't supposed to be provoking; I was supposed to be *peace offering.*

I owed Watt that much, I really did.

I shuffled the grocery bags and stepped closer, appraising the engine. "Could be the alternator. Or a fuel pump problem?" I hadn't the first clue what either of those things looked like, though I knew all too well how much they cost.

"I know cars, Jasper," Watt scoffed. "I've been working on them all my life, remember?" He caught himself, like even saying those few words had been a bridge further than he was willing to travel. "I've got this, thank you. You can leave."

The words *like you left before* were unspoken, but I was pretty sure I wasn't imagining them. I ran a hand through my hair in frustration, not sure what the hell to say.

There were a lot of things I regretted about the way I'd left Copper County all those years ago.

I hated *how* it had happened—my mother showing up unexpectedly and insisting that we had to leave *right then, immediately, not in five minutes, now.*

I hated *why* it had happened—my parents' relationship had limped along for nearly nineteen years, so it seemed ridiculous that it ended with my mom's high-drama flounce to the West Coast.

I hated *when* it had happened—like, within fucking *seconds* of me kissing my best friend... if you could call it a kiss when it was mostly me accosting him and him windmilling his arms in shock.

But more than any of that, I hated the way I'd reacted afterward. I hated that I hadn't gotten his number from Mabel and apologized from the airport, that I hadn't found his email address and sent an electronic apology, that I hadn't mailed a fucking apology postcard or sent an apology Pony Express from Los Angeles.

And really, I supposed I could start by saying any or all of that.

"Watt," I began. "I wanted to say..."

My shopping bag slipped, and I nearly fumbled it. Watt stepped toward me to catch it, but when I managed to save it on my own, his eyes widened, and he took a giant step back like he couldn't believe he'd voluntarily entered my space.

I huffed out an annoyed breath, pulled out my keys, and dumped the bags in my back seat. "I don't *actually* have the zombie virus, you know."

He scowled. "Huh?"

"Nothing. Look..." I slammed the door shut. "I'm trying to tell you, I—"

"Wait, hold up," Watt demanded, flushing an even deeper red. "This is your car? *This* is?" His eyes roamed over my Jaguar's pristine blue finish. "Fuck you, this is *my* car."

I straightened defensively. "Uh, I assure you, it's not. I bought it myself and put a ton of work into it. The paint and top are custom." I mean, technically, *I* hadn't done the work, but I'd signed the five thousand dollar check to Tito "Topper" Guttierez at Topper Auto Care, so potato, po-tah-toe.

"You know what I mean," he insisted. "This is the car I always wanted. It's a Jaguar XK. You know—*knew*—this was my dream car! We talked about it—"

I snorted. "Whoa there, big man. Riding the ego wave much? I recall *I* said I wanted this car. You might have decided later that you wanted one like it... cough-*copycat*-cough, but it was definitely my idea."

Watt produced an outraged squawk that was incongruous with a man so tall and vast. "Your idea? You don't know shit about cars. You wouldn't know a supercharged V8 from a standard inline six," he scoffed. "You don't *deserve* this much horsepower."

I opened my mouth, then closed it again because, gallingly, I had no clue what he was talking about.

But facts had no place in this conversation any more than they ever had, and I felt myself falling into our familiar rhythm. *This* was a language that came naturally to me. One that had been written on my bones when they were still young and soft.

"I know plenty about cars. Plenty. For example, I *know* I look hot as shit driving this bad boy." I leaned against the Jag and folded my arms over my chest. "And if you're the car guy, why am I the one who has a functional vehicle right now? Maybe *you* don't deserve *that* much horse-powder." I nodded at his truck.

Watt sucked in a shaking breath, his hazel eyes alight. I couldn't tell if he was about to burst into laughter or if I was going to watch him have a heart attack in real time. "It's horse*power*, asshole."

My face went hot. "That's... what I meant."

"Sure. So diagnose my truck for me, then, Car Whisperer." He thrust out an arm toward the hood. "Let's see those mechanic skills in action."

Adrenaline rushed and fizzed in my blood like a shot of caffeine. "Pfft. Unlike some people, I don't need to show off my skills for others—"

Watt leaned in, close enough for me to get a whiff of coffee and cinnamon and apples. It made my stomach curl with a hunger that had nothing to do with food. His mouth twisted up in an impression of a smile, and then he said the four words that had always been my personal kryptonite, my Achilles heel, and my biggest turn-on... at least when they came from him.

"I. Dare. You. Jasper."

There was nothing I could do after that, obviously. The die was cast. Because I had never, not once, backed down from a dare when Watt Bartlett challenged me. And whatever else had changed in my life since I was seven-fucking-teen... that, apparently, had not.

"Fine, then. Prepare for humiliation." I lifted my chin and pushed him out of my way before hauling myself up into the driver's seat.

"One of us should be prepared," he said under his breath. "One of us definitely should."

The apple-cinnamon scent was stronger inside the truck, but I ruthlessly ignored it and tried to concentrate on the things I knew about motor vehicles.

There weren't a lot.

I'd seen four tires, so that probably wasn't the issue. I put my foot on the brake and pressed the Start button, hoping for the best, but the truck just chimed a warning at me. I knew trucks—*most* trucks? definitely *some* trucks— needed gas, so I quickly checked the display. No gas light, but...

Aha.

I hopped out. The second my boots touched the ground, I dusted my hands and felt a curious kind of lightness bubble up inside me. "Got it."

Watt lifted his eyes to the pristine blue sky. "Fuck off."

I didn't have to try to smile at Watt. My smile—okay, fine, my *smirk*—just came naturally. I leaned in, the way he'd done to me earlier, and whispered, "Missing. Key."

"Missing...?" Dumbfounded, Watt looked from me to his truck and back. "Don't be ridiculous. This truck doesn't need a key. As long as I carry the fob right here in my..."

He patted the right pocket of his pants and scowled. He patted his ass, patted his chest, patted his left pocket, and just when I thought he might strip down for a cavity search —not really, but a man could hope—he let out a frustrated growl that made goose bumps dance down my spine. "*No.*"

Score one for team "fake it 'til you make it."

"So, what should my forfeit be? Hmmm." I tapped my lips.

Watt ground his teeth together so aggressively I hoped he had his dentist on speed dial. "We didn't specify a forfeit, therefore—"

"Therefore," I interrupted, "per the Rules of Engagement According to Watt and Jasper, Circa 2003, it should be my—" I broke off as a high-pitched shriek filled the air.

Both of us startled and turned simultaneously.

"Oh my heck, if it isn't the two handsomest men in Copper County! Watt, there you are! I was calling out for you earlier, but you disappeared. Oh, look! You found Jasper!"

"More like he found me," Watt muttered.

She stepped between my car and Watt's, a key fob dangling from her finger. "Honey, I think you dropped this."

Honey? Was she talking to…

Oh.

I hadn't been aware just how much I was enjoying the silly interaction with Watt, just how light and buoyant I'd felt, until that one little word sent a pinprick of jealousy straight into my chest, puncturing my happiness balloon.

What the hell am I doing?

I wasn't seventeen, joking around with my best friend. I didn't *have* a best friend anymore. And I sure as hell had no right to be jealous now… not that I ever had.

I didn't know anything about Watt's life these past twenty years beyond the simple facts Mabel had volunteered: his marriage, his kid, his divorce, and his orchard. I didn't know his friends or his hobbies. I didn't know who he was dating.

I wasn't being rational or logical right now, and I hadn't

been making amends. I'd been on the fast train to delulu land.

"Dave found it under the pile of paper turkeys," Kayla was saying. "And Liza said you'd lost your balance." She petted his arm. "You okay?"

"Yeah." Watt's jaw flexed. "Fine," he said gruffly, reaching for the keys.

Kayla took a step back, keeping them just out of reach. "I was *just* telling Jasper I really wanted to go out to dinner and catch up while he's in town. Wouldn't that be amazing? You and me, and Jasper and... ooh, what about Oliver Castillo? I think Jasper and Ollie would really—"

"No," Watt said, the single syllable ringing with finality.

For once, the two of us were in perfect agreement. I assumed Oliver was one of Kayla's many "gay friends," and the idea of a double date with her and Watt was somewhere on my personal must-do list between bamboo torture and self-immolation.

Kayla frowned. "No? But... *Oh, right.*" Her expression cleared, and she smiled knowingly. "I forgot about this thing between you two."

"What thing?" I demanded, suddenly wondering how my voice had gotten so high. Was I somehow emitting Watt-seeking pheromones? Could she smell them? Could *he*?

"There's no *thing* between me and Jasper," Watt said flatly.

"I mean the way you loathed each other back in the day. Always bickering and squabbling, daring each other to do things, getting each other in trouble." She laughed lightly. "The Rivals of Copper County, we used to call you."

Watt's gaze met mine, but I quickly looked down at my boots.

Oh. So... not the pheromones, then.

Was that how Watt remembered our friendship? To me, bickering and squabbling had been my immature flirtation game, and dares had been our love language.

I rubbed absently at my chest. "That was a long time ago," I offered.

"Ancient history," Watt agreed.

"We're all adults now." I set my hands on my hips. "We've matured."

"Some of us, anyway," he said under his breath. He cleared his throat and said more loudly, "I mean, yes. Adults."

Since my hearing was fucking excellent, I gave him a scathing glance. "And *as* an adult," I told Kayla, "I can get along with anyone... no matter how rude or arrogant or dismissive he might be. There's no animosity between us, is there, Watt?"

"Nope." Hazel eyes met mine in challenge. "In fact, there's nothing between us at all anymore, is there, Jasper?"

I plastered on my model smile. "Not a single thing," I lied.

Watt nodded once. "And that's how it's going to stay."

He grabbed his key fob from Kayla's hand, thanked her, and climbed into his truck. "Gotta go. Errands," he said when she protested. "See you later." He pulled out of his spot like he was fleeing a horde of the undead.

Or just one zombie in particular.

I kept my easy smile firmly in place as I waved goodbye to Kayla, got in my own car, and headed out of O'Leary toward the single loop road that fed tiny Copper County— the collection of homes clustered around Copper Lake.

I couldn't lie, I was feeling pretty fucking deflated... while also irrationally angry.

Did I have any right to be upset that Watt seemed

determined to avoid me? Obviously not. It might be argued that I'd low-key avoided him for twenty years.

Did that mean I was okay with it? Also no.

And I wasn't one to give up without a fight... as my ex-husband would soon find out.

Watt could be angry or even hate me a little, but the idea of him ignoring me was unacceptable.

"And that's how it's going to stay," I mocked, imitating Watt's deep voice.

Pfft. We'd just see about that.

I had amends to make, damn it.

It wasn't until I'd passed the turnoff to Bartlett Orchard and was halfway down the driveway to Mabel's place that I realized I still had Watt's fucking peace offering tucked in my back seat... and then I laughed out loud, knowing exactly what I was going to do with it.

"Game on," I whispered.

CHAPTER THREE

WATT

"Fucking *fuck*." I shoved my laptop away with a groan, and it skittered across the kitchen island. "Derry, my child, find a career where you don't have to work on spreadsheets, okay? The fucking things hate me, and I'm concerned it might be genetic."

What should have been a five-minute job updating monthly sales had turned into an hour-long odyssey of beeps and "Critical Error" messages that sapped my will to live, and about the only good thing I could say for it was that I'd been too busy cursing my computer to think about Jasper Wrigley.

It made a pleasant change from every other waking moment of my week.

I. Dare. You. Jasper.

Honestly, what had I been thinking, starting that nonsense?

My son's snort rumbled across the kitchen as he added a third box of penne to the pot on the stove, and I told myself to stop thinking about shit that annoyed me and start focusing on stuff that mattered. Namely, pasta night with my high school senior.

At six two, Derry matched my height, and thanks to his hockey workouts and hard physical labor at the orchard, he was solidly muscled. Ordinarily, he ate clean and tracked his macros, but on our Thursday pasta nights, especially when he was cooking, all bets were off.

"Mom's tech genes cancel out your anti-tech genes, Dad, so I'm tech-neutral," he said. "Lucky for me, Mom's ability to trip over herself while standing still didn't cancel out your hockey genes."

I laughed. "Eh. You're better than I ever was. That's why Utica's going to be scouting you in a few weeks, right? You and Zach?"

Kayla's son was Derry's best friend, fiercest hockey competition, and the snarky, emo counterpoint to my golden retriever child. Zach had gone through a rough patch a while back—picking fights, spray-painting graffiti, and even dating a twenty-four-year-old "older man" before his mom put a stop to it—but he was a good kid, and he'd gotten himself back on track.

For as long as the pair had been friends, they'd talked about playing college hockey together. When Zach had turned eighteen last month, Derry had planned to take him to get a tattoo of Trax the Moose, the Utica mascot... but presumably, Kayla had squashed that idea, at least for now.

"I hope so," Derry said. "Zach's a little worried. He knows he needs a scholarship if he wants to go to college, and I think the pressure's getting to him. His mom says we have this on lock, though, if we focus." He tapped his spoon against the side of the pot and seemed to hesitate before glancing over at me. "Dad... you know I'm cool staying here in Copper County next year, right? That way, you wouldn't have to pay Paddy full-time. I mean, I want to work with you at the orchard eventually, so I don't *need* to go to college at all—"

"Nope," I said just as firmly as I had the last five times we'd discussed this. "Don't worry about the orchard right now. That's *my* responsibility. If you want to take it over someday, it'll be here, but first, I want you to go have the full experience—college hockey, underwater basketweaving, study abroad, a job doing something that actually interests you. I want you to have choices, kiddo."

When losing my virginity had ended with Rachel pregnant my sophomore year of college, it had felt like a giant arm sweeping across the game board of my life, knocking away ninety percent of my own options. It was dumb luck that one of the only ones I'd had left—to leave college, marry Rachel, and build my parents' hobby orchard into a home and business to support my family—was one I didn't regret for an instant.

But I wanted more for my kid.

I'd been busting my ass to pay off the mortgage from when I'd bought my parents out of the orchard years ago, and now I was nearly done. If Derry needed financial help to meet his goals, I had him covered.

"Yeah, but Dad—"

"But nothing," I said. "If you don't get the Utica scholarship, your mom can get you the faculty friends-and-family discount at U of R, and you'll be able to see her and Doug and your little brothers more. Or if you'd rather go somewhere else... we'll see what we can do. Don't be afraid to dream big, okay?"

"Yeah." Derry's mouth twisted up in a half smile. "Right."

"Good," I approved. "Now, tell me how practice went

today. I feel like you've barely talked about hockey all week."

This was unlike him. Usually, the soundtrack to my morning chores was Derry's mile-a-minute recap of practice, his stats (specifically how they compared with Zach's), and his worries about Camp Fair Shot closing.

Some mornings, before the coffee hit, I wanted to beg him to chill a little, but I didn't. Most kids pulled away from their parents when they got to a certain age—I sure as hell had—and I was lucky Derry was an open book with me.

"It was good," he said enthusiastically.

I waited for more, but nothing came.

"And the new coach?" I prompted.

"Great. Yeah. Coach Lancaster's *really* nice. I have him for American History, too, did I tell you? I like him. The other guys like him. You'd like him, too."

I frowned. "Likability's important, I guess, but how is he as a coach? A week ago, you were worried Zach would take your starting spot because his face-off average is better than yours, but his communication on the ice isn't great. You wondered how the new coach would handle it."

"Yeah," Derry agreed. "I'm not worried about that anymore. Coach Lancaster says hockey's about more than getting the puck in the net. It's about being balanced and aligned on a fundamental level because the real game is in your mind."

I waited for him to laugh and say, "*Gotcha.*" He didn't.

"You... mean he's got you drilling on basic skills? Because you said you needed to work on moving the puck out of the zone under pressure—"

"Nah." Derry's voice was muffled as he peered into the refrigerator. "Coach Lancaster says we need to build strong foundations for ourselves physically and mentally before we can work on our skating, so we haven't suited up for practice this week."

"But kiddo, your first game's two weeks from tomorrow," I said, aware I was pointing out the obvious. "You've been stressed about the season getting canceled, stressed about whether you'd start, stressed about Utica, stressed about Camp Fair Shot—"

"I know, right? I'm kind of over it. Coach says it's not good to exist in a high-stress state for too long. He might have us lace up tomorrow, though, to ground ourselves on the rink. That'll be good."

"Ground yourselves," I repeated. "*Ground* yourselves?"

Look, I didn't want to be *that parent*—the one who tries to tell a coach how to do their job or gets whiny when their angel baby doesn't get enough ice time.

I knew the school had so much trouble finding a replacement after Tamsen Monroe had gone on maternity leave they'd considered canceling the season.

I understood that they were hamstrung by some district-wide rule that only faculty members could coach, and I'd heard they'd asked everyone from the principal to the substitute teachers to the cafeteria workers—but no one had been available to take on the task.

I was sure this coach they'd hired was the best of what was around, and the rumors said he'd skated for Boston—whether BU or BC, I wasn't sure—which was impressive.

But also, my kid was coming off a losing season last year and had a real opportunity this year to get a scholarship from his top-choice college, so one could say I had *concerns*.

"Maybe I should speak to this coach—" I began gently.

"Dad, chill. It's all good. Honestly." Derry emerged from the fridge holding a block of cheese and examined it. "Hey, what's Taleggio? Is it like Parmesan?"

"Stop! Don't use that," I barked.

Derry dropped the cheese on the counter and stared at me like he'd never heard me use that tone before... probably because I hadn't. Not since he was little enough to accidentally touch hot stoves, anyway. "What's wrong with the cheese?"

My gut clenched, and I knew my face had to be bright red. I cleared my throat. "It's... not ours."

"Oh." He frowned. "Did Chris leave it over here? Is it one of his charcuterie cheeses that tastes like soap?"

I felt sweat break out beneath my armpits. "Ha. You know Chris," I lied, throwing my friend and his famous charcuterie boards under the bus with zero compunction.

The truth of the matter was not something I wanted to discuss with my seventeen-year-old. Not when it would only lead to questions I didn't know how to answer.

When I'd finally gotten home Sunday (after hitting up Wegmans in Piermonte, where groceries could be acquired without fear of running into your ex-best friend *or* anyone you used to date), the orchard had been jumping. Normally, this would have been my time to get out and glad-hand my customers. To maybe teach them a thing or two about permaculture and sustainable growing while they were petting the goats.

That day, though, I'd craved solitude and a chance to mutter under my breath without anyone wondering whether I'd gone crazy (the answer was a resounding *yes*), so I'd left my employees in charge and set off alone to check the trees and fences for signs of deer incursions.

People didn't want to believe anything so beautiful could be so destructive, but I knew better. If you wanted to minimize damage, you couldn't build your fences too secure.

By the time I'd walked off the worst of my mood, it had been sunset. Derry had already gotten home from Rachel's, and the driveway gate had been closed... which was why I'd been surprised to see a giant brown paper bag sitting on my back porch. As I'd gotten closer, my heart had started to pound, like I'd subconsciously known what I was seeing.

Inside the bag were all the groceries I'd meant to get at Lyon's that morning, along with a few extra items (like a block of weird, unpronounceable cheese) that seemed like they'd been mixed in from someone else's order.

And on the outside of the bag, written in large, black block letters, had been the words MATURE ADULT PEACE OFFERING.

Bag in hand, I'd stalked back out to my garden, peered over the fields and through the trees that marked my property line, and sent a fiery glare up at the house on the hill next door.

How. Fucking. Dare. He.

I hadn't been proud of my behavior that morning, okay? Not of the way I'd provoked Jasper or the way I'd let him rile me. Not proud of how petty and childish I'd sounded—*Christ, had I really told him his Jaguar should be mine?*—or of my smug satisfaction that I'd gotten the last word before driving off.

I hadn't been proud of how much I'd enjoyed our foolish, half-angry banter and teasing, either. Of how weirdly alive I'd felt before Kayla brought us back to reality... if *alive* was the right word to describe the feeling of being whacked in the gut with a cattle prod.

But seeing that bag made all my satisfaction at our encounter evaporate in a heartbeat and my unsettled feeling spread like apple blight.

In short, I'd been pissed.

Mature Adult Peace Offering? Was he kidding?

A peace offering for what, exactly? Coming back to my town and stirring up feelings that should have remained buried? Leaving in the first place all those years ago?

It could have been either or possibly both... from anyone else.

From Jasper, I knew it was neither.

It was no peace offering. It was a declaration of war.

It was him getting the last word.

And every damn grocery in the bag was a consolation prize.

But what was worse—so much worse—than knowing he'd won the battle was remembering how I'd stalked inside, unloaded the groceries onto the kitchen counter with the force of tiny concussive bombs, grabbed that block of stupid cheese to throw it in the garbage... and found myself snort-laughing so hard I'd doubled over with tears in my eyes.

It was *intolerable*.

"Dad?" I blinked out of my daze to find Derry's hand waving in front of my face. "Hellooo? Danger cheese?"

"Sorry." I ran a hand over my face. "I was a million miles away."

"Yeah? Was it warm there?" he joked. "'Cause your face is all flushed."

"Ha." I pulled at my collar. "Must've been."

"Come eat." Derry carried a giant vat of pasta to the kitchen table, where he'd already set out bowls and spoons. By the time I took my seat at the end, he was already filling his dish like he was worried there might not be enough for him otherwise. I smothered a smile.

"Listen, about hockey," I began. "Tomorrow's the parent practice—"

He looked up, mouth bulging. "You're going?"

"Don't I always? Didn't miss a single Friday last year."

"Yeah, but..." Derry chewed and swallowed so quickly he nearly choked. "Promise me you won't say anything to Coach Lancaster, Dad, please? I know he doesn't coach the way Coach Monroe did or the way your old coaches did, but... he's got good stuff to share. He's trying his best, and it was only the first week of practice. Give him the benefit of the doubt. Isn't that what you always say?"

Seeing Derry's earnest face, I couldn't help but grin ruefully. My son was not only a talented athlete and an all-around good person, but he was showing a hell of a lot more maturity than I had this week. Maybe I could learn a lesson from him about being a bigger person. Maybe I could try taking my own advice.

"I promise, Derry," I said, patting his shoulder. "You won't even know I'm there."

———

WHEN I GOT to practice the next day, I had my head on straight for the first time in a week.

Partly, this was because I'd stopped by the bakery with Ollie and eaten a pumpkin pie tart, which was the best thing I'd ever put in my mouth. I hadn't thought it possible to improve on the greatest dessert known to man, but shrinking it down gave it the perfect filling-to-crust-to-whipped-cream ratio, as I'd tried to explain to Oliver... who'd promptly pretended to fall asleep in his chair.

Mostly, though, I was feeling clearheaded because I'd decided I was done being annoyed about Jasper showing up in town. I'd see his "mature, adult peace offering" and raise him an *actual* adult response... by ignoring the gesture and him for the next week or so while he was in town.

Game, set, match.

And I would celebrate by watching my kid kick ass at a sport he loved.

When I pulled into the rink parking lot, I saw I wasn't the only person in town who'd decided to spend a wild and crazy Friday afternoon at hockey practice. Nearly every spot was filled... which shouldn't have been possible, since there were only about twenty kids on the team.

The reason for the crowd became clear when I found a group of hockey parents lying in wait for me by the door to the rink.

"Oh my heck. Watt!" Kayla said, grabbing my forearm and dragging me into their huddle. "Thank goodness."

"Hey, Kayla. Fred. Jasmine." I nodded at each of them in turn while casually (and unsuccessfully) attempting to remove my arm from Kayla's clutches. "What's up?"

Jasmine sighed, pushing back her braids. "Not a problem, necessarily. The new coach is... different," she said diplomatically.

"She means he's filling the kids' heads with mystical woo-woo bullshit," Fred said grimly, running a hand over his bald head. "Now, folks in town have gotten word of it. They're here to watch the show for themselves."

"Ehhh. People are mostly here 'cause the coach is pretty," Jasmine corrected, but at a look from Fred, she admitted, "And also to watch the show."

"Calvin says yesterday Coach told them to *focus on team synergy* and *center themselves with deep breathing.*" Fred shook his head, disgusted. "What kind of bullshit is that?"

"I heard he had the boys line up and tell each of their teammates one thing they really appreciated about them."

Kayla's nose wrinkled. "Do you suppose he learned that when he skated for Boston?"

I glanced toward the building with a frown. Their concerns echoed my own... but I'd promised Derry, and I tried not to break promises to him. "Did any of you email the coach and ask his plan?"

They exchanged a look. "Er, not exactly?" Kayla said. "We figured you'd be the best one to talk to him, given your... history."

My hockey history had ended eighteen years ago when I'd left college, but it was nice that people remembered.

"Just a friendly chat," Jasmine begged. "To ask about the plan, like you said."

"Or a more aggressive chat," Fred grumbled. "To tell him he doesn't know his stick from his dick."

I rolled my eyes. "Dial it back, Fred. Coach doesn't need a bunch of us ganging up on him. Let's see how today goes, and maybe—*maybe*—I'll have a word with him next week."

Kayla gave me a melting look. "Oh, Watt. You're always so... *moderate.*"

Jesus. How did she manage to make the word *moderate* sound like an innuendo?

"Don't be too moderate," Fred advised. "If practice goes tits up like I think it will, tell him we won't tolerate shenanigans with our hockey program. Remind him we pay his salary."

I snorted. Since only an utter asshole would say something like that, I definitely would not. "Keep an open mind," I told him.

I headed for the double doors with the three of them at my heels, planning to duck into one of the seats at the top of the crowded stadium—the better to observe from a distance—but what I saw on the ice was so unbelievable I found myself drawn down the steps like I was pulled by an invisible magnet.

Twenty young men in skates, pads, and jerseys were spread across one side of the rink, all bent over at the waist, their gloved hands braced on the ice in a four-point stance, facing the bleachers packed with gawking spectators.

Most of the crowd, though, seemed to be less focused on the players and more on the coach...

And I couldn't blame them.

Coach Lancaster was facing the players, mimicking their bent stance, but instead of skates and pads, the man wore running shoes and a pair of black compression tights... tights that lovingly cradled every defined muscle of his thighs and ass as he thrust them toward the audience.

I tried to swallow, but my mouth was bone-dry.

My battery was charging—*hard*—and that was seriously unusual for me. It had been ages since I'd been this attracted to anyone, woman or man.

But I was not complaining.

"Remember," the coach said, his voice muffled and distorted from hanging upside down over the ice, "on the inhales, we're aligning our posture and—hey, tighten that core, please, Brandon. I know it's hard on your skates, but double the effort, double the reward. Good!—and now on the exhale, we're siiiinking into the stretch—nicely done, Derry, downward dog *around* your pads!"

I tried to force my eyes away, to find my son among the players on the ice, but the man's ass was like one of those cartoon snake charmers with the swirling eyes, and my cock was a very willing cobra. I was vaguely aware of someone talking to me, but I ignored them.

"This time, on the inhale," the coach went on, "I want

us each to set an intention, guys. Let's all visualize the three p's of hockey: persistence, patience, uh... puck handling. And then, on the exhale, I want you to gather up all your doubts and insecurities and *whoosh*... just blow them away."

"Coach?" A player tried to raise his hand and nearly face-planted on the ice. "How do I visualize persistence?"

"Ha. Good question, Kip." The coach straightened and laughed as he shook his hair into place. "Would anyone like to share what persistence looks like to them?"

I sucked in a shaking breath.

That golden hair. That laugh. That voice.

No fucking way.

I suddenly understood what Kayla meant when she talked about my *history*. It had nothing to do with playing hockey and everything to do with the coach himself.

In what kind of twisted universe was the second man I'd ever lusted after... actually the *first* man I'd lusted after, since the first and the second were the same? What kind of cosmic prank had me wanting Jasper Wrigley again at all?

Why the hell was he even here?

Before I could think twice—hell, before I could think *once*—I found myself marching down the stairs, vaulting over the low wall, and stalking across the ice in my work boots.

Jasper's eyes widened with happy surprise. "Watt! Hey. Did you get my—uh." His surprise turned to alarm as I stalked closer, not stopping until our chests were inches apart.

"What the hell do you think you're doing?" I demanded in a low voice, well aware—finally—of just how many eyes were on me.

I refused to notice that Jasper looked at least as good as he had the other day and better than he had twenty years ago, all flushed, mussed, and bright-eyed. This close, I spotted three tiny freckles that formed a triangle above his eyebrow, and a small white scar that appeared old for him but was new to me bisected his bottom lip. For reasons I didn't want to contemplate, noticing these changes made my temper flare hotter.

"I'm, ah... coaching?" Jasper glanced from me to the team to the audience and back. "Coaching," he repeated more firmly. "Yeah. Because I'm the Fighting Marmots' new coach."

"You are not," I retorted in an angry whisper. "You don't even live here. And the coach is named Lancaster—"

"Jasper Lancaster. Yeah." He lifted his chin a little. "My married name."

The words felt like a punch to my solar plexus, and my lungs forgot how to work for a minute. He was *married*?

"I got divorced but kept the name. And I *do* live here... for the next few months." A beat later, he added, "Why do you look surprised? Didn't your girlfriend tell you all this?"

"My... what? No." I shook my head, heart still racing and thoughts utterly scattered. "How?"

As in, how the hell had I not heard any of this? I mean, yes, every time Mabel had brought up Jasper's name, I'd tried to change the subject... but that hadn't seemed to stop her from reminiscing at will about our summer hijinks or forcing me to admire whatever new magazine Jasper had sent her to show off his ad campaigns.

She'd told me about the gelato he'd eaten after walking a show in Milan, for fuck's sake, and how he'd had ankle surgery the week Abe died, which was why he hadn't made it out to the Cape for the funeral in the Wrigley family burial plot. How had she not shared *this*?

Jasper rolled his eyes and whispered hotly, "How? Gay

marriage has been legal for a hot minute all across the land, Bartlett. Keep up."

I felt like I'd been given a second punch to really round out the first. The universe was definitely laughing at me. "G-gay?"

Jasper seemed shocked by my shock. "Uh, yeah. Super gay. Didn't the kiss I laid on you all those years ago clue you in? And I'm very sorry about that," he added quickly. "*Very*. About the kiss, I mean, not about being gay." Flushing, he darted a glance at the team and then at the crowd. "Look, I would love to catch up with you—honestly—but maybe with less of an audience? I have to get back to coaching now."

My mind was as murky as the lake after a storm and churning with too many slippery new thoughts and ideas— he thought *he'd* kissed *me?*—to catch hold of any one. Instead, I focused on the last sentence.

"But you can't be the coach!" I barked. I remembered trying to talk to him about the sport when we were kids and him nodding blankly. "You don't know shit about hockey."

As soon as the words escaped me, I realized how foolish they were. If I hadn't known Jasper was gay and married and divorced, for all I knew, he had a PhD in hockey.

But Jasper's eyes flashed the way they always had when I'd called him on something and he'd decided to brazen his way through it. "I do so! For example, I know stretching is crucial for core strength and flexibility. So, if you'll excuse me, I'm going to rescue the kids from their downward dogs—"

"Have you ever played a game of hockey in your life?" I demanded.

Mumbled expressions of surprise rolled through the stands. I wasn't sure at which point I'd begun speaking loud enough for everyone to hear, but when I turned my head, I found them all silently leaning toward us, hanging on every word.

Jasper blushed harder. "Irrelevant."

"It's not. That's my kid—" I jabbed a hand in Derry's direction.

"I know," he said softly. "Derry's great. He looks just like you."

Those words and the sadness in his eyes made my stomach twist, but I forced myself to stand firm. "Then you'll understand why it's very *relevant* to me if his coach doesn't know what the fuck he's doing."

Jasper squared his shoulders. "Principal Schmidt hired me. You don't get a say—"

"I do, 'cause I'm a taxpayer in this town, and I pay your —" The minute I heard the words leave my mouth, I shut it quickly, but it was too late.

Jasper's face went purple. "I dare you to finish that sentence."

"Dad?" Derry whisper-hissed. I hadn't noticed him skating over until, suddenly, he was standing alongside Jasper and me, his face a picture of teenage anger and mortification. "You said you'd be cool today. You *promised*."

I squeezed my eyes shut and sucked in a breath through my nose. "Derry, I'm sorry. I didn't..."

"Derry, go finish the yoga sequence with your team-mates," Jasper said in a kind but firm voice. A fucking *teacher* voice. "It's almost time for our affirmations."

My eyes flew open just in time to see my son glance between me and Jasper... and give *me* a look of warning. "Okay, Coach," he said before skating off.

Stung and furious, I rounded on Jasper. "If you think

affirmations are going to win them games, that proves my point. You shouldn't be doing this job."

Jasper straightened. "I'll have you know, I've worked with a mindset coach for years, asshole, and according to the hockey videos I've—I mean, according to my research—many professional athletes find affirmations a key contributor to success. Besides, winning isn't everything."

An unwilling snort escaped me. "News to me. I got your '*mature adult peace offering*,' by the way. Nicely played. *Not* accepted."

Bizarrely, impossibly—*provokingly*—Jasper's mouth twitched. "You do realize that by not accepting it, you're only proving I'm more mature than you are?"

"What?" I scowled. "No."

"Sorry." He smirked. "I don't make the rules."

"That is the most *bullshit*—"

"Oh my heck. Watt?" A pair of hands wrapped around my forearm from behind, and I flinched hard, but Kayla hung on—probably because she'd followed me onto the ice wearing a pair of dress shoes and couldn't keep her balance, I realized belatedly. "Honey, is everything okay here?" Her eyebrows formed a curious little pucker.

"Watt? Buddy, I know I said be aggressive," Fred called from the players' box, "but maybe not this aggressive, huh? Not in front of the kids, anyway."

"What'd you expect?" called a voice I didn't recognize. "Watt and Jasper have been rivals since way back. They *never* got along."

Jasper's eyes met mine, asking a question I didn't know how to answer.

"Oh, dang, I forgot that!" someone else laughed. "Jesus, remember those summers? Everything was *I dare you* and *I bet you*. And who could forget the humiliating consequences they came up with for each other? Remember the mud bath?"

"That was a million years ago, Watt. Let bygones be bygones so the hunky coach can do his job, huh?" another person yelled.

Jasper's blush, which had started to fade, came back with a vengeance.

Someone else piped up. "Watt was a champion hockey player back in the day. If he says the coach doesn't know what he's doing, I believe him. Uh, I mean... no offense, Coach Lancaster!" they added.

I barely paid attention to who was talking and what they were saying. My gaze remained locked with Jasper's, each of us daring the other to look away first, neither of us willing to bend...

Until another man spoke up from the sidelines and drew everyone's attention.

"Watt," Principal Schmidt said mildly. Arms folded across his chest, he stood behind the boards of the rink, watching me and Jasper like we were a pair of misbehaving students. It hit harder because I was acting like one. "I see you've met our coach."

"Sir." I fought not to squirm. "I apologize for disrupting practice, but I had some concerns about Coach Lancaster's methods." I shot Jasper a look. "And qualifications."

Principal Schmidt stroked his mustache. "Then let me see if I can set them to rest. Coach Lancaster has two crucial qualifications." He raised his voice so it carried to everyone in the stands. "First, he's a teacher at the school—and he's turning out to be a fine one. His great-aunt Mabel would be proud," he added fondly.

Jasper blushed.

"You might remember, Watt," the principal went on,

"the school board passed a rule a while back requiring coaches to be part of the faculty? We had a problem where a coach was fraternizing with a student, and the board decided it was easiest to make sure the head coach of every team or extracurricular activity was held to our faculty's contractual standards regarding fraternization and bullying. I'm sure none of us takes exception to that."

"Well... no," I admitted.

The crowd murmured uncertainly.

"Jasper's second qualification," the principal went on, "is that he's *willing*. No other staff member was able to take on the job. His participation is the only way our team's able to play this season. Coach Lancaster was very clear with me about his lack of hockey expertise, but he's been working with Coach Monroe after hours all week to get himself up to speed—"

He had?

Surprised, I darted a look at Jasper, but he was staring down at his running shoes.

"—while also handling a full schedule of courses and taking the required tests for his temporary teaching credentials," the principal went on relentlessly. "I assure you, he's not here on a lark."

Shame made me squirm. "No, sir. I didn't mean..."

My voice trailed off. I wasn't sure what I *had* meant, exactly, but I knew I'd been wrong.

Again.

"Whoa, whoa. Lack of expertise? I thought Coach skated for Boston?" someone yelled.

Jasper stared down at the ice. "In Boston," he murmured, so low only I could hear. "I specifically said *in* Boston. And I was six at the time."

I snickered.

Jasper's gaze snapped to mine, and whatever he saw on my face had his lips twitching again before he looked away.

I clapped a hand over my mouth as a burst of totally inappropriate amusement bubbled up uncontrollably.

Beside me, Jasper bit his lip and ducked his head again, though his shoulders shook with laughter.

"Can Coach Lancaster play hockey or not?" Fred demanded. "'Cause, Mike, the kids need a coach *now*. Why'd you hire someone who can't actually coach 'em?"

Jasper let out a little sigh, and my amusement died.

Fred wasn't wrong. In fact, I agreed with him. Jasper had no business coaching this team—not when our kids' futures might hang in the balance—and I couldn't imagine why he'd thought he could.

But watching Jasper's shoulders sag like his bravado had been pushed to its limits and he was resigning himself to defeat made my chest squeeze against a surge of sympathy or protectiveness or—shit, I didn't know, but it was strange and new and distinctly uncomfortable.

I liked to win, yes. I especially liked to win against Jasper.

But that didn't mean I wanted Jasper to lose. Not to anyone but me.

So when Principal Schmidt finally nodded thoughtfully and said, "I think I have a solution that will work for everyone... if Watt agrees," I was primed to make a decision I would almost instantly regret.

"Sure," I said. "What do you need me to do?"

CHAPTER FOUR

JASPER

"Co-coaches," I groaned, tipping my head back into the couch cushion. Late-afternoon sunshine streamed through Tamsen Monroe's living room window, which was open to catch the chilly breeze. "Me and *Watt*."

"Technically, he's not. He's a parent-coach liaison. And I don't see the problem here." Tam selected another double chocolate cookie from the tin she'd perched on her pregnant belly and stuffed half of it in her mouth. "You know you need help with fundamentals, and Watt knows hockey as well as I do. It's pretty awesome that he agreed to do it for the sake of the kids. If anyone should be upset about this, it's us." She patted her belly sadly. "I don't know who's gonna bring us stress-baked treats every day in exchange for our coaching-coaching now, Bean."

I snorted. "Please. Considering you're my only friend in this town, it'll still be me."

Our new friendship was unexpected, but I was grateful for it. When I'd shown up at the address Principal Schmidt had given me, after delivering my dubious peace offering to Watt's back porch Sunday evening, I'd been flushed with victory and eager for hockey tutoring... but when Coach Monroe had answered the door, I'd been more than a little intimidated.

I'd been told that the woman knew her hockey—that she'd played "division one" in college, which was apparently very impressive, and that a couple of her brothers had played the sport professionally. But no one had mentioned that the former coach of the Fighting Marmots would be a tall, buff woman with glowing olive skin, a stomach the size of a small planet, and a take-no-shit attitude.

"So you're the hockey newbie who's taking my team," she'd said coolly. Her dark eyes had lasered right through the confident smile I'd papered on.

"Er. Well. Not *taking* so much as... borrowing temporarily?" I'd offered, smile faltering. I'd held up one of Mabel's vintage tins like an offering to a goddess. "Will you please teach me your ways?"

Tamsen had sniffed derisively... then she'd sniffed again, deeper this time. Her eyes had narrowed at the tin. "Is that... chocolate?"

"Banana chocolate chip muffins. I made them this afternoon. I'm a stress-baker. You know, a person whose response to upheaval is to produce more baked goods than any one human should reasonably consume? I wasn't sure if you were one of those super-health-conscious coaches, but I thought I'd take a chance since—"

"Shit." She'd rubbed her bulging stomach, then grabbed my arm and hauled me—and my baked goods—into her cozy house. "Sit your ass down. I told my husband I'd planned to give you hairy eyeballs for at least five minutes, but chocolate is my kryptonite."

Just like that, a beautiful friendship had been born.

In a week that had seen me make very little progress

organizing Mabel's cluttered house, zero progress finding an attorney back in California who'd help me sue my ex without requiring an enormous retainer, and negative progress making amends to Watt, it was nice that at least one thing was going right.

Tam and I had spent every evening this week on her couch, sometimes alongside her husband or her brother Delaney—her "non-hockey" brother, as she called him—who was staying with them for a while. She'd provided me with lesson plans for taking over her history classes, along with cheat sheets about which kids needed a little extra help and how to provide it. We'd also watched countless YouTube hockey games, with frequent pauses to explain the rules and formations, and quizzes afterward to check my learning.

One of those things was working out incredibly well.

Hint: it was not the one with the ice.

"Be honest," I asked suddenly. "Am I the most hockey-ignorant person in Copper County?"

Tam's smile softened as she licked chocolate from her lips. "Of course not. Look at Delaney. He's purposefully ignorant, and that's way worse." She pointed at her brother, who was curled up on a chair in the corner, reading a thick hardcover.

"As the official Un-Sportsy Monroe, I do feel I have a certain standard of ignorance to uphold," he said mildly, turning his page without glancing up. He added pointedly, "Tamsquatch."

She narrowed her eyes. "You know I hate that name."

"Do you?" He batted his eyes innocently behind black-framed glasses. "My bad."

"Keep it up," she warned. "I'll FaceTime Wells and

Lawson. We'll take turns forcibly explaining backchecking to you—"

"Oh, I know that one," I said before Delaney could clap back. I recited, "Backchecking is when a player skates back across the ring, from the offensive zone to their own defensive zone, to stop the opposing team's attack."

"Very good," Tam approved. "Except it's rin*k*, sweetie. With a *k*."

I narrowed my eyes. "But it's round... or oval-ish, I guess. Like a *ring*." I looked to Delaney for support.

He scraped his bottom teeth over his top lip and said, almost apologetically, "It's... actually a rectangle with rounded corners."

I pictured the place in my mind and realized he was right. "Shit." I slumped back in my seat.

"You'll get it eventually." Tam patted my knee soothingly... then ruined it by adding, "But for right now, you're definitely the most hockey-ignorant hockey *coach* in Copper County. So explain to me why coaching—sorry, *liaising*— with Watt will be a problem. I've known him for a couple years, through Derry, and he's always seemed like a steady Freddy. A good guy."

"To you," I muttered, squirming deeper into the cushion. "Watt and I have history. Liaising is... not a good idea." Despite the teenage-like libido inside me that wanted nothing more than to liaise the fuck out of him.

She drew her leg up beneath her as though her bones were elastic. It looked uncomfortable but apparently wasn't. "Like... romantic history? You and Watt? I didn't know he was queer." She winced and held up a hand before Delaney or I could object. "I realized that was an incredibly ignorant thing to say the second it was out of my mouth. I don't know if I expected him to flash the secret gay decoder ring or what."

I laughed, and so did her brother. One of the things Tam and I had bonded over was my concern about being an out, gay hockey coach in a small town like Copper County, but Tam had put my mind at rest. Her husband, Lucas, had grown up here, and people had been incredibly accepting when he'd come out as trans a couple of years ago. It was one of the reasons they'd moved back before starting their family.

"No, my history with Watt wasn't a romance. Not for him, anyway. As far as I know, he's straight. Isn't he with Kayla?"

She shook her head. "Nah. Watt's pretty tightly woven into Copper County, and if he was dating anyone seriously, Lucas's Grandma Charlene would've told me more than I wanted to know."

Delaney twisted on his chair and propped his chin in his hand, abandoning all pretense of reading. "So if not romance with you and Watt, then what?"

"Remember I told you I used to spend summers here with my great-aunt and uncle? For a while, Watt was the beefcakey boy next door who made my pre-coming-out heart go pitty-pat." I drew my legs up on the sofa, mirroring Tam. "Part of my personal '*I knew I was gay when...*' story."

"Ah, yes." Delaney nodded. "I had one of those."

"So you worshipped Watt from afar?" Tam asked.

"God no." I laughed. "I worshipped him from up close and personal. We met when we were twelve, I think. The first summer my parents shipped me to Copper County. Watt was larger than life even then—I was a late bloomer and didn't hit my first growth spurt until I was fourteen, so picture this tall, dark, muscly Adonis and this scrawny, tow-headed, bug-eyed little shrimp—"

"A lot like now?" Tam teased.

"Pfft. Lies." I demonstrated by flexing my biceps. While she was distracted by laughter, I reached over and grabbed a cookie from the tin, ignoring her squawk.

"Anyway, Mabel had talked to Watt's mom about me being bored," I said around a mouthful of cookie, "so Mrs. Bartlett forced Watt to come next door and call for me. '*Do you wanna, like, hang out or whatever?*'" I said, in an impression of sullen preteen-Watt. "And I was like, '*Golly gee, heck yeah! Let's swim in the lake!*'" I said in a high-pitched mockery of young Jasper. "But Watt refused to swim because I was too small. Or to play catch or walk to O'Leary for ice cream. He said my little legs would get tired."

"Aw. He was protective," Tam said.

"He was insulting," Delaney corrected.

"*Exactly*. Or... I dunno, maybe he was genuinely trying to be protective at first, like he was with his little sister? But I wasn't his little sister, so I was *pissed*. I got right up in his face. '*Anything you can do, I can do better, Watt Bartlett.*' He didn't believe me, of course." I grinned. "But I showed him."

"Love it," Tam crowed.

"So did I," I said softly. "I got taller and filled out, but the challenges only got wilder every summer after that. I found myself doing things I genuinely hadn't known I was capable of until he dared me to do them. We shimmied up flagpoles, walked along train tracks for a mile without losing our balance, swam back and forth across the lake twice while all the other kids in town watched underwater, making sure we never touched bottom. Once, I ate six ice cream cones in a sitting without puking, while Watt had to tap out at five. Oh, God, and one time, we talked to one of the Copper-plates staying at the campground in a made-up language we called Skaldron that sounded like a cross between Swedish and Klingon." I snort-laughed. "The lady went up to Mabel and said with a straight face that the 'foreign children' staying there were absolutely delightful—"

"No!" Tam and Delaney said at the same time.

"Yup. That one was my idea." I grinned. "When we were older, there'd be consequences for dares you took but couldn't complete, too. Like, one Fourth of July, Watt had to wear Mabel's old flowered sunhat to the O'Leary festival, and he wasn't allowed to tell anyone why. Another time, I had to roll in the mud and not wash off for hours." I squirmed in my seat at the remembered itching. "I convinced a bunch of girls it was a spa treatment, and the next day, they rolled in the mud, too. Good times."

"Holy shit." Tam's grin was fierce. "I bet the other kids egged you on."

"Oh yeah. They'd suggest dares for us. Consequences, too. Highly entertaining for everyone. But..." I hesitated. "It wasn't just showing off or trying to humiliate each other. We were friends. One time, Watt challenged me to jump in Copper Lake naked." I turned my head to give her a rueful grin. "I got pretty comfortable being naked once I started modeling, but back then, I was really shy. That didn't stop me from accepting the dare, obviously—"

"Obviously," Delaney agreed.

Tam nodded. "Teenage boy pride."

"Right. Which is why it really meant something to me that when Watt saw it made me uncomfortable, he called it off. Told everybody *he* didn't want to do it and refused to take anyone's shit. That night, he came over to the campground, and we laid out on the dock and talked. He apologized for accidentally going too far. Said he hoped he hadn't let me down."

That had been the first night we'd sat and talked for hours on the dock. It hadn't been the last. We'd even made up a signal for when I planned to sneak out past Mabel's strict curfew so Watt would know when to join me.

"We made up the Rules of Engagement According to Watt and Jasper that night," I told them. "No dares involving nakedness. No kissing or anything sexual. No involving other people unless we were sure they'd laugh about it. No hurting anyone's feelings. That kind of thing. I think... I think that was when I started falling for him. Before I knew it, I was drowning in the first and most devastating crush of my life."

"Oh, honey. I'd be more shocked if you *didn't* fall for him." Delaney ran a hand over his dark hair. "Damn."

"Uh-huh. God, I'm half in love with him myself after hearing that. *Fuck.*" Tam seemed to have forgotten about the cookies while I talked, but now, she grabbed one and chewed, aggressively eating her feelings. "So what happened?"

Dredging up the past had made me feel too soft and vulnerable to tell them the whole truth, so I hedged. "The simple answer, I guess, is that our lives diverged. My parents got divorced right before senior year of high school. My mom came to Copper County to get me, and we flew to LA that same night... and I didn't get to apologize to Watt for breaking one of the Rules of Engagement."

"Oof. Hold up. You broke one of the rules, then left the man hanging on an apology for almost twenty years?"

I flinched but nodded at Tam. "I know. I *know*, okay? It

was shitty. But I ... I didn't know how to take it back or what to say to make it right. I was embarrassed. And scared. And I wasn't adjusting to the move very well."

This was a huge understatement. My parents' divorce had been acrimonious, moving to a new school as a senior had been awful, and the demands of the modeling career my mom encouraged had made friendships impossible.

That time had sucked.

"The longer I waited," I went on, "the sillier it felt to call him up and apologize for an incident he'd probably forgotten. I figured I'd talk to him when I got back to town." I was aware of how lame my reasons probably sounded, but I didn't have better ones.

"Except you didn't come back... until now." Delaney sounded sad.

"Nope," I whispered.

"And... he hadn't forgotten about it, had he?" he whispered.

I gave a quick headshake. "Based on the few run-ins we've had, I'd guess not."

"And your beautiful friendship is in tatters?" Tam said, her voice rising with emotion.

Reluctantly, I nodded again.

"Dear God, Jasper." She whacked me with a pink velour throw pillow. "You can't tell a story like that to a pregnant woman." She sniffled. "I'm made up of ninety percent hormones and ten percent chocolate right now. I need happy endings only."

I laughed, though I felt the weight of the story, too. "Sorry. I'll make you *triple* chocolate cookies later this week to balance you out. But now you know why Watt and me co-coaching the team is gonna be a thing. Apologizing isn't as straightforward as I'd hoped it would be. The first time we ran into each other after I got back, he decimated a hundred paper turkeys trying to get away from me. The second time, we, um, fell into our old habits and provoked each other just the teeniest, tiniest bit—"

"Ugh." Delaney shook his head.

"—and then the third time, at the parent practice yesterday—"

"Oh, we've heard how that went down," Tam said with clear disapproval. "Lucas's grandmother came by to give me the skinny since she knows I'm bored, sitting here on modified bed rest. She said, '*The Rivals of Copper County are at it again.*' I told her hell no, she was a hundred percent wrong. '*I've never seen Watt lose his temper, Charlene,*' I said, '*and Jasper's awesome. Somebody made that up.*' Guess not, huh?"

I groaned. It had been too much to hope the incident would stay a closely guarded secret between me, Watt, Principal Schmidt, twenty teenagers, and dozens of our heavily invested neighbors.

"So... what do I do?" I demanded. "Our first co-coach practice is the day after tomorrow—"

Tam's eyes narrowed. "Well, you're not gonna lose your shit and argue in front of my team again, that's for sure."

I bit my lip. She was right, of course, but the weirdest part was arguing with Watt... didn't feel like arguing.

Arguments with my ex-husband had felt like stepping onto a tightrope over a viper pit. If I ever expressed dissatisfaction, Martin turned it around on me instantly, either making me feel like an ungrateful idiot for being upset or laughing it off dismissively. It had taken me way too long to realize I'd become scared of my own anger because it never led to anything good.

With Watt, our verbal skirmishes weren't always

productive or pleasant, but it felt like a challenge between equals. Even when I was burning with anger or my feelings were hurt, I never felt dismissed or manipulated.

"I don't want to argue with Watt. Not like that. But I don't know how to make him sit still and listen, let alone convince him to… to…" I faltered.

Tam nodded. "I think step one is to figure out what you're trying to convince him to do. You want him to stand down so you can get through the season as co-coaches? Easy. Tell him you'll sit on the sidelines and babysit practice, so you'll fulfill your job requirements and minimize disruptions."

I frowned. That was one option… but everything in me rejected it. I'd feel too much the guy I'd been during my marriage, avoiding problems instead of dealing with them. It hadn't worked out terribly well.

"I like coaching," I said. "I don't know anything about hockey, but I do know what it was like being pushed to succeed at something from a young age. Maybe I can give the kids a little perspective. Remind them that balance is key, like I've been doing this week, and that they can't get consumed with averages and statistics."

"Agreed," Tam said. "When you suggested starting out with mindfulness work and stretching, I…"

I snickered. "Thought I was crazy?"

"Maybe a little? But then I started thinking of all the well-meaning parents and coaches who've told these kids they need to prioritize their sport as a way to get to college… when there simply aren't that many full-ride hockey scholarships out there." She grimaced. "Don't get me wrong, I love hockey. It made me physically fit, gave me a strong work ethic, and taught me to be part of a team. It's the 'putting all your eggs in one basket' that's a problem. I look at our brothers... I mean, Wells is fine, more or less. But Lawson..."

She and Delaney exchanged a look.

I glanced back and forth between them. "What happened?"

"I forget you don't follow sports. It's so refreshing," Delaney said with a happy sigh. "Lawson tore his ACL last April and needed surgery. He was supposed to take this season off to recover—"

"But the team physicians cleared him to play." Tam shrugged. "Law doesn't know how to exist without hockey, so..."

"So," Delaney agreed sourly. "Like you said, Jasper, it's good for the kids to gain some perspective."

Frowning, I nodded. "I think they know it, too, on some level. I was expecting a lot more side-eyeing than I got at the start of this week. I think some of them are low-key relieved that an adult in their lives is telling them it's okay to step back. Derry, for one. Zach, too."

"Not surprising. Derry's not intense by nature. Really sweet kid. A stand-up guy, like his dad. Natural hockey instincts, disciplined, but he didn't really seem driven to play until recently." Tam selected a final cookie before replacing the lid and shoving the tin away. "Zach's a great kid, too. More cerebral, a little dramatic. Not a natural player, but strong on strategy. Strong work ethic, too. Stronger than you'd expect from someone so good-looking." She grinned. "Or maybe not stronger than *you'd* expect."

I raised an eyebrow. "Pretty people work hard, too, Ms. Monroe. As evidenced by the fact that I'm *here*, learning hockey with you, instead of on some sugar daddy's yacht, working on my tan."

"And we're really glad you are." She licked a spot of

chocolate off her finger. "You do know if you continue to take an active coaching role, that's gonna make things trickier with Watt, right? According to Charlene, he's not a fan of your methods."

I snorted. "I think if I told him the sky was blue, he'd say it was pink rather than agree with me." I dug my elbow into the sofa and turned to face them. "What if... what if I want more than Watt tolerating me? What if I want us to be friends again like we used to be?"

Delaney made a considering noise. "But it wasn't just friendship for you, was it? Would you really want to get close to him again, knowing that's all you could have? Take it from someone who's done that, it's not easy."

I thought of Watt's smile. His bright hazel eyes. How something in me settled when he was near, even when he was angry. I hadn't let myself realize how much I missed that—missed *him*—until I'd seen him again. I wanted it back.

I thought of his lush ass straining against his jeans when he'd bent over his truck. The way his broad shoulders made my throat go dry just as they had years ago. I couldn't lie, I wanted that, too.

But I thought about Kayla calling him *honey*. And about that summer day twenty years ago when I'd gotten greedy and everything had gone wrong.

"Yes. Friendship is more than enough," I said firmly. "In fact, it's exactly right. If I get horny—" Who was I kidding? I already was. "—I'll just dust off my apps. I'm only in town for a few months." The words were meant to remind us both. "Friendship is exactly what I want from Watt."

But Tam's gaze darted to my hand, which was rubbing absently at my aching chest, and when her eyes met mine, they called me a liar.

"Hmm. Well, I don't know what it'll take to get Watt to be your friend again, babes. I don't even know if *Watt* knows." She wiped a cookie crumb off the corner of her mouth. "But I will say... baked goods are always a good start."

CHAPTER FIVE

WATT

I'm not going to the dock to meet Jasper, I told myself firmly as I handed over a couple of U-Pick bags to a family who'd come down from Fairport for a day of apple picking, then rang up another customer for a jug of fresh cider before heading over to the hose to rinse out their baskets.

I'm not.

I'd begun reciting those words when I'd stepped onto the back porch to do morning chores and found an antique house-shaped tin of muffins sitting by the door, along with a Post-it note that said "*FRIENDLY* PEACE OFFERING? Can we talk tonight? Our usual spot?"

Ignoring the happy rush I'd gotten when I'd recognized Jasper's handwriting, I'd glanced around the property—at the bright leaves and the early morning fog on the lake just beginning to burn off, at the fields and gardens separating my property from Wrigley Campground sparkling in dew. The driveway gate had remained closed, and Jasper hadn't been around, but the muffins in the tin had still been warm, leading me to wonder where he'd gotten them so early in the day.

I am not going to the dock, I'd told myself immediately, though the idea had been tempting. Jasper's peace offering game had picked up—he probably didn't remember, but I freaking loved a pumpkin muffin, and these particular muffins were phenomenal. As I'd read the note in Jasper's playful, hopeful voice, I'd considered all the burning questions I had about the parts of his life I'd missed out on and the way he remembered our last day together all those years ago.

I'd actually thought to myself, *What's the worst that could happen?*

The answer was right there in the question, though. The worst that could happen was me getting a happy rush at seeing Jasper's note, at him calling the dock "our spot," at thinking that the answers to those questions would fix things... when the man had walked away before and was leaving town again in a matter of months.

I had no interest in a temporary friendship.

I'd set the muffins in the kitchen, crumpled the note, and gone to do my chores.

But as I'd organized a new shipment of fruit-picking poles, I'd remembered almost laughing with him against my will in front of Principal Schmidt and how the warm light shining in his eyes had made me as foolish as it ever had. I'd even found myself wondering what Jasper was doing at that particular moment—off terrorizing another unsuspecting Coppertian at Lyon's Imperial on a Sunday morning? Learning about hockey from Tam? Or had he simply gone back to bed after dropping off the muffins?—and that... that was when things had gone awry.

My barn had a clear line of sight to the Wrigleys' campground, and I hadn't been able to resist looking over at the house on the hill. I'd noticed that the window in the bedroom that used to be Jasper's was wide open, the curtain fluttering in the breeze. And I'd, you know, imagined him up there... as you do... sprawled on the big brass bed fast asleep.

Except then I'd wondered what if he *wasn't* asleep. What if he was doing something else entirely on this sunny Sunday with his window wide open?

And now, as I hosed out the harvest baskets, my hands grasped the sprayer as I returned to imagining Jasper like that, stark naked, blond hair mussed, one big hand wrapped around his cock. My breath went a little wonky imagining his legs moving restlessly as he pleasured himself, and my cock pushed restlessly against my jeans as I imagined his gorgeous face flushed with need, his head thrown back against the pillows, his—

"Heya, Watt! Got my Jonagolds?" Martha Cushman asked with a merry smile.

My hand spasmed around the sprayer handle, shooting a long arc of water directly into the side of the barn, our electric utility vehicle, a stack of recently rinsed harvest baskets, and, finally, my boots.

Martha blinked at me. "Uh... sorry to startle you?"

"Ah, n-no problem." I managed a wan smile despite the cold water soaking through my socks, causing me to half break out in goose bumps. "Just, ah... remembering the Bills' big victory against the Pats last weekend. Let me help you with your apples."

"I've got it." Derry appeared from wherever he'd been hiding all afternoon and gave Martha a smile. "Over here, Ms. Cushman." He pointed toward one of the large sheds.

"Aw. Thank you, Dermott." She gave him a fond smile

and followed where he led. "You're every bit as helpful as your father."

Derry turned and eyed me up and down, landing on my soaked boots. "Yeah," he said flatly. "Dad's real helpful."

When he turned away, I winced. Derry hadn't been pleased by my interference at practice and, if possible, was even less pleased that I'd agreed to coach the team "without even talking to me, Dad!" Our ride home Friday had been decidedly chilly—nearly as chilly as my damp jeans now—and things hadn't improved. He'd one-word-answered me when he wasn't avoiding me like the plague, so I hadn't had a chance to explain myself… not that I had any explanation beyond "I briefly lost my mind."

And that was why I was *not—definitely not—*going to be meeting Jasper.

In the past week, my calm, settled life had descended into a chaos of challenge, longing, and irrationality. I hardly recognized myself.

I refused to think about Jasper as I smiled, shook hands, and sprayed peppermint oil deer repellent around the property all afternoon. I continued not thinking about Jasper as I threw together burgers and sweet potatoes for me and Derry, as the two of us ate in silence, and as I flopped on my sofa to watch football alone.

Unfortunately, like not thinking about elephants, all this not thinking about Jasper meant I thought of little else. By the time I heard a rustling noise through my open window as I lay in bed, I was too keyed up to ignore it.

"I'm not going to the dock. I'm getting rid of those fucking deer," I muttered as I got out of bed, dressed in clean clothes and a jacket, combed my hair—deer cared about good hygiene—and headed out back.

Surprising no one, I paused just long enough to see the light in Jasper's window before heading out to the lake.

I'll tell him I'm not interested in talking or friendship offerings, I told myself. *More efficient than ignoring him.*

It was almost a relief when I found myself trudging over the moonlit grass toward him, like I'd held a heavy weight for hours and was finally, inevitably surrendering to gravity. The trees whispered in the starlight when I reached the edge of the wooded path that led across the campground from the Wrigleys' Craftsman house to the dock, and the loons on the water gave long, mournful wails.

"If he's not there, I'll go home," I muttered under my breath. "And that will be fine. Better, even. If he's not there, I'll win."

When I paused at the edge of the woods that ringed the lake, though, I saw Jasper *was* there, his sexy body wrapped in a quilt and his face glowing soft silver. He sat facing the guardrail that ran along one side of the dock, the way we'd sat as kids. His booted feet dangled above the water, his chest leaned against the crossbar, and his head rested against one of the tall, worn pilings. He looked... not sad, exactly, but resigned. Weary, even... which might be true, given what Principal Schmidt had said about how many hours he was putting in.

He's not yours to worry about. You're not even friends anymore.

But I was the world's biggest idiot because I felt his weary resignation in my own chest, and I suddenly couldn't stand to see him alone.

I took a step toward him before I could rethink, and my foot broke a branch with a loud *crack*. Jasper turned his head eagerly.

"Watt?"

"Yeah." My boots clomped hollowly across the worn wood of the dock. "You wanted to see me?"

"Yes! Yeah. I... I wasn't sure you were coming." He scrambled around, trying to get to his feet and getting caught in the blanket instead.

I made a *stay* gesture with my hands and stepped up to the railing beside him. "I wasn't." I rubbed my thumb over my lips. That wasn't quite the truth... and somehow, it felt like cheating to lie. "I wanted to, but I also didn't."

"No." Jasper's face fell. "Well. Can't say I blame you." He wiped his hands on his jeans. "Can you... will you sit? I have cocoa in this thermos."

"No, thanks. I assume you want to talk before practice tomorrow. To figure out how co-coaching is going to work—"

"Yes. Definitely. But I also wanted to clear the air. About us. I... Hang on." He pulled his phone from his pocket, unlocked it, pulled up a note, and cleared his throat. "First, Watt, I'd like to thank you for meeting with me tonight. I don't believe I ever adequately expressed to you when we were younger just how much your friendship meant to me—"

I snorted. "Hold up. You wrote me a speech?"

"Not a speech. *Notes.*" He scowled up at me by the light of his phone. "I wanted to make sure I got it right, okay? I suck at improvising, and our last couple conversations have gone off the rails."

Rolling my eyes, I surrendered again and sank to my ass on the wood with my knees bent. "Funny, I remember you being damn good at improvising. Remember the time you explained to my sister for two full, timed minutes why pineapples made the best pets?"

Jasper's bark of laughter seemed to be startled out of him. "Shut up. That was the worst dare. Poor Iris."

"She believed you were totally sincere. My mom still talks about it sometimes. When Derry and I were down in Costa Rica visiting my parents over spring break—"

"Costa Rica?"

"Yup. They retired there when I bought them out of the orchard. And then Iris's husband got transferred to Des Moines... maybe three years ago now?" I said after a pause. "Anyway, my mom made fruit salad in a pineapple half for breakfast, and Derry said pineapple's good, but not as good as mango. Without missing a beat, my mom leaned over and cupped her hand around the pineapple fronds like the fruit had ears. '*Dermott, hush,*'" I said in my mom's voice, "'*Spike can* hear *you.*' And Derry said, '*Holy crap, Grandma, who is in this salad?*'—"

He laughed harder.

So did I.

"Oh God!" Jasper collapsed against the dock beside me, wiping his eyes. "Did you explain?"

"Not... exactly." I hesitated. "I told him it was a joke, but..." I lifted one shoulder.

Jasper sobered. "You never talked to Derry about me, did you?"

I shook my head slowly.

"Right." He sighed. "And that's my fault. I fucked it all up." He rolled onto his side, propping himself up on one elbow. "I'm *truly* sorry, Watt. That's what I wanted to say to you. I shouldn't have kissed you that day. I knew better. I just... I liked you so much. Which isn't an excuse," he added quickly. "We had a rule, and I broke it—"

"No," I cut him off. "*You* didn't. I don't get why you're saying that."

"Uh…" He ran a hand over his face. "Because it's true?"

"I was there, remember? If you're trying to make me feel worse by pretending to take responsibility for something I did—"

"I'm not pretending. I kissed you—"

"*I* kissed *you*," I said hotly. "And we both know it. We were sitting on the shore across the lake by the Observatory House, doing a stupid dare about who could make the other spit water first—"

"Yup, and I kept going for your ribs like I was going to tickle you." Jasper sat up and darted a hand toward my chest in demonstration.

I grabbed his wrist and held it firmly. "Yes, and *I* kept acting like I was trying to head-butt you—" I moved forward and angled my head at his.

"And since I knew from experience how hard your damn head is, I bobbed and weaved like Muhammed Ali—" He wiggled his head up and down like he was pecking at my chest.

"Muhammed Ali?" I snort-laughed. "More like a deranged chicken. But then you angled your head up—"

Jasper turned his head to frown up at me, and I got hit with a whiff of sweetness and woodsmoke that made my gut clench.

"Yeah, like that," I said softly. "And your eyes were… were *right there*—"

"My eyes?" Jasper blinked like he'd forgotten what eyes were. "My eyes weren't doing anything special. It was you. You licked your lips like—*ungh*," he said roughly, eyes transfixed on my face. "Exactly like that."

"My skin felt like it was on fire." My breath came faster now, recalling it. "My brain was staticky, and I couldn't think—"

"Your tongue worried at the corner of your mouth the way it does when you're thinking hard. Yeah, that's it." Jasper's exhale was hot against my cheek, and my mouth tingled where he stared at it.

"And I..." I whispered.

"And I..." Jasper breathed.

"I kissed you," Jasper and I said together.

We pulled back simultaneously.

"No!" we cried in unison. "I did!"

"You waved your arms, Watt." Jasper threw his arms out to the side and made a rolling motion. "You were trying to get away!"

"I wanted to grab you and was trying not to! You *know* the kiss was my idea," I insisted. "That's why you were so horrified that when you heard Abe yelling for you, you ran off without a word. That's why you never called me from California—"

"You know it was *me!*" he returned. "That's why you were so angry when you saw me at the grocery store, you Hulk-smashed a huge flock of paper turkeys, and now O'Leary will have to cancel Thanksgiving!"

We blinked at each other.

"I wasn't angry when I saw you the other day. I felt..." I cut myself off with a headshake. *Like I was seventeen and wanted to kiss you again* might be true, but not helpful at the moment. "It was a shock, seeing you again."

Jasper groaned and fell back against the dock with one hand over his eyes. "Watt, I *couldn't* say goodbye properly. My mom made me leave—"

"Yeah, Mabel told me when I went to see you and apologize the next morning." I hunched my shoulders as a chill breeze blew across the water. "She said your parents were splitting—and *God*, was she angry that they were dragging you into it. She said, '*Jasper'll call you as soon as he can, Watt, 'cause he'll need you. Friendships like yours are the steady hands that lift you when life's too hard to carry alone.*' One of her Mabel truisms." I huffed. "Not so true for us, though, huh?"

"I wanted to call," he said softly. "So many times. But I was scared. To explain why I'd kissed you, I'd have had to tell you I was gay *and* admit I'd had a crush on you—"

"And you thought I'd be mad about that?" I demanded, legitimately horrified. "You were my best friend, asshole. I thought you hung the goddamn moon. Did you really think I'd be homophobic? Me?"

"No!" The word was muffled beneath his arm. "I didn't think me being gay would make you angry. Me admitting that I'd been crushing on you, though? I didn't know. Sometimes you'd overthink things. And it's one thing to know your friend likes guys but another to wonder whether he's been jerking off while thinking about you, you know?"

The arousal that had been rising steadily since the moment Jasper had come back to Copper County slammed into me like a tidal wave, stealing my breath and turning my muscles to jelly. All the blood in my body rushed toward my dick, and my earlier daydream swirled through my mind like a motel TV stuck on a single, relentless channel.

Had he been thinking of me? The question was halfway to my lips before I caught it back.

It wasn't until I noticed Jasper peeking out from beneath his arm uncertainly that I realized I hadn't responded.

"I wouldn't have been angry." Lust made the words come out gritty and harsh. Utterly unconvincing. I swallowed and tried again. "I mean, clearly, I wouldn't since I was the one who kissed you."

Jasper sat up, which put him right beside me. Heat flooded my arm where it brushed against his. "You really think that? Does that mean... are you gay?"

"No." After a beat, I added, "I mean, I'm not *not* gay."

"Okay?" His forehead wrinkled, then quickly smoothed again. "Oh! You're bi? Or pan?"

"No. I mean, sort of. I..." I shook my head quickly. At thirty-seven, it felt ridiculous that I didn't have a solid handle on my sexuality other than "I want who I want with no rhyme or reason," and I refused to discuss it with Jasper. "It doesn't matter."

"Okay." Jasper hesitated for a beat. "I, ah, heard from Mabel that you were married to a woman."

"Yes. And divorced." Thinking about Rachel and our failed marriage wasn't hurtful anymore, but it was a total erection killer. I told myself this was a good thing. "A friend and I hooked up sophomore year of college—you know, one of those wild and crazy, meaningless college hookups you hear about?" I gave him a wry look. "She got pregnant."

"Ah." Jasper seemed to hear some of the stuff I wasn't saying—the weight of the decisions we'd had to make, the terror of getting it wrong, the guilt of even remembering those negative emotions when I'd gotten an amazing kid out of the deal—because he leaned over to gently squeeze my knee. "Sometimes you need to take a wrong turn to get where you're supposed to be—that's another Mabelism for you. Personally, I've had my fill of wrong turns at this point," he joked. "From now on, I'd like a neatly labeled Google map, please and thank you."

His support and gentle teasing made me irrationally angry, both at him—where had he been when my nineteen-year-old self had needed comfort?—and at myself for giving a shit. I felt more exposed than if he'd noticed the semi I'd been sporting earlier.

I quickly changed the subject. "You said you're in town for a couple months, right?"

Jasper pulled his knees to his chest, looping his arms around them. "Yeah. Tam's baby's due next month, and then she'll be off for a while. So I guess... until the end of her maternity leave."

"And you can just abandon your life in LA for that long? Do models take sabbaticals?"

He shook his head. "I haven't actually modeled for years."

I frowned. I supposed it made sense, though. It had been a long time since Mabel had shown me any new pictures. "What have you been doing, then? Please don't say attempting to teach hockey to unsuspecting Californians."

Jasper bumped his arm into mine. "If I *had*, I would have kicked ass at it. But no, I was running a modeling agency with my ex..." His expression darkened. "Until I learned how comprehensively Martin and his new boyfriend, Emilio, had screwed me over."

"'Screwed you over'? You mean he cheated on you?" I literally couldn't imagine such a thing. If the man had Jasper in his bed and Jasper's ring on his finger, what more could he have wanted?

"Not cheating the way you're thinking. We had an open marriage. Martin fucking other guys wasn't a surprise." Jasper's jaw worked for a moment. "I didn't expect him to start a business with one of them and steal all the clients *I'd* worked to acquire, though. See..."

He went on to explain some things about business valuations and divorce proceedings that I didn't fully process because my mind was still back on *open marriage*.

Was Jasper into that? Why the hell did I care?

"Anyway." Jasper waved a hand. "My photographer friend has a lawyer friend, and she and I set up a Zoom meeting. Hopefully, she'll take the case and get back what Martin owes me, and I can use the money to start my own business when I'm back in LA."

I nodded. "Another modeling agency?"

"Yeah." He looked a bit defensive, though I wasn't sure why. "It's not the career I set out to have, I know… but I'm good at it, and I have a lot of connections now. I like the organizing, the mentoring, the hand-holding, the playing therapist. I even liked keeping track of the models' social media stats and financials, though we had an accountant I used for the bigger stuff." He shrugged sheepishly. "Who doesn't love a good spreadsheet?"

"Oh, *ugh*. Are you baiting me right now? You are, aren't you?" I grimaced and shuddered, not bothering to hide my repulsion. "Nobody likes spreadsheets. That's just… unnatural."

Jasper's eyes widened, and my face went hot.

"Sorry. Spreadsheets and I have history—" I began, but I snapped my mouth shut when he started laughing—a real, honest belly laugh that burrowed under all my defenses and lodged itself right in my chest.

The sound of his happiness scattered around the lake like a tangible thing. The breeze stilled, the leaves in the forest stopped rustling, and even the birds on the water went quiet, as though the whole lake was cocking its head and listening to this once familiar sound. The air grew warmer, remembering. The stars twinkled brighter in recognition. The whole world seemed to sigh at the rightness of it. And I…

I found myself staring helplessly at the man beside me.

Beautiful. So fucking beautiful.

Millions of people who'd seen Jasper's face in glossy magazine ads or walking in shows had probably had the same passing thought, but they'd never seen him like this, with his head thrown back, his face contorted, his hair mussed, and his blanket falling off his shoulders.

This view, this Jasper, was *mine.*

He sniffled, trying to bring himself under control. "I tell you I'm gay, I get no reaction. I tell you I had a crush on you, you're all... meh." He waved a hand airily. "I apologize for crossing a line and kissing you, you try to take the blame yourself. But I confess my deep love of spreadsheets, and *that's* what gets you?"

I ignored the last part of this and focused on the important bit. "I'm not trying to take the blame for the kiss. You're trying to take the *credit,*" I said in a low voice. "I kissed you."

"Not this again. You..." Jasper turned his head, and with one glance at me, his breath caught. "Y-you..." He squared his shoulders and lifted his chin, which somehow only brought our faces closer. "Prove it," he whispered.

"Prove it?" I parroted back.

I had no idea what he was talking about because English was beyond me at that moment. Jasper's forearm brushed against my thigh where his hand was braced against the dock, and it seared me through my jeans. My cock was a hundred percent back on board with whatever was happening, stiffening like a fucking divining rod pointing the way to the one person who'd never failed to get him interested. *This guy. This one right here.*

"Yeah." Jasper licked his lips, his gaze holding mine. "I dare you," he said softly.

I moved without thinking, my body processing his

command and obeying instantly, not giving me time to over-think it. And then my mouth was on his.

Our lips met with none of the uncertainty of our first kiss but with a slow, deliberate heat that made the world fall away. I inhaled his sigh and returned it, groaning as the taste of him—sugar and chocolate and Jasper—surrounded me, filling up spaces I hadn't known were empty.

I pushed him down to the dock and spread myself across his chest like a blanket, desperate to kiss him harder, deeper, to crawl inside him if he'd let me. Jasper seemed to be on board with this, if the way he clutched my shirt was any indication.

"More," he whispered brokenly. "Yes, Watt—"

A loon erupted from the lake nearby with an eerie cry, its wings slapping the surface of the water in a frantic rush, and I sprang off Jasper like I'd been scalded.

For one perfect moment, Jasper blinked up at me, dazed and wondering. Then his eyes met mine, and his expression shifted.

"Fuck," I panted. "*Fuck.*"

"No." He sat up and grasped my face with both hands. "Do not overthink this. Please, Watt."

"I'm not." Mentally, I tacked on a *not yet* because I knew myself well enough to know this state was temporary. Once the taste of Jasper faded from my lips, all the reasons why this had been a terrible, complicated, foolish idea would come rushing back.

Like the fact that I barely knew him now, if I ever had.

And that he'd left our friendship in the dust for decades while he lived a fast-paced life in LA and planned to leave again before my orchard was even in bloom.

And that I'd never kissed a man before—well, except for that one time—because Jasper was the only man I'd ever been attracted to... which didn't seem like a thing that should be possible and would therefore likely end in disaster... again.

And that we were supposed to be coaching a hockey team together—my *son*'s team—even though Jasper knew jack shit about hockey.

Oh, look, here come the reasons. Right on time.

"You're definitely overthinking." He sighed and flopped down on his back.

"No. I'm just..." I pushed to my feet and began babbling. "It's late. I have an early morning tomorrow, and you do, too, right? And then we both have practice in the afternoon. So."

Jasper's face was unreadable. "So," he agreed a little sadly.

I reached out a hand to help him up, but he was already scrambling up, so I scooped up his blanket and focused on folding it neatly. When I tried to hand the blanket and his thermos off to him, he seized my hand.

"Watt, I didn't mean for this to happen." His cheeks flushed dark, and his voice turned pleading. "I wanted to talk to you so you'd stop being angry about the first kiss, not to make you kiss me again and then drive you away. I want us to be able to coach together. I want us to be friends again—"

"I was never angry about the kiss, Jasper. Not then. Not now. I kissed *you*, remember? Twice now."

"Debatable," he huffed.

I gently disentangled my hand from his and instantly missed his heat. "And as for the rest..." I gave him a quick, teasing smile I wasn't entirely feeling. "We'll do a fine job coaching now that one of us knows what he's doing. We'll wait and see what happens beyond that, okay?"

I was proud of myself for managing to sound reasonable, rational, and mature. When I saw Jasper's reaction, I wasn't sure why I bothered.

He bristled like I'd issued a direct challenge, complete with narrowed eyes and set jaw. "We *will* be friends again," he declared. "You'll see. By the time Christmas rolls around, you'll be calling me your bestie."

I rolled my eyes. "I've never called anyone that in my life. And this isn't the kind of thing you can bet on, Jasper. You can't force feelings to be something they're not."

"No," he shot back. "You can't. That's exactly my point. So, do we have a deal?"

I opened my mouth to argue, then thought better of it. "What are the terms?" I heard myself ask instead.

"The Rules of Engagement According to Watt and Jasper, Circa 2003, obviously."

I ran a thumb over my lips. I could still feel his lips on mine. "No involving other people, nothing sexual, et cetera?"

"Er. Yes." Jasper swallowed. "Unless... if you wanted to amend it, I'd—?"

"No," I said quickly. That way lay madness. "Nope."

"Right. So, then... I say we'll be friends again in two months' time. Strong as before. All you have to do is open your mind and accept it. And when I'm right, Watt Bartlett's friendship will be my reward. Friends 'til the end." He nodded once. "I won't fuck it up this time."

My stomach did a slow roll. Did it mean that much to him?

Jesus, was I really such an asshole that I'd withhold my friendship from the man like it was some kind of prize?

Could I, even if I wanted to?

Two things kept me from giving in right then and there, though.

The first was that I truly did have reservations about getting close to Jasper again.

I'd believed for years that our kiss was the reason he'd cut me off without giving me a chance to apologize, and that had been bad enough, but knowing it was a misunderstanding that could have been rectified if he'd bothered getting in touch was somehow worse.

I also hated that I was even spending time thinking about unsettling bullshit like this. I should have been sleeping the sleep of the utterly content in my comfortable bed, not out kissing—kissing a *man*, for fuck's sake—on a dock in the dead of night or spending my waking hours fantasizing about him. I didn't *do* this sort of thing.

But the second and more compelling reason was that I simply couldn't turn down a bet from Jasper. Because this unsettled part of me that only seemed to come alive when he was around didn't know how to bow out gracefully.

I raised one eyebrow. "And if you don't succeed?"

He clutched the blanket to his chest. "I... I dunno. I'll be going back to LA eventually, and I won't bug you anymore, so I guess that'll be your prize."

It was a sign of how truly unsettled I was that this didn't feel like a prize at all.

Jasper shot me a wink and leaned toward me confidingly. "Don't worry about that, though. I'm pretty fucking determined." He grinned and turned on his phone's flashlight as he prepared to make his way through the trees and up the hill. "Night, *friend*," he called over his shoulder.

My lips twitched as I watched him go.

My feelings about Jasper might be unsettled, but I couldn't deny that I'd smiled more this week than I had in a long while. This probably meant I'd made a huge error in taking his bet...

...I won't fuck it up this time...

...or else it was the smartest move I'd ever made.

"Good night, Jasper," I whispered when he was too far away to hear me.

And as I walked home, I thought that maybe, just this once, I'd like to see Jasper win.

CHAPTER SIX

REALLY, at a certain point, I either had to get comfortable with bad decisions or stop fucking making them.

"*Fwweeeeet. Fweet, fweet!*" When Watt's shrill coach's whistle split the air for the dozenth time in five minutes, I *tried* to ignore it and focus on the stretching I'd been doing with a small cadre of players on the opposite side of the rink... but like so many things related to Watt Bartlett, ignoring him was easier in theory than in practice.

See also: betting the man I'd become his super-platonic bestie when what I really wanted was to kiss the ever-living fuck out of him again.

"Great job, Kip," I said to the player on my left as he dipped gracefully into a forward bend. "Have you noticed how much your flexibility has improved in the past two weeks? Your reach is longer, and that's really going to help you when you're in the net, I think."

Kip gave me a grin. "Thanks, Coach Lancaster. It's definitely getting easier."

"Awesome. Positive attitude is key. Hey, Zach, engage the front of your thighs and your core, and let your spine hang to get the deepest stretch. Like this..." I bent over to demonstrate. "Perfect. Can you feel your vertebrae realigning?"

"I think so, yeah." Zach shot me a sideways smile that made him look like an upside-down poster of a teenage heartthrob. "Nice trick. Now I'll be *three* inches taller than Derry."

Derry snorted without looking up. "Aw. It's important to have dreams, buddy. Even if you'll never, ever achieve them."

"I don't blame you for not accepting the reality, Dermott," Zach teased. "Having a friend who's better-looking than you *and* smarter *and* taller? It's too much, isn't it?"

"Boys, you are interrupting my peaceful yoga flow, damn it," I snapped, and the kids laughed. "Okay, after a few breaths, round up slowly. Just don't stand too fast, or you'll get light-headed—"

"*Fweet!* Jasper! *Fweet!*"

I snapped up and whirled to face the tallest, broadest, sexiest bad decision I'd made this week—my once and future best friend—and nearly lost my balance as the head rush had me overcorrecting on my stupid, slippery skates.

I pressed a hand to my forehead. "What *now?*" I snapped.

Watt glided toward me with zero effort, grabbing my elbow to keep me from falling. He glanced pointedly from me to the players' bench, where most of the team was taking a water break, to the rows upon rows of parents who'd come to watch another Friday practice and raised an eyebrow.

Right. Shit.

I forced a smile. "I meant... did you have something to

tell me, bestest pal? Some little nuggets of friendly stretching wisdom, perhaps, that you longed to share?"

Watt's lips twitched. "I think you've got the situation well in hand. Hey, good range of motion there, Kip."

"Thanks, Coach!"

"You, too, Derry," he offered. "Zach."

Derry gave a grudging "Thanks," and after looking between them for a second, Zach copied him loyally.

Watt didn't sigh, but I could tell he wanted to. "Water break, guys," he said, nodding toward the rest of the team, who had already assembled in the players' box.

I regarded the box—and, more specifically, the leagues and leagues of ice between it and myself—with resignation. Picking my way out here without falling on my face had been an adventure. One I wasn't looking forward to repeating on the way back.

Watt let me go so he could glide backward, crossing his feet over one another in a move that looked extremely complex to a person who couldn't manage to skate forward while standing upright.

"Something bothering you, Jasper?" he said, his teasing voice pitched low so only I could hear. "Are your skates laced too tight? You seem tense."

I nearly laughed out loud. The tightness of my laces was the least of my concerns.

This week had been five years long, and I was trying to practice mindfulness and stay grounded in the moment, but it was tough. I wanted nothing more than to tell Watt all about what was bothering me—to just throw myself against his broad chest and beg him to wrap his arms around me and tell me everything would be okay—but where would I even begin?

With the house that seemed to breed collectibles while I slept?

Or the attorney who'd told me as a friend of a friend that I'd be better off saving my pennies than filing a suit against Martin that I couldn't win?

Or Martin, who'd decided to break a year of blissful silence by texting three times, begging me to "talk, please, sweetness," making me wonder if he'd gotten me confused with his new boyfriend since he'd never called me pet names in his life?

Or the skates on my feet that refused to obey the laws of physics?

Or Kayla, who'd been giving Watt curled-finger waves from the sidelines since the start of practice today while doing a rhyming song and dance routine she called the "Marmot Cheer," which might haunt my nightmares unto death?

Or Watt, himself, with his sexy grin and broad shoulders, who taunted me in my dreams with memories of our kiss and taunted me in real life by being so freaking kind and funny and *capable* while also daring me to "lace up" for practice to show the kids how to "acquire a new skill" and giving me a bland, infuriating "*Tsk*. That doesn't seem very *friendly*, Jasper" whenever I threatened to make him eat his whistle, but who'd actively bet against our friendship?

I couldn't just dump all of that on him, obviously. I was *Watt's* friend, but he wasn't mine... yet.

"Nope. I'm good," I said firmly. When talking with Watt, it was somehow harder to keep my grip on the practiced smile I usually wore like a second skin. "Just enjoying doing... the hockey... with my good buddy." I winked. "You're the buddy, by the way."

"Uh-huh. You know, it's funny..." He stroked his lower

lip with his thumb. "For someone who's as much of a die-hard fan of *the hockey* as you are—"

"I prefer hockey aficionado," I shot back. I waved a hand in the air before folding my arms over my chest. "Go on."

"Well, I would have expected you to be watching the kids doing their positional drills rather than leaving me to my own devices." He skated in a tight circle—the fucker was *definitely* showing off, and I *definitely* didn't find it hella sexy—before returning to stand in front of me. "I mean, how will they cope without your insightful and thought-provoking critiques? When you yelled, '*Run the puck, Derry,*' the other day, I could see him really digesting that and thinking about hockey in a whole new way."

I frowned fiercely. Was this asshole seriously teasing me out of my mood right now? Why was it fucking *working*?

"I *was* watching. I watched the whole time," I lied. "You see, Watt, when hockey comes as easily to a person as it does to me—"

"Practically second nature," he said solemnly.

"—you don't have to devote your entire attention to it in order to understand what's happening."

"Ahhh." He nodded. "Pardon... just for my own clarification, were you watching between your legs and upside down while you were stretching? Or do you have a different eye somewhere on your body? Your asshole, perhaps?"

I opened my mouth and shut it. "*Neither,*" I bit out. "It's more of an instinctive thing. A... a psychic knowing."

"I see."

"Someday, you'll get there, Watt." I cocked my hip insouciantly...

And promptly ended up chest down on the ice with an *oof*.

"Will I, though?" Watt heaved a sigh and extended a

hand to help me up. "Follow-up question: Is randomly falling also instinctive? Or is that a skill you acquired on purpose?"

I ignored his hand and instead braced myself on my hands and feet—which, like everything with these fucking skates—was complicated by the blades.

"Falling? Pfft. I'm doing push-ups," I said gaily as I levered myself up and down. "It's a little addition to my routine that I like to call *spontaneous conditioning*. Or possibly *stop, drop, and condition*. I'm still workshopping it."

"Astounding." Suppressed laughter bubbled in his voice. "Truly astounding. Just think, I played hockey for years, but I might never have learned this if I hadn't dared you to wear skates for practice this week."

"Yes." I glared up at him—at his gorgeous hazel eyes and sexy, barely restrained grin—and nearly laughed, too, despite the ice stinging my palms. "Just. Think."

"Oh my heck!" a voice called from the sidelines. "Jasper? Or Watt? Could I have a quick word? I have a teeny, tiny little concern about the team."

I sighed as I struggled to my feet. "Come on," I said.

Watt hesitated. "You know, I think *you* can handle the parent interaction," he said as he steadied me. "It makes sense, as the true hockey aficionado of the two of us. And one of us has to go get the guys ready for a quick scrimmage anyway, so…"

"What? No!" I whispered. "She called both of… Get back here, coward!" I cried.

But Watt was already *fweet*ing his whistle at the team as he skated away.

Fuck.

I slowly, painstakingly picked my way over to the side of the rink—the *boards*, as those of us who played professional hockey called it—and gave Kayla a charming paper smile while holding on to the railing with both hands for balance. "Kayla! Hi. Aren't you a vision in pink today?"

"Oh." She glanced down at her shiny pink leggings, oversized pink sweatshirt, pink manicure, and pink sneakers. "Thank you, Jasper. It's not easy being a Bright Spring in autumn, you know."

I nodded with exaggerated seriousness. "Never a truer word. So what can I help you with? You'll have to make do with me..." I shot Watt a glare across the ice. "...since my co-coach is off doing coachy stuff."

"Actually, that's perfect! You're really the one I wanted to talk to, anyway. You know I'm the head of the Marmot Hockey Moms, right?" She pulled her hands up into pink claws and unleashed a vicious marmot hiss. "*Go, Marmots!*"

"Right. Yeah. Go, Marmots." I returned her hiss half-heartedly.

"Well, on behalf of the other parents, I wanted to thank you, sincerely, for helping out with the kids..."

"Oh," I said, touched. "God, no need to thank me. It's my job, and I really enjoy it. Zach, in particular, has a great attitude. Did you see him stretching out there? His range of motion has improved, and he said our mindset work is really helping him. I don't know if he told you, but he got an A-plus on his history assignment, too." I leaned toward her confidingly. "I swear, if there were a higher grade, I'd have given it to him. I told the kids to use their imaginations and think outside the box, but I was freaking blown away when he took the time to turn his essay on the Salem witch trials into a moving, full-blown monologue from a condemned—"

"He mentioned that." Kayla's smile seemed a bit brittle. "That's the *other* part of what I wanted to talk to you about." She knit her fingers together. "The thing is, Jasper, I

—I mean we, the parents—truly do appreciate what you're doing... but when you're asking the kids to think outside the box, have you considered that maybe the boxes are there for a reason?"

I blinked. "I don't follow."

"Coach Monroe understood that being a successful student athlete is all about balance. Schoolwork is important—gosh, I'm *all* about literacy—but it's only one component of success. The kids also need their teachers to support their *non*-academic endeavors."

"Sure. I do support—"

"For example," Kayla interrupted. "Coach Monroe sometimes let the kids do their homework during class on game days. And she definitely would not have given them an assignment that might take up their whole weekend and fill their heads with distracting ideas right at the time when they most need to buckle down and focus on their training if they want to get a scholarship." She cocked her head. "That's not something to be taken lightly."

I frowned. "I... I don't take it lightly, I promise. I've been working with Tam nearly every day and using her lesson plans as a guide—"

"As a *guide*. Well..." She paused. "I just worry that when someone is stepping into a role temporarily, there can be a desire to sort of... shake things up a bit." She did a quick, demonstrative shimmy. "To pal around with the kids, doing yoga and breathing exercises when they should be training, and to be a light-hearted, popular teacher who gives extra assignments that give the kids big dreams—"

I scowled. "It wasn't extr—"

"I don't mean that as a criticism, Jasper! I know you have the very best intentions, and you're trying hard. But... you're not *really* a teacher or a coach, are you? You're stepping up because there's no one else, and that's so, *so* lovely of you." She wrinkled her nose prettily. "I just wanted to make sure you understood the bigger picture. The kids—especially Zach—can't afford distractions."

"Distractions... like the opportunity to reimagine their assignments and actually learn something?" I said slowly, still reeling from the *not a real teacher* comment.

I mean, I knew I wasn't an *experienced* teacher. Obviously. Like everything else in this season of life, I was faking it until I made it. But also... wasn't a teacher someone who taught things? Someone who helped the kids understand and engage with a topic? Someone who cared and showed up?

"*Yes,*" she said with a relieved exhale. "Exactly. And while we're on the subject of distractions, the main thing I wanted to say to you and Watt was..." She bit her lip again.

"Gosh, at this point, why hold back?" I said with heavy irony.

Unfortunately, certain people were irony deficient.

"You're so right," she giggled, clasping my hands tighter. "We've always been friends, haven't we? So I say this as a friend... Jasper, have you considered the toll your constant bickering must be taking on poor, sweet Watt?"

"Our bickering," I repeated. "Poor, sweet Watt?" I looked from her to the smirky, grouchy, teasing man responsible for the torture devices I'd strapped to my feet. "*That* Watt?"

"Yes. I'm sure the kids have noticed you glaring and name-calling—"

"I don't name-call!" I winced, remembering my *coward* comment from a minute ago. "Much."

"I'm sure it's not entirely *your* fault," she said, in a voice that made it clear she wasn't sure of any such thing.

"But Watt has so much on his plate, between running the orchard, and raising his son, and his commitment to participate in the Pilgrim Prance 5K with me the day after Thanksgiving." She ticked the items off on her fingers.

Participate in the... what?

Focus, Jasper.

I blinked. "Okay..."

"He's calm and steady, but I know that deep down, he must find this whole situation with you upsetting..."

"Again, you're talking about Watt *Bartlett*?" I said with a half laugh. "That guy?" I pointed across the ice.

Watt caught me pointing and frowned.

Kayla laughed uncertainly. "Oh, I know you're rivals from way back, but I promise you, everyone who really knows him understands how much he loathes confrontation of any sort. He's a peaceful, gentle soul."

I was stunned speechless... which was probably a good thing since I wouldn't have said anything good.

Fortunately, I was saved from having to respond at all because, at that moment, Delaney came jogging down from somewhere in the stands, his black glasses askew. "Jasper!" He sounded a little breathless, like he'd been hurrying. "Hey. Great practice."

"Hey." I forced a smile. "Did Tam bribe you to come so you could give her a full, in-depth investigative report?"

"Bribe," he scoffed. "As though I need a *bribe* to help my pregnant sister. You wound me, you really do. And that's exactly what I told Tam." After a beat, he added, "*After* I ate the leftover cupcakes she offered me."

I laughed out loud.

"Hey, I'm no fool." He grinned hugely. "You put chocolate chunks in the mix last time, and I'm only human—"

"Um, pardon me," Kayla interrupted, looking wide-eyed at Delaney. "Did you say you're Tamsen's brother?"

He looked her up and down. "I am," he confirmed. "And you are...?"

"Kayla! Kayla Milley." She turned up the brightness of her smile from stun to kill. "My son is one of the starting centers for the Marmots, and... oh my gosh, we're *huge* fans of yours, Mr. Monroe."

"Are you?" He raised one eyebrow. "Did you like my ProPublica piece on climate refugees? Or the one VICE picked up on housing inequality?"

She frowned. "Uh... no. I meant... I meant for the Bruins?"

Delaney nodded sagely. "Ah. My lesser-known work."

Smothering a snicker, I explained, "Kayla, this is *Delaney* Monroe. He doesn't play hockey, his brothers do."

"I swear, I'm doomed to have that as my epitaph," he muttered.

I laughed again.

Watt came sailing over at that moment and caught himself on the railing beside me. His eyes darted between the three of us before focusing on me. "Jasper. Scrimmage time, remember?"

"Oh, right. Sorry. Kayla was just, ah..." I cracked my neck from side to side. "Giving me some feedback."

"All good, I hope," Delaney said lightly. "I know Tam's been very impressed with how quickly Jasper's picked up the game and how dedicated he is. In fact, I'm hoping to buy him a drink at the Hive after practice to celebrate his incredible progress."

I shot him a look that said I knew a lie when I heard one, and he smirked.

Watt cleared his throat.

"Oh, jeez, sorry again." I gestured between the two men. "Watt, do you know Tam's brother Delaney?"

"No." Watt gave him a brusque up-nod. "Watt Bartlett. Nice to meet you."

"Same," Delaney said flatly.

They eyed each other for a beat.

"Well, I'm sure you boys need to get back to it," Kayla said. "A scrimmage is a *brilliant* idea, Watt, honey. I can't wait to see how much the team has improved."

Watt immediately stiffened. "Right. Come on, Jasper. Ticktock."

I opened my mouth to tell him where he could shove his *ticktock*, but Kayla caught my eye and pursed her lips.

"Sure," I agreed easily. "Whatever you say, pal. Let's get after it!"

Watt shot me a look, but I ignored him.

Delaney looked like he was fighting a smile of his own. "We'll catch up later," he promised, sending me a conspiratorial wink.

"Hold my elbow," Watt muttered as I picked my way slowly across the ice, well aware that all the assembled parents and students were watching me. "I'll skate you over to the box."

"Pfft. No way. I'm not a child," I shot back. "Everyone's watching. I might not be capable of getting there smoothly, but I can at least show people I'm capable of getting there under my own power."

Watt glanced over his shoulder at where we'd left Kayla and huffed out a breath. "Yeah, well, if you learned to skate, you wouldn't have this problem."

I shot him an incredulous look. "Wait, what? Learn to *skate*? Is *that* what I need to do? Oh my heck, Watt, what a brilliant idea!" I whispered in my best Kayla voice. "Here

I've been strapping these death-blades on my feet for funsies when all this time, all I had to do was..." I snapped my fingers. "...*learn to skate*."

Watt's jaw worked. "Do you want my help or not?"

The words *definitely fucking not* were on the tip of my tongue, but I felt the combined eyes of the whole stadium watching me step-step-step across the ice, and my chest went hot. Even at thirty-seven, it was zero percent fun to feel pitied.

Plus, while I was almost positive that Kayla was either gaslighting me or just fucking wrong about Watt, I felt a moment of uncharacteristic hesitation as I looked up at him.

Where he'd seemed *teasingly* annoyed earlier, now he seemed genuinely, truly cranky. Like maybe he thought I was wasting his time and making the whole coaching thing even harder on him.

I released a breath that sounded a little too much like a marmot hiss. "Fuck it. Fine," I whispered. "Give me your arm."

Watt seemed a bit surprised, but he didn't say a word as I wrapped my hand around his thick biceps and let him glide me across the ice.

He *was* solid. Kayla was right about that much. Steady, too. I took a deep breath and let it out again, letting myself relax.

"Everything okay?" he asked in a low voice, much as he had earlier.

I ran a hand over my face. *Super great.* Not only was I a failed acting-wannabe, a washed-up model, and half-owner of a defunct modeling agency, but I was now also a shitty fake teacher and a distraction as a coach.

I managed a thin smile. "Been a long-ass week, that's all."

"Mmm. The rigors of coaching, even at your profound skill level, are probably taking a toll."

"Ha. Right." My stomach rolled.

I knew Watt was just continuing our earlier joking. He didn't realize that I was suddenly feeling raw and sensitive, or he'd never have used almost the exact words Kayla had when she'd been talking about me being mean to "*poor Watt.*"

In fact, I should probably explain it to him. Get his perspective on things.

"So..." I licked my dry lips. We were nearly at the players' box, so I blurted in a rush, "Did you want to grab a drink tonight? I wanted to talk about a couple things related to the team."

Watt gave me an unreadable look. "Sure you'd have time for that? I'd hate to take you away from your other plans."

I rolled my eyes. Did he mean my compulsive baking, sorting china figurines, and tutoring with Tam? "I think I can try to squeeze you into my jam-packed schedule, yes."

"Lovely." He looked back across the ice at where Kayla had been, and he looked troubled for a moment before his face closed off. "I can't tonight. I have plans."

"Okay." I stepped over the threshold onto the rubber mat of the box. "Tomorrow, then?"

Watt opened his mouth, and for a beautiful second, it looked like he was going to say yes. But then he glanced Kayla's way again.

"No," he said in a low voice. "Look, I... I think it's probably best that we keep things as they are, don't you? We need to work together as co-coaches, and I don't want either of us to get confused about what this is or isn't, you know?"

Ouch.

It seemed Tam was wrong about Watt and Kayla because the man kept looking to her like she was his personal North Star... even though he'd been kissing *me* the other night.

And that part was... fine.

Obviously.

He didn't owe me anything. The bet we'd made was about being friends. Just friends. With no more rule violations.

But now it felt like he truly didn't even want that anymore, and that hurt.

"I didn't think co-coaches going out for a drink was confusing," I whispered hotly. "Especially when they used to be friends, and at least one of them is trying really hard to be friends again."

"Jasper..." Watt hesitated again.

"But then, I guess I don't know much about coaching, do I?" I folded my arms over my chest.

"Hey, Coach Bartlett?" Zach interrupted. "Did you want us to line up, or...?"

"Huh? Yeah. Shit. Get out there, guys." Watt shook his head as if to clear it, blew his fucking whistle, and turned his attention to the team as each of them stepped out of the box. "Remember what we talked about a minute ago? Kip, you're in goal, and you're gonna play it cautious. Keep it covered, yeah?"

"You got it, Coach," Kip called before skating off.

"Zach, let's see some good communication out there. Remember, you're part of a team."

Zach nodded once.

"Good. And Derry—"

"Yeah, I know," Derry said dismissively as he stepped onto the ice.

I wondered what that was about since Derry was usually incredibly polite and good-natured.

Watt ground his teeth as he watched his son go.

"Do you think Derry is...?" I began cautiously.

"I think we need to focus on the game, Jasper," Watt whispered in a tone that suggested I shut my mouth.

"I know, but..."

He gave me a surly look. "*I* will handle Derry, okay? You... worry about your plans for the evening."

I stared at him, stung. "What are you talking about? Jesus, Watt, I'm trying to be your friend—"

"And *I* am trying to coach this team," he hissed. "You know, the job *both* of us are supposed to be doing? Maybe focus a little more on that and a little less on... distractions, okay?"

Distractions like teasing him and arguing with him?

Distractions like our rivalry and our friendship?

My jaw dropped, and I blinked at him. "But... I..." I swallowed.

Well, shit.

It seemed Kayla had been right.

And wasn't that a lowering thought?

I blew out a breath, and without another word, I turned my attention to the scrimmage, not wanting to distract Watt further.

Jasper, you are such a fucking idiot.

Deep down, I'd thought our friendship resurgence was inevitable, like seasons passing. That the same way autumn always follows summer, what Watt and I had as kids would come around again, the same as before, if I just hung on long enough.

I'd deluded myself into thinking I still knew Watt—that, despite all the surface changes, at his core, he was the same person he'd been at seventeen, with the same needs and wants, the same desire for connection with me—because then I could pretend I was the same person I used to be, too. Maybe I'd wanted to believe my coming back to Copper County now could be one giant, cosmic do-over—a chance to erase all my many failures and get it right—so that when I left this time, the rest of my life would fall into place also.

But I wasn't a kid. There were no do-overs. And faking it until you make it could only take a guy so far. Eventually, you needed to face the reality that you couldn't force things to happen simply because you thought they should.

While Watt blew his whistle and barked instructions at the team, I nodded and smiled and stayed quiet, not offering any dubious or distracting advice of my own.

Unfortunately, the twenty-minute scrimmage was still a shitshow, and the defeated expressions on the kids' faces as they filed back into the players' box, red-faced and sweaty, said they knew it.

"Zach, I thought we were working on your puck control and not trying to play hero," Watt said wearily. "What was that out there?"

Zach's handsome face hardened. "I was trying to make a play—"

"By yourself?" Watt took a breath. "It's a *team* here. Communicate with Derry, and maybe you'll get some-where. And Kip, you were supposed to tighten up your defense—"

"Sorry, Coach." Kip, the shortest and possibly youngest player on the team, hung his head like a kicked puppy.

"Don't be sorry." Watt looked around at the team. "That goes for all of you. Sorry doesn't mean shit. You've gotta put in the effort and change the way you play. If you keep doing things the way you've been doing, you can expect the same outcomes you've been getting. You've got to take what you're learning and put it into practice. You hear me?"

I definitely heard him.

The boys muttered, "Yes, Coach."

I did, too.

After they left, Watt sank to the bench and rubbed both hands over his head. "Christ, that was rough."

"Yeah," I agreed.

He glanced up at me, his hazel eyes tumultuous, and my chest squeezed. "About what you were saying earlier..."

I held up a hand. "I understand, Watt." I sat down beside him and removed my skates, stretching my aching toes for a minute before grabbing the duffel with my real shoes from under the bench.

Watt blinked. "You... do? Really?"

"I hate that you sound so surprised, but I guess I don't blame you. I told you I was determined, and at times, I can be a bit *too* determined. Not unlike a bulldozer." I gave him a quick smile. "But cuter, obviously."

His forehead creased. "I don't know what—"

"That was a joke," I said quickly. "I, um..." I bit my lip nervously. "Look, I realize now that I might have jumped the gun a little the other night on the dock. You said we couldn't force feelings to be something they weren't, right? I did hear you, I promise. I just... didn't listen."

"What are you trying to say?" he demanded.

"I really do want to be your friend, Watt. I'm not giving up on that. But I know things aren't that easy. We don't really know each other anymore, do we?" I said sadly.

"I... I guess not like we used to," he said cautiously.

I nodded. "So the bet and all that other stuff? Let's just..." I waved a hand. "...call it off. According to Watt and

Jasper's Rules..." I paused. "Actually, I don't think there is a rule for canceling a bet, is there? I don't think either of us ever canceled one. Not after we created the rules. Ha. Well, let's just... rewind to Sunday and pretend it didn't happen."

"Pretend it didn't happen," he repeated. "That's what you want?"

No. Jesus, obviously, it wasn't. Even now, when I knew better times a billion, it was a struggle not to run my fingers through Watt's dark hair, to hold his stubbled cheeks in both my hands, and kiss him so hard and so deeply the remaining parents milling around the bleachers would stop and stare—not with pity, this time, but with envy.

But that didn't seem to be what *Watt* wanted, and my wants weren't the only thing that mattered.

"I'm good with it if you are," I said firmly.

Watt stared at me for a long moment, and I wished I knew what the hell he was thinking... or maybe I didn't. At length, he opened his mouth and—

"Jasper?" Delaney appeared in the stands beside us and glanced back and forth between me and Watt as if clocking the tension between us. "Spectating's thirsty work, and I'm about ready for that congratulatory drink. You wanna...?" He tilted his chin over his shoulder toward the exit.

"Oh." He'd been serious about that? That was unexpectedly sweet of him... and pretty damn appealing after the week I'd had. "Yeah. Yes. Totally. Just, um..." I looked at Watt, but he was staring down at his skates. "Give me a minute to finish up here?"

Delaney nodded, but Watt immediately stood and shook his head.

"No, it's fine." He gave us both a friendly smile. "You go have fun. We're done here."

"But—"

"Awesome." Delaney gestured toward the exit like a game show host. "Shall we?"

Still, I hesitated, but Watt had removed his whistle and started packing his stuff, clearly done with our conversation.

I blew out a breath. "Yeah," I agreed. "Let's go."

It wasn't until we'd reached the door that I realized what had been bothering me.

I knew what Watt's real smile looked like. And I knew a fake smile when I saw one.

CHAPTER SEVEN

WATT

"Oh, God, how does this series just get better with every rewatch?" Chris sighed, sinking back into my couch. "John Ruffian in a pearl-snap shirt and tight jeans as he pretends to be a sheriff? And all the delicious tension between him and the suspicious deputy? Ten out of ten gay stars, no notes. I think that might be my favorite episode."

Ollie leaned forward to pick at the huge "Fall Charcuterie Experience" that Chris had brought over. "Cutie, you said that two episodes ago, when John pretended to be a teacher. You can't have two favorite— Oh my God," he groaned as he popped a bite of food in his mouth. "What is this?"

Chris laughed from his usual nest of pillows and blankets on the floor. "Caramelized onion and fig dip. One of my new fall offerings at Cheese and Charm. Good?"

"Mmpfh. I changed my mind. Keep making this dip and you can have as many favorite episodes as you want." Ollie looked at me. "Right, Watt?"

I grunted. It probably made me a terrible friend, but I'd

barely been paying attention to their conversation because I was too busy replaying my earlier conversation.

"Let's just call it off"? "Pretend it didn't happen"?

What had happened to *"friends 'til the end"* and *"I won't fuck it up this time"?*

"...next episode. Right, Watt?"

"Hmm?" I glanced at Chris, who was watching me expectantly. "Yes. Sure." I waved a hand at the television. "Go ahead."

Jasper had been acting off all week—tense, tired, smiling a little too broadly, and trying a little too hard. I'd thought, at first, that it might have been lingering awkwardness from our kiss at the dock—fuck knew *I* felt awkward about it—but our banter had flowed, and he'd seemed comfortable around me, so I'd chalked it up to actual fatigue. I'd been skating practically since birth, and even I found it physically demanding to do a full practice *after* putting in a full day of work, and I wasn't going to Tam's most nights for mentoring.

Now, I was wondering what—or who—else had been keeping him up at night.

"...probably aliens, don't you think, Watt?" Ollie demanded.

"Hmm?" I blinked up at the sound of my name, but I had no idea what he was talking about. *Was* there a John Ruffian episode about aliens? "Er... yeah. Good call."

Ollie pointed an accusing finger at me. "I knew it!"

"You haven't been paying attention at all, have you?" Chris sounded reproachful.

I winced. *Busted.* "Sorry, guys. Woolgathering. Let's start the next episode."

"We coooould," Chris said. "But would you rather talk about why you're looking so upset? We're really good listeners, you know. And we won't judge." He elbowed Ollie's shin. "Will we?"

"Weeeell. Possibly a little judgment?" Ollie held up his thumb and forefinger.

"Oliver!" Chris slapped his leg.

"I'm being honest. And Watt knows I'd only judge him with love."

I snorted. "Because of the *sacred bonds of friendship,* as John Ruffian says? No, thanks. I have nothing to discuss."

"Not a single thing?" Ollie pursed his lips. "Because *I* heard you were arguing with the hot new hockey coach at Derry's practice a week ago. That seems discussion-worthy."

"And very un-Watt-like," Chris added solemnly.

I rolled my eyes, glad Derry was at Rachel's for the weekend so he wouldn't overhear. He'd gotten over the worst of his anger at my "interference," but I'd rather not remind him of how it had started.

"You need to stop listening to your ladies, Ollie. And you need to stop listening to *him*," I told Chris, hooking a thumb at Ollie.

"And then I heard you were coaching the hockey team, despite it being your busy season at the orchard," Ollie went on.

"That's because the new coach doesn't know hockey. Literally, the man doesn't understand the rules of the game and can barely stand on a pair of skates, even when dared —" Though he'd looked damn, damn cute trying this week. "—even though he likes to pretend he's an expert, so I kinda *had* to help out. For Derry and the kids, you know. It's bad enough they might lose their chance at camp this summer, and—"

"Did you catch that, Chris?" Ollie demanded, pointing at me accusingly. "Did you see?"

"I did," Chris said. "That little smile. Dead giveaway. He *like*-likes him."

"What?" I scowled, all thought of a smile gone. "No. Don't be ridiculous. Start the episode."

"Innnnteresting," Ollie mused, one smoking pipe away from being Sherlock fucking Holmes. "Watt with a guy... I can see it. So, Watt, maybe I was on the wrong path earlier. Maybe instead of Kayla as a potential date, I should have been pushing... Kevin from the barbershop."

"Can we not? Start. The. Episode."

"Gender doesn't matter. You know we don't give a shit," he went on. "And I think you're underestimating how stress-relieving a casual hookup could be—"

I shook my head. "I think you're underestimating how stress-*inducing* this conversation is. Casual isn't my thing. And if I'm being honest, neither is serious. Can we drop it?"

"But—?"

"Hush, Ollie." Chris shoved a cracker into Ollie's mouth. "He said he doesn't want to discuss it, so we won't." To me, he said, "Just to say, lots of people aren't into casual sex the way Ollie is. I'm not. And some people aren't into sex, period. We're not trying to pressure you, Watt. We just want you to know we're here if you need us. We want you to be happy—"

"I am happy! Of course I am." I thought for a minute before ticking off all my blessings on my fingers. "I have an orchard, a great kid, work I love. I'm fucking marinating in my contentment over here, okay? *Now* can we start the episode?"

Ollie grumbled around a mouthful of cracker, "Fine."

"Thank you." I folded my arms and burrowed deeper into the sofa.

Chris grabbed the remote while Ollie took out his phone and started messaging someone—probably arranging a hookup for later, as usual.

Which made me start thinking of other things.

Like... whether the Hive would be crowded tonight.

And who might be there "celebrating" over drinks.

And how obnoxiously sexy Delaney Monroe's dark glasses looked against his tan skin.

And the carefree way Jasper had been laughing with him earlier.

As the *John Ruffian: Pretender* theme song played, I found myself blurting, "What if I *was* interested in him?"

Chris immediately paused the episode, and Ollie dropped his phone on the couch.

"Knew it. You argued with him in public," Ollie said, like the logical leap from A to Z was self-explanatory. He grabbed a slice of pita bread off the tray and pointed it at me. "You don't argue, Watt. Remember how Kayla Milley roped you into running a race in a pilgrim costume because you were too easygoing to say no?"

"You make it sound like I'm a pushover. I'm *not*. And," I added confidently, "there's no pilgrim costume involved."

At least, I hoped to God there wasn't.

"You're definitely not a pushover," Chris agreed. "But you don't like to make waves. Reed once said you're like a tree—"

"Yes!" Ollie said, shaking Chris's shoulder enthusiastically. "*Yes.* Wasn't I just talking about this the other day, Watt? You're steady. You're calm. You don't get ruffled because you don't put yourself in ruffly positions. You're a tree, and you might bend to every breeze because you're easy like that, but ultimately, you cannot be moved. Nobody argues with a tree, and the tree sure as heck doesn't argue back." He opened his mouth wide, dropped in his over-loaded pita square, and shot me a wink. "Except, apparently, with the new coach," he said around his mouthful. "'Cause he charges your battery like *vroooom*."

I rolled my eyes.

"Who is this guy?" Chris asked eagerly. "Was it, like, just instant, undeniable animal chemistry? You took one look at him and *wham*, spicy thoughts? Because I've been there, and it's a lot to process—"

"No, nothing like that. We... we knew each other when we were kids..."

I explained our history briefly. About how Jasper had stayed with Mabel and Abe, about our friendship, our teas-ing, the way we'd challenged each other.

At first, I spoke haltingly because those summer days with Jasper weren't something I talked about, ever. I'd boxed the memories up and stuffed them in a corner of my brain, I realized. Until the light had come on in the house, I hadn't let myself think of him, let alone talk about him, because remembering had brought back all the hurt and confusion, all the wasted potential, all the unfinished business.

But by the time I told my friends about how Jasper and I had invented our rules and cemented our friendship, how we'd come up with the signal of the light in the window, and how I'd felt my first stirrings of teenage lust, the words came easier... possibly because Ollie was grin-ning wildly and Chris's eyes were a pair of pulsing cartoon hearts.

"Watt and Jasper's Rules of Engagement. Oh!" Chris

pressed a hand to his chest. "That is so hecking cute, Watt. Jasper was your first crush. Wait until I tell Reed this story."

Considering Chris's mouthy, bodyguard-turned-security-specialist fiancé was built like a giant brick wall and seemed about as sensitive as one, I could make an educated guess. "Reed'll say, 'Why didn't Watt just cowboy up and tell the guy how he felt?' Not sure I disagree," I added dryly.

"Because you're talking as an adult. Reed was a teenager once, too. Heck, even when Reed and I first got together, he had a hard time processing his feelings. He wasn't always the sweet, emotionally mature teddy bear he is today."

Ollie and I exchanged a look. Literally *none* of those were words I'd use to describe snarky, overprotective Reed, but okay.

"Let's focus, people." Ollie waved a hand. "Finish the story, Watt. How'd you guys go from that to... this?"

"I, ah..." I ran my tongue over my teeth. "I kissed him."

"In violation of the rules?" Chris gasped.

"Rebellious." Ollie nodded. "I dig it."

"It wasn't premeditated. It just... happened. And I immediately wanted to apologize because I'd crossed a line. I figured Jasper would be angry—"

"Was he?" Chris asked. "Did he say your friendship was over?"

I shook my head. "Abe called his name literally the second we broke apart, and Jasper had to run home. Worst timing in history. And then... he left town and never contacted me again."

"He left because of the kiss?" Chris whispered. "How tragic, Watt. You poor thing."

"He was *that* pissed his best friend kissed him?" Ollie snorted. "Fuck him."

"It wasn't... it wasn't exactly like that," I admitted before explaining about him moving away suddenly due to his parents' divorce. "Can you believe Jasper told me the other night that he thought *he'd* kissed *me*? He thought I'd be the one upset. It was a huge, stupid misunderstanding." It was still hard to wrap my mind around this. "But the end result is the same. Nearly twenty years, zero contact."

"That's rough," Ollie said, shaking his head.

"Yeah." I cleared my throat. "It was. I was hurt and angry. I—"

"No, Watt, I meant rough for *him*."

When I glanced at him, Ollie pointed at his own chest. "Child of divorce, remember? Not only did my family split up, but I also had to move away from my friends and support system. It's not surprising that Jasper didn't reach out right away. He was probably reeling."

I frowned. "He was, but..."

"But it still hurt," Chris finished loyally.

I opened my mouth, then closed it again. He was right. Even though I understood Jasper's actions better now, they had still left a mark. And getting over it and trusting him again weren't as easy as I thought they should be.

If I were a mature adult, wouldn't I be able to forgive and forget?

Ollie frowned. "And you didn't reach out to him?"

"People didn't really text back then, I guess," Chris mused. "But you probably sent him emails. Or letters?"

"I..." I cleared my throat. "I didn't do any of that. Mabel said... she said Jasper would call me when he was ready because he'd need me, which he clearly *didn't* because he didn't reach out. I thought... I mean, I *knew*... he was done with our friendship after the kiss."

"But Jasper must've also thought—" Chris began. He broke off and bit his lip. "Oh."

There was a beat of silence.

Total, damning silence.

I bent forward, bracing my elbows on my knees, and ran both hands over my face. "Oh, God. I'm the asshole, aren't I? I waited for him to call. I waited for him to give me an opening to apologize. I didn't even think about what he was going through."

The obviousness of it, the selfishness of it, was breathtaking.

"You were hurt," Chris pointed out, patting my shoulder. "And you were a kid, Watt. You both were."

"Do better now," Ollie said practically. "What's happened since he came back?"

"I was an asshole again," I muttered into my hands. "I yelled at him at practice a week ago and told him he didn't know what he was doing. That's the argument you heard about."

"Eeesh." Chris winced. "Really?"

"And then he... he brought me a peace offering. Two peace offerings, really. Sunday, we met on the dock to talk—"

"Just like old times?" Chris said. "Aw. That's good."

"And... we kissed again," I whispered.

Chris's eyes bugged. Ollie punched a fist in the air.

"Let's fucking go! And how was it?" he demanded. "Battery fully charged?" He winked.

"It was... it was..." I spread my hands, trying to put into words that I *had* no words because I hadn't been thinking at all from the minute the kissing had started. "Good," I said simply. "It was really good."

"And was it just a kiss?" Ollie's grin turned sly. "Or did he, you know, polish your apple?"

"Oliver." Chris pushed his leg hard.

"No." My face went hot. "There was no apple polishing. I've never... I wouldn't even know..." I broke off with a headshake, feeling like an idiot. "I don't have any experience with guys."

Chris shrugged. "Neither did I, until Reed."

"And I'd argue that you *do* have experience with guys," Ollie said. "Being a guy yourself. We're not that complicated, Watt. A little rub, a little tug, a little checking in to see what your partner's into, and then providing more of that." He grinned. "But don't you worry. Chris and I will be your gay sherpas. Together, we will help you summit Gay Sex Mountain. The climb will be *hard...*"

"I'm not gay, Ollie." I ran a hand over my face. "I'm not straight. But bi or pan don't really fit either." I hadn't been attracted to enough people to reliably say what I was.

"Meh. Labels are for cheese," Chris said matter-of-factly. "You're attracted to the man?"

"Yes," I admitted. "But he's the only man I've ever been attracted to. What do you call it when you've only ever been attracted to a handful of women and one particular guy?"

"I think you call it being Watt," Chris said easily. "So. What's next? What's the plan?"

"No plan. I'm not going to *act* on anything. I wouldn't even know where to begin." I pushed back into the sofa. "I'm attracted to Jasper, yes. Whatever that means. But he's going back to LA in a couple of months, and..."

"And you're a tree," Chris said. "You can't be uprooted."

"I don't want to be," I said staunchly. "Acting on the attraction would just complicate things."

"Or it might make everything come right," Ollie said

cryptically. He waved a hand. "But never mind. What do you want?"

"I... I'd like to be friends. While Jasper's here. I thought he wanted that, too. After the kiss the other night, he even bet me that we'd be friends again by Christmas..."

"Oh, gosh, I think I like this guy. I think I like him *so* much," Chris sighed. "You need to bring him to our next *John Ruffian* night. Does he like *John Ruffian*? Oooh, do you think he'd like a breakfast board? Because I've been working on a thing with pumpkin waffles as a centerpiece, and—"

"Chrissy, focus," Ollie said, patting Chris's shoulder. "Watt said *thought*, as in Jasper no longer wants to be friends." He narrowed his eyes at me. "What did you do?"

"Why do you assume it was me?" I demanded. "I didn't do anything."

It poured out of me in a confusing tumult: the way Jasper had been just a little off this week, smiling a little too hard. How I'd first teased him into real smiles and then into teasing me back. How I'd thought things were going okay... maybe better than okay... until he'd changed his mind after good-looking Delaney asked him out and canceled our bet.

If I'd expected sympathy, though, I was doomed to disappointment.

"Let me understand," Ollie said in a tone of deep foreboding. "Jasper, the man you kissed and then signed up for a no-commitment friendship trial—"

I winced. "That's not how I'd characterize..."

He raised one dark eyebrow. "—was acting *off*, by your own admission. And instead of sitting him down and lovingly forcing him to chat, perhaps after plying him with charcuterie, in the time-honored tradition—" He gestured at the table. "—you instead made assumptions. First, that he was feeling squirrelly about your kiss"—Ollie ticked off on his fingers—"though you had no reason to believe that, and *then* that he was tired, and *then* that he's too busy giving Tam's brother a nickel tour of his love factory—"

I wrinkled my nose. "That might be your worst euphe—"

"Bupbupbup." Ollie raised his chin. "Just answer the question, Bartlett."

"I love when Ollie gets like this," Chris whispered in an aside. "It's like in Season 5, Episode 2, where John pretends to be a lawyer so he can punish the corporation poisoning the—"

"No comments from the jury." Ollie gave him a pointed look.

Chris startled, then made a show of zipping his lips and throwing away the key.

Ollie's gaze burned me again. "Your answer, Mr. Bartlett?"

"I... suppose... that might be one way of categorizing what happened." I found myself squirming a bit. "Factually accurate, but—"

"A-ha!" Ollie slapped his jeans like a judge with a gavel. "I hereby declare you guilty of Making Emotional Assumptions with Jealous Intent. And this is a Level-Three felony Making Assumptions charge because you're a repeat offender."

"Oooh, Level Three sounds serious," Chris said. He frowned at Ollie. "Wait, I thought I was the jury?"

"I appeal this verdict, Your Honor," I said dryly. "On the grounds that I'm not jealous. Never have been. I attended my ex-wife's second wedding, for goodness—"

"Pfft. Of course you did. Because she wasn't the one that got away," Ollie said, lifting an eyebrow.

I blinked. And deliberately chose not to give that idea another thought.

"Did your muscles get all tight when you saw him with the other guy?" Chris wondered. "Did you get all *grrrrrr*—like low-key embarrassed but also illogically and nonspecifically ragey? Did your fingertips twitch like you wanted to grab Jasper, or whack the other guy, or both, even though you're usually a very gentle human? Because that's what happens to Reed when you pretend to flirt with me."

I instantly regretted every time I'd ever pretended to be interested in Chris for Reed's benefit because those symptoms sounded familiar...

Not just from when I'd seen Jasper with Delaney but from when I'd heard about his marriage a week ago also.

"Fuck," I said succinctly.

"Mmhmm." Ollie sat back on the sofa, satisfied. I could tell he saw right through me. "Appeal denied. Would you like to hear your sentence?"

I gave him an unimpressed look. "Is it being lured into a deep conversation with my friends under the guise of a low-key *John Ruffian* and charcuterie night? Because if so, I think I should be sentenced to time served." I blew out a breath. "Look, if I knew how to handle shit with Jasper better, I'd already be doing it. There didn't use to be all these misunderstandings between us—"

"Except there was at least one huge misunderstanding, wasn't there?" Chris pointed out softly. "And both of you got hurt, which is why you're both messing up now. You're trying to protect yourselves from being hurt again. I don't blame you, but it's also not working."

I sighed, stretching my neck from side to side. I really fucking hated being seen so clearly. And I hated not knowing what I was doing even more.

"Fine, then." I waved a hand. "Sentence me. What is it that I need to be doing that I'm not?"

Chris and Ollie exchanged a look. "Talk to him," they said in unison.

"Find out if you like *this* Jasper as much as you liked young Jasper," Chris said. "Betcha you will."

"And figure out what you really want from him. Because you *saaaay* it's friendship..." Ollie pursed his lips. "...but you and I have been friends for years, and you've never thrown a fit because *I* was mixing up love muffins with a hot, new baker—"

"If you did, you'd be throwing fits all the time," Chris said seriously.

"—so I think you want to throw a benefit or two into that friendship, if you know what I mean," Ollie suggested.

The idea made my stomach jump but in a good way. "I'll... see what he thinks."

"Tonight," Ollie warned.

Chris nodded. "Yeah, like, *now*. Or whenever he gets home from... um..." He winced. "Whatever he might be doing?"

I ground my teeth together, thinking of Jasper with Delaney. "Right."

"I think you need to bring him a peace offering. Something that shows you know what he likes and what he needs," Chris said. "Like, once I was really missing my family, so Reed drove all the way to Syracuse to get me these biscotti, and when he came home, we watched *The Cutting Edge* because it was my nonna's fave." He sighed dreamily before focusing on me again. "So what's Jasper's favorite hobby, or food, or music? What does he really, truly need?"

I shook my head. "I... don't know anymore." I frowned,

pondering what I *did* know about Jasper. The things I knew he liked. The things I knew he wanted.

"When in doubt," Chris went on, "I say you can't go wrong with an emergency charcuterie—"

Ollie patted Chris's shoulder. "Chrissy, my angel, not as many people get jazzed about cheese as you do."

I straightened in my seat. "Actually," I said, thinking of the giant block of unpronounceable cheese still sitting in my fridge. "A charcuterie might not be a bad start. And as for the rest... I have an idea. But I'm going to need your help."

CHAPTER EIGHT

JASPER

I HAD A SURPRISINGLY good evening at the Hive, during which I didn't talk about Watt or worry about my friendship with Watt or even think about Watt *at all.*

When Delaney pulled into the campground's driveway and helped me out of his car a couple of hours and several stiff drinks later, I felt compelled to share my appreciation.

"You're a delight, Delaney." I slung my arm over his shoulder and nearly tripped over my own feet in the process. "Thank you for inviting me to that... to that..." I couldn't quite find the words to describe the Hive, with its diverse crowd of old ladies and bikers playing pool, soccer moms and twinks with sparkly lip gloss losing their shit to Chappell Roan on the dance floor, and quiet farmer-types holding up the bar while chatting with the tattooed '40s-pinup-girl bartender. "To that glorious, neon-lit utopia. To that... United Nations of questionable life choices. It was so much fun."

Delaney laughed and kept us both mostly upright. "It really was... until I noticed that it was barely 9:30 and you were already toasted. I'm thinking we should have gotten you something to eat."

"Me? Nah. I'm fine. I have baked goods in there." I gestured toward Mabel's house, which glowed like a beacon in the moonlight. "Enough for, like…" I counted on my fingers. "A year? Longer than I'll be in Copper County, anyway."

The thought made me sigh, and the sigh made my feet drift onto the grass.

"Whoa. Path's over here, Jasper." Delaney steered me back on course. "You don't sound too excited about going back to LA."

"Hmm? Oh, no, I am. Definitely. Or, like, mostly definitely," I corrected, thinking about the texts I'd received while at the Hive. One had been from Martin, beseeching me yet again to call him, and the other from my mother, demanding to know why I hadn't called Martin yet. This second one, at least, was not unexpected since my mother—and her husband—were huge fans of all things Martin. "Things will be different when I go back this time," I told Delaney. "They totally will, even if Watt and I aren't friends. I'm a determined person. Sometimes too determined." I snorted. "Ask Watt."

"Yeah, you told me about losing your friendship bet. I still don't get it, but… Oops, nope, this way! We're heading for the house, Jasper, not the lake."

"No," I agreed, nodding. "No lake. Watt won't be there. Anyway, this time, when I'm in LA, I won't listen to *Martin*. I definitely won't take his word about anything."

"Martin's your ex?"

"Mmm. My agent first. I won't be that naive next time."

"Of course you won't. Everything will be *very* different," he agreed in the placating voice people sometimes used when dealing with the inebriated... which was weird since I totally wasn't.

"Hey, Delaney?" I stopped walking, forcing him to stop walking, too. "Do you think when I'm in LA this time, I'll miss Copper County as much as I did before?"

Delaney was silent for a beat, looking at me with warm, sympathetic eyes. "I don't know, Jasper. I don't know if location matters so much." He sighed and looked around at the open campground, at the rustling trees, at the clouds scattering across the moon, like he was seeing a different place and time. "Wherever you go, there you are, you know?"

"Whoa." I blinked up at him. "*Wherever you go, there you are.* That's, like, *deep*. Super deep. You must be a brilliant writer."

He snorted. "That's actually a quote from—"

"*Brilliant*," I repeated.

Delaney laughed, and the sound made me happy... but not the belly-swooping, heart-pounding sort of happy I felt when Watt did the same. Which was too bad, really.

"Okay," Delaney said. "Just a couple more steps and we'll be at the porch... oh, no gardening tonight, Jasper," he said as I headed for one of Mabel's flower beds.

During my summers here, the beds had been filled with hydrangeas and snapdragons. All of the blooms were gone now, and a brisk October wind blew off the lake, but someone had covered the beds with straw and mulch, preparing them for next year.

It didn't take a genius to guess who that had been.

"Watt," I sighed.

"You're gonna ruin those boots," Delaney said as he steered me back toward the path to the porch. "I'd think that was against some kind of modeling code, but you're not very model-like."

"Not anymore, nope." I patted my stomach, which was still flat but where nary an ab could be seen anymore.

Delaney stopped *me* this time. "I wasn't talking about your appearance, Jasper. I think you're *very* attractive, and your physical appearance is the least of your appeal."

"Aww." This was so touching I blinked up at him for a long moment. "Thank you, Delaney. I think you're great, too. And I'm glad you decided to buy a house in Copper County. I will totally come back and visit you." I patted his shoulder. "And I'm sorry Watt was so cranky to you earlier. He's usually much nicer." I sighed. "Like, *so* nice. But... not *too* nice. You know?"

He bit his lip like he was fighting laughter. "Yeah," he said ruefully. "I think I'm getting a pretty clear picture."

I wrinkled my nose. "Sorry, what were we talking about?"

"Long-lost loves... or possibly boots? One or the other."

"Huh. I don't know anything about either of those. I actually hate fashion." I whispered this like a confession, but it was probably pretty obvious since I was still wearing the same running tights and Patagonia fleece I'd worn to practice. Not exactly catwalk-ready. "But my mother said I couldn't waste these cheekbones, and modeling paid the bills." I shrugged. "I liked history better. When Martin said I should get a degree for business reasons, I was like, yes. Boom. History. Did you know those who study history are doomed to repeat it?"

"I think it's those who *don't* study history are doomed to repeat it."

"Huh. You sure?"

"Very. Okay, lift your leg onto the step. There you go."

"I thought it was funny, 'cause I like history a lot and I'm terrible at teaching it, which is a sitch... sitch...

sitcheation I've repeated a lot. But Kayla says... *whoa*." I caught myself against the railing as an earthquake rolled over us... though Delaney didn't seem to be affected. "Oh no. Delaney," I whispered, "I think I might have had too much to drink."

"Uh-huh. You'll be okay." He paused beside me while I waited for things to stop spinning. "So... what did Kayla say?"

"Oh, that." I waved a hand. "She said I need to focus more and stop distracting Watt at hockey practice with my arguing and stuff."

"Ha. I'll just bet she did," Delaney said darkly.

"I keep trying—you know I do—to fake it 'til I make it..." I sighed again. "But some things are harder to fake than they look."

"You talking about ice-skating?" he wondered. "Or being friends with Watt?"

I whirled my head to look at him and nearly lost my balance. "Watt? Who brought *him* up?"

"You did," he said dryly. "At least forty times tonight."

"No." I frowned. "Forty?"

"And counting. And given the way he was looking at you earlier... maybe don't listen to Kayla so much, huh?" He grinned and propped me against the wall beside the door. "Where are your house keys?"

"Hmm." I closed my eyes because this made it easier to pat my pockets. "You know, though, what if Kayla's right? About..."

"Watt?" Delaney said, sounding surprised.

"Exactly. I mean, she's right about him being steady and kind. He really is. And I didn't know I had a competence kink until this week—"

"No, Jasper." Delaney pushed urgently at my shoulder. "I meant Watt—"

"And when he's around, even when we're teasing each other, I feel... good. Light. Like a part of myself I don't remember is—"

"Jasper," he hissed. "*Shut up*. Watt is—"

"Strong," I sighed. "Yeah. And sexy. And he looks so nice in flannel—"

"*Here*," Delaney bit out. He gripped my chin hard. "Open your fucking eyes, man."

I blinked my eyes open, and the first thing I saw was not Delaney but a vision of a broad-shouldered, dark-haired man wearing a fierce scowl while carrying a balloon... and a tray of crackers?

"Watt!" I grinned at this apparition. Those drinks had to have been *killer* strong if I was hallucinating something so impossible, but I was too happy to see him to care. "You're here! Damn, you look nice. Delaney, if you could see Watt like I do right now, you'd agree with me about the flannel."

My dream-Watt, who'd been giving Delaney a glower hot enough to peel paint, turned his gaze toward me, and his whole expression softened. "You okay, Jasper?"

"Me? Fuck yeah! I'm great." I started to pitch forward and ended up leaning back against the siding with a *bang*. "I may have had a couple whiskey things. Two? Or... seven?"

"Seven," Delaney said wryly. "Definitely seven."

"They tasted like apples." I smacked my lips. "Kinda like you do."

Watt's nostrils flared, and he growled at Delaney. "What the fuck?"

"Don't look at me." Delaney held up both hands. "He had a bad week, and he made lots of new friends at the bar.

A bunch of people wanted to buy Coach Lancaster a drink—"

"*Seven* people," I repeated happily.

"Uh-huh. And I think he's been eating nothing but his own baked goods for a week," Delaney said. "I'm gonna get him into bed."

"The hell you are." Dream-Watt walked to the far side of the porch where Mabel's (and my) favorite porch swing hung and set down the crackers on Mabel's dainty wicker table. The helium balloon that seemed to be attached to the tray swayed back and forth... or possibly I was swaying? Either way, it made me laugh.

"Oh, fuck off. I meant *alone*, Watt," Delaney scoffed. "Jesus, the man's so drunk he thinks he's hallucinating you. He can't consent to anything."

I blinked. Wasn't I hallucinating him?

Then again, if I was hallucinating him, why was Delaney playing along?

"I'm confused," I said. I made my way over to the swing, paused for a second to steady myself, then sank back into the freshly washed cushions—the first task I'd completed when I arrived—and pulled Mabel's thick porch blanket over me.

"You can go. I'll take care of him now," Watt said in a low voice.

"The way you took care of him earlier?" Delaney demanded.

I wasn't sure exactly what he and Watt said after that, though I heard them speaking in low voices.

"Delaney?" I called a moment later. "I'm okay. I'm just gonna lay down out here for a minute. It's a nice night."

Delaney—I was pretty sure it was Delaney—sighed

heavily. "Call me tomorrow, okay? And come by Tam's this weekend. Bring chocolate."

"M'kay," I agreed. I couldn't bring myself to sit up when every motion of the swing made the world whirl madly. "Drive safe."

A moment later, a finger prodded my hip. "Push over," Watt said. "Make room."

I blinked my eyes open blearily. "Watt? You're here? For real?"

He snorted. "You want me to prove it? I know you had a stuffed whale named Captain Bubbles. You once told me you slept with him until you were thirteen."

"How does that prove you're real?" I demanded, even as I moved over to make room for him.

"Because *I* know that you slept with him until you were fifteen."

I gasped and tried to lift my head. "You knew?"

"Yep. I thought it was cute."

"Oh." I let my head flop down, and when it happened to flop onto Watt's broad, flanneled shoulder, I left it there... and possibly even burrowed further into him, closing my eyes and inhaling his cinnamon-and-coffee scent. "You're warm."

"Funny, I was thinking that about you." He wrapped an arm around my shoulder and pulled me against his chest. "But you always did run hot. Remember how you'd jump on my back and hug me when you were all sweaty, just to piss me off?"

I chuckled low. "It wasn't *just* to piss you off, Watt."

He laughed, too, and his big legs set the swing in motion.

This time, though, the movement didn't make me

nauseous. With Watt beside me, the way the world swung finally began to make sense.

After a long time in the fresh cold air—five minutes or five hours, who knew?—my head was a little bit clearer, and Watt spoke again.

"You want to talk about what happened in practice today?" he asked.

"No?" I sighed. "But we probably should. I'm sorry."

"No," he insisted. "I'm sorry because—"

I turned my head and opened my eyes a crack. "Because you were cranky at practice earlier."

He blew out a breath. "Yeah. Essentially."

"And I'm sorry because I was distracting you. Kayla explained at practice that I've been distracting my student athletes with my history assignments and distracting the team with my stretching and distracting you with our fighting—"

Watt scowled. "We weren't fighting. We were joking around."

I sat up further. "That's what *I* said! But then..." With a sigh, I sank back down against his chest. "I remembered you saying *focus on your job and not on distractions, Jasper.* And I wasn't sure if she was right. I don't want that to fuck things up for the team or for you."

"Okay, so let me be clear. Really clear. Are you listening?"

I nodded, his flannel rubbing against my cheek.

"First, you've been out there every day, in your skates, doing a thing that doesn't come easily to you. I know you've been tired but putting in the work anyway. That's mental toughness, Jasper. That's a thing those boys are learning because they see an adult they like doing it. You with me?"

I swallowed hard. "I'm with you," I whispered.

"And second, Kayla's single-mindedly focused on getting Zach a hockey scholarship right now. It comes from a place of love—when you're a parent, you'll do anything to make sure your kid gets what they need—so I'm not going to criticize. But she's sure as fuck not being objective, so take what she says about your teaching and your coaching with a grain of salt. Yeah?"

"Y-yeah," I said softly. That was exactly what Delaney had said, but hearing it from Watt was different somehow.

"And third... Kayla has no clue what I like or don't like, or what upsets me or doesn't. So when it comes to you and me, don't listen to a damn word she says. Okay?"

I braced a hand on his stomach and pushed myself up far enough to look into his eyes. Every feature on his handsome face looked... sincere. "Okay."

"Okay," he repeated, pushing my head back down onto his chest. But my eyes were open now, and when I wasn't looking at Watt, I saw...

"Um, Watt? Is that a cracker basket... with a balloon on it?"

He laughed, and the sound was like a force field, pushing away the chill of the night air. "That's an emergency charcuterie board—if you stick around Copper County, you'll learn that those are a thing here—using the Taleggio cheese you accidentally brought me a couple weeks ago. More specifically... that's a Mature Friendship Peace Offering."

It took me a second to figure out what he was saying and another to flop-scoot myself off the swing and onto my knees on the porch floor so I could look at the charcuterie more closely.

"Oh my God! There's a piece of cheese in the middle shaped like... Italy?"

"I told him it looked like Italy," Watt muttered. He scratched his head the way he used to when he was feeling unsure. "It's an ice skate. Because symbolism."

"Oh!" I twisted my head this way and that. "Yeah. No, I totally see it," I lied.

"And the balloon is... well, technically, it's a groundhog, but we were working with what Chris had leftover at his catering business, and Oliver said it was close enough to a fighting marmot because... symbolism again."

"You brought me a cheese skate and a flying groundhog?" I demanded. "As a Mature Friendship Peace Offering?"

"When you put it like that, it doesn't sound quite as mature." Watt cleared his throat. "It was the best I could do on short notice. The idea is that I... I'd like to teach you how to skate. If you want."

"Oh," I breathed.

Before my marriage, I'd made a decent living. I'd had a house and a car, a closet with some designer pieces I'd been gifted, and money left over for nice extras.

Later, Martin and I had poured money into an even nicer house, a professional chef, a personal trainer, and closets full of designer clothing because he'd said *looking* like successful modeling agents was the first step to *being* successful, and I'd believed it. If there'd been a tangible thing I'd wanted during those years, I'd probably gotten it.

And yet I couldn't think of a single one of those things —not one—that knocked the air out of my lungs like this had.

"What I really wanted to say is that I'm sorry I let you down." Watt gave me a half smile that said he remembered the first time he'd said those words to me, more than twenty years ago. "I want us to talk to each other. To get to know each other again. To... to stop making assumptions about each other. I want us to be frien—*ooof.*"

Before he finished speaking, I'd launched myself at him. Watt clearly hadn't expected a person packing seven apple cider old-fashioneds to move that fast or squeeze him quite so hard, and since it was impossible to hug a seated person in a graceful way (especially while packing those old-fashioneds), I ended up sprawled against his chest with one knee on either side of his thighs and my arms holding him in a headlock.

"Does this mean yes?" His words were muffled against the chest of my fleece jacket.

"Totally. Yes. Wait, does this mean I win the friendship bet?" I demanded.

Watt dug his fingers into my armpits, probably in an effort to breathe, and when I twisted away, he caught me around the waist so I wouldn't fall off the swing. "Nope. Because you canceled the bet." He shook his head with mock sympathy. "Which was really a stupid move on your part, man, but here we are."

"I un-cancel it!" I cried. "I hereby un-cancel it!"

"No can do—*hey,*" he said when I tried to tickle him back. "That's not fair! Not the ribs! We had a rule—"

"The rule applies to bets. No bet, no rules."

He took both of my hands in his, pushing me onto my back on the swing. Before I could react, he followed, lying on top of me until our chests were pressed together, with both of us laughing wildly.

Our faces were suddenly inches apart, his breath warm against my lips, and the air between us felt charged. For a heartbeat, our eyes locked, and neither of us moved.

I licked my lips. "W-when you say friends, do you

mean... just friends? Like, the Rules of Engagement According to Watt and Jasper, Circa...”

Watt's lips brushed mine with a softness that made my breath catch—a hesitant, barely there touch that felt like a question. Slowly, the kiss deepened, achingly gentle, as if both of us were afraid that too much pressure might break whatever fragile thing was blooming between us.

When he pulled back, we were both breathless.

“Maybe we can figure out some new rules for as long as you're in town,” he suggested softly. “Friends with benefits is a thing, right? I'm not entirely sure what that should look like or if it's even a good idea...”

“I think it's the best idea ever!”

Watt raised one eyebrow. “I'm going to need to hear it from you when you haven't had seven drinks. Right now, you need to get some sleep.”

He had a point. I'd almost fallen asleep on his chest, and I'd hate to pass out midway through... whatever might happen... and drool on his delicious flannel.

“Tomorrow morning, then,” I said, grinning. “Come over early. I'll make you breakfast.”

Watt looked surprised but pleased. “You will?”

“Totally.” I brushed his hair back from his face with one hand. “I'll be the best friend with benefits you've ever had, Watt. You'll see. I bet you anything.”

It was a bet I was determined to win.

CHAPTER NINE

It was cold as fuck the next morning—the kind of unseasonable cold that left a thick cloud of fog hanging over Copper Lake and made the folks grumble about how the weather folks never got their forecasts right.

Personally, though, I didn't blame the meteorologists. If there was one thing I'd learned, it was that sometimes weird stuff happened you could never predict…

Like, for example, kissing the shit out of my former friend last night.

Two weeks ago, I'd have sworn up, down, and sideways I'd never even see Jasper again, let alone *like* him again. If anyone had tried to forecast the chances of me becoming his friend with benefits, the number would have been a negative.

Yet here I was at just-past-sunrise, walking down the damp grass at the campground past the one-room cabins Chris and Reed had fixed up last year, wearing a green sweater Oliver once claimed matched my eyes and grinning like a fool.

Weirder still, I wasn't overthinking it.

Or... okay, I kind of was, but I wasn't letting it stop me.

Last night, as I'd climbed into bed, I'd half expected to toss and turn all night. All the reasons kissing Jasper had been a terrible idea were right there waiting to be stewed over—He was a man. I sucked at relationships! I had no business being jealous over Delaney. Was I gay or bi or pan? Should I have *told* Jasper I was jealous of Delaney and not taken the out he'd given me last night? Was jealousy a thing friends with benefits did? What did friends with benefits even *mean?*—but somehow, I'd slept like a baby.

This morning, when I'd woken from dreams of Jasper's apples-and-whiskey taste and his happy, tipsy smile, not a single shred of regret had arisen.

My cock, on the other hand, had risen immediately, and when I'd taken myself in hand in the shower, I'd come with Jasper's name on my lips and the memory of our kiss searing my brain. This was unusual for me—I didn't usually get off to hot memories, possibly because I didn't *have* many hot memories—but had been seriously fucking satisfying.

Which, come to think of it, might have explained my goofy smile.

And my decision to enjoy this for as long as it lasted because happy times like this didn't usually last for long.

I'd barely knocked on the back door of the Wrigleys' house when it flew open, and suddenly, Jasper was there, barefoot and messy-haired, wearing a pair of baggy, low-slung jeans... and a frilly, pink-flowered apron over his very tan, very naked chest.

My thoughts scattered like leaves in a breeze.

"Hey, come in! Holy shit, you look hot in a sweater and puffy vest. Lumberjack kink unlocked." Jasper gave me a flirtatious grin that softened when a shrill buzzing came from deeper in the house. "Gimme five minutes. I've gotta fold and stretch my sourdough. Pain in the ass, but worth it."

He grabbed my arm and towed me through the entryway lined with family pictures and into Mabel's homey kitchen.

"Grab a seat... wherever you can find one." Jasper waved a hand at the cluttered kitchen table with its half-barrel chairs off to the left before moving past me into the little horseshoe-shaped kitchen.

I was vaguely aware that the room looked clean and tidy but *old*. The white cabinets Abe had built were tired now and the Formica countertops stained and peeling in some spots, though the curtains framing the window over the sink looked freshly washed. It was hard to look at anything else, though, when Jasper was in front of me. "Coffee?" he asked. "It's almost done."

"I... uh..." I rubbed at the back of my neck. The air in the kitchen was oppressively warm... but none of that explained why my whole body buzzed and I already felt myself beginning to sweat. That was pure Jasper. "Yes?"

He bent to take something out of the oven, and I watched the muscles of his naked back flex and stretch beneath the thin apron strings. My fingers twitched with the urge to touch, but I stuffed them in my pockets.

Jesus fuck, that apron. Speaking of new kinks...

"I wasn't sure when you'd be coming. I figured you'd be busy with chores and stuff," Jasper was saying as he did something complicated to a bowl of dough. "Picking apples and... I dunno, milking cows and threshing wheat or whatever."

I blinked out of my lust-daze and forced myself to act normal. I removed my vest, draped it over the back of a chair, and instead of focusing on Jasper, I fixed my gaze on an old hanging calendar on the pantry door that suggested it was still March of 2018. "No threshing. No cows, either. My parents tried the whole hobby farm thing and kept goats for a while there—"

"Chickens, too. I remember." Jasper spilled a pan of muffins onto the counter and then tidied them into neat rows.

I nodded. "Still have those. Sold off the other animals, though, when I took over and focused on the orchard. I've got 1,700 apple trees now, give or take, plus another 550 that are a mix of pear, cherry, and quince. I've got the U-Pick, and I also sell in quantity to a couple distributors. Too much for one person, so I hired a few seasonal employees. Then, I diversified a little. Come winter, I'll offer online classes in sustainable orchard management and permaculture, and maybe a class for fruit-growing newbies this year, too, if I, uh... Anyway."

I broke off with a cough. Christ, I was babbling. It had to be boring as fuck.

"If you?" Jasper prompted, not seeming bored at all. The coffeemaker—which looked new and fancy—beeped, and Jasper poured some into a pair of old-fashioned mugs.

"If I can manage to get organized." I shrugged. "The trees are the easy part. It's the admin that's the killer. I love my orchard... but I'm also pretty damn glad the U-Pick is closing for the season after today."

He gave me a teasing grin that made the butterflies in my stomach settle. "What I hear you saying is that you're a self-made apple magnate."

Laughing, I leaned a hip against the counter. "Yes. Exactly. Like Steve Jobs, but with actual apples."

Jasper's laughing eyes met mine and heated. He bit his lip. "Look, I know you probably want to talk about things and, like, come up with some stipulations and friendship rules." He removed his apron and folded it on the counter with slow deliberation. "I respect that." He moved around the counter. "But first... I want to greet you properly."

"Prop—? *Oh.*"

Before I had a second to anticipate or brace myself, he'd wrapped his arm around my neck and pulled me into a searing kiss.

When our lips touched, it felt like picking up where we'd left off the night before. Familiar and comfortable, brand-new and exciting all at once. I wrapped my arms around him and nearly groaned at the feel of his hot, smooth skin beneath my palms and the tingly sensation of his fingers spearing through my hair.

Jasper's phone vibrated noisily on the counter, and he pulled back just far enough to shoot it a glare but didn't pull away. He looked up at me almost shyly. "Hi."

"Hi," I managed.

He bit his lip and looked away. "I'm jumping the gun on our rule-amending, but I'd been thinking about it since last night, and—"

"Jasper." I turned his face toward mine.

"Yeah?"

I bent my head and kissed him again, harder this time. My hands roved over his back, my thumbs snagged on his waistband—

This time, it was my phone chirping that interrupted us.

"Fuck," I said against his lips.

Jasper laughed. "People are *so* inconsiderate." He nudged me toward the table and pulled out a chair covered in books, papers, and old magazines. He grabbed up the stack, looked around for a place to put them, and finally stacked them on the floor. "Go ahead and check it. Might be Derry or something."

Because he was right, I pulled my phone out even as I said, "Doubtful. Derry's at his mom's until tomorrow, and his little brother has a piano recital that—*fuck*." I clicked my phone off and quickly set it facedown on the table.

Jasper delivered my coffee and a muffin before clearing off another chair so he could sit opposite me. "What's up? Crisis with the apple empire?"

"No, just Kayla asking when I can train with her for the 5K she's coordinating—"

"Oh, right! The Pilgrim Prance." Jasper's blue eyes were gleeful. "Kayla mentioned it. Folks at the bar last night said the runners are all wearing little buckled hats, which is a sight that I, for one, will be extremely *thankful*—"

"There are no costumes!" I said in genuine alarm. "Why do people keep saying that? It's a charity thing to benefit the local hockey summer camp." I briefly outlined what Camp Fair Shot was about, how important it was, and how it was in jeopardy.

"Aw. That sounds like a great cause." Jasper leaned across the table to pat my arm. "And you're gonna rock those buckles, buddy."

"I hate you," I muttered, ripping off the top of the muffin and sticking it in my mouth. I stopped abruptly. "Oh my God. What is this?"

"A pumpkin muffin?" Frowning, Jasper grabbed the rest of my muffin off my plate and took a bite. "What's wrong? It tastes fine—"

"It tastes fucking perfect," I corrected. I stole the rest of my muffin from his greedy paw. "You made these?"

"Yes? I brought you a batch the other day, remember? I found some of Mabel's recipe cards—" He waved a hand impatiently toward the living room. "—hiding in various locations, and I remembered you liked these." He shrugged.

It was a simple thing, really. It shouldn't have felt like such a big deal that he remembered. But it did.

"I had no idea you were the one who'd made those muffins," I said softly. "I didn't even know you baked."

Jasper's mouth twisted. "We know each other just enough to think we know each other entirely. But..." His hot, hopeful gaze caught mine and held it. "Maybe it'll be fun learning about each other again?"

My heart gave a wild thump. "Yeah," I croaked. "I—"

Jasper's phone clattered against the counter again, and his smile became a little forced. "Ignore that."

"You don't want to see who it is?"

He shook his head. "There are four people in the world who text me regularly. My mother's already sent her weekly text, and she's off to Fiji with her husband. I've already told Tam and Delaney I survived the night with no hangover. So by process of elimination, it's my ex trying to get in touch with me..." He paused for a moment. "...from wherever he is in the world, since it's practically the middle of the night in California. And before you ask, no, I don't know what he wants, and no, I don't care. Marty got a little too used to me coming when he called. I refuse to play his game anymore."

Marty sounded like an asshole, and I wasn't just thinking that because I felt... some kind of way... about him getting to spend years with Jasper, and share a *name* with Jasper, and have an "open marriage" with Jasper.

I suddenly had a shit ton of questions about his ex—and about Delaney—that I probably had no right to ask.

"So..." I began. I pushed my chair back to get comfortable, but the leg of the chair caught the pile of papers and books Jasper had stacked on the floor, and they toppled. "Shit. Sorry—"

Jasper huffed out a laugh. "God, don't worry about it. Add it to the rest of the mess." He waved a hand at the living room again.

"What mess?" I wondered. "You mean Mabel's collectibles?"

He laughed again, though he sounded desperately unamused. "That... and the other stuff. When was the last time you saw Mabel's living room?"

"I..." I shook my head. "I dunno. A few years?" *More*, I realized. "After Abe died, I tried to keep up with the property for her—mowing and gardening and stuff—and I brought her groceries in the winter. We'd sit here or out on the porch, and she'd give me a cold drink..."

Jasper nodded like this confirmed something he'd expected. He stood and held out a hand. "Come see."

I let him grasp my wrist and tow me through the swinging door on the far side of the kitchen, and then I stopped, pulling back in shock.

Mabel and Abe's home had always been filled to the brim with a variety of eclectic souvenirs from their cross-country road trips—kaleidoscopes and fancy teacups, vintage quilts and antique tools, souvenir spoons from all fifty states—and Mabel had loved to tell the story of where and how she'd acquired each item. Abe had even filled his garden with a collection of flowers and shrubs—some native to Copper County and some he'd gotten by "seed trading" with folks he met while traveling.

As a kid, I'd thought it was utterly fascinating, and I'd envied Jasper the opportunity to live in their cozy house full of treasures.

I was not feeling envious now.

Mabel's handmade braided rug was now buried under piles of boxes, suitcases, papers, clothing, and collectibles. Atop what I imagined was the couch sat a pile of magazines, a stack of blankets and old T-shirts, and a steamer trunk that must have been hundreds of years old, while a stained glass lamp sat like a cherry on top. The piano Mabel loved was heaped with books, a set of socket wrenches, board games, sweaters, and a box of empty mason jars.

"Jesus," I breathed, taking it in. "It's..."

"A mess," Jasper said softly. He entered the room and toed gently at a pile of afghans on the floor. Something in the pile clinked ominously. "And it's not just in here, though this is the worst of it. I found Mabel's Royal Doulton scattered around the house in various places—including one in the bottom drawer in the upstairs bathroom and another in the garage next to a can of old paint. There are family photos tucked into nearly every book..." He pressed the heels of his hands into his eyes. "Sorting through it is like trying to unpick a knot, and the knot is Mabel's brain."

"But... how?" I demanded. I knew I sounded angry, but it wasn't directed at him. *How the hell had it gotten like this? How had I missed the signs?*

Jasper shook his head. "I don't know. I talked to Mabel every week, and she seemed... fine. Truly. I mean, looking back on it, she did sometimes ask about my parents like she forgot they were divorced. And some-times she'd talk about Abe like he was still around—like, *'That dang leg on the piano bench is wobbling again, Jasper! Should've gotten a new one years ago, but you know Abe loves a project.'*—but at the time, I... I guess I thought that's just how it must feel when you've loved someone for so long. Like they're still with you even when they're not."

I nodded. She'd done the same with me. I'd pitied her and hadn't pointed out the obvious truth.

"She'd also tell me how she was getting together with her luncheon club, and whatever funny, outrageous thing Arabella Collins did this week, and what was blooming in the garden, so I thought—" His voice choked off. He sounded lost and guilty, and my heart squeezed.

"Jasper," I said softly. "Arabella Collins died ten years ago. Maybe before Abe did. And... Mabel was living in an assisted-living place about an hour from here for a long while before she died. I think... I think your dad might've been paying for it. She had a stroke a couple years back, and she wasn't too steady on her feet after that."

He squeezed his eyes shut. "Yeah. The attorney explained all that when he called to... to say she was gone. He said you'd been taking care of the property. I wish... I wish he'd called me before, but we all thought my father was her heir. When I went to the Cape for her funeral, I found out he'd been lying to me about her, and she never said differently. I imagined she was still right here. That she'd be here forever."

Jasper took a shaky breath. "I hate him for that, Watt. But I hate myself for it, too. I should have known."

"She probably asked him not to tell you," I said. And I could hardly blame Jasper for not suspecting the lie from thousands of miles away... when I'd been living right next door and hadn't realized how bad things had gotten even before Mabel's stroke. It was all too easy to accept what you saw on the surface.

Jasper nodded and smiled a ghost of his beautiful smile. "Probably. God, she hated for anyone to make a fuss over her. I'd ask how she was doing, and she'd say, *'Don't you worry about me, Jasper. I'll be around to bother you for a good long time yet.'* And I get why... but it's annoying, too, you know? I would have come back. I wish... I wish she'd wanted me enough to ask me and let me choose." He swiped at his nose and bent to pick up a teacup from a stack of photographs on the piano. "Anyway. I'm not sure what to do with any of these things yet. I'm trying to pick out the best things to send to various extended family. Mabel had some grandnieces over in Barton who were at the funeral. I guess there's some stuff I could donate—"

"You're trying to sort it all yourself." It wasn't a question.

He stood stiffly, arms wrapped around himself. "Well, yeah. Since my staff is busy this week—"

"I meant, I'm surprised you aren't getting help."

Jasper lifted one light eyebrow. "From you?"

I winced. *Fair.* I would have helped if he'd asked... but there was no way he could have known that. "Why not hire someone? There have to be companies—"

"Not all of us are apple billionaires, Watt," he teased. "But even if I had the money..." He set the cup down on the piano with a *clack.* "I can't bring myself to let someone else sort through Mabel's treasures and decide what's worth keeping. What if they got rid of all the teacups because they have no resale value? What if they said there were too many quilts? You can't just throw away a person's whole past because it's not trendy anymore."

"You shouldn't keep it all, either, if it doesn't serve you. Keep the things *you* want, Jasper. The things that are important to you. Get rid of the rest."

"Yeah. Yeah, you're right. But I still owe it to her to do it myself. I was a shitty great-nephew, no matter what she said." He cleared his throat. "I should have come back a long time ago."

"Why didn't you?" I whispered, coming up behind him and setting a hand on his shoulder. He straightened defensively, and I hurried to add, "That's a *question*, Jasper. Not a judgment. I'm asking because I want to know. The whole truth."

He sagged back against me. "When I said I wanted us to figure each other out and be friends with benefits, I was expecting there to be exponentially fewer clothes."

I laughed. "Not sure you could be wearing much less than you are. Not that I'm complaining."

Jasper laughed, too, and then sighed. He stepped away and turned to face me, determined and a little defiant. "The truth is... I don't have an amazing reason. I have a lot of little stupid ones. My parents' divorce, for one thing. My career, for another—my mom was determined to make sure I succeeded at something, mostly as a giant *fuck you* to my dad, and since I had no other skills besides this—" He lifted his hands to frame his gorgeous face. "—my options were limited."

I scowled. "Bullshit."

"And Abe and Mabel came out to visit me a couple times, so I told myself I didn't need to fly east. And... shit, Mabel *hated* Martin—" He shook his head. "Even though he was only my agent when we met. *If it smiles like a snake and talks like a snake, best believe it's got the fangs, too, Jasper.* I thought she just didn't get LA culture. But she was right. Martin was a snake. The strangling kind."

"Is that why you didn't tell her you got married?" I wondered.

Jasper shook his head again. "Oh, no, she knew. If she didn't talk about it, it was probably because she was disappointed I married someone I wasn't in love with, and she didn't—"

"Wait, what?" I said, holding out a hand to pause the conversation. "You weren't in love with him? Why did you agree to get married?"

He paused. "We were together casually for a while, both physically and professionally," he explained. "But then Martin heard about some study where married men earn, like, twenty percent more than unmarried men. He and I were already running our modeling agency together, already sharing a house because it was owned by the business, and he thought it would be good for our professional reputation if we could tell people we were married and maybe make more money, look more established and trustworthy. '*It just made sense,*' he said. This was only..." He paused to consider. "Three or four years ago now? At the time, I agreed because he was right. It did make sense. We had so much shared history, and he seemed like the most constant part of my life at that point. But now... well, I've spent a lot of time trying to figure out what the hell I was thinking."

Jasper inhaled and exhaled. "I guess... I guess I thought making it official would change things. It sounds so stupid and cliché when I say it out loud. I just... I wanted a partner. Someone to respect and love, even if we weren't *in* love. Someone who'd respect and love me in return. I wanted security. I thought when Martin brought up the idea of marriage that meant he was ready to settle down and embrace those things, too, you know?"

"Yes. I definitely do know," I admitted. "Rachel and I had similar thoughts. That getting married would suddenly make everything fall into place like satisfying puzzle pieces."

"Except you loved her," Jasper said, folding his arms over his bare chest. I may not have known him well as an adult yet, but I still knew him well enough to recognize his pretend-chill stance.

"I did. I loved her for being my first. I loved her for caring about me and my feelings when we found out she was pregnant. And I loved her for giving us a shot and trying to make it work. For giving me Derry and for loving him and helping me give him the best life we could. Yes. I loved her. I love her still, in a way."

I made sure to meet his eyes before continuing. "But I was never in love with her."

The air seemed charged around us, but I wasn't sure if it was just enough to shed warm light on the emotions between us or a dangerous surge that would blow every-thing to smithereens.

"Oh," Jasper said softly.

"It sounds like we took similar paths."

"Except it wasn't the same at all," he said, looking devas-tated. "You tried to make a family, to give Derry a good life. I..."

"Jasper." I didn't know what I wanted to say, but I could tell he was overwhelmed.

"It wasn't just about Martin. The longer I stayed away from Copper County, the more it felt like I needed to make the time and distance worth something. Like, I... I needed to earn a billion dollars or become famous or whatever, and *then* when I came home, I could say, '*See, I stayed away because I was doing this brilliant thing that you can be proud of, and now all the years away are worthwhile.*' Like a gambler who keeps betting... and betting... and betting, because... because if they stop, they're a failure who's gambled away his family and his home, but if they can win just once, then they're a... a *hero*. And they'd deserve to go home again."

"Oh, Jasper." I took a step toward him, but he took a step back, nearly into the piano bench. His eyes sparkled with unshed tears.

"And the truth is... I was scared, too," he went on. "Mabel and Abe and Copper County were this perfect utopia in my memory. Like a safety net. If I came back and things were different, if this place wasn't my safe harbor anymore..." His voice broke, and he sniffled.

It had literally never occurred to me that beautiful, confident, teasing, challenging Jasper could be so damn insecure. That he might feel like he had to prove something in order to come back or earn his place in his own family.

Every inch of space between us felt intolerable. I needed to hold him.

"Come here," I whispered. I opened my arms as I walked toward him. "Please..."

Jasper heaved a shuddering breath and stepped forward until his forehead rested against my chest, and his tears soaked my sweater. His back felt cold under my hands, so I pulled him in tighter, trying to warm him.

"I just thought I'd have more time. Even after twenty years," he whispered.

I knew he was talking about Mabel, but it felt like he could have been talking about us, too. And I really didn't want to waste another second trying to keep my distance from him.

"Mabel loved you exactly as you were," I whispered into his hair. "She liked knowing you were living your life and having your adventures. And she knew you loved her and this place, too. She refused to sell it because she wanted you to have a home to come back to."

Jasper's arms snaked around my waist, and he sucked in a shuddering breath.

"She was *so* proud of you, Jasper." I rubbed a hand up and down his back soothingly. He smelled delicious—like soap and baked goods—and my gut clenched with want.

Jesus Christ, Bartlett. Not the time!

"She'd show me pictures of you in magazines," I continued. "She'd say, '*You see that boy, Watt? You can see the goodness in him, and that's what makes him so pretty.*'"

Jasper snickered and pulled back to look at me. His gorgeous eyes were red-rimmed and puffy, and just like the other night on the dock, I was struck by the idea that this was a Jasper no one else got to see. The real Jasper. My Jasper.

The only man I'd ever wanted.

"And what did *you* say?" he demanded. "I mean, you agreed, obviously—"

I ran my thumbs over his cheeks, wiping away his tears. "Fuck no," I said, deadpan. "I said, 'Mabel, that right there is a picture of a shit-stirring asshole who'd tickle a man to win a bet so often we had to make a fucking rule about it—'"

Jasper's whole face creased with laughter, exactly as I'd hoped. He punched me lightly in the stomach... but then rested his head against my chest again.

It should have felt strange, holding him like this.

It did *not*.

"You know," he said finally in a much calmer tone. "I had all these people with expectations of me. My dad, pressuring me to visit him. My mom, pressuring me to make money. Martin, telling me how to behave and what to wear, and how to talk to people, and what he thought I should study when I finally decided to go to college. But you know who never gave me one shred of guilt or expectation?"

"Mabel," I said softly. "Because her love didn't come with expectations."

He nodded against my sweater, then pulled away. "Ugh. Jesus, I suck. I had a plan here, Watt. I invited you over this morning so I could *seduuuuce* you with baked goods, and instead, I vomited emotions all over you." He shook his head angrily and turned toward the kitchen. "Come on. I'll get you another muffin, and we can start over—"

I grabbed his shoulder, spun him against the wood-paneled wall, and kissed him hard and fast.

"Jasper Wrigley," I rasped out. "You seduce me by breathing." I paused. "Which is a little overwhelming, honestly. I've never had a friend with benefits before."

"No?" Jasper blinked up at me. "Wow." He licked his lips. "Well, for a, um, first-timer... you're doing okay."

I took a deep breath. I knew he was teasing, but his words were an unwelcome reminder that I didn't know what I was doing. Talking, flirting, kissing... with Jasper, those were easy. But I had no idea what came next or how to ask for it...

Until Jasper made that easy, too. "So, Watt..." He smirked and lifted his arms to my shoulders like we were slow-dancing middle-schoolers. "When you said we'd amend our friendship rules... how amended were you talking?"

"Uh... pretty amended? I don't know," I admitted. "I've never been with a guy before."

I could have said more—that I'd never really been *attracted* to a man besides him or that I'd never been attracted to anyone the way I was to Jasper—but I held back.

I liked being with Jasper. Hell, in my entire life, I'd never felt so fucking consumed by anyone. And because I hadn't, this felt like a big deal to me...

But it wasn't.

I was still a guy who had no clue how to *relationship*. And even if I miraculously got a clue, Jasper was leaving in just a few months anyway. The last thing I wanted was to ruin our second shot at friendship by trying to turn it into something it couldn't be. I'd seen that film before, and I knew how it ended.

For once in my damn life, I would try not to overthink this and simply enjoy it while it lasted. I would take whatever Jasper offered. I'd follow his lead.

Like Mabel, I wouldn't put pressure on him to do something he didn't want to do.

"You are definitely attracted to me, though?" Jasper said, jolting me out of my thoughts.

I laughed out loud. He actually had to ask?

"Um. *Yeah*." I palmed my cock, which was still half-hard, and his eyes lit with interest. "But I don't know exactly what to do..."

"And you *hate* not knowing what to do." He grinned slyly. "It's gonna kill you that I'm better than you at this, isn't it?"

The provoking little shit knew exactly how to play me. He always had.

"You won't be better," I shot back. "Lack of experience is not the same as lack of talent. I mean, just look at your skills on the ice."

He shook his head and gave me a smile that promised retribution. My cock throbbed against my jeans. "I bet I'll make you scream my name, and if I do..." He hesitated for a second, probably trying to think of some dire punishment.

"If you do, I'll help you clean out the house," I said promptly.

Was this a foolish offer, when him cleaning out the

house faster meant he'd disappear faster, too? Probably. But after witnessing his raw emotion earlier, it also wasn't something I'd let him do by himself.

"And if you don't..." I paused, tapping my lip thoughtfully.

Jasper turned us around so I was the one backed against the wall. He twisted his fingers in my hair and kissed me messy and deep. His evil grin widened as he reached for the hem of my sweater. "Then I'll keep trying until I do."

He pulled off my sweater and T-shirt at the same time, leaving me as bare-chested as he was. But where Jasper's chest was a hundred acres of smooth, golden, tanned skin... mine was not. My shoulders and chest were pale and covered in dark hair.

Before I could feel self-conscious about that, though, Jasper let out a shuddering breath, and his eyes glazed with lust.

"Oh, fuck," he breathed. "You are *so* hot."

Was I?

Before I knew what was happening, Jasper had sunk to his knees between my feet on the hardwood floor. His palms slid up the front of my jeans in a way that felt both careful and deliberate. Like he was savoring the moment.

Every inch he touched sent a ripple of heat through my body, and I couldn't help hissing in a breath.

He looked up at me, blue eyes dark with mischief and so intense my pulse raced.

"Relax," he murmured, like such a thing was possible when his hands were now on the button of my jeans. The teasing lilt of his voice was gentle. "You trust me, right?"

There was something electric in the way he said it, and the words curled through me, making me feel both exposed and grounded.

I nodded, swallowing hard. Part of me couldn't believe I was here with him like this. The other part couldn't believe it had taken so long—literal decades—for us to get here.

My heart hammered in my chest as he oh-so-slowly slid down the zipper over my straining cock and pulled my jeans to my knees.

My cock jumped out with embarrassing eagerness, already rock hard just from his teasing, from his scent, from Jasper existing in the same room with me.

"Oh, Watt," he said approvingly. "Now, *this* is a mature *adult* peace offering that might just have been worth waiting twenty years for."

His lips quirked in that familiar, bright smile that had gotten me into trouble more than once, and his fingers traced lazy patterns on my bare legs. I felt like I was unraveling under his touch.

"Are you going to talk about it?" I demanded. "Or are you going to do something?"

Jasper leaned in closer, his breath ghosting over my hip, and pressed a chaste kiss there... so close yet teasingly far from where I needed him. The warmth of it sent a shiver up my spine, and I exhaled a shaky laugh.

"Contrary fucker," I muttered. "Stop teasing."

His smirk widened. "But Watt... teasing is what we do."

I opened my mouth to retort, but before I could, his lips moved up to trail soft, wet kisses across my lower abdomen. There was zero rush to his movements, like he had all the time in the world... like he was savoring every part of me, including my frustration.

Heat pooled low in my stomach, tension building with each slow, sensual glide of his lips and every breathless pause as he got closer and closer.

And then, finally, his mouth closed over the tip.

The hot, perfect clasp of it sent a shock wave of pleasure through me—a pleasure that was echoed by Jasper's low groan. His long, smooth fingers gripped my base as he pulled back to lap greedily at my slit.

"God, you taste good," he breathed.

I wanted to say something clever... to say anything at all... but all I could do was moan. "Please. *Please*, Jasper."

Endless blue eyes locked on mine, and the lust in his gaze sent an extra jolt of heat through me as he slowly took me into his mouth.

His head bobbed slowly and rhythmically as he sucked me down, teasing and exploring and learning exactly what drove me insane. It felt like he was mapping out every sensitive spot—or, *fuck*, like he'd somehow known them innately—finding the perfect balance of pressure and softness, and bringing me closer to the edge with every passing second.

My breath quickened, hands trying to find purchase on the wall behind me to hold myself up as my legs turned to jelly. Just when I thought I couldn't take any more, he eased back with a maddening grin while his hand gently massaged my balls.

"Am I winning?" Jasper asked, voice rough. "Just checking." He sounded arrogant, but the way his cock bulged insistently against the front of his jeans said he was just as into this as I was.

I could not, for the life of me, force my mouth to make words. My head swam. My body trembled under his touch.

He was winning. He was *so* winning...

And so was I.

He chuckled softly, clearly pleased with the effect he was having on me. "Don't worry," he whispered before swallowing me down again. "I'm just getting started."

The warm suction of his mouth was indescribable as he

found his rhythm again, this time more focused and more intent, as if he knew exactly how to push me to the brink.

I was vaguely aware of him jerking himself beneath me—the sway of his arm moving and the little *huh huh huh* of his breath as he got closer. I wanted badly to see him come—to *make* him come—but I couldn't make myself move. My whole consciousness was focused on the heat rising in waves from my balls to my stomach and the way every nerve in my body seemed to come alive under his touch.

"F-fuck!" I cried. "Yes. Shit, Jasper. I'm coming..."

He groaned eagerly, and the vibrations were the last straw.

My orgasm hit so hard I felt like I'd had the wind knocked out of me. The world narrowed to pinpricks, and my body forgot how to breathe automatically—I had to force each gasp of oxygen into my lungs because my muscles were too lax with pleasure to function.

So *this* was what sex was supposed to be about.

Jesus Christ. How had I gone thirty-seven years and never known?

Jasper pulled off and licked me slowly, his lips curving into a wicked smile as he lapped up every drop.

I hissed at the pressure on my oversensitive flesh and pulled him to his feet. After pressing a kiss to his lips, I pulled him against my chest, buried my face in his neck, and muttered, "Holy. Shit."

He laughed. "Good, huh?" His hands roamed up and down my back, soothing me as I caught my breath.

Suddenly, the worries I'd been holding off began creeping closer to my consciousness. *Why him? Why now? Why am I letting myself go down this path when I know it's a dead end? This isn't a real relationship. Would I want it to be? He's leaving soon. We're barely friends again. This would complicate everything—*

"You know," Jasper began, "I feeeeel like I heard you say something right at the end there...? I can't *quite* remember, but it sounded like... my name?"

Amusement flashed through me like lightning, pushing back the too-serious thoughts. "Did I?" I pretended to think about it, then shook my head against his shoulder. "Sorry, I can't recall. I might have nodded off there for a minute and muttered something in my sleep..."

Jasper's clever fingers dug into my ribs, making me squirm.

"Hey!" I grabbed his hands in mine. "New rule. Absolutely no tickling when anyone's dick is out."

"Hmm." He cocked his head. "Denied." He broke my hold and aimed for my ribs again.

Laughing, I pulled him against me. "Okay, okay. I'm way too blissed-out to deny it. You won." I pulled back to meet his eyes and added, "This time."

"This time? So... we're doing this again?" The words sounded like a tease, but something in his eyes suggested he was serious. That he really didn't understand the effect he had on me.

"Hell yes," I said. "As often as possible."

Jasper smiled up at me—his genuine, gorgeous smile—and the cold morning air around Copper County had to have grown ten degrees warmer.

There were still a billion reasons why this was a terrible idea, but right then, I was only too happy to let that smile get me into trouble one more time.

CHAPTER TEN

JASPER

I stood outside my classroom door, watching the students buzz up and down the hallway on their way to their second-to-last class of the day.

"Hi, Mr. Lancaster." One of my students held out her hand for a fist bump.

"Esther," I said. "Great job on your quiz."

"Yo, Mr. L!" A football player in my Western Civ class gave me an up-nod. "You coming to the homecoming parade, or do you have lame hockey shit?"

"Much as I'd love to see you riding on a float, Marco, hockey is my life," I said wryly.

"Mr. Lancaster." James came to a skidding halt in front of me, eyes wide and pleading. "Please, I really need my phone back—"

I shook my head. "You know the rule, James. If I catch you texting in class, you get it back at the end of the day."

"I know. I *know*." He practically vibrated with urgency. "But could I please have it back a period early? I'm really sorry I was using it during class, and I swear I won't do it again. I was just waiting for an important text earlier. Like, high-key important—"

I lifted an eyebrow. "Are you on a kidney transplant list? Or was the president calling to ask your advice on the latest TikTok dance?"

"I mean, no... but..."

"But you asked Rory to homecoming this weekend, and you wanted to see if she said yes."

His eyes widened further, this time in horror. "You *know*? About me and Rory?"

"That's what I do, James. I teach, and I know things," I said in my best Tyrion Lannister impression. Taking pity on him, I added, "I haven't heard what her answer was." I nodded toward my desk. "Go ahead. Top drawer. But James, remember that no one who's worth being in your life is gonna want you to disregard your priorities for them," I called as he darted into the room.

"You got it, Mr. L." James took his phone from my drawer and immediately turned it on. A grin lit up his face. "Fuck, yeah. Locked *down*. Shit, I am so vibing with this girl." He punched a fist in the air and grinned as he danced past me into the hallway.

Laughing, I shook my head as I watched him go.

Arlene Da Silva, the French teacher across the hall, caught my smile and returned it. "Kids, huh?" she said, just as my phone buzzed in my ass pocket.

"Ha. Yeah. *Kids!*" I agreed before heading back to my now empty room and closing the door.

I was very glad no one was around to see me practically tearing my pants in my haste to get my phone out.

Watt had started texting me yesterday afternoon ("*Now five people text you. So there.*"), and since then, I'd become a Pavlovian what-not-to-do, practically salivating every time the damn phone vibrated, even in the middle of class. It could be argued that I should take my own advice...

Except that my situation and James's weren't similar in any way. I mean, I wasn't trying to "lock" Watt down. He and I were *friends*.

Friends with benefits.

And, yes, admittedly, I really hoped to... you know, *benefit*... from those *benefits* again tonight when Watt came over to help with Mabel's house, because they'd been very, um... *beneficial*... Saturday morning, but that didn't mean I was trying to "vibe" with Watt.

Whatever the fuck that meant.

I was just grateful that Watt had meant it when he said he wanted to be friends again and had been sincere in his offer to help with the house. That was all. Hearing his calm, practical "We'll go room by room, little by little" made the overwhelming task seem *possible*. And getting his ridiculous texts—"*Bet I can make you laugh. You ready?*"—brightened my day.

In a friendly way.

Unfortunately, *friendship* didn't entirely explain the wave of disappointment that whacked me in the chest when I unlocked my phone and saw the text wasn't from Watt... but residual marriage bitterness might.

MARTIN

Jazz, this is silly. We still co-own a business. You can't ignore me forever.

I snorted. *Couldn't I, though?* Our business, which no longer had any clients, thanks to Martin and his boyfriend, had ceased doing business over a year ago.

And I fucking hated when he called me Jazz.

I marched over to my desk, threw myself into my chair,

and opened my laptop to prepare for my final class of the day. As part of the process for getting my temporary teaching credentials, I had one class a week observed by either Principal Schmidt or Raj Wickramasinghe, the school's humanities chair, and I wanted to be on my game, just in case Kayla had taken her concerns about my teaching methods to the principal. After that, I had a practice to get to. And then *benefits* to think about...

So I couldn't explain how I ended up hate-scrolling Lancaster Modeling Worldwide's Instagram.

I'd made a study of Martin's new business after our split, pretending it was market research on a would-be competitor for when I started my own business while really searching for reasons why Martin had screwed me over. Unfortunately, the smiling faces of his clients hadn't told me anything I didn't already know.

Mabel had called Martin a snake... and she was right.

Strangely enough, back when I first met him, snakiness had been part of his charm. Martin made decisions based on his own bottom line, and after all the complex emotional upheaval of my last summer in Copper County, the simplicity of that had been comforting as fuck.

The first time he'd propositioned me, when I was twenty, I'd laughed it off. The second time, a day or two after Mabel had told me about Watt's marriage... I hadn't.

I'd told myself that having an affair with a man twice my age was adult and worldly. Exciting in its secrecy— because it *had* to be a secret since forty-something Martin might be a horny enough bastard to fuck his twenty-something client, but publicizing it might hurt his brand. I'd thought I was free from emotional entanglements, and I'd felt powerful.

In short, I'd been an idiot.

By the time we'd started our agency, I'd been wiser. Business was the one area where I'd trusted Martin, and I'd believed that as long as I kicked ass as operations manager and let Martin focus on glad-handing and networking—as long as I proved I could keep our bottom line nice and high—he'd have had no reason to fuck me over. Our marriage, such as it was, had felt like an extra level of security.

Until it wasn't.

I'd had to lose everything, but I'd finally learned my lesson.

I would never again give my power away or make life decisions based on hopes and dreams instead of reality. Nobody was that trustworthy.

Which was why Watt and I being friends suited me perfectly.

My phone vibrated on my desk, startling me so much that I accidentally like-hearted one of Martin's old posts.

Fuck.

I un-liked it immediately, then clicked my browser window closed just in case. It was past time for me to block Martin entirely.

But when I picked up my phone to do just that, my stomach swooped giddily at the message on the screen.

WATT

WHY DID THE BOSTON TEA PARTY GET
SO WILD? <laugh-cry emoji>

Already grinning wildly, I typed out a response.

Is this another dad joke? Because your dad
jokes are the worst. There's no way you're
winning the bet at this rate.

WATT

I am literally someone's father, Jasper. All
my jokes are dad jokes. ANSWER THE
QUESTION.

> *sigh* I want you to know this is done out
> of pity, okay? This is a pity-ask.

> I DON'T KNOW, WATT? WHY?

WATT

Oh my god, you're dying to know now,
aren't you? Maybe you don't deserve to.

I laughed out loud in the empty room.

> Ugh. This is painful. Truly painful. You're
> embarrassing yourself. Frankly, you're
> embarrassing both of us.

WATT

BC THE COLONISTS WERE STEEEEEPED
IN REVOLUTION. lol. Get it?

> No! Nobody could get that. It doesn't even
> make sense! What the fuck?

WATT

You're laughing.

> Am not!

WATT

You are. I can just tell. It's an instinctive
thing. A "psychic knowing." Like you with
hockey.

> It doesn't count if I'm laughing at YOU
> instead of the joke.

WATT

My work here is done. Goodnight.

Watt? That doesn't count!!!

OMFG, I hate you.

I was still staring dopily at my phone when someone knocked on my classroom door. "Come in."

"Hey, Mr. Lancaster?" Derry Bartlett's dark head popped into the room, and his hazel eyes—Watt's eyes—met mine. "D'you have a sec?"

I slid my phone guiltily into the drawer.

"Yeah. Of course. Have a seat." I motioned toward the rows of desks and closed my laptop so I could give him my full attention. "Having trouble with the essay?"

"No, it's not that. It's, um..." He folded his large body onto one of the desks and kept his eyes trained on the whiteboard over my head. "Mr. Lancaster, you know a lot about life and shi—*stuff*—right?"

I blinked. "Depends on the day, really. But definitely some shit, yes. What's up?"

"Well." Derry shifted in his seat. "I have a... a friend..."

My eyes widened, and I fought to keep my expression neutral. In my whole life, I'd never heard an *I have a friend* story that ended well.

"He, uh, he's having some trouble planning out his future, kinda."

"Oh." I relaxed back in my chair. "You mean deciding what college to go to, what to study, what career he wants, that kind of thing? Because your friend could talk to Mrs. McReady at the guidance office. She—"

"N-no. No, it's not that, exactly." Derry licked his lips. "It's like... what do you do when your parents want you to do one thing and you want to do something else?" He glanced behind him, as though checking to make sure no one was listening, and lowered his voice to a whisper. "Like, if you don't want to stay in New York for college or play hockey anymore?"

"*Oh*," I said again. My phone in the drawer vibrated with a text notification like the thumping of a tell-tale heart. "Do you... I mean, does your friend... know what he'd rather do instead?"

"Not really?" Derry stretched out his long legs beneath the desk. "He has a billion ideas. Law school, maybe. Or acting." He rolled his eyes. "He doesn't really know. He mostly knows what he *doesn't* want."

"Oooh." I nodded. "Yeah, I feel that. Uh... I guess the most straightforward plan would be to talk to your dad... er, *his* dad. I mean, his parents. Let them know what he's thinking, even if he doesn't have it all sorted yet."

"Well, yeah." Derry spread his hands like this was the most obvious thing in the world. "But, like... how?"

"How?" I repeated.

"Yeah." Derry shook his head impatiently. "People say 'talk about it' like it's easy. It's not. We've been planning on going to Utica and playing hockey forever. It's been decided. Set in stone. You can't just say, '*Sorry, changed my mind.*'" He ran a hand through his hair in a frustrated gesture that was so exactly like his father's I nearly smiled. "Or, I mean, I guess you *can*, but it sucks when you know they're gonna be pissed and disappointed and worried."

"True story, bro," I said with feeling. "And lots of things get better as you get older, but that one?" I shook my head. "It never *doesn't* suck, feeling like you're disappointing someone. When I was your age, I started modeling because my mom wanted me to, and since I was the human equivalent of a wind-up car, once I got pointed in that direction, I kept going for a loooong time. But eventually, I ran out of steam and thought... wait, why am I doing this? I realized I didn't have a reason. I never had. Took way too long for me to get there."

"But… she was okay with it, right?" he asked hopefully. "When you did tell her?"

"*Noooo*. Nope. It's been five or six years since my last modeling campaign, and to this day, she likes to pretend I'm just going through a phase. Every time she meets an up-and-coming new designer, she tries to convince me to come back for just one more photo shoot." I smiled. "I got to a point where I was more okay with disappointing *her* than I was with disappointing *me*."

"Yeah." He frowned thoughtfully. "Yeah, I get that."

"And I wish I could tell you that after I woke up and made that change, my whole life sorted itself out," I said gently, "but it didn't. Living your life to please other people becomes a habit if you do it long enough, and you start to lose touch with what *you* want altogether. I've only just started to understand that." I leaned toward him. "I wish I'd started being honest with myself and the people I love when I was younger. Maybe I'd've made *that* a habit instead."

"Yeah." He heaved a disappointed sigh.

"I guess what I'm telling you is, even if it's hard, you need to live your life for yourself. Parents might have an idea of what they think will make you happy, but in the end, you're the only one who has to live with your choices."

"I get what you're saying, but…"

"It's still not easy," I said with genuine sympathy. "I wish I had a magic answer, but any adult who says they've got their shit figured out is lying."

"My dad does," Derry said unhappily. "He always knows what he's doing."

"Ha! Right." I laughed without thinking. Only when Derry looked at me in surprise did I realize he'd been sincere. "Uh. I mean…" I cleared my throat. "I don't think it's that simple. He probably second-guesses himself a lot and just doesn't share that with you."

Derry shook his head. "You don't know him well enough yet, but you'll see. He's the chillest guy ever."

I forced myself to nod slowly. Obviously, I wasn't going to talk about Watt to his kid—hashtag *beyond inappropriate* —even if Derry was wrong. But it bothered me a little… or possibly more than a little… that Derry didn't know Watt and I had ever been more to each other than reluctant co-coaches.

"If that's the case," I offered, "then maybe your dad will be more understanding than you think when you talk to him about this."

Derry cocked his head suspiciously. "But we're not talking about him. I said this is about my *friend*."

"Right," I agreed. "Sorry. Your friend." Hesitantly, I added, "I'll tell you this, though: sometimes you need to take a wrong turn to get where you're supposed to be. Someone used to say that to me a lot—" I grinned, thinking of Mabel. "—but I didn't really understand it until I was older. There are a billion ways to be happy in this life, Derry, and if we all had to follow the same path, the traffic would be ridiculous. Just make the best choices you can—er, that your *friend* can— and trust that it'll all work out."

He smiled a little. "Thanks, Mr. L. You're, like, weirdly easy to talk to."

I laughed. I'd been on the cover of *L'Officiel* twice, but somehow, this felt like a much bigger win.

"Knock, knock," Principal Schmidt said, pausing in the doorway. He saw Derry and beamed broadly. "Mr. Bartlett! My favorite student."

Derry and I exchanged a smile. Every student was Principal Schmidt's favorite student, and he told them all so.

"Hey, Principal Schmidt. I was just, uh..." Derry pushed to his feet. "Getting Mr. Lancaster's help with an essay." He gave me a significant look.

I nodded. "Yup. You sure were. You think you've got a handle on it now?"

Derry grinned. "No? But you've given me a lot to think about. See you at practice, Coach." He rapped his knuckles on his desk and hotfooted it out of the room.

"Sorry to interrupt," Principal Schmidt said. He looked toward the hall, where Derry had disappeared. "Everything okay?"

"I... I think so." But when my phone vibrated in my drawer again, I frowned.

Was my conversation with Derry something I was supposed to talk to Watt about?

I wouldn't even consider it if Derry had been anyone else's kid. Nothing we'd discussed concerned his health or safety, and as an almost adult, he deserved to have some privacy and autonomy... especially when the very thing we'd been discussing was how to talk to his parents—or his "friend's" parents—about complicated or disappointing things. I didn't think my friends-with-benefits-ship with Watt changed that.

"Principal Schmidt," I began.

"Jasper," he chided, "it's *Mike*. You work for me, and you were never actually a student here, remember?"

"I know. It just feels weird. I keep expecting Aunt Mabel to pop out from behind a door and give me a *look*."

He laughed and rocked up and down on the balls of his feet excitedly. "I stopped by to let you know that I won't be observing you next period. Based on Tam Monroe's recommendation, and my own, the board approached the state licensing agency, and your temporary authorization has been approved."

I stared at him in surprise for a moment, my brain struggling to shift gears. "But I thought... I've heard some of the parents are concerned I'm not following Tam's lesson plans faithfully enough. I, uh, I've been trying to get the kids engaged, but I think maybe I'm making the assignments too time-consuming." I lowered my voice to a stage whisper. "Don't tell anyone, but I'm not actually a history teacher." I winked.

Principal Schmidt frowned. "Well, your temporary certificate says you are, and Raj has been signing off on all of your assignments. Unless you're telling me he doesn't know what he's doing?"

"No!" I hurried to say. "Of course not."

"And Tam told me that she's going to implement a lot of your ideas into her plans when she gets back. I believe her exact words were, '*I'm so stealing all the good shit Jasper's coming up with.*' Do you think she's wrong?"

I chuckled. That sounded like Tam. "No, I just..."

"You *just* need to trust yourself a bit more. You're helping your students learn and helping them think critically about things. That's priceless. And remember, Tam didn't set out to be a history teacher, either."

"She didn't?" I wrinkled my nose. "Really?"

"Nope. She wanted Celia Govostes's job. Celia's nearly seventy and she's got a trick hip, but she's feisty. She'll probably be running the Phys. Ed. department until she's a hundred." He smirked. "Once you give a person a whistle, it's hard to pry it away from them."

I laughed, thinking of Watt. "No kidding."

"So, like your great-aunt used to say, sometimes you take the elevator, sometimes you take the stairs." He cocked an eyebrow. "Don't think that just because Tam was doing this job before you that she's somehow *better* at it than you arc. More experienced, sure, but that's not the same thing. Speaking of which..." He flashed a knowing smile. "How's hockey going?"

We chatted for a few minutes about my progress (or lack thereof) before he excused himself and left me to prep for my final class of the day.

Which, of course, meant me grabbing my phone from my drawer as eagerly as James might have.

> **WATT**
>
> Hey, can we talk before practice?
>
> Jasper?
>
> I assume you're ignoring me because you're still laughing at my joke. Pull yourself together.

I bit my lip as a smile stretched across my face. God, I liked having Watt in my life again.

And, I realized, I couldn't wait to tell him about my day. Not just the shitty, sad panda bits about Martin, where I wanted to lay my head on Watt's chest and have him hold me, but the really good stuff, too.

I wanted him to know that one of my students had trusted me enough to ask for advice and that Principal Schmidt had given me a huge vote of confidence. I wanted to tell him about Martin's bullshit attempts to contact me and how I was ignoring the fuck out of him because I didn't care about his approval anymore.

I wanted to explain how fucking *good* and strong I felt in my own skin these days and my sense that I was slowly figuring things out...

And that he was part of that.

> Sorry. I was searching the rule book for a clause that allows me to cancel this friendship due to attempted murder by terrible jokes, but I'll have to get my revenge in other ways. Tonight. <eggplant emoji>

WATT

You wish. Tonight's my turn.

A shiver of want raced up my spine. *Oh, yes, it was.*

> We'll see... Coach.

WATT

Nope. No. You're not turning Coach into a THING.

Speaking of which... meet me in the lobby by the box office before practice?

I knew Watt wasn't planning for us to get it on in the box office right before we coached—though I wouldn't be opposed to a little make-out sesh—but happy anticipation of just seeing him and being in his presence had me practically floating as I taught my last class and drove out to the rink...

Where Watt was already waiting for me, just as he'd promised.

"Hey! God, I have so much to tell you," I began, but before I could finish my greeting, Watt pulled me into a nearby maintenance closet and pulled the door closed.

"Well now, Coach Bartlett, this is unexpected," I

purred, wrapping my arms around his neck. The tiny space smelled strongly of industrial cleaner, and the light from a single pull-chain bulb was weak, but I was here for it. "I'm kinda wishing I hadn't taken the time to change into my running tights before I left school because if you get handsy, we're gonna have a situation—"

"Jasper," Watt began in a low, pained voice. Then he stopped and squeezed his eyes shut.

"What?" I demanded, dropping my arms to cup his jaw. "Is there a problem with the team? Or a problem with..." I gestured between the two of us. "Are you rethinking the friends-with-benefits—"

"No! No." He pressed a quick, chaste kiss to my lips. "Not rethinking... exactly."

"Okay." I narrowed my eyes. "Can I buy a couple consonants and some vowels, Pat?"

Watt took a step back—which might as well have been a mile, in a closet that was only four feet deep—and ran a hand through his hair. The frustrated gesture reminded me of Derry, earlier, and I would have smiled if I hadn't felt the anxiety pouring off him.

"It hit me a couple hours ago that you and I haven't really talked about... how we're going to talk about... us," Watt said.

Nose wrinkled, I stared at him. "Uh. Maybe try *different* consonants and vowels?"

"Derry is out there." He waved a hand toward the ice impatiently. "I don't know how to tell him that I... that *we*..." He broke off with a headshake. "He's at an impressionable age, and you're his coach, and... it's not like you and I are actually dating. He doesn't even know that I'm attracted to..." He blew out a breath. "*Fuck*. I'm not saying this right."

After my divorce, one of the mindfulness coaches I'd worked with had been a huge fan of ice plunges—daily mini torture sessions where you lowered yourself into frigid water and kept yourself there as your balls curled into your torso in an attempt to seek shelter. I'd tried it precisely once before vowing never again.

This conversation was having roughly the same effect on me. All my happy, bubbly thoughts froze and sank to the pit of my stomach.

It wasn't even that anything Watt was saying was wrong or hurtful—I didn't imagine many parents wanted their teenagers to know about their sex lives—but suddenly, it was like Martin was standing in front of me, telling me that we had to keep our sexual relationship quiet because nobody would understand.

"You're saying you want to keep it a secret?" I asked in a small voice.

"No! Or... maybe? Shit, I don't know. I *do* know my timing sucks, though. We should have talked about all this over the weekend when we decided to... to get physical, but I let myself get carried away. I didn't think, and I was happy not thinking. It feels unfair to dump this on you, but it involves you, and I want us to be on the same page—"

"No, I'm glad you brought it up," I cut in, and I meant it. "We're friends, above anything. If you're worried about something, I want to know."

"I can't even tell you what I'm worried *about*, exactly. Derry's dated girls and guys—he tells me kids today aren't 'into labels'—and he knows my closest friends are gay. Nobody's going to clutch their pearls. But I... I think I *am* into labels, and it bugs me that I don't have one that fits. I can't explain it to him when I can't fucking explain it to myself."

Something about what Watt was saying, or maybe the despair in his voice, broke through the protective bubble I'd been trying to pull around myself.

This conversation wasn't about me. Watt was *not* Martin. And I wasn't a twenty-year-old idiot anymore.

"Watt, Derry's a smart kid. You don't have to have all the answers. In fact, maybe it would be good to let him know you struggle sometimes. That way, he can talk about his own struggles more easily."

Deep hazel eyes met mine. "So you're saying I should tell him? Is it even worthwhile? You're leaving in a couple of months, aren't you?"

"Yes," I said without hesitation. "I am. And no, I'm not saying you should tell him if it doesn't feel right. Coming out, in any capacity, has to happen on your own timeline." I believed that to my core. "I'm just saying that you don't have to hold back from having hard conversations with him." I stepped forward and put a hesitant hand against the front of his sweatshirt. "It's okay to let him see that your life is as messy as everyone else's."

Watt blew out a breath and drew me tightly against him. He pressed a kiss to the top of my head and buried his face in my neck. "I know you're right. But..."

"But you're not ready to do it today." I put my arms around his shoulders and scratched lightly at the hair on the nape of his neck, loving the way he arched against me as some of the tension bled from his shoulders. "That's okay."

"Is it? Is it going to bother you to not be open about it?"

"To have to restrain myself from throwing you against the boards at the end of practice and having my wicked way with you in front of the kids?" I laughed. "Somehow, I'll manage. Can Derry know we're friends? Or should I pretend I hate you? If so, you're gonna need to tell me a few more dad jokes—"

"Of course he can know." Watt pulled back to frown at me seriously. "He likes you a lot."

"Well, good. I like him a lot," I said softly. I pushed Watt's hair back from his forehead. "He's a sweet guy, and he tries hard to do the right thing. Reminds me of someone I know."

Watt smiled. "Thanks."

"Hmm? Oh, I didn't mean *you*, silly," I teased. "I meant *me*. I've only known him a couple weeks, but I think we've really connected over the mindfulness exercises, so—*mpfh*."

Our lips met in a fierce kiss that was both playful and longing. The way his tongue moved against mine sent a bolt of crackling heat through me, displacing my earlier chill.

Fuck, Watt was good at this.

A second later, he pulled back and rested his forehead against mine.

"Thank you," he breathed against my lips. "I am so damn glad I accepted your peace offering. You make things better."

His words and the warm, affectionate look on his face made my stomach lurch in a happy, hopeful—and distinctly un-friends-with-benefits-y—way, but I ignored it. "I'm happy to help. You're still coming over tonight, right?"

"Mmhmm. I said I'd clear out your den."

"*Clear out your den*." I snorted. "Not a euphemism I'm familiar with, but—"

Watt groaned and clapped a hand over my mouth. "Never meet my friend Oliver. The two of you would get along a little too well." He frowned. "Actually... maybe a *lot* too well. You're not, ah, clearing dens with anyone else, are you?"

I made a show of looking right and then left. "Not at the moment, no."

"I mean, you and Delaney aren't..." Watt cleared his throat. "And I ah, I know there are hookup apps you can use..."

"Delaney's not on any of the apps," I said sweetly, deliberately misunderstanding him. "Tam made him promise. But he said all bets are off once he actually moves here for good in a few months."

"He's moving here for good?" Watt's jaw worked.

It wasn't possible Watt was actually jealous—that wasn't what our friendship was about—but the idea gave me a little thrill I didn't want to consider too closely.

"Yup. He's buying a fixer-upper on the far side of Copper Lake from the campground. We'll all be neighbors! Won't that be awesome?"

"Yeah," he said flatly. "Awesome. But for the next couple of months... I mean, as long as you're here, while we're being friends with benefits, you and I can..."

I ran my tongue over my teeth. It was probably smart that Watt kept reminding both of us that what we shared was temporary. There was no reason it should bother me. So I took pity on him.

"Watt," I whispered into his ear. "Tonight, I want my mouth on you... and only you."

A shudder moved through his body from head to toe. "Fuck, yes."

"But for now," I said, stepping away and throwing open the door, "let's get to practice... *Coach.*"

Watt shot me a glare and took a second to adjust himself in his pants before he followed.

"Still not a thing, asshole," he muttered as he brushed past me.

I laughed out loud. "Bet you it is," I called as I hurried to catch up.

Was I worried I was making bad decisions?

Maybe. Yes. Just a tiny bit.

But at that moment, I was enjoying myself too much to care.

CHAPTER ELEVEN

WATT

For a man who kept getting compared to a tree, I was feeling pretty fucking uprooted these days... but when my phone dinged as I stirred the pot of bubbling tomato sauce, I decided I wasn't mad about it.

> **JASPER**
>
> Why do hockey players make terrible
> comedians?

I grinned down at my phone. Our silly bet from the other day had evolved into a constant string of jokes so terrible I would have to delete my text history or risk my future great-grandchildren thinking I'd lost my marbles.

I put my spoon down to type.

> They don't. As evidenced by the fact that I
> am HILARIOUS.

> Bet-winningly hilarious.

JASPER

Pfft. You made me laugh once. ONCE. And
it was mostly AT you. And anyway, it's your
fault my jokes don't hit. A comedian is only
as good as his straight-man and you never
play along.

I snorted.

After this week, I don't know that I'd pass
as anybody's straight man. Or do I need to
remind you what happened Monday night?

The answer was a mind-exploding repeat of Saturday
morning's blowjob that had left me staggering home as
crookedly as Jasper after his seven cocktails.

I hadn't gotten a chance to return the favor—Jasper had
gotten himself off again, which had kind of been a relief in
the moment—but I'd been thinking about it a lot since then,
and it felt like a missed opportunity. Next time I got a
chance to put my mouth on him, I would take it.

Possibly even tonight.

JASPER

Don't you dare get me hard when you're
not coming over for hours, asshole. Answer
the question.

And then, before I could tease him again, Jasper added:

JASPER

NEW RULE: those who don't play along
don't get their dicks sucked.

I smirked.

> Fine. Why do hockey players make terrible comedians, Jasper? I'm DYING to know.

JASPER

> Because their SCHTICKS are lame!

> Do you get it? SCHTICKS?

I actually chuckled out loud, not because the joke was funny—Jesus, no. Even at twelve, I'd had better taste—but because *he* was. And because texting with Jasper had become one of my new favorite—

"Dad?" Derry called, walking in from the living room. "I said, can I go over to Zach's?"

"Huh?" I glanced up and almost fumbled my phone in my haste to put it down. "Sorry, kiddo. Didn't hear you come in. Didn't you just drop Zach off?"

"Yeah. I came home 'cause it's pasta night. Duh." He strolled into the kitchen and snuck a slice of cucumber out of the salad I'd prepped. "But I meant after dinner. He and I have, like, school stuff to do. His mom says it's okay if I stay over."

Stirring my sauce again, I narrowed my eyes. "You also have school tomorrow, remember?"

"Dad, we're seniors. This time next year, I might be chanting fraternity pledge songs by the light of the moon, and you'd never know about it."

I stared at him, arrested, and he laughed out loud. "Oh, my God. The look on your face. Aren't you the one who wants me to have the full college experience? Doesn't that include pledging a fraternity if I want to?"

"Fuck." I shook my head. "There was *nothing* in the parenting manual about this. Yes, fine, you can go. This once. Did you do your English essay?" I demanded.

"Yep."

"And your history assignment?"

"Uh-huh."

"And your…" I took a wild guess. "Math?"

"Actually, no. We're working on *spreadsheets*, and I was wondering if you could give me a hand—"

"Go pack your stuff for Zach's," I said, unable to stop the grin from spreading over my face as Derry laughed his ass off. "Then get back down here." I pointed at the pasta timer with my spoon. "You have exactly three minutes, fifteen seconds."

Derry saluted and ran out of the room. After giving the sauce another stir, I opened my phone again.

> Dear Jasper, I am writing this text from beyond the grave because that joke was so desperately unfunny, it killed me. Remember me fondly, Watt.

JASPER

Oh, I'll remember you. Here lies Watt. He didn't have a Jaguar convertible and I'm funnier than him. SUCK IT.

Smiling, I took a deep breath and typed back.

> Okay. I will.

It took a minute for Jasper to respond.

JASPER

Wait, what?????????? Explain.

> Gotta go. Pasta night with Derry. See you later.

"Dad? The timer's going off. Dad!"

"Shit." I clicked off my phone and jumped into action, scooping the pasta out of the water and into the sauce.

Derry dropped his duffel bag on the floor by the island and came over to mooch more cucumbers. "You and I are going to have to have a talk about this constant phone usage, young man. When I was a lad, we didn't *have* phones. We communicated by tying carrier pigeons to stone tablets, and we *never* sent them off at meal time—"

"Yeah, yeah. Grab the salad and bring it over," I instructed. I nodded down at the pasta pot. "I've got this."

I slid my phone into my pocket before bringing the pasta to the table.

"Soooo," Derry said, grabbing the tongs and dishing out noodles before I was even seated. "What's new with you?"

"Me?" I shrugged. "Oh. Ah. Not much. Slow week, now that the U-Pick's closed. Posted sign-ups for my January course on integrated pest management. Finished winterizing the back garden and planted some rye. Constantine and I met with Chris and Reed to talk about the landscape design for their place—have you been over there to see it yet?"

Derry shook his head, mouth full of pasta.

"Looking good. I mean, it's actually in the middle of renovations, so it looks like shit, but they took my advice and hired Brew Barnum to do the kitchen for them, and Brew's gonna knock it out. I don't care how much you love DIY, if you're trying to turn an '80s laminate monstrosity into a Craftsman revival, you need an expert—"

"Uh-huh." Derry set down his fork, folded his hands, and looked at me. "You gonna tell me who you were texting?"

I blinked. "Texting?" I said, like I'd never heard of the

word. I was pretty sure my face was as red as my pasta sauce. "What do you mean?"

"Don't be weird about it. You're nearly as bad a liar as Chris. I know you were texting someone earlier, and I'm pretty sure you were doing it last night, too." He narrowed his eyes. "Are you dating someone?"

"No." I shook my head, probably a little harder than the situation warranted. "Nope."

"Because it would be okay if you were. More than okay." He picked up his fork again and twirled more noodles. "Like, if you and Zach's mom—"

"No," I repeated. "Kayla and I are friendly, and that's all there is to it. I told you that when we went on those dates a couple years ago, remember? I'm not dating anyone."

This wasn't a lie, technically... but saying it felt wrong anyway.

I had a policy of being honest with Derry. I didn't share every detail of my life, but as he'd grown, I'd been pretty frank about stuff I thought might affect him—puberty, dating, drugs, alcohol, mental health.

This thing with Jasper, though, felt like it was in a category all by itself.

As I'd told Jasper, it wasn't that I wanted to keep our hookups a secret because I thought Derry or anyone would have a problem with Jasper being a man—they wouldn't, and I wouldn't give a shit if they did.

The reason I didn't want to talk about it was because the whole situation—our friends-with-benefits relationship *and* my first steps into hooking up with a man—felt delicate and new, like the first green shoots of a sapling that had sprouted unexpectedly out of a seed that had been planted twenty years ago. I wanted to protect it from the elements and let it grow. To see what it developed into, without explaining or dissecting it, even in my own head.

This tree, whatever kind of tree it was, was never going to bear fruit. Who knew how long someone as smart and determined and beautiful as Jasper would want to keep up the -with-benefits part of our friendship? And even if it lasted for as long as he stayed in town, Jasper *was* leaving, and that would be that. Which was all the more reason to keep it to myself, to enjoy it while it lasted, and to not give the town gossips anything to pick over when it was done.

It wasn't only Derry I wasn't talking to about it. I hadn't updated Chris or Ollie, either, though Ollie had texted me eggplant emojis and question marks repeatedly, and Chris had given me several significant looks earlier in the day.

Derry *was* the person I felt guiltiest about not telling, though, not because he needed to know about my sex life—he most definitely did not—but because I hated hiding that Jasper and I were more than just co-coaches who'd gotten to be buddies.

Jasper had been my best friend once. He was my friend now. And it bothered me that I'd been so hurt and resentful I hadn't talked about someone who'd been incredibly important to me.

I'd tried to erase Jasper from my history, and that wasn't fair.

"What about you?" I asked Derry distractedly. "Anything new happening with you this week?"

He made a thoughtful noise. "The usual," he mumbled around a mouthful of pasta. "School. Practice. Homecoming's this weekend. I think Zach and me and a bunch of the guys are gonna go to the dance. Zach's been having kind of a rough week."

"Yeah? Rough how?"

Derry finished chewing, swallowed, and took a deliberate sip of water. "He wanted us to go to a festival in Syracuse this Saturday to have a little fun and blow off steam. But his mom's, like, obsessed with him getting a hockey scholarship, and she's convinced the scout will be coming to the game next week."

"Hmm. I haven't heard anything about it, but if that's true, the team's in pretty good shape. We have a solid shot against Baxter." I cocked my head. "You worried?"

"No," he said, but the way he bit his lip suggested a *yes*. "Zach's mom said he couldn't go to Syracuse, though. That he needs to stay home so he can train, rest, and focus. He's super bummed."

I nodded. "I get it. Frankly, I see both sides. I'd be disappointed too, but Zach's been a little bit distracted lately, and it shows." I'd told Zach the same thing earlier at practice. "He was doing better with his communication on the ice last week. This week, not so much. He's got to impress those scouts if he wants to wear navy and orange for Utica next year."

"I know. He knows, too." Derry looked at me intently. "But hockey's not the only thing in the world, right?"

I felt like I'd found myself transported to a conversational minefield.

"No, of course not," I said carefully. "It *is* pretty important if it's what's getting you through college, though, right? I was under the impression Zach couldn't afford it any other way."

"That's what his mom says." Derry frowned down at his plate. "I told him there are other scholarships. Academic ones. Or, like, he could defer college for a year and save up." Troubled hazel eyes met mine. "The best part of our Utica plan was that we were doing it together. I want him to be happy, but it wouldn't be the same going without him—"

"Hey, hey." I shook his shoulder gently. Apparently, overthinking was as genetic as hazel eyes and dark hair. "You're stressing about something that might not even happen. Let's talk about it next week, after the game. We'll have a better idea then, okay?"

Derry hesitated for a second, then blew out a relieved breath and nodded. "Yeah. Okay. We'll hold off until next week. Good plan."

I grabbed his chin gently. "I'm so fucking proud of you, Dermott. And not just because you're a good student and a freaking amazing player who's going to kick ass at college hockey, whether you get a scholarship or not." I winked. "You've got a huge heart. Zach's lucky to have you."

Derry lifted one shoulder. "I'm lucky to have him. He's a pain in the ass sometimes. Or, like, *all* the time." He huffed out a laugh. "But... I dunno. He and I are a team."

I nodded and picked up my fork again. "I know exactly what you mean. Did I ever tell you I had a friend like that when I was your age?"

"You did?" He wrinkled his nose. "Who? Oliver?"

"Nah. Ollie hadn't moved to Copper County yet. It was, ah... Jasper, actually."

Derry laughed again, but when he saw I was serious, his eyes widened. "Jasper, as in Coach Lancaster? But... Zach's mom said you guys were rivals. That you, like, *hated* each other."

I shook my head. "No. Never. We were rivals the way you and Zach are. We competed all the time—mostly over silly stuff, and occasionally about important stuff, too. But I could tell him... just about anything."

Derry frowned fiercely, pasta seemingly forgotten for the moment. "What happened? How did I not know this?"

"Because he left town, and we lost touch." I looked at him squarely and admitted, "And I've started to realize, since he came back, that it was half my fault. I was hurt and maybe a little jealous because he was living a big life on the West Coast. I figured he'd forgotten all about me."

Derry pursed his lips thoughtfully. "Do you regret it? Do you... do you wish you'd stuck together? Stayed friends?"

I dragged the tines of my fork through the last bits of sauce on my plate and considered this. The simple answer was to tell Derry with confidence that I had no regrets, but I remembered Jasper saying *Derry's a smart kid. You don't have to have all the answers.*

"I don't know, bud," I said slowly. "On the one hand, yeah, I do regret it. I didn't act like the person I want to think I am. Because of my own hurt, I wasn't a good friend to him when I could have been. On the other hand, no, because I have you and this place." I waved a hand to indicate the orchard. "And I like my life. I'm content. If Jasper hadn't left when he had and the way he had... I don't know if I'd have this. Maybe I'd have something different that I liked just as much. Maybe not. It's... complicated."

To my surprise, Derry nodded. "If we all followed the same path to happiness, the traffic would be ridiculous," he said sagely.

I blinked at him. "That's... true."

Derry smiled. "Coach Lancaster told me that the other day. I like him," he declared. "Maybe it's his mindfulness stuff or whatever, but... he's got a good vibe."

"Yeah." I chuckled. "He does."

"So... you're friends again now, right? And that's why you took the coaching job all of a sudden?"

"I told you, I did that for the sake of the team," I said. "Though I'm sorry I didn't talk to you first—"

"Meh." Derry waved this away. "I'm over it."

I mentally rolled my eyes. *He's been one-word-answering me for a week, and now he's over it?*

But then I thought about my newly recharged friendship with Jasper after I'd been a cranky shithead for *years*... and decided maybe that was genetic, too.

"Yeah, Jasper and I are friends again. I'm, ah, helping him clear out Mabel's place. She collected a lot of stuff over the years, and he needs to sort through it before he puts the place on the market."

"Whoa, whoa. He's leaving again?" Derry's brows knit together. "What for?"

"Because his life is in LA, Derry, just like mine's here. He's only teaching while Coach Monroe's on maternity leave."

"But... did you tell him he could have a life here, too? Like, there's so many reasons for him to stay," he said, all fired up. "Do you know if he even likes his life in California? He said he was over the whole modeling thing. Isn't it your job, as his friend, to call him out when he's being dumb?"

I shook my head patiently. For all of Derry's maturity, sometimes he just didn't understand the way the world worked. "It's my job, as an adult, to give my friend the respect and space to make his own choices. Remember, living in Copper County isn't for everyone. Lots of people like to come here for the summer, but most folks don't stay. Your mom wasn't a fan of this place. Your grandparents couldn't wait to leave. Besides..." I spread my hands on the table. "Not everyone is meant to stay in your life for the whole of it, Derry. Some people are just there for a season. They change you, and they... they *grow* you, but you can't hold on to them too tightly. You need to let them go so they can grow, too."

Derry chewed on the inside of his lip. "You really think that? That you need to, like, support your friend, no matter what? Even if they want to leave?"

I raised an eyebrow. "As long as they're not making choices that are going to harm themselves or others—which includes, but is not limited to, drunk driving, face tattoos, and skipping school?—then yes." I gave him a wistful smile. "I do."

"I still say that's dumb, but..." He sighed, resigned, and pushed his plate back without even going for seconds. "Maybe you're right."

I wished I wasn't.

But it was all the more reason not to waste the limited time I had with Jasper.

———

Two hours later, after Derry had left, I found myself pushing Jasper against the wall in his back hallway with a sense of urgency I could barely control. My hands fisted in his worn T-shirt, tugging him against me while my lips crashed into his.

His breath hitched in surprise, but he quickly matched my intensity.

Fortunately, Jasper was pretty damn practiced at balancing after managing to stay upright on his skates this week, or we might have ended up on the floor.

Then again, maybe that wouldn't be the worst outcome.

"Holy shit." Jasper's voice was ragged. "I had no idea my jokes would have this effect on you. Wait until... you hear the one... about apples..."

I chuckled breathlessly, and my lips found Jasper's again, harder this time. When I pressed my body against his, our hips ground together in a way that sent sparks shooting down my spine.

I'd fantasized about this a bunch of times during the week—as in, every day—but it just wasn't the same. My memory couldn't quite capture the perfect pressure of Jasper's cock when he rubbed his body against mine or the way his fingers felt when they tangled in my hair to pull me closer. I deepened the kiss, sliding my fingers down Jasper's chest, my fingertips mapping out every inch of him through his thin T-shirt.

But when I got to his waist, I faltered like I'd reached the edge of a cliff. In our previous times together, this was the part where I'd stop and let Jasper take over. I didn't want to do that this time, but I definitely needed a minute.

"So. Tomorrow," I said. "You and me, skating lesson? I haven't forgotten. I talked to Ollie. My friend Ollie? One of his physical therapy patient's grandsons is the maintenance guy at the rink, and he's letting us in early. Like, five o'clock early. I can pick you up. Or maybe it'd be better if we took separate cars since you'll need to get to school? Your call."

Jasper blinked those beautiful blue eyes like he wasn't sure where my babble tsunami was coming from or why. "N'kay. Whatever you want, Watt." He licked his lips and added in a drugged whisper, "Kiss me again?"

Laughing softly, I kissed the corner of his mouth, then his jaw, letting my tongue trail down his neck. He shivered against me, and that small reaction made me bolder.

"You are so damn sweet," I breathed against the shell of

his ear. I slid my hands lower to rest on Jasper's hips, my fingers pressing in just enough to keep him grounded. "Sweet smile. Sweet heart. But how sweet do you taste?" The heat in my voice made the simple words sound like a promise.

Jasper groaned, his hand tightening in my hair as if he didn't want to let go... and that gave me the courage to drop to my knees.

I paused for a second and looked up. Jasper's gaze met mine, his pupils blown wide with want, and he nodded frantically.

I swallowed hard as nerves fluttered in my chest—I really *hated* not knowing what I was doing—but my desire was way stronger than my nerves, and although this was new... *fuck*, it felt right.

I wanted to learn every part of Jasper while he was here with me.

And I'd have plenty of time for overthinking later.

Pressing a kiss to Jasper's stomach through his shirt, I moved my hands to his belt. My pulse raced as I undid the buckle, the *click click* of the metal feeling like a countdown to something I couldn't turn back from... and didn't want to. My fingers trembled, but I pushed on, unzipping Jasper's jeans and sliding them down, down, down... and then off entirely.

Jasper's dick was long and hard and cut, his length already flushed red and his head shiny with precum. Hands pressed into his thighs, I leaned in and took a cautious lick... and moaned.

He *was* sweet but also salty and a little sharp, like a green apple. It was perfectly Jasper... and so fucking delicious I lapped at him again, needing more.

Jasper let out an answering groan that went straight to my dick.

It was hard to be nervous when he was already so hard just from kissing and rubbing off on each other. And the look on his face—half-lidded eyes, mouth slightly open, completely lost—made me feel ten feet tall. Like a dick-sucking prodigy, even before I'd fully gotten my mouth on him.

I wanted to make him feel just as good. To show him how fucking gorgeous he was, inside and out. To tell him without words how badly I wanted him.

Taking a deep breath, I leaned in and licked a slow, wet stripe up the softness of Jasper's skin from root to tip. More precum welled, and I eagerly licked it up.

Jasper hiked up his shirt with a frustrated noise like he was pissed that it was blocking his view, then, in a single smooth move, dragged the offending garment off and threw it somewhere on the floor beside us.

"Y-yes," he said unsteadily. "Do it."

Eyes locked on his, I leaned in and suckled lightly at his tip while my fingers tracked the firm planes of his body —*fuck, he was cut*—up the thick golden-brown of his happy trail, over the dip of his navel, across his smooth, muscular chest, to toy with his small, dark nipples.

His back arched, and I caught his hip with one hand, pushing him against the wall to hold him in place.

Chuckling slightly, I ran my hands up Jasper's thighs. I knew what I liked when I jerked myself, what felt good to *me*, so I cupped his balls firmly in my hand and rolled them while still sucking him gently.

Jasper's arms flew out to catch the wall like he'd been electrocuted, and his legs trembled. *Excellent.*

Jasper's body quaked and shivered as I sucked him in another inch, then pulled back.

"Is this... payback?" he demanded. I was pretty sure he meant to sound outraged, but he only sounded dazed. "Oh, God. Suck me. All the way. *Please*, Watt."

To be perfectly honest—and for maybe the first time ever—I hadn't meant to tease him. I'd simply been drawing it out because I was lost in the glory of his body and figuring out what made him craziest. I wanted to lay him out and feast on him for days. I wanted to taste every inch of him— to know what his balls felt like on my tongue, to rim him until he came apart. To taste every freckle that dotted his hard, muscular thighs.

But his plea made my pulse race, and taking a deep breath, I sank lower, taking as much of him into my mouth as I could—which wasn't nearly as much as I wanted— before I gagged a little bit. Clearly, I was going to need some practice before I could take all of him.

Jasper didn't seem to mind, though. His fingers were threaded through my hair on each side of my head, his face flushed and clenched, blue eyes glazed with pleasure.

"Watt," he breathed, almost in disbelief. "Fuck, baby. So good."

Those whispered words lodged themselves in my chest. I took him deep again and felt Jasper's body react, fingers clutching at me while his hips moved in an abortive thrust.

I wanted that, suddenly. Wanted him to fuck my face and take control. Maybe not today, but... yeah. Definitely soon.

I curled my fingers around the base of his cock and started stroking him in time to the up-down of my mouth, setting a rhythm that I'd swear echoed my own heartbeat and the steady throb of my cock against my fly.

I spared a single moment of regret that I hadn't thought to take my own pants off, or at least unzip them, before starting this, but I didn't have the hands or coordination to do anything about that now. I was too busy worshipping Jasper with my mouth, savoring his gasps and whimpers like I was saving them up for a long, cold winter.

"Don't stop," Jasper warned, as though that was even possible. "Please, baby. I'm so close. Watt... I'm coming. *Watt!*"

Jasper said my name like a prayer, his dick growing even harder in my mouth. I guessed he was warning me so I could pull off, but I didn't want to. I wanted to feel him come in my mouth. I wanted to taste it. I wanted the proof that I'd made him lose his mind.

His fingers gripped my hair painfully tight, his cock throbbed, and his whole body clenched as his cum flooded my mouth. I caught every pulse and wave of his pleasure, swallowing them all down and making them a part of me. It was raw and... well, beautiful.

Unforgettable.

Before I knew what was happening, I found myself flat on my back in the middle of the entryway rug with a very naked Jasper on top of me, kissing me wildly.

"Holy fuck," he muttered, his voice as rough as though he'd been the one with a dick in his mouth. "Holy fuck, baby."

I sucked in a breath, not because I didn't like Jasper calling me *baby* or because it felt wrong, but because I liked it a little too much.

It felt a little *too* right.

Temporary, I reminded myself, even as Jasper's hands—gratifyingly clumsy now—reached for my fly. *Friends with benefits. Do not ruin this with expectations.*

But when he tugged my jeans down and got his hand around my length, I couldn't stop myself from pulling Jasper on top of me, wrapping my arms around his shoulders and plunging my tongue into his mouth to taste him again.

It was too late. I was already addicted to him. I didn't know if I could ever get enough.

Mind reeling, chest heaving, I forced myself to stop thinking about the future—a future where Jasper would be back in Los Angeles while me and my big, complicated feelings would be here in Copper County—and to focus on the present. On the perfection of Jasper's hand on my cock and the hot affection in his eyes as he stared down at me.

"Jasper!" I shouted desperately, back arching off the floor as I came and came and came. "Fuck."

"I may... have been wrong," Jasper said a long moment later. I was still sprawled on the floor half-naked—which was distinctly chilly—but with Jasper's forehead pressed directly over my thudding heart and his naked leg slung over my thigh, I didn't have the will to move.

I was pretty sure my heart kicked up an extra notch, though I tried to make myself sound easy. "Wrong? About what?" *Please don't let it end yet.*

"About being better at that than you." He lifted his head and narrowed his eyes at me, teasingly suspicious. "Are you sure I'm the first guy you've been with?"

"Oh," I croaked. I dragged a hand through his messy golden hair. "Yes. Very sure."

This would have been the time, maybe, to tell him that he was the only guy I'd ever felt this way about. That I could count on one hand the number of people I'd been sexually attracted to ever and still have fingers left over. That my feelings for him were utterly unique to anyone I'd ever met... and that he wasn't just my *first* guy, he was probably also my *only*.

Hell, maybe Jasper could explain it to me since I still didn't understand it.

But I didn't want Jasper to get the wrong idea. Friendship with benefits was the rule we'd laid out, and I had no expectation of that changing. Like I'd told Derry earlier, sometimes you couldn't hold on to things for more than a season. And if there was one thing I'd learned, it was the tighter you tried to hold them, the more it hurt when they left anyway.

"Ridiculous." Jasper slumped back down with his cheek to my chest.

I blinked, wondering for a second if he'd read my thoughts, then craned my neck so I could see his face. "What is?"

"That you're so good at that." He sounded peevish. "I know we tease each other a lot, but it would be nice to be better at *something* than you are."

I found myself laughing in disbelief. "You sucked my brains out through my dick twice this week. I've been making notes, dumbass."

"So... you're saying I taught you everything you know?"

"Mmhmm. You're an excellent teacher."

Jasper grunted, apparently mollified, and cuddled closer.

My heart squeezed. I carded my hand through his sweat-damp hair again, and he shivered.

"Come on." I slapped his flank. "I don't want you to get a chill. You've got an early skating lesson in the morning, remember?"

He groaned and rolled onto his back. "You were serious about that?"

I laughed as I pushed to my feet and reached out a hand to help him up. "Yep. That's the only time the rink is free."

Jasper reached for his jeans and dragged them on, then set his hands on his hips and sighed tiredly as he faced the living room. "I guess... we should start cleaning, then, huh? Before it gets too late?"

"Probably," I agreed. I ran my thumb over his cheek. He didn't look quite as weary as he had a week ago, but it was clear this process was taking a toll on him. "Were you working on the house late last night?"

Jasper nodded. "And the night before, too, after I got home from Tam's. It feels kind of endless. I can't imagine what it'd be like if I had to work on the campground, too." He hooked a thumb over his shoulder in the direction of the cabins spread through the woods by the lake. "I need to thank your friend Chris and his fiancé for the renovations they did. I'll pay them back somehow."

I shrugged. "They don't expect payment. Though, you know, maybe some pumpkin muffins wouldn't go amiss." I patted my stomach.

Jasper's eyes lit with humor. "And I suppose I could make you some at the same time?"

"It would be the friendly thing to do," I agreed fake-seriously. I slid my hand down his arm, threading our fingers together.

He laughed... and then yawned. "M'kay. This weekend. For tonight, let's finish up the den. There are only a couple more piles to sort since I got the rest done yesterday. Turns out, the couch is still in great shape, and the television's only a couple years old—" He tried to tug me down the hall.

I resisted. "Now, that's an idea," I said. "How about we take the night off and watch television?"

"Television," Jasper repeated, his eyes searching mine. "Like, Netflix and chill?"

I laughed. "We already chilled." Though, who was I kidding? I'd be ready to go again in ten minutes... five if Jasper remained shirtless. "I mean actual television. I mean the two of us sitting on a sofa together, with blankets, and watching the single greatest television show of all time."

"Oh." He sounded surprised. "What show?"

"Jasper," I said seriously. "Have you ever heard of the show *John Ruffian: Pretender*?"

He shook his head. "No? Should I?"

"Oh, baby," I said, pulling him down the hall. "I am about to rock your world."

CHAPTER TWELVE

JASPER

By our third skating lesson, I was feeling pretty cocky. Not *skilled*—I wouldn't go that far—but cocky. I hadn't wiped out spectacularly in our first two sessions, which felt like a win. And while I still wobbled like a newborn giraffe half the time, I was getting the hang of the whole "let go and glide" concept...

At least, as long as Watt was holding me.

Watt was skating backward around the empty rink, his grip on my hands firm but easy as he pulled me along. His hazel eyes held mine, and I knew without a doubt that he was trying not to smirk... and also that the smirk would break through soon enough.

"Keep breathing," he teased. "The key to skating is not passing out."

"I'll keep that in mind," I shot back.

I did sound ridiculously breathless, but it had nothing to do with the skating. Even with only a single set of lights turned on above the middle of the rink—not the best lighting to show *anyone* to advantage, but the best Watt's friend was able to do for us since the rink technically didn't open for a couple of hours—and dressed in an oversized hoodie, Watt looked really good on the ice. Then again, the man looked stupidly good all the time. I didn't understand how a person who was so incredibly tall and broadly built should be so effortlessly graceful with a pair of thin blades strapped to his feet, but he was, and his confidence and competence made my heart thud in my chest.

Or maybe it was just *him* and the fact that in some ways, I felt closer to him now than I had twenty years ago.

Watt pulled me closer, dropping one of my hands and resting a palm on my waist to steady me when I wobbled again. "Relax. Remember, it's all in the knees. Bend 'em a little more."

"You're obsessed with my knees," I muttered.

He laughed. "Definitely obsessed with you bending them for me," he said in a low voice that made my stomach flip and my knees weaken just slightly—

"There you go," he said proudly, displaying the smirk he'd been holding back. "Perfect knee bend."

I scowled. "Did you just flirt with me on purpose to help me achieve the right form?" I determinedly ignored that it had worked... and that a smirking Watt Bartlett was the sexiest thing I'd ever seen.

"A stellar coach—that's me, by the way—adapts to the needs of his student." He booped me on the nose. "That's you."

Hmph.

Watt and I skated side by side, and I was temporarily so annoyed that I forgot I didn't know what I was doing. It turned out bending my knees *did* help. My legs wobbled less, and I glided more confidently.

"There's a reason there isn't an episode of *John Ruffian*

where he pretends to be an ice-skater," I complained. "This shit is difficult."

"Maybe there is and you just haven't gotten to it yet." He narrowed his eyes. "Wait. You didn't keep watching without me last night, did you?"

"Where is the trust, Bartlett?" I demanded. "I told you I wouldn't. Which, I'll point out again, is massively unfair since you've already seen the whole series fourteen billion times."

"Yeah, but I like watching your face when you watch it. It's even more fun than watching it on my own," he said, which was the sweetest thing ever and made my stomach flips turn to handsprings… until he ruined it by adding, "*Oh my god, Watt! Why couldn't John keep his mouth shut? Now, Duane the illegal lumber trafficker is going to throw John in the giant woodchipper!*"

"Hey! It was a tense moment for me, asshole," I argued. "And I was a John Ruffian newbie then."

"It was a week ago."

"It was thirteen episodes ago!" I shot Watt a glare and added menacingly, "And I'm starting to understand where Duane was coming from."

Watt's grin widened, and he glanced pointedly down at my skates, which were moving in a reasonable facsimile of skating. "Look at you go. When you forget to look at your feet, you're unstoppable. Next thing we need to do is put a stick in your hands."

I shot him a sidelong glance. "I think my stick-handling skills are in top form. I haven't had any complaints, Coach."

He chuckled, his hazel eyes darkening. "*Coach* is still not a thing. It's not ever going to be a thing."

"The bulge in your jeans says diff-erent-ly," I

singsonged. "I think you've got some unresolved fantasies—"

He shuddered and made a sound like he was vomiting in his mouth. "Shut your mouth. My old hockey coach is *Joe Cross*."

"Who?"

"The mechanic in O'Leary. The guy who looks like Santa Claus and—"

"And wears nothing but decade-old Tom Brady T-shirts?" I widened my eyes. "Oh. Wow. I mean... no judgment, Watt. When I was in college, I had a thing for one of my drama professors who sounded just like David Attenborough, and—hey!" I cried as Watt let go of my hand and skated two feet away.

"I have never had any unresolved sexual *anything* for any of my coaches," Watt said firmly.

"Fine." I scowled. "You're a saint. A very overgrown, repressed saint. Now, come back here and help me..."

"Or what?" he taunted. He skated in a slow arc, close enough to catch me if I fell but too far away for me to lunge at him. It was maddening. "Why don't you come and get me?"

I gritted my teeth, digging the toe of my skate into the ice as I pushed off. My legs were still embarrassingly shaky, and my arms flailed a bit as I tried to balance and reach for him at the same time.

Watt's eyes widened in surprise, but his grin was brighter than the sun—though maybe that wasn't saying much since it had been dark o'clock when we'd gotten here.

"Eyes up, Jasper. Stare at your feet and you're gonna fall," Watt called, skating just out of reach. "Did your mindfulness gurus not teach you that?"

Fuck.

I pushed off again, trying to do it smoothly, the way he'd shown me a dozen times. *One foot out, then glide. One foot out, then glide.* But my skates kept slipping at awkward angles as I overbalanced. Instead of smooth, I probably looked like I was doing a strange kind of dance. A sort of hiss-less version of the Marmot Cheer.

"Get back here," I ordered.

"Pardon?" He slipped away again. "Can't hear you."

I let out a sound like a boiling teakettle and pushed off again, except this time, I wobbled a little too hard, nearly toppling over. The ice rushed up to meet me... but at the last second, Watt swooped in and caught me by the waist, pulling me close enough that our noses brushed.

"Fucking *excellent*," Watt said, kissing me hard and twirling us in a circle before I had a chance to be embarrassed. "You did it." He sounded nearly giddy.

I opened my mouth to protest, but I realized he was sort of right. I *had* done it. Until I hadn't.

Team fake it 'til you make it was almost, kinda... making it.

"Now we just need to see this kind of fire from the team in their game this afternoon, and we'll be golden," Watt said.

I snorted. The team was doing really well, in my inexpert opinion, but I couldn't help adding, "Gonna provoke the shit out of them, too?"

Watt laughed out loud. "If they were all as contrary as you, I would." He ignored the look I shot him and kissed me again, more deeply this time. "You know, I never had a thing for my coach," he whispered when he pulled back, "but my *rival*... Yeah, I definitely had a thing for him."

My stomach did a triple cartwheel, and I wrapped my arms around Watt's neck. "Is that so? Tell me mo—"

Wham.

The sound of a door slamming shut echoed through the empty rink. Watt shoved me away from him immediately and turned, one hand shielding his eyes from the overhead lights as he scanned the empty stands. I couldn't help but notice the look of panic on his face.

I wavered on my skates, arms whirling like propellers as I tried to keep my balance.

"Shit," Watt muttered, exhaling in relief. He turned back just in time to catch me before I landed on my ass. "Sorry. I was startled. I didn't know if it was one of the kids, or one of the hockey parents, or someone else..." He swallowed hard, and we both realized how he'd meant to end that sentence.

Or someone else who might have seen him kiss me.

"I get it," I said. And I did. I'd been down this road before, after all. I just hadn't expected to be traveling it again.

I extricated myself from his grasp and picked my way over to the gate that led into the stands. A moment later, Watt skated over to join me.

"Fuck. Jasper, I'm sorry. I overreacted. I didn't think."

"I know." Sighing, I sat on the bench and bent to unlace my skates. "Did I ever tell you about how my ex and I first got together?" I asked, though I knew the answer.

Watt scowled fiercely. "No. Just that he was your agent before anything happened. Which is kinda skeevy."

I ignored him and continued the story. He wasn't wrong, but that wasn't the point. "It happened in June—I remember because I was in Miami doing a shoot, and I couldn't believe how hot it was. I'd just gotten off the phone with Mabel, and she'd filled me in on all the gossip from Copper County. My mom usually traveled with me back then, but she was in Arizona at a spa retreat, so it was just me and Martin—"

"I don't want to hear this story." Watt jammed his hands in the pocket of his hoodie.

"It's not a bad story. I was feeling lonely and homesick and a little lost. Martin was... a friend, sort of. The closest thing I had to one at that time, anyway. And I wanted sex, which was exactly what he was offering." I took off one skate and flexed my toes. "It wasn't my first sexual experience by a long shot, and it was totally fine. Good, even. When it was over, he said he hoped we could do it again... and asked me to keep it quiet because it would be complicated to explain to people. I agreed."

"What?" Watt demanded. "That's—"

I tilted my head and looked at him, silently daring him to continue.

Watt sucked in a breath, and his face turned red. "No way... I don't... It's not the same situation. I don't care if people know I'm with a *man*—"

"Neither did Martin."

Watt's nostrils flared. He stalked off the ice and threw himself onto the bench. "My wanting to keep this quiet has nothing to do with *you*, though. It's about *me*. I thought... I mean, you said you understood that. You said I should figure things out on my own timeline."

I bent to untie the other skate. "I did. I still do. You have mental baggage to unpack and sort through. I get that. I'm carrying some luggage of my own." I tapped at my temple. "Part of us getting to know each other again, being friends again—or friends with benefits or whatever—is me sharing how my luggage sometimes doesn't coordinate with yours." I gave him a half smile. "I'm not angry at you, Watt, and I'm *not* pressuring you. I'm explaining why your reaction just now made me feel... not great. And that's *my* shit to sort through. Okay?"

He pressed his hands to his eyes. "I don't want to be like Martin. I don't want to treat you like he does."

"You're not like him," I assured him. "Jesus, no, Watt." I scooted over and bumped my arm into his. "That's not what I was getting at, I swear. You couldn't be like Martin if you tried." This was true. "And I'm not the same person I was back then, either. I know all that." I pointed to my head again. "Sometimes I just don't *know* it." I tapped my chest. "And I need a second to remind myself."

Watt considered this for a moment, then nodded. "Thank you for explaining. I do want to hear these things... even when I don't want to hear them."

I grinned. If I needed further proof that Watt and Martin weren't remotely the same person, there it was. In no realm would Martin ever thank me for sharing something he might take as criticism. "You're welcome."

"I don't ever want you to feel bad because of me, Jasper," he said softly.

I bumped my arm against his again, and this time, I let it rest there. "Please," I teased. "This, from the man who once challenged me to ride the Tilt-A-Whirl with him after downing four milkshakes?"

His lips twitched just a little. "As I recall, I'd had *five*."

"From the man who once bet me that I wouldn't stand up at the O'Leary Fourth of July festival and do a dramatic reading of the ingredients on the back of a potato chip packet?"

"Not a dry eye in the house when you got to the bit about the malic acid," he said solemnly.

"From the man who dared me, just this morning, to tie

knives on my feet—" I kicked at my skates. "—and glide around a rink?"

"I held your hand almost the whole time. And you did it," he pointed out.

"I did do it," I agreed. "I've done a lot of things I didn't think I could do, thanks to you." I winked. "And possibly a few I *shouldn't* have done."

Watt laughed, and so did I, and when he wrapped one arm around my waist, pulled me down against his chest, and pressed a kiss to the top of my head, it felt genuinely soothing. Like he was healing some old hurts I hadn't even known I had.

"I care about you," he said softly. "Always have. Even when I was stupidly angry, even when I was blaming you for leaving, even when I was being an ass. You matter to me, Jasper. I don't want to fuck things up and lose this again."

"Same." I turned to face him and caught his stubbled cheeks in my two hands. "You're a pain in the ass, Watt Bartlett, and you're the best man I know." I pressed my forehead to his. "So let's not fuck it up. Some coach I know once said that if you want different results, you've got to put in the effort and change the way you play."

Watt's smile broke over his face slowly. "He sounds brilliant. Probably really hot, too."

"He has his moments," I agreed.

———

WHEN GAME TIME came that afternoon, I was feeling a whole lot less cocky. In fact, I was forced to recite my own mindfulness mantras to keep my nerves from showing. It had been a whole lot easier to believe that winning and losing don't matter when I hadn't known twenty hard-working kids who'd be crushed if they lost.

The first two periods went by in a blur, and despite Calvin wrenching his knee pretty badly in the first period, we'd managed to keep the game tied at two apiece. Then, three minutes into the third period, Derry had completed an elegant one-handed pass that shot the puck over to Zach, who'd sent it flying to the back of Baxter's net. While the team had erupted into cheers, more than half of the home-town crowd that packed the stands had let out a coordinated, feral, truly bloodcurdling marmot hiss.

Kayla was ecstatic.

I'd tried to stay mostly quiet throughout the game so as to not distract Watt or any of the players, but when we were down to ten minutes left on the clock, I couldn't help screaming encouragement.

"You've got this, Rodney!" I shouted at one of the players. "Focus on the ice, no distractions."

He tossed me a jaunty salute. "Got it, Coach."

"Nice try on the last play, Kip!" I called toward the goal as the kids lined up for a face-off. "This time, try to *extend* your arm a bit further to make the save." I extended my arm like a ballerina in demonstration. "Remember those stretches I showed you?"

Kip nodded back.

Watt made a noise that sounded suspiciously like a laugh, and I caught him side-eyeing me. "Enjoying yourself, Coach Lancaster?" he asked.

I snorted. *Enjoying myself? Is he kidding?* My heart was racing so fast my Apple Watch kept telling me I was suffering a cardiac incident, and every time a Fighting Marmot got checked against the boards too roughly, I wanted to stalk out onto the ice and crack a few of the opposing players' helmets together.

"I... am," I admitted, shocked to find it was true.

When we won the next face-off, I found myself leaning over the boards of the rink, practically jumping up and down with excitement.

"Yes! Go, Derry! Skate the puck!" I screamed as he flew past us on a race to the net.

But one of the Baxter Badgers appeared out of nowhere, stealing the puck from Derry's stick and turning to skate back up the ice.

It seemed I wasn't the only one surprised because I was pretty sure our defense wasn't in position like they were supposed to be. And before they could scramble to correct, a Badger built like a brick shithouse was bearing down on our goal... with only little Kip, the smallest player on our team, standing between him and a flashing score light.

I gasped. "Kip!" I clutched Watt's shoulder with both hands. "Oh, crap. Ohhhh, *crap*. I can't look, Watt," I cried. But despite my words, I was unable to turn my head or stop watching.

The Badger player wound up his stick and swung at the puck like it was a golf ball, sending it arcing toward the goal in what even I recognized was an absolutely flawless, unmissable shot.

Time slowed as we waited for the flashing light that would signal their goal and, effectively, our first loss of the season. In that fraction of a second, I decided I hated sports with a passion, that I was bringing five dozen consolation cookies to practice on Monday, and that I needed a stiff drink or a hard fuck, possibly both.

But at the last possible second, Kip sprang into action,

stretching his arm out like it was made of rubber as he lunged across the net and caught the puck in midair.

For a second, there was stunned silence throughout the rink as we all processed the fact that we'd witnessed a walk-on-water-level miracle. Then Kip pushed up his mask and called, "Hey, Coach Lancaster? I think the stretches are working!"

The crowd jumped to their feet, exploding into screams and whistles, and the players around us went wild.

"Oh my God!" I crowed triumphantly. I hadn't let go of Watt's shoulder, and I found myself shaking it violently... not that it moved him much. "Did you see that? Holy shit, Watt, did you see?"

"Yeah, I saw it." Watt glanced at me from the corner of his eye and smiled the smile I loved—I mean... in a friendly way—then grabbed me up in a hug so fierce my feet left the ground. "Yeah, I *fucking* saw it!" he repeated, spinning me in a giddy, dizzy circle. "You did that, Jasper. You! I'm so proud of you."

When he put me down two seconds later to congratulate the team, my giddiness didn't go away.

Fortunately, the clock had run out. The remaining players streamed in from the ice shortly thereafter, with Rodney carrying Kip in front of him like the mermaid on the prow of a ship. The players tapped the ends of their sticks against the ground forcefully, chanting first Kip's name, then Calvin's, since he was our wounded warrior, and then... mine.

My face went hot, and I shook my head. I took zero credit for Kip's awesome move. But Watt grinned at my discomfort and let the celebrating and chanting go on for a long-ass time before finally calling the kids to order.

"Awesome job, everyone. Kip, I really hope your parents

caught that because that save was highlight reel material. And here I've been encouraging you to tighten up your form and work on your speed when all you really needed was to extend yourself." Watt shot me a wink that had my blush ramping up exponentially.

"But this win is about more than one person or one moment," he went on. "You *all* got us there. Zach, Derry—amazing job on that last goal. Rodney, you really stepped it up." For every player, Watt pointed out something they'd done particularly well, reminding them that they were part of something bigger than themselves and that their fortunes rose and fell together.

It did things to my insides, watching Watt interact with the kids. A strange and new addendum to my competence kink, maybe. Or maybe *Watt* wasn't the one of us with a coaching kink after all.

His eyes met mine over the players' heads, and he lifted an eyebrow like he could read my thoughts. "Anything to add, Coach Lancaster?"

I blinked. Was I supposed to say something meaningful? I was totally unprepared. "Uh. No? Just... celebrate your win this weekend, and on Monday, let's start preparing for our next game."

Apparently, that was the perfect thing to say anyway, judging by Watt's warm smile and the way the team broke into exuberant catcalls again. Within seconds of Watt dismissing them, they were heading to the locker room to shower, grab their gear, find their families, and enjoy their victory.

"I get it now," I told Watt in a low voice as we stood by the back of the box, watching the kids file out. Derry had been the first to pack up his stuff and was already headed to his mom's house near Rochester for the weekend. "The hockey thing, I mean. I can be competitive—"

"You?" Watt feigned confusion. "I had no idea."

I rolled my eyes. "My point is, I hadn't fully realized how much bigger it is when you're on a team. When you're not just winning so *you* can win but so everyone can win."

He stepped a bit closer, almost crowding me against the back corner of the box. The stands were only inches away, but nobody was paying attention to us. "You're saying *the hockey* has converted you to team sports?" he teased.

"I'm saying I think the coach is more brilliant than I gave him credit for," I said softly. "Nice job... *Coach*."

"Never ever gonna—" he began.

I laid a hand on his forearm where it rested against the wooden gate that separated the players from the spectators. "Oh, it's a thing," I said in a low voice filled with promise. "Yep. As in, I might need some remedial *coaching* later."

"You... *oh*." Watt's eyes flared with heat, and he leaned toward me slightly. "Well, then. I—"

"Watt, honey! Oh my heck, Watt!"

Watt closed his eyes and exhaled through his nose.

I stiffened and snatched my hand off his arm, immediately aware of just how close Watt and I were standing.

I was stuck in the corner, unable to move much, but I braced myself for Watt to spring away.

And you won't make a big deal of it, I told myself firmly. Once per day was plenty.

Watt did *not* move away, however. In fact, he left his arm braced against the board exactly where it had been so that when we turned to watch Kayla approach us, his hip came to rest just slightly behind mine, overlapping us like dragon scales. I was completely surrounded, suspended in a bubble of Watt.

"Kayla. Hi," he said with easy politeness, as though nothing were unusual about our proximity. "Great game, huh? Were you coming to congratulate Jasper? It's thanks to his amazing coaching on foundational skills that we were able to pull off the win."

I turned my head to blink at him in surprise, vaguely aware of Kayla doing the same.

"Well... yes, actually." Kayla smiled gamely. "I was coming to congratulate *both* of you. Wonderful game, well coached. I'm glad to see you were able to put aside your rivalry. Pity that Calvin couldn't push through and left the team shorthanded, but the others stepped up *so* well, thanks to you, Watt... er, and Jasper."

"Calvin hurt his knee pretty badly," I informed Kayla. "I imagine his parents are taking him to get it checked out."

"Pfft. I used to get injuries like that all the time when I was cheerleading. As I tell Zachy, if you want something badly enough, you push through. Oh, speaking of which..." She lowered her voice. "I tried to keep an eye out for the Utica scout. I didn't see him, but I'm sure he was here."

"Was he?" Watt frowned. "I didn't hear anything about him coming. Jasper?"

I shook my head. "It's common for scouts to introduce themselves to the coach first, right?" When Watt raised an eyebrow, I shrugged. "I've seen *The Blind Side*."

Watt chuckled. Kayla looked slightly annoyed—whether at my joke, or my proximity to Watt, or the idea that the scout hadn't come, I wasn't sure—but I found I couldn't care much about that because in the next second, Watt's hand, hidden by both the box and my body, where no one could possibly see, came to rest firmly on my ass.

I sucked in a sharp breath as my cheeks heated—both

sets of cheeks—and narrowly resisted the urge to ask Watt what the fuck he was doing.

"Well, if not this game, then certainly the next," Kayla said. "Or perhaps there's been some confusion since Tam Monroe is still the Marmots' coach, and Jasper's only her substitute."

She turned to me for agreement, and I nodded eagerly… though, frankly, I would have agreed to just about anything she said. Watt's hand had moved just the tiniest fraction so the full weight of my ass cheek was cupped in his large palm. The heat of him seeped through the thin material of my running tights, making my cock swell instantly.

"T-Tam might have gotten a call," I blurted. My voice came out like a chipmunk high on helium, but I couldn't stop it. "I… I mean, I would think she would have told me. I was over there last night. And Tuesday. And Sunday morning. But she was super uncomfortable yesterday. Like, in a pregnant way. Lucas said it was probably almost g-go time, and Tam burst into tears because she didn't want it to be over. And then Delaney said he was m-manifesting that the baby wouldn't come until December so he could win their family betting pool, and Tam whacked him in the face with a cushion for dooming her to four more weeks of pregnancy. And Charlene said Tam was—"

Watt's fingers flexed, digging into the muscle and pulling my cheeks apart. I sucked in another breath like a deep-sea diver preparing to submerge. "She said Tam was close. Really close," I said in a desperate rush. "*Too* close."

Kayla waved a hand. "Nonsense. There's no such thing as too close, Jasper."

Watt's chuckle was laden with so much pure *sex* I couldn't believe Kayla didn't notice it.

With his arm blocked from view, no one could see how

tantalizingly close Watt's fingers were to rubbing over my hole. Thanks to the hang of my fleece jacket, no one could see the effect his touch was having on me, either.

To anyone looking, we probably looked like two men crowded a little too close together. Not particularly remarkable. And yet, Watt had freaked out earlier at the idea that anyone might see us being more than friendly. So what the hell was he thinking now? Why had he suddenly become Mr. Risky McRisktaker?

"Speaking of things that are close, though." Kayla's smile widened a fraction. "The Pilgrim Prance is only two weeks away, Watt. We should coordinate. Maybe go for a practice run this weekend? I'll text you."

Watt's hand hesitated for a second before journeying on, and I decided I was dying.

Or, okay, that might be a bit dramatic. Possibly more like... dying-lite.

Lightly dying.

"I already have plans this weekend," Watt said, managing to sound both apologetic and uncompromising. "But don't worry. I'm not as young as I used to be, but I can run a 5K."

"Oh my heck, I'm *sure*." Kayla fluttered her lashes in open flirtation and set her hands on Watt's arm—by which I meant the arm that wasn't busy defiling me. "But then you've always been so athletic. Watching Derry make that pass to Zachy at the end there was like stepping back in time and watching you on the ice again! Isn't it exciting to think about us going to their games next year and reliving our glory days?"

So much of my concentration was locked on the movement of Watt's fingers, and on assessing whether anyone could see us, and on trying very hard not to groan or squirm,

I probably shouldn't have had enough left over to notice the way Kayla's fingers clenched possessively on the sleeve of Watt's hoodie... but I managed it.

And I was therefore very aware of the way Watt's free hand clenched into a fist before he shifted his weight and casually pulled his arm away from her.

"It's exciting to think about the boys doing something they want to do," Watt agreed. "But I have no interest in reliving the past. I've spent twenty years learning from my mistakes... and I try not to make the same ones twice."

I turned my head and found Watt was already looking at me. Though his expression was bland and neutral, his eyes carried a weight of regret, pride, and affection that would have stolen my breath... if I hadn't already been seriously breathless.

"In fact," Watt went on, "I'm pretty excited about the present. Wouldn't you agree, Jasper?" He trailed one thick finger down my ass crack.

"*Yes!*" I yelped, jumping in place. My cock throbbed, and though I refused to look down, I knew it was tenting the front of my thin tights. I was two seconds away from a public decency violation.

"Gosh, I'm so sorry." I pressed my hands to my flaming cheeks. "I just remembered that I have to... to do something. At home. *Immediately*. Can't be delayed."

"Wow." Kayla looked genuinely concerned. "Is everything okay, Jasper?"

"Hmm? Yes, fine. It's just that I need to, uh..." I turned to Watt in desperation.

"Stretch his sourdough," Watt said with perfect solemnity.

"Stretch..." Kayla wrinkled her nose. "Huh. Really?"

"Oh, yes," I managed to say, torn between laughter,

annoyance, and desperate arousal. I yanked my fleece down as far as it would go and grabbed the bag I'd left under the bench. "You know how finicky sourdough is."

"A pain in the ass, but worth it." Watt hurriedly grabbed his own bag. "I'll come in case you need a hand. See you, Kayla!"

"You're so helpful, Watt," Kayla sighed as the two of us ran up the stadium stairs and out the door.

I managed to hold back my laughter until we'd escaped into the twilight chill of the parking lot. Fortunately, most of the crowd had departed while we were chatting with Kayla, and hardly anyone was around to see me looking deranged and aroused. I felt strangely euphoric—like I'd committed a bank heist and gotten away with it.

"What the hell was that, Bartlett?" I demanded in a whisper as I wiped my eyes. "You went from shoving me away this morning to practically making me come in public."

Watt's answer when it came was more serious than I'd expected. "I told you, I never want you to feel shitty because of me." He shrugged. "I'm not taking out an ad in the *Gazette*. I'm not ready for that. But I'm not pushing you away again, either." His eyes glinted in the streetlight as they met mine. "That's not a compromise I could live with."

"Oh." I swallowed and felt my heart stutter in my chest. "Right. Good."

He glanced down at the front of my pants and licked his lips. "I... may have taken it a little too far."

I stared down also. My bulge was obscene, and the way Watt stared at it while licking his lips wasn't helping anything. "You think?"

"I'll make it up to you. Race you to your house?"

"Yes—no, wait, fuck." I ran a hand through my hair. "I

forgot, the engine on the Jag wouldn't turn over this afternoon, so I left my car at school and got a ride with Ms. Govostes."

"And you couldn't diagnose the issue yourself and fix it immediately?" Watt teased. He bleeped the lock on his truck. "What a lucky coincidence that you and I are headed in the same direction."

"You're so *helpful*, Watt," I said, channeling a smidge of Kayla's simpering tone.

"Move your ass, Jasper."

We sprinted through the chilly twilight shadows toward the flashing lights...

Heedless of anyone who might see.

CHAPTER THIRTEEN

WATT

"Come on, open! Stupid fucking lock," Jasper whimpered as I lavished wet kisses down the side of his neck. "Shit. I'm a righty. Why am I doing this left-handed?"

I grinned against his skin. I couldn't remember the last time I'd felt as thrilled with life as I did standing on Jasper's back porch, watching him fumble his keys as he tried to open the door in the dim porch light.

There were a lot of reasons for this.

One, my team had just scored an incredible win. I'd known the kids had the puck-handling skills to beat Baxter since the teams were evenly matched, but given the late start to the season and then losing Calvin to an injury early on in the game, we'd had to really pull together and battle for the W. That required adaptability and focus... skills they'd gotten thanks to my co-coach.

Two, I felt like I'd scored a win of my own today. This morning at the rink, I'd panicked. One minute, I'd been lost in Jasper's eyes and our silly teasing, riding high on the thrill of watching him learn to skate. The next, the door had slammed, and I'd imagined a horde of Copper County gossips standing there watching, ready to cluck their tongues over Jasper's inevitable departure and Watt Bartlett's continued failure to *relationship*. It was totally irrational—even the most hardened busybody in town wasn't that cruel, and I cared more about Jasper than their opinions anyway—but I'd reasoned that through a second too late.

Listening to Jasper's story about his marriage had sucked, but it had shone a spotlight on my behavior too bright to ignore. I needed to adapt and focus, too, if I didn't want to lose Jasper's friendship.

So I had.

Possibly too well, I thought smugly as Jasper dropped his keys to the dark porch floor for the third time.

"Let me help," I said, swooping down to grab them up.

Unfortunately, on my way back up, I got slightly distracted by the *third* reason I was feeling euphoric: because there was nothing as purely enjoyable in the world as kissing Jasper.

Jasper's mouth was already distractingly damp and swollen from our earlier kisses in the truck, so obviously, I had to kiss him again, more deeply this time, taking the time to appreciate the softness of his lips and the way his taste had already become familiar.

"Not helping," Jasper groaned breathlessly, breaking our kiss. "I'm two seconds from blowing you out here, and... *no*. I want a bed this time. We still haven't made it to a bed, Watt."

I chuckled. He was totally right. In the two weeks we'd been together—er, together as friends with benefits, that was—we'd managed some up-against-the-wall blowjobs, an up-against-a-tree handjob down by the dock, and an under-a-blanket frot on the porch swing, where

Jasper had guided me as I worked both our cocks together. We'd also had a couple of couch-based orgasms, including one memorable one where Jasper had rocked his naked body against mine while John Ruffian did some heroic cowboy shit on television, and the two of us had come simultaneously a second before John had declared, "And that's how it's done, partner." We'd promptly laughed ourselves silly.

The fact that we'd had so much sex in such a short time was mind-blowing, considering how many years I'd gone without having sex with another person at all. Maybe even more mind-blowing was the fact that in only two weeks, we'd established a kind of routine—practice, sex, decluttering, sex, and sometimes morning skating lessons—all of it woven through with our banter and texting. Sometimes it felt like I'd forgotten how to stop smiling... until I reminded myself that it was temporary.

That thought had me pulling Jasper back in to kiss him again.

The chilly night air clung to our skin, but I didn't care. Jasper pressed me up against the door, his erection grinding into my hip, practically shaking with need and impatience— or maybe that was me.

"Fuck it. I can't wait," he breathed. The words sent a shiver through both of us.

The keys hit the porch with a loud *clank*. Jasper cursed, but I laughed.

Blood fizzing urgently through my veins, I reached down to unbutton my jeans while Jasper pushed down those sexy-as-fuck running tights, and then I curled my hand around both of our shafts, jerking us together.

"Oh, yeah. Shit, that's good," Jasper muttered against my lips, his cock already leaking. "I'm not gonna last."

He pressed his forehead to mine and clung to my shoulders, his body trembling with every stroke of my fist.

"Don't. I wanna see you come for me. Love the way you lose control," I murmured.

Jasper's breath came in shallow pants. "But I... had plans..." With two hands, he pulled my head back just far enough to look at me. "I want you to fuck me. In a bed."

My hand tightened around us. *Fuck, yes*, I wanted that. I hadn't realized how badly until Jasper had said he wanted it, too. I wanted to be inside him, to touch and know every damn part of him.

"You want me inside you?" I growled. I reached a hand around behind him and fondled his ass the way I had earlier, this time without the barrier of his tights between us. His ass was as perfect as the rest of him, compact and firmly muscled. I tried not to worry too much about my lack of experience as I nudged his cheeks apart and slid my finger firmly over his pucker.

Jasper let out a low whine. "Yes. Fuck. Oh, God, Watt."

His whole body locked down, his fingers dug into my shoulders, and he came all over my fist. The sounds he made, combined with the heat of his release, were enough to trigger my own, and I came so hard it was nearly painful, crying out into the still night.

"Fuck. I'm dead. Absolutely dead." Jasper had face-planted into the front of my sweatshirt and did not lift his head. After a moment, he added, his voice soft with amusement, "The afterlife is chillier than I thought."

I wasn't quite ready to laugh yet. "You want that? For real?"

He lifted his head. "Death? Not at this moment, no."

"Jasper," I warned. "I meant... the other thing."

"Anal sex?" He sighed and pushed himself off me. With

a grimace of distaste, he pulled up his pants and knelt to retrieve the keys. "Yes. But let's have this conversation inside after we've cleaned up. I shouldn't have mentioned it that way."

"No, I'm glad you did," I argued. Jasper managed to open the lock on the first try this time, and pulling up my jeans with my clean hand, I followed him into the warm house. "It worked for me. Clearly. But I need a minute to… to wrap my head around actually doing it."

"To overthink it, you mean?" Jasper teased. He led me upstairs to the pink-tiled hall bathroom, where we washed our hands side by side. "I'm kidding, to be clear."

"I know. And I'm not… I mean… I think it would be hot as fuck, but I hadn't really imagined going there because…"

"Because…?"

"Well… is it a friends-with-temporary-benefits kind of thing to do? Isn't it, like, special? Or meaningful?" I blurted, then immediately blushed. "That's probably some stupid heteronormative thing, right? If I knew what I was doing here, if I had any experience whatsoever, I'd know…"

"Watt." Jasper crowded between me and the sink and framed my face with his hands. "I don't expect you to have the answers *or* experience. I *definitely* don't want to do anything you're not comfortable with. Believe me when I tell you that what we're already doing is fucking amazing. Thrilling. Incredible. Best sex of my life."

I frowned. "Really? That's…"

Impossible, I was going to say, but was it? It was sure as fuck the best I'd ever had. The kind that made me under-stand what people like Ollie had been talking about my whole life.

More to the point, I didn't think Jasper would lie.

"…that's good to know," I finished.

Snorting, Jasper stepped back. "It's really not fair that you're cute when you're cocky. As far as the other thing goes, plenty of gay people think anal is a bigger deal. For me..."

I held my breath. I wasn't sure what I hoped he'd say.

You are *special, Watt.*

It would *mean something to me, Watt.*

We're more than friends with benefits, Watt.

The last one made me suck in a breath. Did I actually want that?

"...for me, the significance of the act is less about what I'm doing and more about who I'm doing it with," Jasper said, which was reasonable and honest... and not at all the clue I'd been hoping for. "Just kissing someone you care about means more than getting railed into the mattress by somebody else."

I sucked in a breath as I imagined that. Jasper beneath me... Jasper *taking* me...

"Yeah," I said hoarsely. "I can see that."

"I think you'd really enjoy it, though." He raised one teasing eyebrow. "In fact, I *bet* you would..."

I opened my mouth to say something—probably a whining *yes, please*—but before I could get the words out, the doorbell rang downstairs.

Jasper and I exchanged a startled look.

The campground was set pretty far back from the road that looped around the lake, down a long, unlit, unpaved driveway. Much like over at my orchard, there weren't a lot of folks who "happened to be in the neighborhood" and just stopped by. Those who were—the other folks who lived around Copper Lake—generally came on foot and used the back door.

"Maybe something with Tam?" Jasper said, pushing past me to the hall. "But nobody texted."

"Maybe a camper who doesn't realize you're closed for the season," I said, following him down the stairs and into the living room.

We were both wrong.

———

"M-MARTIN?" Jasper stared blankly at the man on his front stoop.

I couldn't blame him for staring. The man was a picture of curated perfection. His salt-and-pepper hair was artfully tousled, and his skin glowed with good health. He was dressed in tailored pants that were probably nicer than anything I'd ever owned and a button-down shirt from a designer called Lanvin... which I knew because it had the word LANVIN printed stylishly across the front.

"There he is!" the man said with an affectionate grin, opening his arms in anticipation of an embrace. I had to admit, Jasper's ex seemed more genuine than I'd imagined. I'd pictured a shifty-eyed asshole in a shiny suit. "Hi, Jazz."

For a split second, I thought *jazz!* was some kind of niche LA greeting until he stepped inside the living room and grasped Jasper's upper arms before leaning in to kiss his cheek. "Damn, you look good, sweetness. Country air must agree with you."

Jasper, who looked like he'd been in a daze, jolted to life at the touch of the man's mouth. "What the hell are you doing here, Martin? Where's Emilio?"

"Back in LA, I'd imagine." Martin turned himself in a circle, studying Mabel's living area. Though we'd eliminated the worst of the dust and the towering stacks of hodgepodge, Jasper didn't use this room, so we'd been storing bags of items to be donated in one corner, and the couch was covered in folded quilts. "Your mother mentioned you'd inherited the property here. How utterly... charming!"

Jasper planted his hands on his hips. "Why. Are. You. Here, Marty?"

Martin frowned. "You knew I was coming."

I frowned. "You knew he was coming?"

"No, I didn't know he was coming!" Jasper said furiously.

Martin turned his head as if realizing he wasn't alone with his ex-husband. "Oh, hello there." He took a step closer and then moved around me in a slow circle, studying me the way he had the living room. "You're a big one, aren't you? And that face. Stoic. Grumpy, almost. The shy, silent type. It's rare to find untapped talent in these places, but I could see you for someone like Balmain..."

Jasper moved quick as water, putting himself between me and Martin... which was probably a good idea since I had half a mind to teach him I was neither shy nor silent. "Leave him alone. Watt has no interest in modeling."

For a fraction of a second, Martin froze, and then he turned back on the charm. "*This* is Watt? Your Katy Perry teenage dream of young love?"

I blinked. This asshole had heard of me?

"My *friend* Watt," Jasper shot back.

I couldn't see Jasper's face since he was standing in front of me, but his spine was tight, muscles locked down. I wanted to reach out a hand to touch him, but for the first time since we'd rekindled our friendship, I wasn't sure it would be welcome.

"I can see it." Martin sized me up again with no hint of

jealousy—which was more than I could say for myself when I was assessing him—then gave me a knowing smile. "I guess I should thank you. If it wasn't for you, Jasper wouldn't have hooked up with me at all."

I glanced at Jasper, wondering what in the hell Martin meant by that, but I couldn't see his face. All I could see were the reddened tips of his ears as he stood protectively in front of me.

"You need to leave," he said, emotion grating his voice.

Martin exhaled, allowing his shoulders to drop. "Jazz, when you didn't reply to my texts... that was you upping the stakes. Practically an invitation for me to come and check up on you—"

"Jasper," Jasper snapped. "And no, it wasn't. Don't pretend you came here for me at all. You came because it affects your own bottom line somehow."

"You always could see right through me." Martin shook his head sadly. "I miss that about you, Jaz—Jasper."

Jasper crossed his arms in front of his chest but didn't say anything, so Martin continued. "The truth is, I have a lead on an incredible opportunity for you, and your mother and I thought you'd be perfect for it. They're looking for fresh faces, but I think I can convince them that you've been out of the game long enough for—"

"No."

I watched the back-and-forth like a very tense set of passes on the ice. Jasper's single word was like a powerful shot on goal.

"N-no?" Martin asked, as if he'd never heard the word out of Jasper's mouth before.

Jasper stood up straighter and uncrossed his arms. "I'm not interested in modeling anymore, nor am I interested in any lead you and my *mother* think might be best for me. If you had just taken the hint when I ignored your previous messages, you could have saved yourself—"

"Not sure you can afford to be so dismissive, Jazz," Martin said, losing all hint of attempted charm from earlier. "The job pays fifty grand."

I could hear the *clack* as Jasper's mouth shut. "Fifty..." He coughed lightly. "Fifty thousand? Let me guess... less a standard fifteen percent to you and Emilio for representing me? How cozy."

He shrugged and levered himself off the couch. "That's only fair since I'm bringing you in. But, hey. I'll give you some time to think about it. Your mother mentioned you only have a temporary gig here in town. This would be a fantastic way of getting momentum for your new business once you're back home."

I sucked in a breath. The reminder that Copper County wasn't *home* to Jasper sat like jagged glass in my gut. I'd gotten used to him here.

"You need to leave, Martin. Leave town and don't come back."

My chin dropped in a nod of agreement without thought. I didn't want this man anywhere near my town. Anywhere near my... Jasper.

Martin held up his hands in surrender. "I'll go. But I'll be at the Crabapple Bed and Breakfast for a few more days when you change your mind."

"I won't," Jasper assured him.

As Martin made his way to the door, he glanced back over his shoulder and met my eyes. "Great job at the game today, by the way. Really inspiring win, the two of you."

Jasper's jaw dropped open in surprise. "You were at the game?"

"Mmhmm. A lovely lady in town told me the hockey

rink was the best place to find you, so I stuck around all day. *All* day, Jazz. I would've talked to you this morning, but you were with your..." He paused for a perfectly timed second. "Friend." He smiled and clapped his hands together once, falling right back into the friendly, charming man who'd first entered the place. "Anyway! I'll let you get back to your evening. Jasper, I look forward to hearing from you soon. Take care."

He walked out the door and shut it behind him.

Jasper and I stood side by side, watching in silence through the glass in the front door as Martin's headlights came on, turned around, and headed back down the driveway.

He exhaled long and slow. "Watt," he began, voice dripping with apology.

"So," I said brightly. "That was your ex, huh? Quite a guy. I feel like I might have accidentally just been sold a used car."

He let out a sound that was halfway between a laugh and a sob. "Oh, God, don't joke."

"No, no, really. He's very... uh." I scratched my head. "Slick?"

Snorting, Jasper turned and leaned against the door. "That was awful. I swear he wasn't quite that bad before."

"Maybe he was abducted and this is his pod person replacement?" I suggested. Misery was pouring off Jasper, and I needed to make him smile. "Maybe he signed up for some kind of Freaky Friday personality swap with Charles Manson? What do you think, *Jazz*?"

Jasper's eyes popped open. "New rule: never, ever call me that."

I nodded instantly. "I won't. I'm sorry."

He threw himself against my chest with such force I

staggered backward and wrapped his arms around my waist. "Ugh. No, *I'm* sorry. I just can't believe I ever… What does it say about me that I was…"

"Wrong? And made a mistake? Baby…" The endearment slipped out unintentionally for the first time when we weren't… *benefitting*, but I didn't try to take it back.

It killed me to see him hurt.

I held him with one arm and cradled his head with the other. "Most of us are easily fooled by a wolf in sheep's clothing, and you were a kid when you met him. Derry's age."

"I wasn't a kid when we started our business. Or when I agreed to marry him."

"Well… okay." I stroked his hair. "But by then, you were too close to see him for what he was, and the two of you had a complicated business relationship all wrapped up in it."

The better question, I thought, was where the fuck had Jasper's mom been when he was a teenager? Had she really signed him up with this guy? Had she supported their romantic relationship? Had she encouraged their marriage? Had Jasper really not had a single friend who'd said, "*What are you thinking?*"

It hurt to realize that while Jasper had been meeting this asshole, I'd been here in Copper County, misunderstanding. So much for my philosophy that when you loved someone, you were there for them when they needed you and didn't wait for them to ask for help.

"You shouldn't be comforting *me*, Watt." Jasper pulled away, looking troubled. "Did you hear what he said at the end? He was at the rink *this morning*. He… he knows we're more than friends. What if he says something to someone?"

"Then he does." I pulled Jasper back against me because I was simply more comfortable that way.

Jasper huffed. "Then everyone in town could think we're in a relationship. I know you're not ready for that."

He was right, but not for the reasons he thought. "To be fair, we are in a relationship... of sorts," I said carefully. "And we can figure that out if it becomes necessary. My primary concern here is *you*."

"But—"

"Are you okay?" I demanded, tilting Jasper's head back so I could see his eyes. "I know that was rough. You're not tempted to take the job he offered, are you?"

"No! I mean..." Big blue eyes blinked. "No?"

"Fifty grand is a lot of money," I began diplomatically, "but—"

"*But* Martin is an asshole, and I don't want to leap at the poison carrot he dangled? Yeah. I know." He screwed up his mouth. "I can't lie, it *is* tempting. It's a lot of money. A midlevel model like me doesn't earn that much for a campaign. Not when they've been out of the game as long as I have, and don't have a social media following to speak of, and are thirty-seven. The money would help me get back in the game professionally and financially. And... I guess at least I'd know what I was getting myself into, right? Unlike when I was seventeen."

Jasper stepped back and glanced around the room abstractedly, much the way Martin had done. "But I... I think I want to do things differently this time. I don't know how or what, exactly, but it won't involve modeling, and it sure as fuck won't involve Martin, not even for $50K."

"Good," I croaked out.

I had a lot of other things to say about Martin, and California, and how much Jasper deserved out of life, but I could see from the way he held himself and the bleakness in his eyes that Jasper wasn't in a position to hear them... and anyway, what I really wanted was to make Jasper feel better.

To make him feel *the best*.

To let him know that Martin might only have seen Jasper's pretty face or his usefulness, but when *I* looked at him, I saw his strength, his resilience, his warmth, his honesty, and the soul-deep beauty of his heart. And I treasured them.

And wanted to protect them.

"Let's go to bed," I said instead. I wanted Jasper in my arms with nothing between us.

Jasper turned to me curiously, and though his eyes looked weary, he managed a smile. "Bed? Meaning..." He quirked an eyebrow. "You sure? I don't want you to feel like you have to—"

God, he was sweet. Reassuring me, even when I could see the toll Martin's visit had taken on him.

I stepped toward him and ran a thumb over his cheek. "You never make me feel like I *have* to do anything, Jasper. You make me feel like I want to do things. And like I *can*."

It was true and always had been, back to our very first days together—to our summer days on the dock and our silly dares.

I walked around the house, methodically locking the doors and shutting out the lights while Jasper watched in bemusement. I must have had a goofy grin on my face. Since Jasper's return, I'd become grateful for the nights Derry spent at his mom's. Never in all these years had I looked forward to the time to myself the way I did when I knew it meant I could share it with Jasper.

I took his hand and led him up the stairs to the little dormer bedroom that had always been his.

The space was small and utilitarian—a perfectly tidy

oasis in the midst of Mabel's collections. A wrought-iron double bed with a hand-pieced quilt sat in the middle of the room, flanked by a large chest of drawers on one side and a steamer trunk at the foot. Beside the bed, in front of the far window, was a spindle table that held a phone charger—Jasper's, probably, since it was the only modern thing in here—and a squat, stained glass lamp. Our old signal light.

I smiled when I saw that it was already switched on. "You wanna meet me down at the dock?"

Jasper's lips twitched. "I keep it on most of the time," he said, blushing slightly. "It's comforting. And I mean, it's not like we need a signal now that we have cell phones—"

I stopped his words with a quick kiss. "Get in bed," I said softly.

He screwed up his mouth at my phrasing and blinked at me tiredly. "Uh. Okay? I mean, did you want to talk first about..." He gestured between us. "Or... no, I guess we don't need to. Just remember, we can stop and switch gears anytime, Watt. I'm down for whatever with you." He stripped off his sweatshirt and pulled the quilt down the bed.

The sight of Jasper's naked torso made my mouth go dry and my brain turn to static, but I forced my cock not to react. I wanted to have sex with him. I very, very much did. But at the moment, I had a different goal in mind.

I stripped off my own shirt and jeans and came to stand before him in only my briefs. "You ready?"

"Yeah." He stifled a huge yawn behind his hand. "Sorry! Sorry. Early morning skate, plus roller-coaster afternoon, plus weird fucking evening. But... Jesus, you're hot, Watt Bartlett." Jasper gave me an intent look that made my cock twitch with hope despite my warning. "I'll rally. Fuck, I'm already rallying. Kiss me again."

A wave of tenderness swamped me.

Christ. Seriously, *so* fucking sweet.

"You're down for whatever, huh?" I gently pushed his hair back with my fingers.

"Hell yes." Jasper twined his arms around my neck. "With you? Totally. I'm vers, and I'd be more than happy to top if you wanted to try that at some point. And I meant what I said about no pressure. Whatever you want—"

I coasted my hands up and down his bare sides, and he broke off with a little shiver.

"You know what I *really* want?" I said roughly.

"Tell me." Jasper's voice was practically a purr as he pressed himself against me. "Don't hold back."

"I want to get in bed with you..."

"Liking it already," he sighed happily. "Things are so much better when you're not trying to stay vertical. And?"

"I want to pull the blankets up..."

"Oh...kay." Jasper blinked. "That's a little... restrictive, but I guess it's kinda chilly, so... sure. And then?"

"And then..." I bit my lip, trying to look seductive while also trying not to laugh. "This idea's a little wild, so I'm not sure if you'll be on board with it..."

His blue eyes widened. "Really?"

"Mmm." I leaned in closer to whisper against the shell of his ear. "I want to cuddle."

Jasper pulled his head back, gaze narrowed. "What?"

"I think you need rest more than you need sex right now. You're exhausted, Jasper."

"Am..." He yawned again, so hard his jaw cracked. "...not!"

I pulled him into my arms, rolled us onto the bed, then yanked up the quilt and arranged us on our sides with Jasper's back to my chest. "Remember how we used to lay out on the dock, playing truth or dare and telling secrets? Pretend this is that."

"Except then it was summer. And we were children. And sex wasn't an option," he grumbled, but I could tell by the way he stretched out and nestled back against me that the grumble was for show. "Whose secrets are we telling here? Because I'll warn you, I'm not feeling very share-y."

"That's okay. You're not going to last long. I'll bet you fall asleep before we get very far." I stroked a hand down his arm. "I'll go first. Ask me a truth or dare. I guarantee you a truth for this first round."

Jasper thought about it for a long moment. Because I knew him, I could read the tension in his body as he thought of a funny question, then quickly dismissed it in favor of something he actually wanted to know. I pressed a fond kiss to the top of his head.

"Okay, tell the truth: what was your first thought when you found out you and Rachel were having Derry?"

I sucked in a breath through my nose. "Ooof. Do you know, I don't think anyone's ever asked me that."

"You don't have to..."

"I know." I laced our fingers together and considered my answer. "I guess... I felt all the things you'd think I'd feel. Sad and angry at myself because a lot of things had to change. Nervous, once it really sank in, because everybody seemed to think Rachel and I were too young to handle it." I snorted, thinking about the look her parents had given us when we'd told them. "But that was later. At first, I thought... I thought it couldn't be right. It happened the very first time we had sex, so..."

Jasper turned to look at me. "You mean with each other? Or ever?"

"Both. I was a twenty-year-old virgin. I, ah..." I hesitated because it *still* wasn't easy to talk about, but I'd seen Jasper at his most vulnerable tonight, and it felt right to share this with him. "I haven't been truly attracted to a lot of people. Ever. Men or women. I could count them on one hand."

He digested this for a moment, then squirmed until he was flat on his back. "Why do you sound like you're confessing something?"

I watched my fingers trace a pattern over his chest. "Because it feels weird? I've never known anyone else who felt the way I do about sex. Because when it seems like the whole world is obsessed with sex and you're not, you feel out of step... or broken? Because I've been truly attracted to so few people in my life that I don't know how to classify myself—"

"And you hate not knowing things." Jasper raised himself up to press a kiss to my lips. "*That's* why you want a label. Because you want to make sure you're doing sexuality right, and you assume you're doing it wrong."

It sounded ridiculous, but also... "Yes." That was exactly it, though I would never have been able to articulate it that way.

Hearing him say it out loud simultaneously made sense of my feelings... and also put them in perspective.

"You're not broken, Watt. You're just a competitive bastard," he said confidently. "And you think too much."

Laughing, I dropped my forehead to his neck. He wasn't wrong about those things, either.

My whole life, I'd been praised for doing the right thing, for settling down and being responsible, for putting others first, for being grounded and safe. "Watt's so stable," people would say. And "Watt's so calm." And "Watt's a fucking tree."

And I was. I *was* those things. That part of me had

always existed, and I was proud of it. I *liked* that about myself.

I knew Jasper liked those things about me, too.

But Jasper saw that there was another part of me—an aspect of Watt Bartlett I didn't display openly and most people didn't get close enough to see.

That part of me had always enjoyed a challenge and thrived on honest competition. That part of me was an over-thinker, with my mental feet paddling furiously beneath the surface, assessing and mitigating risks, while I glided across a lake of calm. That part of me had taken the shock of becoming a parent (and our families' doubts) and thought, *watch me*. That part of me had taken the reins and turned my parents' hobby farm into a working orchard to provide a stable life for my son and had a thriving business to show for it.

I liked that part of me just as much, and it meant something that he saw it.

"Thank you," I said, "for understanding."

Jasper yawned. "Pfft. You're not that complicated." He trapped my hand against his chest with both of his. "Go ahead, then. Your turn."

"Okay, truth or dare?"

"Mmm. Truth, I guess?" He shut his eyes like he was bracing. "Hit me with it."

I briefly considered all the things I wanted to know about Jasper. Despite all the talking we'd done over the last couple of weeks, there was still a lifetime's worth of infor-mation I didn't have, and I was greedy for every drop.

I wanted to know more about his relationship with Martin and whether there had been good times mixed in with the bad. I wanted to hear about the most exciting places he'd traveled and the weirdest thing he'd ever worn for a photo shoot. I wanted to hear about the friends he'd made and why he didn't seem to be in touch with many of them anymore. I wanted to know about the most off-the-wall parties he'd ever been to—Pride parades in WeHo, music festivals, and galas—and whether he'd ever worn glitter in his pretty hair.

I wanted to know why he thought sex with me was the best. And what books he'd read (and which ones he'd absolutely hated because I knew those would be the ones he'd remember off the top of his head). I wanted to know when he'd started baking, and why he'd studied history, and how he'd gotten to be a spreadsheet genius. I wanted to know what he'd miss most about Copper County when he left and what he'd told Martin about me.

I wanted to know if he realized that he made me feel strong and capable—like his confidence that I could do or be anything made me so fucking comfortable being exactly who and what I was.

In the end, though, I didn't ask any of those things.

"Okay. Tell the truth," I said softly. "When you bought the Jaguar—*my* Jaguar—did you do it because you knew how much I wanted one?"

Jasper snorted without opening his eyes. "Are you asking if I paid twenty thousand dollars to buy a convertible ten years ago—a full *decade* after the last time we spoke— then spent thousands more fixing and restoring it, on the off chance that someday I'd drive it back through Copper County and score a point in an unspoken teenage dick-measuring contest against you? Don't be stupid, Watt..."

I supposed when he put it like that...

He rolled away from me again, burrowing back against my chest while keeping my hand trapped against his own, and sighed sleepily. "...of course I did."

JASPER

When I woke up, it was still pitch-dark outside the dormer window—the kind of darkness I'd only ever experienced in Copper County, where streetlights weren't a thing—and I was cozy and warm under the quilt in my room.

I closed my eyes and stretched... before suddenly remembering the night before. The hockey game. Martin. *Watt.*

My eyes popped open, and I rolled over.

Watt was lying on his side facing me, his stubbled cheek mashed against my pillow. My stomach flipped happily, then settled.

He'd stayed.

He'd taken care of me.

He'd *cuddled.*

The lamp on the table behind him still glowed, turning his dark hair into a bright corona and making the smooth skin of his broad shoulder glow gold. Relaxed in sleep, his face looked younger. Not quite like the teenager he'd been—baby Watt could never have managed that thick scruff—but more carefree than he was now.

I sighed softly and tucked one hand under my cheek, marinating in the safety and utter contentment I felt at knowing Watt was within touching distance.

Seeing Martin on my doorstep last night had been like the part of a scary movie where the bad guy pops back to life, and I was still shaken by it. It wasn't just knowing that he'd followed me to Copper County and shown up uninvited—although, yeah, that was definitely bothering me—it was that he'd assumed I'd jump at the lure he'd dangled. Had been so sure I'd take his offer, in fact, that he'd hopped on a plane and driven all the way out to my house when I hadn't answered his texts.

Had he not known me at all, despite being in my life for twenty years?

Or had he known me really well... as a money-motivated and success-focused person who'd agree to work with a snake like Martin if it would help me reach my goals?

Had I changed since moving to Copper County? And what would that mean for me if... er, *when*... I moved back?

I didn't want to think about it.

Instead, I thought about how Watt had stood beside me in silent support while Martin was here, giving me the courage to stand taller.

Then he'd comforted and cared for me in the exact perfect way, not forcing me to talk but teasing me and protecting me.

He'd been my rock.

And I couldn't help wondering what my life would have been like if I'd had him in it all along.

Gently, gently so as to not wake him, I glided a fingertip up the sharp curve of his jawline and over his scruff. Even in sleep, he looked strong and determined. I watched my fingers track higher, over his smooth forehead, then down the perfect jut of his nose. With the barest pressure, I traced the outline of his perfect Cupid's bow and his full lower lip, which opened slightly—

"Stop being creepy." Watt's voice was thick with sleep and rough as sandpaper.

"Stop being gorgeous," I shot back.

Skeptical hazel eyes blinked open. "I'm definitely not the gorgeous one in this bed."

My heart thumped unsteadily. He was wrong. I wouldn't deny that I was handsome—I'd been paid to be, after all—but Watt was truly beautiful inside and out. His beauty was weathered like the rugged cliffs of Jane's Peak, sturdy and resilient like the bark of a sugar maple. The sort of beauty that sometimes went unnoticed because it was simple and rooted in the landscape of everything familiar.

Scooting closer, I replaced my fingertips with my mouth, kissing him more fully awake. "You stayed last night."

Beneath the blanket, his hand wrapped around my back. "We were in the middle of a game. Leaving would have meant forfeiting."

I laughed softly. "That's why, huh?"

Watt's eyes creased with a teasing grin. "I also heard that you were *down for whatever*—"

My heart skipped a beat, and I moved a hand to his chest. "With you," I finished just as I had the night before. I wasn't sure he understood the distinction... or if I fully understood it myself. "Yeah. Definitely."

His grin was slow, and even though we were joking like we always did, there was something deeper behind it. Something that made my chest tighten and my cock fill. "Careful." His voice went lower. Deeper. "*Whatever* could mean a lot of things."

"I can handle anything you dish out." I raised an eyebrow, trying to hold on to the teasing edge of our conversation. "Can *you*, though? You seemed to have concerns yesterday, and that's okay..."

His eyes darkened, and his hand drifted down to rest below my hip, dragging the quilt with him. The air between us shifted subtly—the teasing still there but muted by something hotter and more intense. His thumb stroked along the waistband of my pajama pants, then dipped just beneath the fabric.

My breath hitched.

"I want to do this," he said. "I just don't wanna fuck it up."

I couldn't help the chuckle that slipped out. Watt really had no idea how much I wanted him. How badly he turned me on. "You can't fuck it up. It'll be awesome because it's us, and we're... friends. Bet you."

Watt's gaze softened, and he let out a breath. "You make it feel easy."

"I was kinda hoping I'd make it feel... *Oh*." I moved my hand under the sheet to cup his length and found that his shaft was already tenting his briefs.

Watt snorted. "You definitely make it hard, too." Kicking off the covers, he moved his hand down to cup my ass and pull me against him for a long, thorough kiss.

Kissing Watt was familiar ground by now, though it never got old. The familiarity of his taste and the feel of his hands on my body made my pulse pound. In no time at all, I was painfully hard and grinding against him, seeking his friction and hardness.

"Tell me how this works," he demanded breathlessly,

breaking our kiss. Before I could say anything, he added, "And don't be cute. That was a genuine question."

I was so worked up I didn't have the brainpower to tease him, though I loved that he'd thought I would.

"Lube," I said. I pushed him flat on his back and crawled over him to rifle through the drawer in the bedside table... which Watt took as an opportunity to yank my flannel pants down so he could knead and stroke my ass.

"So fucking perfect," he growled.

Nearly trembling with desire, I tossed the lube on the bed and stood to shuck my pants the rest of the way off. As he watched me, Watt's large hand stole under his own waistband, and he groaned as he gave himself relief.

Saliva pooled in my mouth. Before I knew it, I was on the bed between Watt's legs, sucking his cock. "Jasper," he hissed. "*Fuck.*"

I fucking loved the sounds he made when I sucked him. Every time, he sounded surprised and delighted and desperate, like he'd forgotten how good it would feel. I remembered what he'd said last night about not wanting many people, and it was a hell of a drug, knowing *I* was the one who got to be in this bed with him, that *I* was the lucky bastard who got to reduce this strong man to a writhing mass of groans and shudders.

It made me want to give him more, and more, and more pleasure—so much that he forgot to be surprised and learned to expect it as his due.

I pulled off and moved lower, drawing his balls into my mouth one at a time and swirling my tongue around them. The musky scent of him had me rocking against the mattress.

I simply couldn't get enough of this man. I wanted to do everything to him at once. To take him down my throat, to turn him over and stroke his hole with my tongue until he lost his mind, to kiss him and swallow down all his hot noises.

Watt's fingers threaded through my hair and tugged, and I let him draw me up to kiss him again. "Let me get you ready."

Yes. I wanted that. I'd been wanting it since the first day, if I was being honest.

I hadn't been lying yesterday when I'd told Watt that the particular variety of sex wasn't what made the experience meaningful; it was the person you were with. I believed that wholeheartedly.

What I *hadn't* said was that sex with Watt—sex of any variety—was a whole separate experience for me than sex with anyone else. I'd tried just about everything over the years, and it had all been excellent. I didn't know why it was different with Watt... only that it was.

"Turn around," he murmured, reaching for the lube.

I complied, crawling onto my hands and knees beside him, but he seemed to hesitate. Probably overthinking again.

"If you want," I croaked out, "I can stretch myself this first time, and you can watch."

"And deprive me of the enjoyment? Don't think so."

"You seemed hesitant," I said with a grin, enjoying his attempt at bravado to hide his nerves.

"I'm just... considering."

"Uh. Okay. Good. Great." Meanwhile, I was dying. My cock was leaking, practically begging for relief. "But it'd be faster if I—*ohmotherfucker!*"

Watt had grabbed one asscheek in his capable, *capable* hand and, with the other, squirted a generous stream of cool lube down my crack.

"Watt," I said helplessly, shifting my knees wider.

He trailed one blunt finger through the slickness and tentatively slid the tip back and forth over my hole.

All the breath in my lungs exited in a rush. *Just from one finger touch.*

I was so fucking into it, it took me a second to realize that he hadn't gone any further, and when I turned my head, I found that he was staring at me with his brow furrowed.

"Watt?" I demanded. "You okay?" *Please don't change your mind. Please.*

He huffed. "I am *so* good, Jasper." When his eyes met mine, they were hazed with want, nearly drunk with it. And with our eyes still locked, he sank one lubed finger inside me.

I clutched at the sheets when his finger began to move but couldn't help rocking back against him.

The small movement made him groan and fist his cock with his other hand.

"More," I panted.

He poured out more lube before sinking another finger inside to join the first. The fingers of his free hand splayed against my back as if holding me in place while his dick rode against my hip like he needed relief.

The burn and stretch were real. Watt wasn't a small person, and his fingers were proportional to the rest of him. And it had been a long while since I'd bottomed. But the man moved his fingers with purpose, like he knew what he was doing—or had done a real quick google after I fell asleep—and before long, he slid his fingers over my prostate.

I sucked in a breath so fast I nearly choked. "*Fuck. Watt. Yes.*"

"Told you I'd be good at this," he teased.

"I never doubted it," I said fervently. Followed quickly

by "*Christ*" as he glided over the same spot again. I reached down to give my poor dick a bit of attention. "Oh, shit. You're *so* good at this."

I was rocking back and forth, riding his fingers, but it wasn't enough. "Watt..."

"Jesus Christ, I want you," he whispered.

I was pretty sure that was supposed to be my line.

I was feeling genuinely frantic as I pushed him back onto the bed and moved to straddle him, like I might die if I didn't get him inside me. I grabbed the lube from where he'd thrown it on the bed and poured some down his length, loving the way he hissed and threw his head back into the pillows at the sensation.

I leaned forward to give him a quick kiss because his mouth was my favorite thing ever, and I couldn't resist tangling my tongue with his.

Then, I slid my hand down to the base of his cock, holding it in place so I could sink down on it.

"Jasper." Watt groaned my name like it was a please and a thank-you all at once, and I got it. I did. Because I felt the same way.

Knowing it was Watt... *my* Watt... made all the sensations explode exponentially. My heart was in my throat, my stomach in my chest, and Watt's fat cock deep in my gut.

The sound of his hot breaths as I felt them against my ear. The taste of his salty precum still on my tongue. The rough feel of his body hair against the tender skin of my ass. Everything about the situation revved me up until I was breathless with it.

Being with him like this was incomparable to any experience I'd had before with anyone else. It was everything I'd never even imagined. The fact it was with Watt made sense in a way I couldn't describe.

"You okay, sweetheart?" he murmured next to my ear.

"Watt," I breathed, overwhelmed with emotion.

"I know." His deep voice vibrated through me as I turned to kiss him, stubble scraping across stubble as he continued to push in and out of me. "You feel so fucking good, Jasper. So damned good."

I moved my hand between us to grasp my cock. As soon as he realized what I was doing, Watt pulled back enough to watch me stroke myself. His eyes moved between my cock and my hole as if mesmerized.

"You're so beautiful like this," he said in a ragged voice. "So fucking hot taking me. I won't last. Need you to come. Jasper."

My dick didn't need any encouragement. My balls were already drawn up tight, and the sight of him turned on like this was doing a number on my self-control.

The orgasm hit as I noticed his stomach contract with another thrust. Pearly white fluid landed in the hair of his lower belly as I shot over and over again, crying out his name or a strangled version of it anyway.

"Oh fuck," Watt groaned before shoving himself deep inside me and leaning in to kiss me hungrily as he groaned into my mouth and shuddered.

I ran my hands up and down his broad back and tried to memorize what it felt like to be completely owned by Watt Bartlett.

This was no longer in the same stratosphere as friends with benefits. Our connection was deep and true, unlike anything I'd ever considered with anyone other than Watt.

After we got cleaned up and returned to bed, we shared tender touches without saying much of anything. Words seemed unnecessary, and it turned out to still be the middle of the night.

We settled back into bed, wrapped up in each other to seek a few more hours' sleep, and as Watt's breathing began to slow, I heard him murmur, "My Jasper. *Mine.*"

I drifted off with a stupid grin on my face.

And the knowledge that, for the first time in my life, someone cared enough about me to want to stake a claim.

CHAPTER FIFTEEN

AFTER THAT PIVOTAL DAY, I put Martin's visit into a mental box and closed the lid. I definitely wasn't going to take his offer, so it wasn't worth thinking about.

Besides, I had Watt to think about, as well as my temporary but glorious life in Copper County to enjoy.

As the days flew by and cold, drenching rains came to strip the leaves from the trees and turn them into a brightly colored carpet lining the roads around Copper Lake, I fell into a joyful and unexpectedly busy routine.

I went to school every morning, and practice every evening, and had Watt to fill my nights and weekends.

In between getting my house organized and watching four seasons of *John Ruffian*, Watt finally allowed me to take a look at the spreadsheets he'd been keeping (and breaking) for the orchard. I was not only able to get his current inventory tracking numbers updated, but I also set him up with brand-new harvest tracking and labor management spreadsheets and showed him how to use them.

He took to my lessons about as well as I took to ice-skating—which was to say low-key not-well—but I found his frowny concentration face and muttering at the keyboard about as adorable as he found my flailing on the ice—which was to say *highly* adorable—which made doing admin a little bit like foreplay.

And I had the best sex of my life.

The best.

Bar. None.

Midterm exams passed (and so did all my students).

The Fighting Marmots beat Fairport by a wide margin. The Utica scout Kayla predicted hadn't come, so Watt had reached out to their coaches to set up a visit, and he (and Derry) seemed hopeful.

Watt casually mentioned us spending Thanksgiving together since Derry would be at his mom's and Watt's sister, Iris, and her family weren't coming for the holiday this year.

I got invited to the Bartletts' for Thursday Pasta Night... and after Derry sent a video of me and Watt bantering over garlic bread to the team chat, he and Zach had come up with the idea for a Co-Coach Cookoff at Watt's place last Sunday, which the whole team and a few of our Copper County friends, including Watt's buddies Oliver, Chris, and Brewer had attended.

I'd won, which wasn't a surprise. As I'd told the crowd in my humble victory speech, I was basically a culinary Energizer battery—when it came to food, I just kept going and going—so Watt really needed to stop betting against me. For some reason, this speech had Oliver rolling on the floor with laughter, but Watt had distracted me with a blowjob that night when I'd asked him to explain.

Then, three days later, my happy bubble popped... in the most predictable and expected way.

I woke up on Wednesday—the first day of Thanksgiving

break—to a message from Martin, which was never the best way to start a day.

> **MARTIN**
>
> Alright, sweetness. I've given you time, and now I'm calling your bluff. Call me today, or I'm going in a totally different direction with this campaign. And it will definitely be your loss.

I ignored it, obviously, and the day improved after that.

Later in the morning, Lucas sent a message to a group chat he'd called "The Uncles" saying that Tam had gone into labor and baby Tierney had arrived at 12:23 a.m.

The attached video showed Tam looking exhausted but enraptured and the baby looking... well, if I was being honest, Tierney looked like a scrunched-up, pissed-off sweet potato with really good hair, but I wasn't judging. Girlfriend had been fighting a tough battle last night. I'd probably squall, too.

> Congratulations, Monroe Fam! <heart-eye emoji>
>
> **DELANEY**
>
> She's so cute! Congrats, Tam and Lucas!
>
> **UNKNOWN NUMBER 1**
>
> Seriously cute. Just like her Uncle Wells.
>
> **UNKNOWN NUMBER 2**
>
> Totally! So cute! Just like her Uncle LAW!
>
> Delaney, are babies supposed to look like that? I don't wanna worry Tam, but she's VERY wrinkly. Have you seen Benjamin Button?

TAM

Lawson, you asshole!! My baby is not Benjamin Button!!

DELANEY

Lawson, you're still messaging the group chat, dumbass.

WELLS

Ignore him, Tam. He's been hit by too many pucks. Tell Tierney her Uncle Wells, Aunt Heather, and her cousins can't wait to meet her. I'll bring her a jersey with my number on it at Christmas.

LAWSON

Shit!! My bad. We played last night and I got to Copper County really late. I'm still half asleep. And back off, Wells. You have your own kids to wear your jerseys. Tierney's mine.

I snickered.

So, Delaney, who won your family betting pool?

DELANEY

Ugh. Lawson did. Lawson and Wells, meet Jasper. He's an unofficial Monroe now. Tam and I have adopted him.

WELLS

Welcome, Jasper!

LAWSON

Oh! The hockey padawan Tam's been Yoda-ing. Excellent! Welcome to the fam. Wanna drive your local bros to the bar for drinks later? My treat. Gotta celebrate little Benjamin's arrival.

TAM

I swear to god, Lawson.

I laughed out loud. Tam and Delaney's brother was hilarious, and I thought I might really enjoy being adopted.

I floated around most of the day working on an improved pumpkin pie recipe for Thanksgiving dessert, tweaking some accounting sheets I'd been playing around with for the orchard, and texting with Watt, who was busy working with his friend Constantine over in O'Leary to build a trampoline for Con's kids.

WATT

Going out with Delaney, huh? Does he
know you and I are FWB?

Of course not! You weren't ready and I
respect that.

WATT

He needs to know you're not on the
market.

I felt nerves jangle in my stomach.

I'm not?

WATT

And that if he wants to flirt with someone,
to look Ollie up.

I poked my tongue into my cheek, grinning at my phone like an idiot. I'd always thought jealousy was wildly imma-ture, but I found I liked it a lot... with Watt.

> What about Lawson? You know, the hot
> hockey player? He's going to be there.
> We're probs gonna have an intimate chat
> about stick handling and our favorite...
> pucks.

It took Watt a long time to answer, but when he did, it was well worth the wait.

WATT

> Compare notes all you like. But Jasper...
> you'd better let them know that when you
> get home tonight, the only one handling
> your stick will be me.

"Game on, Watt Bartlett," I whispered to my empty house, grinning so much it made my cheeks ache. "Game on."

———

I REALIZED PRETTY QUICKLY after picking up Delaney and Lawson that I'd made a slight miscalculation. There would be no intimate chats about anything because the O'Leary Bar and Grill was packed to the rafters with O'Learians and Coppertians enjoying pre-Thanksgiving revelry.

Fortunately, we got there just before the rush and managed to get a booth near the back of the bar. Lawson immediately sprawled across most of one seat, his baseball hat pulled down low on his handsome face, while I slid into the other.

It surprised me when Delaney crammed himself in next to Lawson, but I understood the reason quickly enough.

Everyone in town seemed to have heard about Tam's baby, and every one of them decided to stop by our table with a congratulatory round of drinks for Lawson and Delaney while I stuck to sparkling apple cider mocktails.

Most folks were polite and left after saying hello, but quite a few recognized Lawson and wanted to hear *allllll* about last season's injury. A few more wanted autographs or —in a couple of cases—to give him their phone numbers. The longer these conversations went on, the more forced Lawson's smile became and the faster his leg jiggled under the table.

Whenever this happened, Delaney would straighten in his seat, becoming a physical and conversational brick wall in front of his much larger brother until the person sighed and walked away.

It was the kind of brotherly thoughtfulness that made me wish I had a sibling.

A few drinks in, Lawson's discomfort faded. By the time we'd been in the bar an hour, Lawson's presence had become old news, and Lawson himself was red-cheeked and adorably tipsy.

Meanwhile, Delaney had scowled harder with every neighborly visitor who stopped by.

"This town is weird," he pronounced. "No human beings are this friendly. I'm not sure what kind of cult they're peddling, but I refuse to join."

I laughed. "You're ridiculous. They're *kind*. And... yeah, okay, a little up in your business, but it's sweet. You're going to be one of them soon, remember?" I wiggled my eyebrows. "How's the house thing coming, by the by?"

Delaney raised an eyebrow. "We don't talk about the house, Jasper. Besides, I'm only establishing a home base here because I love Tam, and I like Lucas, and I want to be close to Tierney—"

"And because of what happened with that guy in Providence," Lawson piped up helpfully.

Delaney whacked his arm. "We don't talk about him, either. The point is, I'm not drinking the Kool-Aid. I might be *living* in Copper County, but I'm not becoming a Copper-person."

"The word is Coppertian," I informed him. "And I don't see what's wrong with being one. You seemed to know and like everyone at the Hive the other night. And you like Theo and Bennett—" I pointed at the couple who was sitting at the bar, chatting with Jamie and Parker, the O'Learians who owned the place. "You said it was really generous of Bennett to open up the Observatory House to kids for science field trips."

Delaney sipped his martini. "It is," he muttered.

"And that older guy over there? Hen Lattimer from the hardware store?" I gestured with my drink—the one Parker had gifted me when he'd heard I was the designated driver tonight. "He's showing that other couple pictures of his great-grand-dogs in their Halloween costumes. That's adorable. Admit it."

"Adorably *weird*," Delaney grumbled.

"And that lady over there in the pink? That's Kayla Milley. She's... well, I wouldn't say we're friends..."

"More like frenemies," Delaney declared. "Isn't she the one who tried to convince you that you were a shitty hockey coach?" He downed half his drink. "This ought to be good. How's *she* adorable or weird or nice?"

"Well... she's organizing this fun-run fundraiser thing Friday to save the kids' summer hockey camp. And she has great taste in men. And she's got genuine enthusiasm and... and determination. I appreciate that." I watched Kayla across the room as she and a couple of other parents demonstrated the Marmot Cheer for the crowd. "Also, she made up a whole cheer routine for our hockey team that really gets the crowd on their feet."

Lawson grinned. "Aw. That's kind of cute."

"It is. You know it's a nice town when even your frenemy has redeeming qualities," I informed Delaney.

"I suppose," he grudgingly admitted.

"And... oh, you know Brew Barnum, the builder guy, right?" I pointed to the man sitting at a table with Brian and Dare Turner. "I met him the other day, and he seemed lovely. Isn't he helping you fix up your new, uh... thing we're not supposed to talk about?"

Brew had told me at the cookoff that he'd be happy to give me an estimate to repair my saggy front porch steps, too. I'd told him there was no rush, though, since I wouldn't be listing the house for a while yet.

"Yes," Delaney bit out. "I know Mr. Barnum."

Lawson and I exchanged a look. His eyes widened comically, and he mouthed, *"Mr. Barnum,"* before hiding his smile behind his hand.

"And that's one of my coworkers." I exchanged a friendly wave with Arlene across the crowded room. She was sitting in a booth with Ash James, Reed Sunday, and the local librarian. "She's starting free dance lessons in February to make sure people don't feel too cooped up during the winter. I told her I'd be there to get my salsa on." I pressed one bent arm to my stomach and lifted the other like I was holding an invisible partner while swaying to an imaginary beat.

"There's more to do here than I expected," Delaney allowed. "The Hive is really cool. And this bar has great cocktails, but it's..." He wrinkled his nose at the television set, where a bunch of commentators appeared to be discussing college football. "Not entirely my scene."

"It's too low-brow for Delaney. He likes dark jazz clubs where people wail heartfelt songs about single-use plastics." Lawson chuckled at his own joke.

Delaney blushed. "That was *one* time. And anyway..." He turned back to me. "Easy for you to say it's great to be a Coppertian when you're a short-timer, Jasper."

I blinked. "Huh?"

"A short-timer. Temporary. A... what do they call it around here? A Copper-plate? You're moving back to LA," Delaney explained when I only stared at him. "You kept talking about it the other night. You insisted that Los Angeles was where you belonged and that you had a plan to start a modeling agency as soon as Tam's maternity leave was over. You said it nearly as often as you talked about your friend Watt."

"Ah, dude! An Angeleno." Lawson held his fist above the table for a bump. "I've played there. Great weather. Shit traffic."

"I... I guess." I bumped his fist half-heartedly.

"Countdown's started now, huh?" Lawson covered his mouth to hide a burp. "Tamsquatch has popped her bambino, so you'll be leaving in... what, a couple months?"

Delaney nodded. "Twelve weeks. Tam was super clear. She was bored out of her skull on bed rest and can't wait to get back."

Twelve weeks.

My mouth opened, but I couldn't make it form words.

Because, yes, *obviously*, I was heading back to LA. I had a whole plan... or, like, seventy-five percent of a plan.

Definitely at least fifty percent, with an outline for the rest.

But for some reason, the thought of leaving made me feel vaguely nauseous.

Twelve weeks.

When I'd first come back, I'd told myself to focus on the immediate challenges: sorting through the twin messes of Mabel's treasures and my friendship with Watt, deciding which pieces of each to keep and which to let go. Learning to teach and to coach and to skate. Refining my business plan and networking with people in LA had felt way less urgent. There'd been plenty of time.

Twelve weeks.

At some point, I'd gotten comfortable. I'd made a routine and reveled in it. I'd made a friendship with benefits and reveled in *that*. I'd started calling Mabel's place *my* house.

But the reminder that Tam would be coming back to her job soon—in *twelve fucking weeks*—had started a timer in my brain, and I could practically hear the seconds ticking away.

How many more days could I justify spending here? Would I be around for the Marmots' hockey playoffs? Would I get to take those salsa lessons? How many more nights would I get to spend watching *John Ruffian* with Watt's strong arms around me? How many more times would I have him in my bed? Who would make him laugh and stop taking life so seriously when I was gone?

And why was I even thinking of this like an ending when it was supposed to be a beginning?

"Whoa. Y'okay, man?" Lawson demanded, peering over the table at me. "You look like you got bodychecked."

"Huh? N-no." I shook my head. "I'm fine. I'm... I'm great."

"Uh-oh." Delaney's eyes narrowed. "You did it, didn't you? You drank the Copper County Kool-Aid."

"Me? Pfft. No! No way. I just had a moment of... of *pause*. That's all." I took one shallow breath and then another.

I really wished Watt was here to ground me.

Delaney rolled his eyes. "My keen investigative reporting senses suggest that's not all." His eyes flicked down to my hand. "You're rubbing at your chest." He leaned closer. "And you're literally sweating."

"It's warm in here!" I lied. "That's all. I *am* going back to LA. I... I definitely am." Hearing myself say the words out loud should have helped them feel true, but it didn't. "My career is there. M-my life is there. I... I'd regret it if I didn't go."

Lawson cocked his head. With the insightfulness of the inebriated, he asked, "Would you regret it... if you left?"

I stared at him in panic.

"Ooooh." Delaney sat back in the booth and regarded me with pursed lips. He elbowed his brother. "You know what he needs, Law?"

Lawson frowned, then brightened. "Ohhhh. Yup. Yuuuup. Our new bro needs a yaysnnays."

"I'll get the supplies," Delaney said. "Be back."

"A what?" I demanded, but Delaney had already pushed himself out of the booth and headed for the bar. "He'd better not be going to get me alcohol," I warned.

Though... shit, I might need some.

"I really do have to go back to LA," I babbled. "I mean... I won't have a job once Tam's back. And last time I checked, there weren't a lot of other job openings here that I'm quali-fied for."

"Uh-huh." Lawson had taken out his phone the second Delaney left the table and didn't look up from whatever he was scrolling.

"And I've been running a modeling agency behind the scenes for years." I blurted out a brief recap of my career history, ending with Martin's betrayal and how it had essen-tially left me penniless before I came back to Copper County. "That's my career."

"Yup." Lawson didn't appear to have heard a word I said. He had his tongue stuck between his teeth while he messaged someone.

Delaney returned carrying a stack of napkins and caught sight of Lawson's phone screen from behind as he slid into the booth.

"Lawson Harvie Monroe! You stop that right now!" he gasped. "You're not allowed to use Grindr, especially not while drinking!"

Lawson pressed his phone to his chest and blinked drunkenly around the bar. "I'm not? Who says? I'm a grown man! Aren't I?" he added uncertainly.

"No, you're a very large toddler. And *Tam* says." Delaney grabbed Lawson's phone, clicked it off, and set it on the table. "She gave me a whole speech about how this town is her home, and she'd really rather not have her broth-er's one-night stands knocking on her door, and blah blah. She said she'll consider removing the restriction once I offi-cially own property here."

Lawson sulked back into his seat. "She didn't give *me* the speech."

"Because she was busy pushing a nineteen-inch human

out of her body when you arrived. But if she gave it to me, you know she would've given it to you... *Player*."

Law stuck out his tongue. "*Misfit*," he shot back, repeating a word I'd heard Delaney's siblings used to tease their non-sporty brother.

Delaney ignored him. "Anyway, we have a higher calling than getting our dicks sucked right now," he said loftily. "We're helping Jasper."

He set the stack of napkins in the center of the table.

"I, uh... I don't know if that's a higher calling, per se." I eyed the napkins dubiously. "And I don't think napkin origami—or whatever a yay-yay is—is necessary. I know what I need to do—"

Lawson sat up, his good humor immediately restored. "But you don't *need-dah* do *anything*. That's the wrong way to look at life, Jasper."

Delaney nodded. "Our mom was big into self-determination. So when we'd say, '*But I* need *to drink and do drugs, or I'll be a loser*,' or whatever, she wouldn't lecture us about the evils of peer pressure. She'd say, '*Tell me more about why you* need *to do that. Let's think this through.*'"

"She had us make a pros and cons list. A 'Yays and Nays.'" Lawson grinned. "Or as Delaney put it when he was little, yaysnnays. How old were you when you figured out that wasn't an actual word? Twenty-five?"

Delaney ground his teeth together. "The point is, it's a great way of making decisions."

He took two pens out of his pocket and uncapped them, then grabbed a couple of napkins from the stack. Across the top of one, he wrote, **YAY FOR LA!** before passing the napkin and the pen to Lawson.

On the second, he wrote, **YAY FOR COPPER COUNTY!**

He looked up at me expectantly. "Whatcha got for us?"

"Well, uh… I've been planning to move back all along." I nodded for Lawson to write that down on the LA list, but he didn't.

Lawson wrinkled his nose. "Your top reason to move back to LA is 'I planned to'?"

"No!" I frowned. "Not the *top* reason. But I mean, it's *a* reason. You're supposed to have goals and plans and then to achieve them. If you don't achieve your goals, you've failed."

"You can, like, *change* the goal," Lawson began.

Delaney nudged him. "That's rich, coming from you, Mr. Give Me Hockey or Give Me Death. Besides, you're not supposed to give your opinion. Write."

"M'kay." Lawson sighed and scratched **Has cunning plan** under LA. "What else?"

I shrugged, not really sure what to say. There were a lot of things I liked about LA. Was I supposed to list them all? I traced the wood grain of the tabletop and considered.

"Well, there's this BBQ place in Koreatown that makes killer short ribs and a place in Brentwood with great matcha scones. Watt says my version's really good, but it's not as good as theirs." I glanced up uncertainly. "Is this the kind of thing you mean?"

"Sure." Lawson obediently wrote **Unique food.**

Delaney scratched something down on his list also, but he covered his napkin with his hand so I couldn't see.

"Oh! And there's this beach," I offered, "called Malibu Lagoon. I'd go there sometimes to think because it reminded me of Copper Lake. I mean, the lagoon doesn't have a dock, and it's not as secluded, and there are seagulls instead of loons, but I was telling Watt the other morning that if you squint hard, it's close enough. And he said that if *he* squinted hard, I look like Shaggy from *Scooby-Doo*, and then I tickled him—which, yes, was a rule violation, but honestly, he deserved it."

I noticed Delaney and Lawson exchanging a glance. "What?"

"Uh. I'm just not sure if that's for *my* list or his." Lawson nodded at Delaney.

The poor guy had to be even drunker than he looked. "Yours," I said. *Obviously.*

"Right." Lawson scribbled **Beach like Copper Lake.**

"What about some other things?" Delaney prompted. "Like... what are the best things about your job?"

"That's easy." I waved a hand. "I love fostering relationships with people and helping them reach their potential."

I thought of the ways I'd helped the models I'd worked with—making sure their calendars were updated and that they got paid, that their contracts were fair and that they understood them, that their taxes were done and that their social media stats were strong.

"I might not have been someone they thought of as their closest friend or mentor—" That had been Martin, with his charming smile and his marketing contacts. "—but I made a difference in their futures. I'd been just like them once, and I knew that unscrupulous people like to take advantage of the naive and uneducated. I gave them information so they could feel empowered. And I was good at it," I added. I waved a hand at Lawson. "Write down *competent.*"

Lawson nudged Delaney with one meaty elbow. "He's talking to you, D. Write it down."

Delaney nodded. "I'm writing. **Teaching, helping, empowering. Purpose and meaning. Competent.** Got it." He flashed me a grin. "And there you were the other night, telling me that those who study history are doomed to repeat it... but not when they have you as a teacher, huh?"

"Wait, no." I looked back and forth between them, wondering if *I* was the drunk one. "I was talking about my actual career. As a modeling agent. Being a teacher is totally different. I mean..." I frowned as I tried to think of the reasons *why* it was different. I hadn't thought the Venn diagram of teacher and modeling agent would have much overlap, but it turned out they did.

"Why don't you talk about your friends," Delaney suggested. "Who are you excited to see? Who's been blowing up your phone like, '*Yeah, man, I can't wait for you to get back so we can... insert thing here.*' Who are your business associates, even? Do *not* say Martin." To Lawson, he added, "Martin is his evil ex who cheated him out of their company and left him broke—"

"Yeah, Jasper told me all about it when you were..." Lawson waved a hand at the bar. "Doing the napkins."

When he saw me gaping at him, Lawson looked offended. "What? I was listening! I'm not just hot abs and a... a killer slapshot, Jasper. I've got a brain. I've got *feelings*." The word was punctuated by a killer pout.

"No, I know, of course you do. I'm sorry. I—" I began.

But Lawson burst into raucous laughter. "Nah, dude, I'm messing with you. I'm all abs and slapshot. Zero smarticle particles." He tapped his temple a little too hard. "At least I've never gotten romantically involved with my agent, though."

"Only because you don't get 'romantically' involved with anyone," Delaney muttered.

I winced. "Look, I recognize *now* that it seems a... a little strange, but at the time, it felt normal. Martin had been in my life for a long time. He was more likely to… to be a good partner to me than some random guy, right?"

"I don't know about that. I *do* know it's easy to be manipulated when someone gets their hooks in you young," Delaney said flatly.

Lawson nodded vehemently.

I stared at them for a long moment. Watt had said something similar, but I'd dismissed it. Obviously Watt was on my side because he was always on my side, even when he'd been pissed at me. Hearing the same thing from people I'd only met recently hit differently.

"Martin came to see me last week," I confessed. "He offered me a job, but I told him no." I filled them in on Martin's indecent proposal.

"Hold up. Fifty thousand?" Lawson repeated. "Now, *that* is a reason, broseph, especially under the circumstances. If you're goin' back anyway, why wouldn't you take that job, too?" On the top of the LA list, he wrote ***Fifty thousand dollars is A LOT of money.***

Then he underlined it five times. And circled it.

Delaney scowled. "Fifty thousand is peanuts if it means selling your soul and working with your asshole ex," he said passionately.

Lawson winced. "Thought we weren't giving opinions, D."

Delaney darted a guilty look at me, and his shoulders slumped. "Fine. Continue. Other, non-Martin people you're dying to see?"

"Dying? No," I said slowly. "Most of our friends were industry friends, and Martin got custody of them in the divorce. My mom is there. We're not close, but she's a patron of a lot of fashion designers, and she'd like showing me off and helping me build a new wardrobe."

"That could be good." Lawson wrote **Mom. Nice clothes.**

I made a face. I wouldn't say *nice*. I was gonna need a moment of silence for my comfy coaching tights and teacher khakis.

I took a sip of my drink and thought harder. "I also have a photographer friend, Javier. He's selling his downtown loft, and he might offer me a good deal. The space could double as a living and office situation."

"Fun." Lawson wrote **Fancy apartment (Javier).**

"Yeah. I'll just, um, have to sell my house here… Mabel's house… to afford it," I said quietly.

I stubbornly ignored the voice in my head telling me that even then, I'd have to take out a mortgage. That this hadn't actually been a plan; it had been a dream. One that didn't even feel like mine anymore.

"If there's one thing *I* know after being traded a bunch…" Lawson pressed a hand to his chest with slightly inebriated sincerity. "…it's that you can make friends anywhere if you're a fun guy and you… you have fun. As long as no one's asking you intrusive questions about your freaking injuries, dude." He added that last part into his glass as he took another slug of beer.

I nodded. "Well, yeah. I mean, I've already made a bunch of good friends just since I've been back here. Tam, and you guys, and Arlene, and Chris at the cheese shop, who gave me a discount because I mentioned that I liked the *John Ruffian* sticker on his laptop. Besides, I already have a *best* friend, and Watt's still going to be in my life, no question."

"Sure," Lawson agreed with a nod.

"I mean, it won't be the same," I hurried to add. "Like, he won't be able to teach me to ice-skate from LA. A-and we won't be able to hold hands and run off the dock into the water like we used to in the summers as kids, which is the most freeing feeling in the universe, let me just tell you. And we won't be able to sit on the porch on chilly evenings and talk like we did this week. And there won't be any sweet little happy hello kisses, or deep, passionate kisses, or the kind of kisses where you feel like you've been *owned* on a fundamental level, or my personal favorite, the kind of little carelessly affectionate kisses you give each other when you come into the room because the person is just standing there and you love them."

I stopped for a sip of liquid when another thought occurred to me. "Oh, and did I tell you that the other night when Martin came to visit, he tried to be all smarmy-charmy, and Watt totally didn't buy it." I sighed dreamily. "And I got really upset afterward because... seriously, how did I ever marry that guy? But Watt..." My face broke into what was probably a dopey smile. "He held me all night long afterward. He made me feel so much better. And then in the morning we, uh..." I broke off with a cough. "Never mind. Not relevant."

"Jasper." Delaney's eyes were wide. "You just said a *lot* of things. Do you realize...?"

"Don't worry. Watt said I could tell you about us." I leaned over the table and looked around, but nobody was paying attention. The crowd had thinned out a bit, and most folks appeared to be watching Kayla demonstrate her cheer routine. She'd even climbed on a chair so more people could see her marmot hiss.

"Watt and I might have crossed into friends-with-bene-fits territory at one point," I whispered. "And, then, um... *kept* crossing into it at various other points. And now we're firmly in benefits territory."

"Friends with benefits?" Delaney repeated. He frowned. "But you just said…"

Lawson nudged him. "Jasper, keep going. Tell us what else you like about Copper County."

"Oh. Well. There's the house. Mabel's house. I love the dormers that look out over the campground and the lake." I smiled. "And over the Bartletts' property next door. I used to leave a light on in the window when I wanted Watt to sneak out when we were kids," I told Lawson.

Delaney propped his chin in his hand. "Go on."

"Well, uh, there's the campground and the lake, too. The campground used to be super popular, but now it just breaks even financially, which is a shame because Copper County is probably the most gorgeous place ever. I think now that the campground is renovated, someone should advertise it. Explain what makes it so special."

Lawson's phone buzzed on the table, and he gave Delaney a guilty look as he stuffed it in his hoodie pocket. "Er. Tell us more about… about that," he said quickly.

I laughed, but as I stared at the ceiling over Lawson's head, I considered. "It's… it's not just the way the place looks. It's not the way the sunshine looks on Copper Lake, or the fog in the morning before the clouds burn off, or the way the loons call. Copper County has this… this magic about it, this crazy positivity. It's like all the people who've lived there over the ages have loved the place so much, and loved each other so much, that the land soaked it up. There's love in every leaf and tree branch, in every drop of water in the lake. You don't need to drink the Kool-Aid because the happiness and steadfastness soak right into your pores. You can't help but feel like *you're* loved when you're here. Like there's no task you could accomplish that's too impossible for you to handle, no mistake you could make that's too big to be forgiven, no misunderstanding so complex you can't straighten it out. It feels like... home."

I broke off, realizing I'd been rambling and that Delaney and Lawson were staring at me slack-jawed. "Wow." I picked up my glass and peered down into it. "They did say this was nonalcoholic, right? 'Cause I went *way* off topic. Sorry. Back to the list?"

"Jasper—" Delaney cleared his throat. "Remind me again why you need to go to LA when you so clearly want to be here? You can be a substitute teacher for a while or manage someone's business from afar... You can set something up here *way* more easily than in Los Angeles."

"I... I mean..." I shook my head. "It doesn't make sense to stay..."

"Honey, it makes *no* sense to go." Delaney flipped both lists to face me.

Lawson's short list contained food items I liked, an apartment I didn't want, clothes I'd hate, $50K I'd have to sell my soul to get, and a plan that was not a plan.

Delaney's list was two napkins long, and it mostly contained...

"Holy shit," I whispered. "W-why is Watt's name on here twenty times?"

"I wrote it once for every time you mentioned him," Delaney said. "Watt's friendship." He tapped the list with his pen. "Watt teasing you, Watt liking your scones." *Tap, tap.* "Watt holding you, you loving Watt..."

My eyes filled as the truth hit me. "I... I did say that, didn't I? Oh, shit. Oh, *shit*. You guys..." I looked at Lawson and Delaney with wide eyes. "I'm in love with Watt Bartlett."

Delaney and Lawson looked at each other.

Lawson shrugged. "Sure seems like it. Bummer about the $50K, though."

I laughed, then grabbed the LA list, tore it into scraps, then tossed the scraps in the air like confetti. "I don't want $50K. I want…"

"Watt," Delaney said.

"Yeah." I bit my lip. I still couldn't believe I'd been so blind. "He's just… he's the best person in the universe. And… and maybe he's not down for a relationship right now, but I think he will be. Probably. Eventually. And if he only wants to keep doing what we've been doing forever, I'll still be happier than I've ever been because…"

"*Watt*," Delaney insisted, his eyes wide.

"*Exactly*." I scrubbed both hands through my hair. "That's what I'm saying. And I can't thank you guys enough for helping me with this yaysnnays. You're both brilliant. Now I need to go find—"

"Watt!" Delaney said as a figure appeared beside me. "How are you?"

I glanced up to find the man I'd been thinking about standing right beside me. "Oh my God! Hi! I had no idea you were here!"

"You might have," Delaney muttered under his breath. "If you ever learned to take a warning."

Watt smiled, and instantly, the whole world calmed and settled. My future slid into place with a *click*.

"Hey, yourself." He glanced from me to Delaney and Lawson and then to the napkin scraps on the table. "Having fun?"

"Oh." I grabbed the Copper County list and jammed it in my pocket. I wanted to show it to him later, when we were alone. "Yeah. It's… it's been a heck of a night." I moved over so he could sit beside me and collected the torn napkin shreds in a pile. "You know Delaney and Lawson, right?"

Watt exchanged greetings with the men.

"When did you get here?" I asked.

"About five minutes ago." Watt's arm rubbed against mine as he glanced around the bar, and it sent a shiver through me. "Ollie and I were out, but he got a call from one of his PT patients who wasn't feeling well, so he abandoned me."

"That's too bad," I said, though my wide smile probably told a different tale. "But I'm really glad you came to hang with us." Beneath the table, I set my hand on his thigh.

"Except we're nearly done here," Delaney piped up. He made an exaggerated sad face.

"No we're not." Lawson shook his nearly empty drink glass. "I was just going to get..." His body jolted, and he shot Delaney a look. "I, ah... I was just going to get *going* after I finish my drink... is what I was going to say."

Delaney nodded. "Yup. Same. Besides..." He gave me an intent look. "I feel like you and Watt have a lot to talk about, Jasper."

"Do we?" Watt looked at me curiously. "Like what?"

"Oh, this and that." I gave him a big smile. One might even say a *loving* smile. "I just need to use the bathroom, and then we can go. I need to drop Lawson at the B&B and Delaney at Tam's—"

"No, no, don't worry about us," Delaney said. "I'm perfectly sober, and we're gonna go meet some new friends. Really get into the Copper County vibe, like you were suggesting."

"We are?" Lawson's body jolted again, and this time, he glared at his brother. "I mean, we are. Yep." In a lower voice, he added, "You're lucky that's my good leg."

"It's not luck, dumbass," Delaney shot back.

I stifled a laugh behind my hand. I liked both of these guys so much.

Watt squeezed my hand as he stood to let me out of the booth. "Don't take long," he said so softly only I could hear.

"I won't," I promised.

I was feeling confident and happy.

I had a *new* plan in mind, and I was done wasting time.

But by the time I got back from the men's room, all hell had broken loose.

CHAPTER SIXTEEN

I sat back down in the booth after Jasper left and offered the Monroe brothers a smile. "Sorry to break up your night. Looked like you guys were having fun."

"We were. Jasper's good people." Delaney adjusted his glasses. "But we'll hang out another time. He's an honorary Monroe now."

I blinked in surprise. "Is he? That's... great." Actually, if Delaney considered Jasper a brother, that was *awesome*.

For many reasons.

"Delaney needed another non-hockey person in the family," Lawson confided with an exaggerated wink.

Delaney and I exchanged a look, and he grinned. Apparently, taking care of tipsy Monroes—and honorary Monroes—was his thing.

"I don't know if Jasper's a non-hockey person anymore," I told Lawson. "He's getting pretty good at skating now. Slapshots won't be far behind."

Lawson chuckled. "I heard he keeps skating forward until he finds something to grab onto. That's a... whaddya call it, Delaney?"

"Serious problem?" Delaney suggested. "Deadly accident waiting to happen?"

Lawson frowned. "No. Jeez. Negative much? I meant a... a metaphor. For Jasper's life. Skating forward..." He laid his palm on the table and drove it toward me like a car. "Until he's got a reason to stop." He bumped his hand into my arm.

Delaney and I exchanged another look, and it was clear he was trying not to laugh. "Sure, Law." He patted his brother's arm. "You're great at metaphors."

He lifted his chin, offended. "My verbal skills are unappreciated. And after I helped you teach our bro-ski how to yaysnnays and everything."

Delaney did laugh now, even as he shook his head. "Dude. We need to get you back to the B&B. You are one drink away from making some poor choices."

"Do I want to know what a yaysnnays is?" I asked Delaney.

"Oh." He looked startled for a second and darted a glance at the napkin scraps on the table. He waved a hand. "Nah. It's just a silly thing our family used to do—"

"A pros and cons list," Lawson volunteered. "For when you need to make decisions. *Big* decisions." He leaned toward me again and confided, "The *biggest*."

"Wow." I looked from Delaney to Lawson and back. "Everything okay?"

"Yes," Delaney said before Lawson could volunteer anything. "Everything's fine." He tugged his brother's arm. "Let's go, uh..." He glanced around the crowded room, and his eyes brightened. "Wish Kayla a Happy Thanksgiving. I bet she'd really appreciate that."

Lawson wrinkled his nose. "Who?"

Delaney pointed across the room, and all three of us

turned to see Kayla fist pumping like she was in the middle of a cheer routine and giggling wildly with her sister, Mandy, to the delight of several onlookers... including Fred Palmer, who wore a surprisingly besotted expression.

"Ohhhh! Cheerleader lady!" Lawson said happily. He shoved Delaney's shoulder. "Yeah! Let's go."

"Good to see you, Watt," Delaney said.

"Have fun *benefitting* with Jasper!" Lawson laughed.

I shook my head as I watched them go, but I was smiling, too. When I wasn't being unnecessarily jealous, Delaney was actually a really nice guy.

I glanced behind me, where a short hallway led to the restrooms, and noticed a long line of people waiting. I sighed. Jasper was going to be a while.

I took a sip of his drink while I waited and toyed with the napkin scraps on the table, shaking my head at my own impatience.

I hadn't lied to Jasper when I got here—I *had* gone out with Ollie tonight, and he *had* gotten a call from one of his favorite clients, Doña Ruth, who'd taken a fall while her daughter was out of town and needed to be checked out—but I wasn't feeling disappointed or abandoned about the change of plans.

Not even a little.

I was actually pretty thrilled that the night was ending this way. That I'd gotten to see Jasper's warm, welcoming smile when he'd spotted me... and that we'd be going home together.

After the special night we'd shared last week, my feelings for Jasper had changed... or maybe it was more accurate to say that I was finally ready to stop pretending I wasn't having any. It was definitely time to tell him how I felt.

I wanted Jasper around all the time, and not only

because he was the most gorgeous man on the planet and I craved his touch, but because something in me came alive when he was near. And I was the luckiest person in town, because of all the people he could've been spending time with, he chose me... over and over again, despite all the misunderstandings in our past.

I was ready to take out that ad in the *Gazette* we'd joked about. I was ready to write on a billboard ten feet tall so that every gossip in Copper County could see: *I'm with Jasper. Jasper's with me.*

Until I looked down at the napkin confetti and saw the words written there.

YAY FOR LA!
Fifty thousand dollars is a lot of money!

I sucked in a breath through my nose. The daydream of confessing my feelings and having them reciprocated popped and disappeared like an impossibly thin soap bubble knocking against the tip of a blade.

Was he thinking about taking the modeling job after all? Was *that* the decision Jasper and his friends had been talking about? Was that what Jasper wanted to discuss with me? Was he going back to LA sooner than expected?

It shouldn't have been—wasn't—a surprise. Unlike last time Jasper left, I'd known this was the plan all along.

But shit, the reminder that he was leaving hurt. Badly. Sometime in the last couple of weeks, I'd stopped over-thinking the ending and started letting myself hope Jasper would change his mind.

I crumpled the napkin scraps and stuffed them in Lawson's empty glass.

Disappointment and sadness sat like lead weights in my

gut. That wasn't Jasper's fault, of course. None of it was. And I was his friend—whatever else had changed between us, *that* would never change. I wanted him to be able to talk to me about these things. He deserved that from me, and I would make sure he got it.

But... I didn't know if I was capable of it tonight. I needed to get my shit together first. I needed to figure out how to talk to him rationally and tell him how I was feeling... ideally without collapsing to my knees and begging him to stay, which was what I felt dangerously close to doing at the moment.

It wouldn't be fair to put that kind of pressure on him. I needed to think.

"Oh my *heeeeckkk*!" a familiar voice cried, and I stiffened. I really could not—could *not*—handle Kayla tonight. But then she continued. "It's Lawson Monroe! Omigod, I'm *such* a fan! Yoo-hoo, Lawson!"

When I glanced over, Kayla was standing on top of a chair, waving wildly at Delaney and Lawson, who were still making their way through the crowd.

I barely had a chance to feel relieved that she wasn't yoo-hooing me when Kayla launched into her cheer routine, complete with arm movements and strange little jumps. "Ready? Okay! Go, Marmots, fight, win, score! Show them what we're fighting for! We're Marmot-strong! We're Marmot-true! Victory is what we dooooo—*oof*!"

Kayla's chair shot out from behind her, and she fell to the ground.

Before I knew what I was doing, I'd pushed myself out of the booth to help, but I saw that a dozen other people, including Fred, had already rushed forward to assist her.

A second later, Kayla stood with assistance. She waved and gave the crowd a big smile that seemed only a little forced. "I'm okay! Silly chair can't keep a Fighting Marmot down!"

Someone in the crowd let out a feral marmot hiss... and the rest of the assembly returned it.

I shook my head. I'd lived in Copper County my whole life, and even I couldn't believe our antics sometimes.

"Whoa." Jasper came up beside me and laid a hand on my arm, though, like everyone else, his attention was focused on Kayla. "What's going on over there?"

"Kayla fell from grace," I said, amused. "She's okay. I'm guessing Lawson wasn't the only one who had a few too many tonight."

Jasper winced. "At least she's got her friends." He grinned up at me. "Speaking of which, you ready to go... friend?"

I laughed unsteadily. "Uh... yeah. Sure."

"Hey." He touched my arm like he needed the connection as much as I did. "You okay?"

"Yes. I just... have a lot on my mind."

Jasper darted a glance across the bar again. "You worried about Kayla?"

"Huh? No. Like you said, she's got a bunch of people who are taking care of her." I rested my hand on the small of Jasper's back as we made our way to the front door. "One of the benefits of staying in a town like Copper County," I couldn't help adding, then bit my tongue.

I was *not* going to put expectations on him the way the other people in his life had.

"Ahhh," Jasper said once we were on the sidewalk. "I get it. You're thinking about Derry. Did he talk to you?"

"Derry?" I gave him a quizzical look. "Talk to me about what?"

Jasper bit his lip. "Um. I don't know. Just... he's got some big stuff coming up, right? Moving away from home. Choosing to go to college or… not." He shrugged.

I raised an eyebrow. "Or not? What do you know, Jasper Lancaster?"

"I don't *know* anything," he said quickly. "Just a… a vibe I got, as the kids say, when he and I were talking one day. I'm sure he'll talk to you about it, once he's ready." He hesitated. "Should I have said something to you earlier?"

"No," I said automatically. Then I thought about it fully and repeated, "No. I trust you to give him good advice."

Jasper's eyes widened and softened until they were practically glowing in the light of the bar windows. "That might be the nicest thing you've ever said to me." He sniffed loudly. "I can't wait until we get home. I have so much to tell you—"

I hesitated, and Jasper caught it.

"Seriously, baby, what's up?" he demanded as we reached my truck.

The *baby* was a reminder of everything I wanted and probably wouldn't have.

I pulled Jasper close, heedless of anyone who might see, and pressed a kiss to his forehead. "I want to talk to you, too. And I want to hear whatever you've got to tell me. But not tonight, okay? My head is a mess."

"Like… a headache? Shit. Come home and I'll get you some Tylenol—"

"Actually." I chafed his upper arms through his fleece jacket. "I think I'm gonna go to my own place, if that's okay. Derry's there, and he's heading to his mom's in the morning."

"Oh," he said in a small voice. "I mean, are we… are we still on for Thanksgiving dinner, or…?"

"Jesus, yes," I said without hesitation. "You're one of the things I'm most thankful for this year."

His expression cleared immediately, and he grinned. "You just want the pies I baked," he teased. "Pumpkin whore."

"Pies, plural?"

"Somebody I know prefers his pie in tartlet form. Some bullshit about ratios…"

I wrapped my hand around the back of Jasper's neck and kissed him hard, trying to convey all I felt in the press of our lips and the way our tongues tangled together. *I want you. Please stay. Help me figure out how we can make this work. I want this to be our first Thanksgiving together, not our last.*

When I pulled back, Jasper's beautiful blue eyes were glazed, and he was breathing hard. It took everything in me not to say *I love you* right then and there.

But I had other things to say, too. And I needed to figure out how to say them right.

"Drive safe," I told him. "Text me when you wake up, okay?"

"Feel better, Watt," Jasper said softly as I climbed into the truck.

I smile. "I'm gonna try."

———

I REGRETTED LEAVING Jasper almost immediately. I'd gone from feeling unsettled when the man was around to being unsettled whenever he wasn't.

Which was a real problem if he planned to not be around on a permanent basis sometime soon.

When I opened the back door, Derry was sitting at the

kitchen island with his phone in his hands and a giant plate of food in front of him, as usual.

"Hey," I said as I tossed my keys on the counter wearily. "Not hanging with Zach tonight?"

"Nah. I told Mom I'd leave here at ten tomorrow, so I'm turning in early. Doug's deep-frying the turkey this year, and I want to be there to watch the carnage." Derry grinned.

I returned his smile as well as I could... which apparently wasn't too well because Derry frowned.

"What's wrong?"

I shook my head. "Nothing worth talking about. Just a lot on my mind."

Derry lifted one eyebrow. "You mean big, grown-up, important shit that my tiny brain couldn't comprehend?"

"No!" I huffed out a laugh as I grabbed a soda out of the fridge. "More like overthinking *personal* stuff I'd rather not discuss with my son."

"Ohhh." To my surprise, Derry nodded. "You and Coach Lancaster have a fight?"

I froze with my hand on the can and turned to look at him. "No. You know we're over that. We tease each other, Derry, but—"

"Dad," he said, exasperated, "come *on*."

"Pardon?"

He rolled his eyes. "I've been waiting for you to talk to me about this, but you haven't, so I guess I'm diving in. You and Coach Lancaster... you're together, right? He's the one you're always texting with and giggling like a little kid?"

I opened my mouth, then closed it again. "I do *not* giggle like a little kid."

Derry just laughed.

"But... yes," I admitted, exhaling. "We're together. Sort

of." I paused, trying to gather my thoughts. I'd imagined coming out to all of Copper County at the Bar and Grill earlier, but telling my son was different. "It's not..."

I trailed off, the word *serious* on the tip of my tongue. But I wouldn't start lying to Derry now. The truth was, my feelings for Jasper *were* serious. At least, to me. I wasn't sure how he'd feel when I finally laid it all out.

"Knew it!" Derry crowed, way too pleased with himself. "Dude, you guys are hilarious together. I kinda suspected last week on Pasta Night, and I was like, '*I gotta get them to hang out again so I can be sure,*' and then at the cookoff—"

I stared at him, stunned. "You set that up?"

"Pfft. Obviously. And when I saw you guys cooking together in the kitchen, I was like, '*Suspicion confirmed.*' The way you smile at each other..." Derry grinned wickedly. "It's fucking disgusting. He's such a simp for you."

Startled, I laughed. "But you're not... surprised? Or... anything?" I'd known he wouldn't have a problem with it, per se, but I'd expected questions about why I was dating a guy for the first time at my age.

Hell, I'd questioned it myself.

But apparently, I really didn't need to have it all figured out for everyone else. *Apparently*, when people cared about you, they accepted you and rolled with it... like Jasper had.

"Maybe a little." Derry shrugged. "But honestly... not after I saw you together outside of practice. You guys just fit. It's like, if you were looking at cars and you found one that was, like, absolutely perfect for you in every feature, but the color wasn't the one you expected you'd want, would you say, 'Nah, sorry, I only drive blue cars'? That'd be dumb. And anyway, he's cooler than Zach's mom." He pulled a face. "But don't tell Zach I said that."

"I definitely won't," I agreed. I pulled out a chair at the kitchen table and sat.

"So, Coach Lancaster's staying, then. Not going back to California." Derry made it sound like a foregone conclusion.

"Eh." I winced. "No. I think he's still going back."

"Ooof. Even though you guys are in love and all? That's rough." His face creased. "Oh, shit, is that what you were fighting about?"

"We're not fighting," I said. "And I don't know how Jasper feels. We have a lot of stuff to talk about, and..." I huffed. "I don't know what the fuck I'm doing, to be honest, Derry. I need to figure it out."

Derry cocked his head, considering. "Huh."

I glanced up. "What?"

"Nothing, really. I just... I don't think I've ever heard you say that before." He shrugged offhandedly.

I snorted. "Maybe because I hate not knowing what I'm doing. But that doesn't mean I haven't felt that way," I said with feeling. "Trust me."

"Coach L was right." Derry gave me a slight smile. "He said any adult who has their shit figured out is lying. I told him you were the exception, and he looked like he was trying not to laugh. I get it now."

"I'm definitely not the exception. You'll find, my child, that just when you *think* you know what you're doing in life... life changes the rules."

Like, say, by dropping your childhood best friend back into your life... and making you fall in love with him.

To my surprise, Derry gave a heartfelt sigh. "God, yeah. I know exactly what you mean."

I frowned at him, Jasper's words from earlier coming

back to me. "Hey, Der... are you thinking about not going to college?"

He glanced up in surprise. "Me? No. I mean... not really. I've thought about it off and on, but it makes sense, what you've said. The orchard will be here after I've gone to school and traveled and stuff. But probably I'll be coming back sooner than you think. I love it here."

I nodded slowly. "I definitely wouldn't say no to that. If it's what *you* want, not because you think it's what *I* want."

Smiling, Derry rolled his eyes. "I know, I know. You've only said it about a billion times."

"And I'll say it a billion more," I said firmly.

Derry's smile faltered. "I, uh... I wish every parent felt that way. If I tell you something, can you not tell Zach's mom?"

Ohhhh.

"Zach doesn't want to go to college," I guessed.

"No! I mean, he does. Eventually. But he definitely doesn't want to play hockey anymore, which means it's gonna be hard for him to go to college at all. His grades are okay, but not for, like, an academic scholarship..." Derry's mouth screwed up. "So he's kinda stuck."

"I'm sure there are other kinds of scholarships, though, no? And there are loans. Or he could get a job and earn the money."

"Yeah." Derry looked troubled. "That's what he's planning to do right now. And it sucks because he can't talk to his mom about any of it. She's *only* focused on hockey and getting a scholarship. So he's trying to figure out a new plan on his own." He shook his head. "She keeps saying, *'Trust me, Zachy, you'll thank me when you're older and don't have student loans.'*"

Derry stood and took his plate to the sink. "But I've

been thinking about what Coach Lancaster told me a while back. That there are a billion ways to be happy, and sometimes you have to take a wrong turn. And about how *you* said that if you love someone, you support them and don't put expectations on them. So, like, why won't Zach's mom let him make this choice, even if it turns out wrong?"

I considered this for a moment. I didn't disagree... and I understood Kayla's position, too.

"It *is* Zach's life," I agreed. "And maybe his mom does have some expectations. I think she's also probably made some wrong turns herself, like the rest of us, and wants to save her kid from that. When you're young, you tend to consider the choices that are right in front of you." I held my hand up close to my face. "When you're older, or even just further away from the situation, you see how those choices lead to other choices." I pulled my hand further away. "I think it's good to give the people you love all the information you have so they can make an informed decision. In the end, though, the decision has to be his."

He nodded seriously as he digested this, and then his eyes took on a teasing light. "Hey, Dad? If age means you're zooming out on life... how come you look like *this* when you're staring at a spreadsheet?" The little shit pressed his palm against his nose.

"Dermott Bartlett." I shook my head sadly. "Here I am passing on my wisdom, and you mock me."

He dropped his hand and smiled. "Nah, I heard what you're saying. When you love someone, you make sure they have all the information they need to make good decisions," he recited. "I'm gonna talk to Zach because I think there are some things he's not considering."

"Good man," I approved.

"What about you?" he wondered.

"Me?"

"Are you going to tell Jasper how mixed up you feel about him leaving," Derry said, "and how much you care about him? So he has the information he needs to make his decision?"

I nodded. "That's my plan."

But as I did some final preparations for Thanksgiving dinner the next day and cleaned up the kitchen, I still couldn't figure out how to tell Jasper that I was in love with him without that feeling like a weight on him when it came time to make his choice.

Restless, I wandered out into the November night and headed for the orchard. The air was crisp and cold, filled with the lingering scent of apples and the deep, earthy fragrance that said the land was settling for the winter. Renewing itself so it could bloom again in the spring.

A rustling noise stopped me in my tracks, and a pair of shining eyes appeared out of the shadows.

The deer and I both froze—me, with my hands in my pockets, it, with a fallen apple in its mouth—and I nearly laughed.

For months, I'd been trying to keep these invaders out, like if I built a wall high enough, I could keep the orchard safe. Now... I felt like I understood that deer on a fundamental level. It wasn't reckless; it was simply drawn toward something that felt right, something it needed to survive... something more important than all the obstacles in its path.

Same, buddy.

Derry was right. In the morning, first thing in the morning, I would tell Jasper how I felt. Give him all the information he needed, all the messy truth of how much I loved him and wanted him to stay but never wanted to tie him down.

I'd stop worrying so damn much about how I packaged it up and perfected it.

I'd trust us not to misunderstand each other again.

———

WHEN I GOT to the kitchen the following morning, I was in a great mood, and it only got better when Jasper texted.

> JASPER
>
> Happy Thanksgiving! I made pumpkin muffins. Want me to bring some over? On the one hand, we're having tartlets later and that's a lot of pumpkin, even for a pumpkin whore. On the other, you're supposed to carbo-load today for the race tomorrow…

I bit my lip and grinned.

> Jasper. Baby. There's no such thing as too much pumpkin.

He took a moment to reply, and I knew it was because of the endearment I'd thrown in there.

> JASPER
>
> Well. If that's how you feel… I am definitely on board.

I really hoped he was agreeing to more than just the pumpkin.

> Let me know when you're coming over. Derry's leaving for his mom's in an hour or so.

JASPER

Oh. I can wait, if you want.

Nope. Not at all. I thought you'd like to wish him a happy Thanksgiving. Derry and I had a long talk last night.

Another long pause, and then...

JASPER

???? You can't leave me hanging like this.

Come over.

"Aw. You and Coach Lancaster figured stuff out, huh?" Derry appeared in the kitchen with his duffel bag slung over his shoulder and made a beeline for the fridge.

"Not yet." My stomach fluttered with excited nerves. "But I'm feeling hopeful."

When my phone rang, I answered it without thinking. "Hello—"

"Oh my heck," a voice on the other end said sadly. "Happy Thanksgiving, Watt. I have terrible news."

"Uh. Happy Thanksgiving, Kayla," I said. "What's going on?"

Something in my tone had Derry looking up from the juice he'd been pouring.

"I know this is going to absolutely crush you, Watt, and I... I'm *so* sorry... but I'm not actually going to be able to prance with you tomorrow."

"Oh." In all that had been going on, I hadn't given a single thought to the Pilgrim Prance... except to hope that there really wouldn't be costumes. "Oh, that's..." *Amazing.* "Not a problem. Is everything okay?"

"I'm afraid not." She sighed. "I sprained my ankle last

night. Nothing serious, but I'm on crutches for a couple of weeks. I can't drive."

"I'm sorry to hear that. Let us know if you need anything, okay?"

"Yeah, about that... I'm gonna need you to send Zachy home, I'm afraid."

I frowned. "Zach's not with us, Kayla."

Derry's eyes widened, and he suddenly got very busy drinking his juice. He headed for the living room, and I moved to block him.

"Yes, he is," she said with so much certainty I almost doubted it for a minute. "Zach told me last night that he and Derry had plans this morning. Watching the parade, I think."

"Hang on, Kayla," I said. I pulled the phone from my ear. "Derry? Anything you'd like to tell me?"

Derry winced. "Uh. No?"

"Dermott."

Derry sighed and rubbed at the back of his neck. "I told him not to, Dad. After you and I talked last night, I texted Zach, just like I said I was going to. I told him my concerns. He swore he wouldn't do anything until we talked."

"What was he going to do? Where is he?"

"I... I don't know exactly," Derry admitted.

"Watt?" Kayla's voice called from the phone. "Watt, are you there? What's going on?"

"I'm trying to figure that out, Kayla. Zach's not here," I said. "But Derry might know where he is. We're going to look into it, okay?"

"But... where could he be?" she said, her voice high with stress and worry.

"He... he was thinking about meeting a guy who offered him a job. He wanted an alternative way of paying for college instead of a hockey scholarship. That's all. And Zach's an adult," he reminded me.

"A *job?*" Kayla's tone suggested a job was about as strange and unwelcome as a pet boa constrictor. "What in the world? He knows I don't want him working during the season. Where is he, Derry? Where can I find him? I... oh my heck, I can't even drive!" she wailed.

"Kayla," I said calmly. "We'll find him and get him home, okay? Hang tight." I disconnected. "Start talking," I told Derry.

"We can try to find him..." He shook his head. "But it might be too late. He might have already left town."

"Left town?" I demanded. "He hasn't graduated yet! Derry, what the hell—?"

A knock sounded on the back door before it was pushed open, and suddenly, Jasper was there, holding a plate of muffins and looking fresh and gorgeous. I drank him in like sunshine after a long winter.

"Uh. Hey." Jasper looked between us in concern. "I heard you from outside. What's going on?"

I sighed. "We're gonna need to postpone breakfast. Zach's missing."

"Missing?" Jasper gasped. He set the muffins on the counter with a *clack*. "Oh my God. How?"

"I don't know." I turned to Derry and tilted my head. "Dermott was just going to tell us."

Derry blew out a breath. "Okay, so like... me and Zach were in town a few days ago at Fanaille because there's this girl he likes who loves the cupcakes there."

"Okay," I said impatiently, trying not to rush him.

"Right. Sorry. Um, so we were at the bakery, and Zach was talking to me about how he doesn't want to play hockey but doesn't know how else to pay for school, you know?" His eyes met mine, and I nodded.

"Oh my God," Jasper breathed. "It really was your *friend?*"

Derry frowned. "Well, yeah. That's what I told you, right?"

"Yes. Yes, you did." Jasper waved a hand. "Go on."

"Anyway, this guy was sitting at the table right near ours —you know how the tables are so close together? And he was like, hey, if you're looking for a job, I'm hiring!"

Jasper and I made identical *what the fuck* faces, and Derry huffed before continuing. "And Zach immediately said, '*Yeah, no. Go away.*'"

I let out a relieved breath. "Good."

"Zach's not an idiot, Dad. He's not gonna step into some weirdo's candy van down by the river. But... the guy wasn't a creeper. He was old. And nice. He mentioned that Zach had the potential to make decent money, and... look, I know it sounds weird the way I'm telling it, but it wasn't. The guy recognized the quote on Zach's laptop sticker, and we got to talking. He seemed really smart and like he knew what he was doing, so they followed each other on Instagram, and... and the guy DM'd him. Zach thought about it for a while, but he was really intrigued by what the guy had to say, so they talked on the phone, and then... I don't know."

He bit his lip. "If I'm being honest, something about it gave me the ick. I remember you saying if something sounds too good to be true, it probably is. But I didn't wanna tell Zach that when he was all excited and finally thought he had a decent alternate plan, you know? And plus... like, Zach knows that I'm bummed to think he and I might not be playing together next year. I didn't want him to think I was telling him because I wanted to guilt him, you know?

But then last night, you and I talked, and you said you need to give people all the information they need to make a solid decision. That you need to tell them how you really feel."

Derry glanced back and forth between me and Jasper. "Right?"

Jasper and I looked at each other. Our gazes caught. Held. Warmed. His eyes widened in question, and I smiled slowly. He let out a breath that seemed to weigh a thousand pounds, and the tension left his body in a rush. Then he smiled back— a smile filled with so much pure love and promise my heart lurched crazily in my chest.

Okay, then, I thought, taking a deep breath. *Okay*.

I still didn't know what the future held—and I really, really could not wait to actually sit down and talk about it—but at least Jasper was feeling feelings, too. We would figure it out together.

"...so I texted Zach that he should talk to Coach Lancaster," Derry was saying. "Since *he'd* know better than anyone if the company was legit. And Zach said he—"

Jasper wrenched his head around when he heard his name and held up a hand. "Sorry, wait, back up. What company? What kind of job was the guy offering Zach?"

"Oh." Derry looked back and forth between me and Jasper again. "Modeling. The guy was an agent. Didn't I say?"

CHAPTER SEVENTEEN

JASPER

"Mother. *Fucker*," I shouted, my voice trembling with rage.

"Shit." Watt—the beautiful, beloved, warm, and wonderful man I'd spent my whole morning dreaming of being alone with—hung his head in frustration. "You don't think..."

"Oh, I think. I *definitely* think. That unmitigated asshole." I yanked my phone from the pocket of my jeans, pulled up Martin's message from yesterday, and handed the phone to Watt. "I guess we know what new direction he's planning on moving in, huh?"

"Fuck," Watt agreed after skimming the message.

I paced the stretch of kitchen between the island and the sink, back and forth. "And here I was, so proud that I was ignoring him. *Ha ha*, I thought, *looks like you don't know me as well as you think. You lose.* And meanwhile, he's doing *this*. Charming one of *my* kids..."

"Hey." Watt stepped in front of me, blocking my path, and I ran into him. "I know you're pissed—"

"Understatement," I bit out.

"—but if any part of you is feeling like this is on you, please don't."

Until he'd spoken, I hadn't realized that guilt was exactly what I was feeling, along with anger. Guilt that I was the one who'd brought the Martin plague to Copper County. Guilt that I hadn't foreseen this... somehow.

I blew out a breath. "I know you're right," I said softly.

Eyes still warm on me, one side of Watt's mouth pulled up in a facsimile of his teasing grin. "Because I'm always right."

That startled a laugh out of me, which brought my anger down to a reasonable level.

I leaned my forehead against his shoulder. "Thanks," I whispered. "You help, too."

"And I always will." He spoke just as softly as I did, but his words sounded like a promise.

It was absolutely not the right time for us to have the conversation we needed to have or to discuss the napkin list I had in my pocket—a list I'd added a few items to overnight—but the way he was looking at me, the warmth in his eyes, felt like a minor miracle. Like the good that would always temper the bad of whatever life would throw at us.

"So," Watt said. "What's the plan?"

"I don't understand what's going on," Derry said. He sounded young and a little scared. "Is this guy dangerous? For real?"

I pulled away from Watt so I could lay a hand on Derry's arm. "No," I said firmly. "Absolutely not. Martin, my ex-husband, is an actual modeling agent. *My* agent, once upon a time—"

"That's his name!" Derry said excitedly. "Martin something."

"He's not going to hurt Zach. But he's probably going to try to get him to sign a contract—"

"And move to Los Angeles." Derry's face fell. "Yeah. Zach mentioned that. That's when I was like, 'Wait, dude, you haven't even graduated yet!' I guess the guy—Martin— told Zach that people do that all the time. They finish school out there..."

"Yeah," I agreed. "Some people definitely do. I did. And in my case, it worked out okay. It's *not* a path I'd recommend, though, Derry. Not unless someone truly knew what they were signing up for. Not unless they knew just how hard that life can be and that there are no guarantees of success. I didn't know any of that..."

"I remember you saying." Derry frowned.

"And I don't believe for one second that Martin will explain any of that to Zach. Martin can be very convincing. He offers you whatever you think you want most... even if he can't actually deliver it."

Derry's jaw worked. "I want to say I don't think he'd have signed anything or left without saying goodbye... but then, I didn't think he'd be stupid enough to go meet the guy and tell his mom he was *here*, so... I guess I don't know."

"He's not stupid," Watt said. "Zach wouldn't be the first person to sign a contract and regret it. Older and wiser people than him do stuff like that all the time..."

I nodded.

"...but let's try to prevent that from happening if we can," Watt said. "Any idea where Martin might be?"

Derry already had his phone in his hand. "I'll text Zach and see if he'll answer."

I waved a hand at the phone Watt was still holding. "Those messages are the only communication I've had with him, other than the time he came to—" I broke off as I recalled a snippet of conversation from that day. "Wait, didn't he say he was staying at the Crabapple in O'Leary last week? He's probably staying there again. There aren't many hotels around here."

"It's worth a try." Watt grabbed his keys from the counter. "Derry, come on. You can text Zach from the car."

We piled into Watt's truck with Derry in the back seat, and Watt drove us down the deserted road to town at a breakneck pace.

At literally any other time, I would have been really turned on by the way he handled the wheel—and probably would have made a teasing remark about it—but I was way too wired.

Concern for Zach tangled with my own thoughts, vying for attention. As worried as I was, part of me couldn't stop thinking about Watt, about *us*, about finding out for sure where we stood.

I wanted to tell him how I felt and finally put it out there. More than anything, I needed to hear him say it back. I'd seen the love in his eyes earlier in the kitchen, the soft intensity that had been building between us for so long finally acknowledged and unguarded, but I needed the words. I needed the certainty.

No more confusion.

No more misunderstandings.

But first, I needed to make sure another kid didn't wander blindly into making the same mistake I'd made, all starry-eyed and full of misplaced dreams.

"Fuck," Watt muttered under his breath, yanking the steering wheel hard as we were forced to detour around Weaver Street, which was closed for some O'Leary festival or another. I clenched my jaw, fighting to stay calm as Watt maneuvered down a maze of side streets and finally parked at the library, across from the elementary school.

"Dad, I see him!" Derry cried, pointing toward the elementary school playground.

A lone figure in a yellow jacket sat on the swings, slouched over and head bowed. *Zach.* His lanky form was unmistakable, even with his face hidden under his messy mop of hair.

But then something else caught my eye, freezing me in place. Across the street, I saw another figure, dressed head to toe in designer crap. His stupid, tousled hair caught the sunlight as he hefted a giant suitcase into the trunk of his sleek rental car.

My blood boiled. My heart pounded, adrenaline rushing through me. Before I even knew what I was doing, my legs took off, carrying me straight for him.

"Jasper!" Watt called after me, but I didn't stop until I was right next to Martin. I ripped the suitcase out of his hands and slammed it to the ground.

"What the hell do you think you're doing?" I spat.

"Jazz—"

"Don't even try it. How dare you! I cannot believe that you thought you could come to *my* town and pull this crap. Was taking my business and my career not enough? Now you think I'm going to let you take one of my kids away from everything he loves? Hell. No."

"Chill out, Jasper. Jesus. You make it sound like I'm signing him up for hard labor. I made a career for you. I can do the same for him—"

"Zach is barely eighteen, you predatory asshole," I fumed. "You know damn well he shouldn't be signing contracts on his own. You *know*. Did you tell him about all the casting calls? The constant workouts? The people who'll be judging his body? Did you tell him about the rejections? Did you tell him he might spend *years* low-key feeling like he's not good enough... and that you'll make him think he should be grateful for the privilege?"

Martin opened his mouth, but I had no interest in anything he had to say. This time, he needed to listen to *me*.

I jabbed a finger into his chest. "Zach has roots here, Martin. *Friends* here. You might not understand how important that is, how valuable it is, because you can't put a price tag on it, but *he* knows. Did you tell him he's going to have to kiss that goodbye for a couple years because he'll be too focused on his career to come back and probably too poor to afford it? Or did you offer him all the shit you think he should want and plan to manipulate him into believing it's what he wanted all along?"

"Baby." Watt's strong arms came around my waist from behind, grounding me... and pulling me out of Martin's reach. "It's okay."

"It's *not*," I argued. "I cannot believe I married this man. I cannot believe I spent so many years giving a shit what he thinks. I cannot believe that when he told me the best way to get over someone was to get under someone else, *I fucking listened*." I jabbed a finger in Martin's direction. "I would never have hooked up with you in the first place if I hadn't just heard the news that Watt was married," I yelled. "And you know it."

I felt Watt's arms tighten reflexively around me, and I froze.

Crap. I hadn't planned on connecting those dots for Watt ever, and definitely not in a screaming match in the street. But as far as I was concerned, it was just one more part of our past. One more part of how we'd finally come back together. One more wrong turn that had gotten us where we needed to be.

"Jasper," Watt whispered. "Baby. It really *is* okay. I've got you now. And Zach is fine. Derry says he didn't sign anything."

"He..." I deflated. "He didn't?"

"For fuck's sake. No, he didn't." Martin drew himself up, brushing his suit sleeves and straightening the cuffs of his shirt. He looked thoroughly annoyed. "I offered Zach a very good, very fair contract. And he was going to say *yes*... but then he chickened out. Started spouting some crap about '*balance is key*' and '*only stretch as far as it feels right, listen to your body.*'" He snorted. "Sounded like the mindfulness bullshit you always used to go on about."

My anger flared again, briefly, but before I could lunge at him, Watt whispered in my ear, just low enough that only I could hear. "Please don't kill him. If you get caught, they probably won't give conjugal visits, and it would be a real bummer for me, discovering gay sex at thirty-seven only to lose it. But, you know, your call. I'll support you either way."

I snickered. Then I snorted. Then I doubled over right there on the sidewalk as laughter bubbled up uncontrollably. Even as Martin drove off, muttering something about crazy small towns, I couldn't stop laughing. And through the laughter, as tears welled up in my eyes, it hit me like a ton of bricks:

This was my life now.

I got to keep this.

I wasn't a Copper-plate, and I would never have to leave again when the season was over.

And best of all, I got to keep Watt. The man who *got* me, who calmed me, who fired me up.

Who loved me.

I turned around in his arms. "I love you, Watt Bartlett," I whispered.

This wasn't the right place, and possibly not the right time, but I didn't care. I couldn't keep the truth in one second longer.

Watt didn't bat an eyelash at the public declaration. Instead, his face lit up with a smile that made my chest tighten, and he replied loud and clear so that everyone would hear it and believe it. "And I love you, Jasper Wrigley Lancaster."

I let out a ridiculous sob-sniffle, completely uncaring about the tears prickling in my eyes. *Twenty years*. It felt like twenty years I'd been waiting to hear those words. And I wasn't sure when I'd evolved into a crier, but I was rolling with it.

"And I'm staying in Copper County," I added, wiping my eyes with the back of my hand.

"You are?" he demanded. "Wait, really? For sure? Because I saw part of your pros and cons list for Los Angeles at the bar last night, and I know you have big dreams—"

"I ripped that list up, Watt. That's what I wanted to tell you last night. None of those dreams are actually mine anymore, if they ever were. I was clinging to what I thought would make me happy, but when I thought about what actually makes me happy..." I pulled my **YAY FOR COPPER COUNTY!** list from my pocket. "It turns out they're all right here, and they all involve you. I bet you I can convince you—*mpfh*."

Watt kissed me soundly, his strong arms wrapping around me, locking us together so tightly I knew we'd never truly be separated again.

Then he pulled back and grinned, eyes glinting with mischief, and took the list from my lax fingers. "Let's see this—oh." When he looked at me again, his eyes were soft and warm. "Jasper... my name is written on this paper like thirty times."

I nodded.

"*Making scones for Watt*," he read.

"Having someone appreciate my baked goods is a real plus," I assured him.

"*Jumping in the lake with Watt. Leaving the light on in the window for Watt. Being there for Watt when Derry leaves for college. Kissing Watt. Skating with Watt—*"

His smile was contagious. I couldn't help smiling back just as giddily, so I didn't try. "I've mastered gliding forward, I think," I told him seriously. "I'm ready to learn how to stop."

"*Telling Watt that he's a way better cook than I am, and also better at blowjobs, and that he can drive my Jag whenever he wants... Aw,* Jasper. Baby, that's *so* sweet—"

"Hey! That's not on there. That's *definitely* not on there." Laughing, I tried to steal the list back but got a little bit distracted when Watt kissed me again.

"I'm convinced," he said a little while later. "You should definitely stay in Copper County. You win the bet."

"Watt Bartlett," I said mock-severely, twining my arms around his neck. "Is this what our bets are going to be like now that we're in love?"

"That when you win, I win, and vice versa?" Watt pressed our foreheads together. "Yeah, Jasper. That's exactly how it's going to be because that's how it's always been. You and me. Rivals. Best friends. Lovers. Building a life together in this town. And I bet you're gonna love it."

That was one bet Watt would win for the rest of our lives.

EPILOGUE
WATT

Since Jasper had come back to Copper County, I'd found myself doing a lot of things I would never have imagined.

Some things—like coaching high school hockey, having my best friend and rival back, and learning that I didn't need to have my life or my sexuality a hundred percent figured out, *and that was okay*—were pretty freaking wonderful.

Other things—like falling head over heels in love with Jasper, having him fall just as hard for me, and beginning to plan a future where every day began and ended with him in my arms—were nothing short of amazing.

But there were a few things—okay, *one* thing—that I absolutely refused to do. Categorically, empirically, fundamentally refused, no matter how gorgeous Jasper was, or how sappy I got when his big blue eyes danced, or how my brain blanked when he kissed me.

"Watt." Jasper glanced around the little parking lot off the Ring Road—the imaginatively named two-lane street that ringed Copper Lake—where almost all of Copper

County and a sizable portion of O'Leary had gathered to run off the calories from yesterday's Thanksgiving feasts in the name of charity. "You *have* to."

"Do not," I shot back immediately.

I meant what I said—I truly believed a man had certain core principles that were nonnegotiable, and he should not be swayed for anything—but if I was being honest, there was a strong chance I might have disagreed with Jasper anyway, just for the fun of it.

Betting, bantering, and teasing were some of the things we both liked best about our relationship—along with the way we loved, accepted, and supported each other fiercely and unconditionally, of course. Jasper challenged me every single day to be the best version of myself, to do things I hadn't known I was capable of, and I would never take that for granted.

"Please?" Jasper wheedled softly. He stepped close—much closer than he would have gotten in public a couple of days ago, but not nearly as close as I wanted him—and whispered in my ear, "I'll make it worth your while."

My mind turned to static.

You might imagine, given our pumpkin-tart-fueled Thanksgiving sex-fest at my house yesterday (after dropping Zach safely at home for a long talk with his mom and after Derry had left for Rachel's, of course), that I might be just the tiniest bit less susceptible to Jasper's sexual wiles today.

You might think it only logical, since we'd followed yesterday up with long, lazy shower blowjobs this morning, and since I'd come my brains out mere minutes before leaving for the race, that I wouldn't be overly affected by the heat of Jasper's body—clad in those damn running tights—pressed against me or his hot breath tickling my ear.

You'd be so, so wrong.

"Jasper..." I swallowed hard, tangling my right hand with his left. "You're asking me to compromise some deeply held beliefs here. Can't do it."

Jasper chuckled. "Watt. Baby." His grin was warm, amused, and full of love. "You're being *so* dramatic right now. I'm only asking if you'll—"

"Yoo-hoo! Watt! Jasper!"

Jasper closed his eyes and sighed briefly before turning and grinning at the newcomer. "Kayla! Hey. Feeling better?"

Kayla made her way through the crowd on a pair of hot pink crutches that coordinated with her pink pants and pink Pilgrim Prance 5K T-shirt. Her foot and ankle were wrapped in matching hot pink gauze.

When she reached us, Kayla gave Jasper a genuine smile. "Much better, thank you. What a beautiful day for a race, isn't it?"

"Couldn't be better," Jasper agreed. He gestured toward the huge Pilgrim Prance sign hanging above the lot. "You did an amazing job organizing all this."

"Aw. Well. Some things about today didn't turn out *quite* the way I hoped." She glanced from her injured ankle to our joined hands and gave a rueful little shrug... but then her face brightened. "Other things have turned out even better than I dreamed, though. Lawson Monroe asked me how I was doing today!" She bit her lip and leaned closer as she confided, "He remembered me from the bar the other night, can you believe it? I really think he and I have a connection of sorts. Not romantic, of course," she hurried to add. "He's just a *tiny* bit younger than me. But friendships are important, too."

"Absolutely," I said, squeezing Jasper's fingers a little bit tighter. "Friendship is the *most* important thing."

Kayla's face softened. "I can't thank you both enough for helping us out yesterday. Zach and I had a long talk last night. We haven't come to any decisions yet, but I'm... I'm listening now."

"Good," Jasper said. "Knowing he has you in his corner will help him make good choices."

"I hope so." Grinning, she wagged a teasing finger at Jasper. "I told you that day at Lyon's Imperial that everyone would be glad you came back to Copper County, didn't I, Jasper Lancaster? I just hadn't expected it would be because you'd excoriated that awful man just so you could save my Zachy."

Jasper and I both knew his anger with Martin yesterday had been years in the making, and Zach had only been the final, final straw, but Jasper didn't tell her any of that.

Instead, Jasper's smile deepened, and he said, "Actually... it's Jasper *Wrigley* again." He lifted his left hand... which was still joined with mine. "Got a new life, time to ditch the old name."

My stomach flipped. Jasper and I had spent a long time down at the dock last night curled together under a quilt, talking about what his future here in Copper County might look like—substitute teaching until a full-time position opened, starting a business doing remote admin work for small businesses like the orchard, keeping and renovating his house while advertising the campground to tourists—but he hadn't said a single thing about changing his name back.

"Jasper," I said softly.

He turned to give me a smirk that said he knew exactly how I was feeling about this revelation—darkly, possessively thrilled, hopeful, and *happy*.

"That's wonderful news," Kayla said. "I'm really glad... for both of you." She clutched her crutches a little tighter and leaned toward us. "And I've got some wonderful news of my own. Camp Fair Shot has a new sponsor." She beamed. "An anonymous benefactor donated thirty thousand dollars overnight, and the camp is safe for the next year or two at least!"

"Whoa! Any idea who?" I wondered.

"Not a clue," Kayla said. Her eyes narrowed. "But I'm going to find out."

I didn't doubt her for a second.

"So does that mean...?" Jasper blinked around the parking lot at the crowd assembled near the starting line. "Is the race... canceled?" He looked strangely—adorably— crushed by the prospect.

"Oh, honey, gosh no. Not when so many people have put so much time and effort into making this happen! I'm so glad you were able to partner up with Watt since I couldn't." She touched a hand to the sleeve of Jasper's T-shirt—one she'd custom-made along with some other stuff and had Zach bring over yesterday in a box labeled, appallingly, *Costumes*. "Copper County will be thrilled to have our favorite rivals running on the same team for once... and poor Watt would have been *so* disappointed to miss the prance."

I would *not*.

"Oh, yeah. Watt's a hell of a prancer," Jasper said solemnly. He gave me a sly look and added, "Though not as good as me. And he's *definitely* not as well-dressed as I am." He ran a hand down the front of his shirt and adjusted his hat proudly.

I shook my head, fighting a smile. He was not going to get me to change my mind by teasing me into it.

I refused.

I was stronger than that.

Probably.

"Don't forget to get changed, Watt. The race is starting in just twenty minutes," she said.

She didn't give me a chance to express my opinion about that before hobbling away.

"I brought the outfit she made you, you know," Jasper said softly. "It's in the back seat of the Jag… which I might let you drive home if you play your cards right."

I scowled. "That's not—"

"Jasper!" a feminine voice called. "You look *epic* in feathers."

Tam walked over, a baby carrier strapped to her chest. Lucas, loaded down with a baby bag that probably could have doubled as a suitcase, walked beside her.

"Congratulations, you guys," I said, shaking Lucas's hand.

"Oh my God!" Jasper gave Tam a gentle hug, mindful of the small person between them. "You look amazing. *Tierney* looks amazing. Hi, baby. I'm your Uncle Jasper. Wait, Tam, should you be standing so soon after giving birth?"

Tam laughed. "It's been days, Jasper, so yes. I'm only staying for an hour because she'll be hungry, but I couldn't miss this." She looked utterly gleeful as she took in the sight of all her fellow Coppertians in their multicolored T-shirts. "I needed to show Tierney exactly the kind of wacky and wonderful place she'd be calling home." The satisfaction on her face said she wouldn't have it any other way.

"I heard you might be staying in Copper County," Lucas said.

"I am. It's the right move for me. I had some big plans, and I was holding on to them pretty tightly, but…" Jasper gave me a look and stepped back to take my hand again. "I found something better to hold on to."

"I feel that," Tam said. She peeked at the baby nestled against her chest and ran a hand over her daughter's head. "Speaking of which... Lucas and I have been talking, and I'm not sure I'm coming back to school this year." She gave Jasper a small smile. "I'm gonna need more time with her. I'm planning to speak to Mike Schmidt next week about taking the rest of the school year off, so maybe you'll have a job for a while longer, if you want it."

Jasper and I exchanged a glance, and I nearly laughed at how giddy he seemed about this development.

"And then next year..." Tam glanced up at Lucas.

"Next year, we'll see," he said.

Tam nodded.

"That would be *awesome*," Jasper said. "Let's talk about it after you talk to him. I'm bringing you muffins this weekend. Gotta keep both my girls fed."

"We'll hold you to that," Tam promised. "Ooh, gotta go say hi to Angela Ross. She made Tierney the sweetest little hat... See you later!"

"About the costume," I began as soon as she left, but then Ollie and Brew Barnum appeared out of nowhere.

"Brew," I said, clapping the man on the back. "Good to see you."

He gave us each a friendly nod.

"Jasper!" Ollie exclaimed. "Oh my fucking God, that shirt! That hat! Tell me you made them!"

"Nooo." Jasper shook his head. "This was all Kayla's creativity. I'm afraid I can't take credit—"

"Responsibility, you mean," I muttered, gazing at his front. A giant puff-paint turkey covered with dozens and dozens of glued-on feathers glared malevolently from the center of his chest. Another thick layer of feathers adorned the bottom hem, the edges of both sleeves, and the neck. On his head sat a small, jaunty, glitter-encrusted pilgrim hat attached under his chin with an elastic strap.

He looked utterly ridiculous... and somehow was still the sexiest thing I'd ever seen.

"Credit," Ollie insisted. "Definitely credit." He grinned down at Jasper's and my joined hands. "You hear that, Brew?" he asked apropos of nothing. "That *vroom vroom* sound? What could it be? It's like a... a battery..."

Brew's brows lowered in confusion.

"Oliver," I said flatly, though my lips twitched. "Fuck off."

Ollie grinned as he looked me up and down. "And where are your feathers, friend?"

"I have no feathers. And before you start trying to change my mind," I added when he appeared ready to argue, "I'm a hundred percent secure in myself and this decision. Nothing is going to get me to change my mind."

Though I was talking to Ollie, I gave Jasper a look of warning. His eyes danced in response as if to say *challenge accepted*.

My heart skipped a beat.

"Brewer Barnum!" someone called angrily.

All four of us turned our heads as Delaney stormed over. His cheeks were bright pink, and the air around him fairly crackled with annoyance. "Did we, or did we not, have an *extensive* conversation about moldings for my dining room four days ago?" Without waiting for Brew to reply, he went on. "Yes. Yes we did. And did we, or did we not, agree that I want white cyma recta molding. Specifically *cyma recta*, Brewer. Convex below, concave above." He moved his hand in an inverted S-shape. "And I said, '*Do you see, Brewer?'* And what did you say? Hmm? What did you say? You said, '*I see,*'" he said triumphantly. "*I see.* Do you remember?"

"Uh..." Brew cocked his head to one side and scratched his neck. "Yep."

"But when I go over to my cabin today, what's stacked up on the floor?" Delaney threw both hands in the air. "Shaker molding. Shaker molding, which has no currrrrve at all!" He jabbed both arms in the air at forty-five-degree angles like he was doing a strange sort of dance. "And it's stained wood. *Dark* stained. The exact, literal, absolute opposite of white!" He huffed out a breath and said more calmly, "And look, I... I *know* I'm throwing a lot of stuff at you. I know I can be picky. But I have very high standards. And if you don't understand something I want, you just need to ask, and I'll... I'll explain better. I just want the house to be right. Okay?"

Brew pursed his lips thoughtfully and tilted his head in the other direction. "Okay."

Delaney huffed. "Okay." He glanced guiltily from Brew to the rest of us. "Sorry to be so agitated."

Brew nodded.

"So... thanks." Delaney gave a single nod. He turned to Jasper, then darted a glance at me. "Talk to you soon? Drinks, maybe?"

"Definitely," Jasper said. "I'm buying."

With another nod, Delaney walked off in Tam's direction.

"Uh, Brew?" I cleared my throat. "What's cyma recta molding?"

Brew shrugged. "No clue."

"But..." Ollie frowned. "You said you understood and you'd get him what he wants, buddy."

Brew gave Ollie a small smile. "I said I understood that he wants the house to be right. So do I. So I'll give him what he *needs*."

"Ah. Sure." Oliver nodded, still frowning. Apparently, he didn't understand the distinction any better than I did. "Anyway, Chris is over there, and I'm ninety-nine percent sure he has a charcuterie board, so…"

He raised his eyebrows at our friend, and Brew nodded.

Ollie gave us a little salute as he stepped back. "Later, guys."

"Later," I agreed. I turned to Jasper. "Now, about the costume thing. For once and for all…"

"You know, baby…" Jasper smoothed his hands up the front of my plain blue Henley and arranged his face into a look of feigned concern. "Delaney's not the only one who seems upset. You seem pretty agitated yourself."

I did *not* look agitated, and we both knew it, but if it meant keeping Jasper's hands on me, I was willing to pretend.

"Do I?" I said. "Wonder why."

"Irrelevant. The point is, you shouldn't exist in a high-stress state for long." He walked his fingers up over my collarbone, and I shivered. "Since I'm all about mindfulness—pretty much an expert, really—I could help you with that."

"You do help with that," I said gruffly. "You make things better. Cleaner. Brighter."

It had nothing to do with mindfulness, either. It was because of Jasper himself.

Because he'd been smiling nonstop since he'd decided to stay in Copper County, and his happiness made me happy, too.

Because I'd become that sappy guy who found himself

existing in a feedback loop of joy and optimism with the man he loved—a tree in full fucking bloom—and I had zero desire to change that.

Jasper was it for me. Forever.

"I could help *more*," he purred in my ear.

I snorted. "Let me guess. It would involve me wearing a *befeathered* T-shirt and a *bedazzled* pilgrim hat? No. No, thank you. I cannot be bought, Jasper Wrigley, or charmed by your wiles. I'm shocked that you'd think so little of me."

Jasper leaned his head against my shoulder, and the tiny, elasticized pilgrim hat perched on his blond hair glittered in the sun. "It's because I think so *much* of you, Watt. I want to run this race, and I want us to do it together, in the true spirit of this weird and awesome town. I have drunk the Kool-Aid. Copper County 4-eva. Come be weird with me. Everything's more fun when we're a team."

"I adore you," I told him, not entirely unmoved by his heartfelt words. "But..."

"But you still don't wanna wear the sparkles or the feathers." Jasper gifted me my favorite Jasper smile—the smile he only smiled for me.

It was the kind of smile a man could bet his future on... and I planned to.

"Still don't," I agreed.

He sighed. "Probably for the best. If you wore these feathers today, then when we got home..." He twined his arms around my neck. "I'd be really, really tempted to pluck you."

"To..." I glanced down at him, my mouth suddenly dry. "To pluck me?"

He nodded. "I'd be thinking about it alllll morning long, while we did this run around the lake. I'd probably end up running behind you, just so I could watch your… tail feathers. I'd replay all my favorite… plucking fantasies."

"You…" I coughed slightly since my throat had somehow gone dry, too. "You have plucking fantasies?"

"So many, Watt." Jasper pressed a kiss to my cheek and whispered, "So many."

I took a deep breath. "You win. Get me the fucking T-shirt," I growled.

"Yay," Jasper breathed. His smile widened until it was brighter than the sun. "Though I'm pretty sure this means we'll *both* win, and that will always be the best win of all."

Did you catch a little hint of something… brewing between Delaney and Brew? Find out in The Misfits of Copper County *→ https://readerlinks.com/l/4386760*

Need a little more Watt and Jasper? To sign up for my newsletter and get Plucked, *a free swoony and steamy bonus scene, go here → https://readerlinks.com/l/4386741*

ABOUT MAY ARCHER

May is an M/M author who lives in Boston. She spends her days planning vacations, mainlining diet soda, avoiding the gym, reading M/M romance, and when all other forms of procrastination fail, writing it.

Visit her website at <u>mayarcher.com</u> to sign up for her <u>newsletter</u> to hear about sales and upcoming releases, freebies and behind the scenes info and more! Or join her Facebook group, <u>Club May</u>!

facebook.com/may.archer.author

instagram.com/mayarcherauthor

amazon.com/May-Archer/e/B075JQVGLX

patreon.com/MayArcherRomance

bookbub.com/authors/may-archer

9 781964 685168